Look Again

Stephanie Rogers

ALSO BY STEPHANIE ROGERS

Look Closer: The Webcam Watcher Book 1
Look Now: The Webcam Watcher Book 3

The Dark Place

1

'ARE YOU SURE YOU want to do this?' Leanne asked. She folded her arms and leaned against the door frame to my bedroom. 'You don't seem too keen, if you don't mind me saying.'

I just shrugged. She'd hit the nail on the head but I wasn't about to admit it. I applied a second coat of mascara. In the mirror, the face looking back at me was more like Ann Boleyn might have looked as she walked to her execution rather than someone going on her first date in six months. I'd been cajoled into going and felt like a condemned woman.

'But he's such a nice, kind man.'

'He's mad keen on you, Sarah.'

'He's a good catch. He has a good job and a lovely house.'

These were all the things I'd been told by my bosses, Jenny and Sandra, as I worked, captive and unable to escape the barrage. Yet they meant well.

'Who is he again?' Leanne asked, scratching her nose.

'Sandra's friend's son. Apparently, he came into the deli one day, saw me, and has never stopped going on about me. Sandra says he's smitten.'

I don't like that word, smitten. It borders on obsession too much for my liking, and any crossover with obsession isn't good. I'd had enough obsession to last me a lifetime, thank you very much.

'Are you just going out with him to shut them up, then?' Lee asked.

I shrugged again. I couldn't really deny it.

'Well, you shouldn't be.'

I replaced the lid on the mascara and dropped it back into my make-up bag.

'I know. But I've been thinking, maybe they're right, and I have hidden away for too long.'

Lee didn't look convinced. 'Can't they see you're not keen?'

I turned to face her. 'It's not their fault, really. They don't know the full details of what happened, do they? They don't even know about the baby. I asked Mum to back me up when I told them it was just a stomach bug, and she did.'

At the mention of the baby, my throat tightened. I'd put it on Facebook, but only to get to *him*. And now I didn't even have a Facebook account. I'd closed it down ages ago.

Lee just shook her head. 'I think you're mad,' she said.

'Thanks.'

I was ready. She took in my ripped jeans and old sweater but didn't comment. It was clear I'd made no effort whatsoever. We both knew the old Sarah would have had every outfit out of the wardrobe and consulted with her on what to wear. She'd have sat on my bed with a glass of wine while we chatted. I would have had an expertly applied face full of make-up, crafted to make the most of my features whilst looking like there was barely any there, instead of the two coats of waterproof mascara I'd gone for tonight. My hair was unwashed and still in the low bun I'd pulled it back into for work this morning, and it wasn't what I'd call tidy.

'I won't be too long,' I told her, picking up my bag. 'Is Sam here?'

She nodded. 'He's staying over, if that's okay?'

'Yes, it's fine with me.'

2

'Well, dare I say, have fun.' She pulled a sarcastic face. 'What film are you seeing?'

I sighed. 'I let him pick, and he went for a rom-com with Cameron Diaz, so that's a black mark against him.'

She sniggered. 'Oh, dear.'

'Don't wait up,' I said, rolling my eyes.

'I thought you said you wouldn't be late.'

'Yeah, well. I won't be.' I pushed my feet into my battered old trainers. Lee said nothing.

'No funny business after the film, then?'

I stuck my fingers down my throat and mock-gagged. 'If he so much as touches my sleeve, he'll get a punch in the knackers.'

'Wow! I actually feel sorry for him now.'

She followed me to the door, and I waved to her as I left. It wasn't too late to text him and cancel. Except, of course, it was. I was going to be late (having taken so long deciding what to wear!) and he was probably going to be waiting outside for me any moment now. The cinema was a good ten- to fifteen-minute walk away.

It was dusk outside, and I zipped my jacket up, shivering at the thought that it would be dark when I got out. I couldn't see what the shadows may be hiding, but I felt there were eyes everywhere, watching, waiting. Sounded like paranoia, but once it had happened to you, the feeling never went away.

I'd arranged to meet David outside the cinema. I hated the cinema. All that popcorn-munching and bag-rustling and whispering. And that all-encompassing darkness so you couldn't tell who else might be in there, right behind you.

I tried to clear my mind. It was hardly a good state to turn up in, being on your guard and thinking about escaping or punching your date. I tried to relax and practised a smile. How hard could the next two hours be? And I was probably being too hard on him. He was a nice guy, by all accounts, and I needed to give him a chance. I'd met him twice in the deli and he seemed alright. He wasn't bad-looking.

When I got there, he was waiting outside with a bunch of flowers! Wilting yellow chrysanths that had seen better days. I gave him a weak smile and took them. What the hell was I supposed to do with them all night? I felt like a right berk.

He got my ticket before I could pay for it myself, then joined the end of a long line for popcorn. I knew it! It was the worst start to a date ever. I waited by the ladies' loos for almost ten minutes. It gave me enough time to decide that I found nothing remotely attractive about him. I clutched the bunch of flowers like an idiot. Would he notice if I found a bin for them?

'I got the sweet one, not the salted,' he said when he came back, looking pleased with himself. He'd also got the biggest size, by the look of it. 'You ladies like your sweet stuff, don't you?'

Wow! Great generalisation of women, mate! I wanted to say. Instead, I just smiled and wondered how much more fun I'd have had staying in and shaving my legs with a blunt razor.

We went in to the screen while the lights were still up, and he decided where we would sit. He talked about his job (something in finance), his house (a semi somewhere I'd already forgotten), his interests (watching *The Big Bang Theory*, and metal detecting at weekends). True, he did ask about me, but I didn't want to tell him anything. Instead, I diverted attention back to him, and he was only too happy to oblige and tell me more about his life. Every time I moved my feet, I accidentally kicked the flowers I'd jammed under the seat.

All the while, his hand dipped into the oversized bucket of popcorn again and again, scooping it into his mouth. It was like watching a digger scooping up earth. I felt sick at the smell: vanilla, buttery and cloying. And he offered me some every time, even though I kept refusing.

Before the lights went down, I cast surreptitious looks all around, looking for Chris's familiar dark brown eyes, black hair and stubble, the powerful frame, the sheer maleness of him, that I found so hard to ignore back then. Nothing. I relaxed a bit and settled back into my seat as the trailers came on.

As soon as the film began, my head started to throb with the noise, and grew steadily worse for the next half hour. All I could think about was how easy it would be in a place like this for someone to creep up behind you and get really close without you noticing. Would I feel their breath on the back of my neck?

I glanced over both shoulders. My headache was worsening every minute. If it turned into a migraine, I'd be stuffed. I needed to go.

I turned to look at him. He was glued to the screen, still eating popcorn and chewing with his mouth open. Some fell onto his lap, and he picked it up and ate it, his eyes never leaving Cameron Diaz's bare legs that were currently filling the screen as the camera panned slowly up them, culminating in the smallest knickers I'd ever seen.

'I've got a horrendous headache,' I told him. 'And this noise is making it worse. I'm going to the loo.'

I got up to go, and, to my horror, he got up too. A barrage of tutting came from behind us, along with a male voice muttering, 'Get out of the damn way before she puts her clothes back on.'

I stumbled out of the darkness with David close behind. Fingers of panic clutched at my chest at the thought of his proximity.

'You didn't need to come with me,' I said.

'It's okay. I'll be out here when you come back.'

That's what I was afraid of. As I pushed the door to the loo open, I couldn't help noticing his hand was back in the popcorn box again.

In the toilet, I splashed some cold water on my face as hot tears stung my eyes. I shouldn't have come. I should have stood my ground and said I wasn't interested in dating anyone. Why was I so damn weak all the time? An overwhelming need to be home consumed me, and I couldn't stand to be here a minute longer. I hated the dark cinema, populated with strangers and more hiding places than I could count.

I rested my forehead on the mirror, hoping for the cool glass to offer some relief, but it didn't. The racing of my heart was causing blood to rush in my head, making me feel even worse. I was in the beginnings of a panic attack, and I needed to stop it now. Deep breaths, in, out, I told myself for the next few minutes. Nothing helped and my legs turned to rubber. I sagged against the wall. I had to get out of here, back to the safety of my flat. ('Where it turned out you weren't safe at all,' the ever-present voice in my head informed me).

David straightened when I left the toilets, pulling the door open a little harder than I intended.

'You've been ages,' he said, frowning. 'We're missing the film. Ready to go back in?'

He went to place his hand on my back and I leaped away, as if scalded.

'Actually, I think I'm going to have to go home. This migraine is getting worse, with all the flashing lights and noise in there.'

He peered closer at my face until I could smell the vanilla sweetness on his breath. I turned my head away.

'You don't look that bad,' he said. 'Are you sure you're really ill and not just trying to get away from me?' He let out a braying laugh, then stopped in shock when he realised what he'd said in jest just might be true. 'My God! You are, aren't you?'

'Look, I really do have a terrible headache. I'm sorry. The truth is, I shouldn't have come. I've just come out of a long relationship that ended badly and I don't think I'm ready. I'm sorry to have wasted your time. The last thing I wanted was to mess you around.'

He blinked, then his lips twisted into a sneer. I stepped back and stopped when I hit the wall.

'Right,' he said, scrunching up the popcorn box and ramming it in a nearby bin. He crossed his arms. 'So you thought it was okay to string me along, did you? All that chatter in the cafe, flirting with me and giving me the eye? Was it just a free night at the pictures you fancied?'

I couldn't believe what I was hearing. None of that had happened, and a spark of anger made my mouth go into gear. 'Now, just hang on a minute! *You* asked *me* out!'

He took a step toward me, and I took one to the side. A flash of alarm made my pulse double. He was so much bigger than me. He could really hurt me.

'You're just like all the rest,' he spat at me, his gaze travelling slowly up and down my body.

My anger ignited, momentarily driving away the fear. 'I never flirted with you even once, for your information. And here's the money for the damn ticket.' I fumbled in my purse and fished out the exact change while he held his hand out. 'I never asked you to pay. You insisted. I did *not* fancy a free night at the pictures, and I certainly do not fancy YOU!'

I shoved the money at him, turned on my heel, and started to walk away from him. Thankfully, he didn't follow me.

'I know what you are,' he shouted after me. 'You're nothing but a frigid cow. I'm sorry I wasted my time on you.'

I stopped and turned to face him, rage blazing right through me now. 'What did you just say?'

'You heard,' he said, glaring at me.

'You're a dickhead!' I said to him. 'No wonder your mum is desperate to find you a girlfriend. You've got no charisma or charm to find one yourself, have you? Why don't you stick to metal detecting and leave the female population alone? Do us all a bloody favour. Oh, and stick your manky flowers where the sun doesn't shine.'

He waved his hand in my direction. 'Whatever. Go and waste someone else's time.'

And with that, he stalked back off to the film, pulling open the door and disappearing into the darkness once more.

I leaned against the wall, suddenly weak. It took a huge effort to summon up enough strength to start moving. Back on the street, I gulped in air and pushed him from my mind as I walked home, concentrating instead on the fact that someone could be following me right now. How fast could I go without actually breaking into a run? In my pocket, my fingers curled around the can of pepper spray that I now carried around everywhere I went. Was I imagining it, that *he* was following me or watching me? That he was even back here from God knows where he went? I had no idea. My perspective was so skewed I didn't know anything for sure. This was all *his* fault. A sob caught in my throat. I broke into a light jog and didn't make eye contact with anyone. As I passed a gang of teenage boys, one of them tittered and said something in a high-pitched voice. I jogged faster, my bag banging against my hip, and didn't look back.

When I got home, out of breath and red-faced, I could hear Leanne and Sam laughing in her bedroom. At least she wouldn't be able to see the state I was in if I was quick.

The front door banged behind me, and I scurried for my bedroom. She must have heard it, as her bedroom door opened as mine closed.

'Sarah?' she shouted.

'I'm okay. I'm going straight to bed, Lee. I'm knackered.'

'Are you alright?'

'I'm fine. Just tired. Can we talk about it in the morning?' *Where you'll want to rehash every last detail, no doubt.* I knew she meant well, but I just didn't have the energy for it.

'As long as you're alright,' she called back. Her bedroom door closed.

I got ready for bed, throwing my clothes on the floor and leaving them in a heap, exactly as Chris would have hated. Before he'd got into bed with me (if sex wasn't on the cards), he'd have folded them neatly and put them somewhere tidy, while muttering about creases.

I took out a bag from my wardrobe and pulled out a tiny mint-green babygro. It was soft against my cheek and I could almost imagine the smell of the baby in it. Although my chest tightened, the rest of my body relaxed at the feel of it. What would my baby have smelled like, had he or she made it? Soft, pink skin, talcum powder and milk. I climbed into bed, still clutching it tight. At least the sight of it didn't make me cry anymore. I didn't know if I'd ever have my own baby, feeling about men the way I did now. It was looking more and more unlikely, as what I did know was that it would be a long time before I went on another date. With anyone. If ever.

2

'STAY,' I SAID, POINTING at the mutt.

Unbelievably, the little white dog lowered its backside onto the sand, beside the T-shirt and shorts I'd just taken off. It was learning fast. It now understood English, it seemed.

The waves were cold around my feet as I stepped into the Atlantic, the Brazilian sun doing little to warm up the water even though the air temperature was 24 degrees Celsius. This place, the State of Espirito Santo, was much nicer than the shit hole I arrived in when I first left the UK and came to Brazil six months ago. Okay, fled the UK, if you want to be pedantic. I'm not gonna argue.

The sea here was much cleaner, the churned-up clouds of sand at the bottom visible. I waded a few more meters in, shivering, took a deep breath and threw myself forward, right about where I knew the sea floor dropped sharply away. This time I got it right, and I didn't knock my knee on the rocky shelf that jutted out to my right. I'd been mapping this place out in my head for the last month or so, and now it was paying off.

I flipped over onto my back, raised my head and looked back to the beach, which was still maybe only twenty metres or so away. The dog was still there, panting now, its eyes fixed on me. She was a good girl. She'd followed me around practically since I arrived and we'd got a bond now. It was funny, really. Back in England, I never really thought about animals, other than how much of a damned nuisance they could be, with their stink and noise, but she was alright. She paddled in the sea every day with me, except for now, when I was going too far out. I wouldn't want her to get swept away or anything. Anyway, the water kept her smelling quite nice. She'd come in with me later on.

But now, I wasn't here to mess about. I turned onto my front and fixed my eyes on the massive rock that jutted out of the water. It must be twenty feet tall, about a fifteen-minute hard swim away. I pulled my goggles down from the top of my head and over my eyes, and began a front crawl as fast as I could. There was nothing in between me and the rock.

My breathing and arm and leg movements were perfectly in sync now. I'd been doing this two or three times a day for the last two weeks, and my muscles had responded well. Back home, as a kid, I was never a good swimmer. I doggy-paddled at the local baths occasionally with my mates, but I never had proper swimming lessons. My folks would never have stumped up to pay for them. But I'd studied technique and form on YouTube. It was amazing what was on there. Want to learn just about any skill? Hack a mobile phone or computer? Make a bomb? YouTube was the answer. It'd taken a while, but I could feel the stroke coming together now. It was a lot smoother, and I swallowed a hell of a lot less water than when I started. I actually really loved it now.

Also, some evenings, when it was cooler and just getting dark, me and the mutt ran along the beach. The faster I went, the more she kept pace with me. Now I'd fed her up a bit. She was so skinny when she first started following me; all her ribs were sticking out. Poor thing was starving. She had fleas and worms, so, after another YouTube session, I got them sorted. She'd also had a bit of a gammy leg that made her limp, but that seemed to have healed by itself.

When I reached the rock, I was panting. It felt good. I hauled myself onto it and looked back at the beach, trying to locate the dog. If I stared hard, I could just about see her. I knew she'd be there, whatever. She wouldn't let anyone near my stuff. Not that there was anything valuable there. I'm not an idiot. Although my wallet would probably be safer in my short's pocket on the beach with her guarding it than the hovel I was staying in. Let's just say it wasn't The Ritz and leave it at that.

I lay back on the rock and looked up, squinting at the sun, at a plane climbing in the distance. Looked like it'd just left Eurico de Aguiar Salles Airport. I wondered where it was going. Manchester? Heathrow? Could be going anywhere in the world, really. I wasn't sure how I was going to get back to the UK yet. But swimming gave me good thinking time and cleared some of the fog out of my brain that the beer caused. I should cut down, but the local brew was a cheap enough pleasure around here. This place wasn't as well known to tourists, and I liked it that way. Even though I supposed to the locals, I was a tourist. Most of the tourists travelled south of here, to Rio de Janeiro, where there was more going on.

As soon as my breathing returned to normal, I slid off the rock, back into the sea, and set off back to the beach. I upped my pace, trying to make it back faster. I think I did, by a small margin, but I was distracted from counting down the seconds and minutes by thoughts of Sarah once again. It seemed I just couldn't get away from her. She inhabited my head and consumed me from the inside most days. She was like battery acid, burning and eating away at me. Not the nicest analogy, but the most accurate. I could still feel the sting of her slap on my cheek that day, just before she collapsed, and I saved her life. The last time I saw her.

I reached the shallows and stood up, shaking my head to clear the water from my ears and her from my brain. The mutt wagged her tail and darted forward to greet me.

'Hey Leanne,' I said, bending down to rub her head. Her tail wagged more, madly now. She was totally devoted to me, this dog. Every time I called her by the name I gave her, Leanne, it made me smile. Leanne, Sarah's best friend and flatmate, was a bitch and so is the mutt, but the dog is only one through biology. The other Leanne, well, who knows why she was, but she certainly was. To me, anyway. To say our dislike of each other was mutual would be putting it bluntly, to say the least.

I pulled my shorts and T-shirt on over my wet swim shorts, and sat on the sand, letting the heat of the sun warm my bones. Leanne rolled onto her back, pushing her belly into my hand. Although she looked little more than a year or two old, her teats were swollen and saggy, like she'd had at least one litter. God knows what to her babies. I rubbed her hard, and she squirmed, ecstatic, under my hand.

'You hungry?' I said to her. 'Come on, then. Time to eat.'

She was on her feet quicker than me, though I doubted she understood a word of what I just said. More like she didn't want to let me out of her sight. We walked together, off the beach and up a nearby side street, to the place I was staying. It was rough, but had a bed and its own bathroom. There was little more to say about it.

There was a small supermarket on the way, and I ducked inside for some orange juice, bread, milk and dog food. The miserable old bastard behind the till barely glanced at me as he put my stuff through and held out his hand for the coins. Suited me. Talking to him was the last thing I wanted. Not that I'd have understood much of what he said if he did speak. I hadn't picked up much of the lingo. No point. I wasn't sticking around long term.

Leanne was waiting for me when I got out. I swear she wagged her tail at the sight of the carrier bag.

3

THE NURSERY DISPLAY OF painted cots, frilly Moses baskets and rocking chairs in the window called to me. I shouldn't go in. What was the point? Yet my feet carried me into the shop as if they had a will of their own.

The assistant was busy at the back of the shop, demonstrating folding down a pushchair to a heavily pregnant woman. A man stood next to her with his arm resting on her waist.

Feeling like an interloper, I made for the baby clothes to the left of the entrance, and immersed myself in the rows of them. It was incredible that anything tiny enough to fit into them could grow to be an actual person. My fingers reached out and trailed across the front of a velvety pale-pink dress for a newborn. It was the softest thing I'd ever felt. I resisted the urge to bring it to my face and rub my cheek on it for fear someone might see and think me mad. I lifted it off the rack. It had tiny white bunnies all over it. I put it back. I should go. Then I saw them: teeny-tiny bootees with bows at the back. They were lemon-yellow and also velvety soft, even more than the dress. On the left foot, it said *BABY* in mint-green and the right one said *LOVE*. They were smaller than my palm when I sat them in my hand.

When my phone started ringing, I put the bootees back on the rack, and pulled it out of my bag. *Unknown caller*. A mobile number. Who was it? I stared at the screen while the ringing seemed to get louder and more shrill. Then I slid my finger to the left, silencing it mid-ring and cutting the call. Maybe they'd leave a message. But hardly anyone knew this number. I'd had it for six months and I was very selective about who I gave it to. It couldn't be *him*. There was no way. It'd be those damn tele-marketers again, most likely. Every time you wanted to buy something online, you had to give them your bloody phone number. Same with your email address. If you didn't fill it in, you couldn't buy anything. You just knew damn well they were going to sell it on, no matter how many boxes you ticked to say they couldn't. It was the way of the world now. I hated it.

I put the phone back and whirled around when a voice at my ear said, 'Hello again. Your friend's baby must be due any day now, right?'

The assistant had come from the back of the shop, and I never heard a thing. My heart lodged somewhere in the back of my throat.

Her smile faltered. 'I'm so sorry. I didn't mean to make you jump.'

'It's okay,' I said. 'I didn't see you, that's all.'

She reached past me and plucked the bootees off the rail. 'They are lovely, aren't they? Almost makes you want to be pregnant just for an excuse to buy them.'

I swallowed hard as my eyes fixed on them again. She handed them to me. I resisted the urge to clamp them to my chest.

'When is she due?' she asked, her smile firmly back in place.

'Oh, er, she has another three weeks yet,' I lied. This time, no heat rose in my cheeks; I must be getting good at it.

'She's so lucky to have a friend like you. You're spoiling her.'

I smiled back. No words came.

'Are you taking them?' she asked.

I held them in front of me. *BABY LOVE*. I brushed my thumb over the elasticated ruffle of the top.

'Yes, I'll take them, thanks. She'll love them.'

'Does she know if she's having a boy or girl yet?'

'No, she's adamant they don't want to know until it's born. They're so looking forward to it being a surprise.'

The pregnant woman waddled past us, her partner steering her from behind like a hulking cruise ship through a narrow harbour. My eyes lingered on her bump and I tore them away, back to the bootees, as a growing lump in my throat threatened to choke me.

'Thank you,' the woman called to the assistant. 'We'll be back when we've decided.'

'Lovely. You know where to find me. And we're open late on Thursdays, until seven,' the assistant informed them. She had on a small name badge that I'd never noticed before. It read *JANICE*. Her closeness suddenly made me feel claustrophobic.

'I'll just get those, thanks,' I said briskly, hoping she'd take the hint and get a move on. She did, and I followed her to the till, trying to blot out her chatter as I paid for them. She put them in a bag with *STORK* in pink and blue lettering on it and handed it to me. A small picture of a stork standing on one leg with a tied-up bundle hanging from its beak sat atop the letters.

'Thank you,' I said before hurrying out of the shop.

On the street, I gulped in a lungful of heavy London air. It tasted acrid, like petrol or diesel or whatever. I shoved the *STORK* bag right down to the bottom of my handbag, pulling a scarf over the top of it. Immediately, I was angry at myself.

What the hell was wrong with me? On one hand, it was no one's business if I bought clothes for a non-existent baby. On the other, why did I keep doing it? What was the point?

But really, I knew what it meant. You didn't have to be Brain of Britain to figure it out. Ever since my ectopic

16

pregnancy caused my tube to rupture six months ago, I'd been fixated on babies and, if anything, it was getting worse. I leaned back against the wall of the shop next door and dropped my head in my hands. Some days, I felt like I was going mad. I'd never even wanted a baby, but now it was all I could think about.

I took a deep breath in and got out my phone. Whoever called had left a voicemail. I dialled it to find a computerised voice droning on about something. I knew it.

I dropped it into my bag, pushed away from the wall and walked to the Tube. I'd prefer to be on my own when I got back to the flat, but Leanne would probably be there, seeing as her commute now took her less than five minutes to walk. The thought of plastering a smile on my face and mustering up fake cheeriness filled me with dread. But I had to go home. I couldn't walk the streets forever, like a vagrant. I'd end up like Ben.

At the thought of Ben, my heart lifted a bit. Ever since he'd gone back home to Scotland with his wife, Kate, he'd stayed in touch. He emailed or rang me at least once a week. I struggled to equate the scruffy homeless man I'd got to know with the photos he sent of a clean-shaven, shorn-haired, laughing bloke. Kate looked happy in the photos and little Sofia, well, she was like kids are, accepting of most things and resilient. Ben told me it was like he'd never gone away in the first place, as far as Sofia was concerned. But sometimes, as I looked deep into his eyes in the pictures, I could see a shadow of something there. Was his smile fake? He was obviously still haunted by what he'd seen on tour in Afghanistan. To see your best friend blown up right next to you, plus all the other horrors he must have been through—well, how do you even begin to get over that?

He was forever telling me how he could never repay me or Leanne for helping him and returning him to his family. But all I wanted was for him to recover and be happy again. I wasn't sure he was.

On the Tube, I listened to some music while appearing to scroll through some new cake recipes for vegans that I'd found the other day. Determined not to make eye contact with anyone, I did an odd mix of keeping my head down whilst at the same time doing a sweep of the faces in the carriage. I had it off to a fine art, although it did hurt my neck if I did it for too long. Everyone looked—I hesitated to use the word *normal*—but they did. No one looked like *him*. Like Chris. I'd tried to stop freezing whenever I saw a bloke of over six feet in height with almost-black hair and attractive stubble, but men fitting that description were everywhere. And you couldn't change your height but hair colour was easily changed. Would I know him if I saw him? I couldn't see how I wouldn't.

I hadn't heard a thing from him since that last day, when I collapsed in his flat, when my fallopian tube ruptured and he called an ambulance. When I got out of hospital, he'd disappeared. I still found it hard to believe, even now, that he would be capable of hacking my computer and spying on me through my webcam. Yet that's what he did. Course, he didn't admit it at first when I confronted him, but he had to eventually.

My head jerked up as the hairs prickled on the back of my neck. Was someone watching me? I scanned around the carriage to find a red-haired guy staring at me. He smiled immediately when my eyes locked onto his, no doubt to appear less intimidating. It took me about three seconds to assess him. I was safe. It wasn't Chris. There were no similarities at all,. I didn't smile back at him, just turned away. No one else was looking at me or showing me the slightest bit of interest. Openly now, I studied everyone methodically until they were all eliminated. Red-hair got off at the next stop after glancing at me again. He attempted another smile. I looked away again. He should have got the message clearly enough now. I wasn't interested.

My stop was next, and I left the Tube, walking fast, surveying the faces around me. I had to work hard to not run down the road in order to get home quicker. I would not let him make me dash like a scared rabbit down my own street.

It was almost six o'clock and the streets in Shepherd's Bush were busy enough. A pleasant breeze blew my hair off my face, which was sticky after the humid air of the Tube carriage. I wished it was greener around here. It was like a concrete jungle with its stagnant air and row after row of identical houses. I used to like it here, but not anymore. What used to feel buzzing and vibrant now seemed tainted, stale, and dull. People sat outside pubs in pavement beer gardens, shirt sleeves rolled up and jackets slung casually on benches beside them. It was just a normal September evening.

I tried to relax, but it was like the weightless bootees I'd bought were suddenly heavy, and were pressing my bag towards the floor, causing the strap to dig into my shoulder. I was being stupid, but I couldn't help it.

I reached our building, adjusted the scarf in my bag, and headed up the steep stairs with the grubby brown carpet to our flat on the third floor. Leanne's perfume lingered outside the doorway, so she must have been home. Or maybe I was just imagining it.

'Hi,' I called out after I unlocked the door and pushed it open. The TV blared out at me from the living room at the far end of the corridor, and I kicked off my shoes then went through.

'Oh, hiya,' she said, from her position flat on her back on the sofa.

'You okay?' I asked when she didn't get up.

'No. Done my back in unpacking boxes when a delivery came in.'

'Ouch! Is it bad?'

'Yeah. I can hardly move.'

'Were the clothes worth it?' I asked.

'Well, yes, they are gorgeous, but I'm not sure they're worth this.'

'Which ones were they?'

'That order from that new designer who does lots in silk.'

'Oh yeah. I remember.'

'We've been waiting for them forever. Who knew silk could be so heavy? There again, it was a massive order.'

'Do you think they'll sell?'

'Yeah, I know they will.'

I believed her. She had an uncanny eye for spotting new trends and the shop she was a buyer for had increased its turnover by over twenty-five per cent since she'd started working there. They also stocked some of her own designs, too, and she was slowly starting to get a name for herself.

She winced as she struggled to sit up. 'So, how was your day?'

I pushed the bootees to the back of my mind. 'Busy. Sold all our stuff again.'

She pulled a face. 'I can't believe there's never any cake for you to bring back. I never get to eat your stuff anymore. It's not fair.'

'I'll make you something special before I leave,' I said, flopping onto the chair opposite.

She closed her eyes. She was reluctant to talk about me leaving, but she'd finally realised there was nothing more she could do to try and talk me into staying. My mind was made up.

I laced my fingers over my stomach, rubbing where it hurt that day. Leanne said I did that a lot. I didn't normally notice, but today I did.

Leanne pouted, still with her eyes closed. 'Can I get to pick?' she asked.

I stopped rubbing. 'Pick what?'

'What you make me. Can I choose?' She cranked open one eye.

I smiled. 'Yes, course you can. As long as it hasn't got three bloody tiers, because that would be taking advantage.'

She laughed. 'I won't. Maybe a nice red velvet cake would be nice.'

'Oh, come on! Red velvet is so overrated. It's tasteless. Style over substance. Something chocolatey, perhaps?'

'Ooh, no, I know. Something with treacle and coconut. But not a tart. You can invent something new.'

I thought for a second, my mind already whirring at the thought of a new concoction. Something with a thick shortbread base might work. Ginger shortbread, maybe.

'Alright. I'll see what I can come up with.'

She nodded and tried to stretch, then abandoned it with a grimace. 'I wish you weren't going, Sarah.'

I sighed. 'I know you do. But it'll be great for you and Sam after he moves in. You and him living together. It's exciting. A new adventure.'

She looked at me. 'I know, but I'm going to miss you so much. I want you here to share my new adventure.'

'Well, if I wasn't moving out, he probably wouldn't be moving in, would he? And I've had more than enough adventure to last me a lifetime.'

She closed her eyes again. 'I know you have. But I'm still going to miss you,' she says, her voice quiet and teary.

'No, you won't. You'll be coming to see me all the time, won't you?'

'Yeah, you know I will. But it won't be the same, will it? This place won't be the same without you.'

I shook my head. 'No, it won't. But that's why I need to go, Lee. I don't want it to be the same. I want a fresh start.'

I leaned my head back onto the cushion and closed my eyes. If I ever needed a fresh start, it was now.

4

THE MOPED WAS, AS usual, parked around the back of the motel. Leanne was in my arms, eager to get into the basket on the front. She started wriggling around the moment she saw it. She fit in so snugly it was a wonder she could breathe, but it didn't seem to bother her. In fact, she loved it.

I placed her in it, and she started panting. It was excitement rather than fear. She barked when I got on and started the engine. Her tail would be wagging, I was sure, if there was any room for it to move.

The 'office' was a twenty-minute drive away, but the moped didn't go much above thirty-five miles an hour. I could probably run faster. It was a ball-ache, but I wasn't going to the trouble of getting a car. The irony of me being seen on this puny little sack of shit wasn't lost on me. My last set of wheels was a Mazda MX5, a beautiful machine. With gleaming silver bodywork, the convertible, the best car I'd ever owned, was one of the things I missed most about my past life. I had to give her up when I left London fast. They took her in part payment, in exchange for a private flight out of the UK. It was either that or go to prison for murder. That's what would still happen if they caught me.

The ride to the office a shit one, through an industrial area where tourists didn't go. It was noisy and dirty and ugly, despite its proximity to the beach. But the air whipping past my face cooled me down, at least.

The office was a glorified shack on a run-down industrial estate that I was getting to use for next to nothing, seeing as no one in their right mind would want to rent it. I got it through the landlady of the hovel I was staying in. It was her bloke's place, and he was just glad to get anything at all for it.

I'd had to get phone lines installed, and the broadband was surprisingly good. You had to have a decent set up for the sort of thing I was doing. I just hoped my workforce was in a good mood. It was true about Latin blood running hot. These lost their shit at the drop of a hat, but only with each other. Never with me. They knew what was good for them, and who was paying their wages.

I turned into the estate and shut the moped off, glad to get rid of the annoying whine of the engine. It was more like an irritating fly than a vehicle. Nothing like the deep, throaty purr of the Mazda. God, I missed that car. She was so smooth once she was running, you could barely hear her. I breathed in deeply and could almost smell the leather of her interior, rich and strong, hear the crunch of her tyres over gravel. She was worth every penny. If I ever got back on my feet, maybe I'd get another. Well, I had to keep some dreams alive.

My unit was the first one on the left, next door to a welding place. The welder was in there now, and the crackle and spit of welding noise bled through the closed door. Further down, a man was doing something with a car that looked like it needed scrapping. He pulled his head out from under the bonnet, nodded to me and carried on. The other three units were pretty much derelict, with wooden boards across the windows and doors. My unit was the best of the six, and much more secure. It needed to be, with the three computers that were inside.

The door to my unit was locked. I liked it that way. Around here, you didn't ask questions. If someone wanted you to know their business, they would tell you. The women who worked for me knew to keep their mouths shut if they wanted the money to keep coming in.

I lifted Leanne out and put her on the ground. She instantly ran to the nearest hummock of dead grass and peed on it.

'Come on,' I said when she was done, and she raced back to me, her tongue lolling out of one side of her mouth.

I took my keys out. The women knew to keep the door locked from the inside but to remove the key so I could get in. They never knew when to expect me. I liked to keep them on their toes so they didn't take the piss. They knew full well I wasn't a good boss to cross. I could hear raised voices from inside, like they were arguing again. So no one was on a call, then. Great start!

I unlocked the door and went inside, shutting out the welding racket. Thankfully, it was quieter in here, or it would be if they weren't arguing. It was also boiling hot, despite the desk fans I'd supplied. They shut up instantly when they saw me. Margot, the oldest woman, jumped up from her chair and started stubbing out a cig in a dirty cup. She knew how much I hated smoking.

I crossed my arms and stood with my back to the door.

'It stinks in here,' I said. 'How many times do I have to tell you to smoke near a window?'

'I am sorry, Mr Carson. I cannot open the window, it is jammed closed,' Margot said, her eyes dipping to the floor.

I rolled my eyes as she called me Carson. No matter how many times I said it was Frost, it made no difference. Something to do with Downton Abbey or something.

I looked over at the window. 'What's wrong with it?'

She shrugged. 'I do not know. I have kept trying.'

I walked over to the window nearest her and pushed it. Nothing happened. I thumped it at the bottom with the side of my fist twice, and it swung open. I looked back at Margot and raised my eyebrows.

She was back at her desk, her eyes fixed on her computer screen. The other two women, neither of whose names I could either pronounce nor remember, were studiously looking at their screens, too. I called them Number One and Number Two in my head.

'You.' I pointed at Number One. She could have been anywhere between thirty and fifty; I was no good at guessing ages. Although I knew Sarah's. She was twenty-six. It was her birthday two months ago. 19th of July. I wondered if she'd got any nice presents, and if so, who from.

'Yes, Mr Carson?' said Number One. She wasn't bad looking, if you liked scrawny and weather-beaten. Which I didn't. A smattering of grey was coming through in her dark hair, which was scraped tightly back off her face into some sort of bun thing. Deep grooves cut into her face, around her mouth. Not a good look. She wasn't even a three out of ten. But I wasn't getting into the numbers thing right now. I had a ten and look where that got me. She called the police on me. Was that unforgivable? I hadn't decided.

'How's it looking? The list?'

The women spoke good English. I couldn't believe it when I got here. It was a turn up for the books, and the last thing I was expecting. I had no intention of learning Portuguese. I wasn't sticking around long enough to make the time investment worthwhile, but a language barrier would have put a damper on the whole enterprise. Apparently, the reason they were so good at English was the huge influx of American and UK TV programmes. In other words, they were lapping up the same shit we were back home, and they'd been doing it since they were little. It was subtitled in Portuguese, but the spoken words were English. I supposed some stuff was overdubbed, but a lot wasn't. It was why their speech could sometimes be peppered with lines straight from a bad soap opera. I loved it. It was hilarious.

'We have a new list, Mr Carson. The leads are good. This list should last us another two weeks, at least.'

Those damn lists cost me a fortune sometimes. 'How many calls a day?'

'We are doing two hundred on a good day.' She smiled hesitantly, obviously hoping to make me happy, which I wasn't yet.

'And you?' I pointed at Number Two. She was younger than the others but not fitter in any sense of the word. Blotchy-faced, podgy and stank of B.O. I'd told the other women to tell her to wash more, but it seemed they hadn't. I could smell her from here. I kept her on because she was the best one. She had the most amazing voice. Not a voice you would ever put with her face. When she spoke, her voice kind of oozed into your ears. It was soft and husky and all seductive. She was either your best friend or your favourite whore. It said *You can do anything you want to me.* But it also said *You can trust me. You know you can. And you want to make me happy, don't you?* It was an amazing thing to behold.

Number Two stared at me like a rabbit caught in the headlights. She'd told me she needed this job because her baby brother was desperately ill and required a lot of hospital care, which was either expensive if you could afford it, or cheap if you'd rather die than pay. I guess they'd rather pay. The ties of family, eh? Except mine, of course. I always found the most dedicated workers were the ones in the most desperate need, but wasn't that the same anywhere? Or at least, where there wasn't the generous welfare state we had at home.

'The figures?' I said, with a tut. God, I asked the same questions every time. You'd have thought they could have pre-empted them by now.

Two pulled a sheet of paper from a pile beside her computer and handed it to me. I ran my eye down it. The columns were neatly filled in. Good. Everything was as it should be. I reached the bottom. Wow, they were better than I'd been expecting. Seemed some people never learn. When would people wise up about scams and stop being so trusting? It was pathetic that they still fell for it with all the information that was out there. And if they got Number Two, it could be goodbye life savings, if I was lucky. It'd happened more than once, and it wasn't as if the women were averse to it. They knew exactly what they were doing. The bank balance looked more than healthy. After paying the women, I'd be left with more than I was expecting.

Margot was still engrossed by her computer. I didn't know what was on there that was so good. Number Two was reaching down, stroking Leanne's ears under the desk. Leanne was leaning her head into the girl's hand, her eyes closed. Every so often, her back foot came up and pawed at the air. I gritted my teeth at the sight of it. If Number Two rubbed any of her vile B.O. onto Leanne and I could smell it later, I wouldn't be pleased. The fans were running, but they only shifted the air directly in front of them. I went to stand in front of the closest one. At least the air smelled better here.

'Why were none of you on the phones when I came in?'

Margot jumped. She was so nervy today. Something to feel guilty about, maybe?

'We have been, Mr Carson. We about to make more calls right away.'

I narrowed my eyes, trying to work out if she was shitting me. In the end, though, the figures spoke for themselves.

'Alright,' I said. 'Good work this month, all of you. I will pay bonuses.'

I could almost hear a collective sigh of relief. I might be a tough boss, but they knew I'd make it worth their while if they came through. They'd be earning a lot less working as chambermaids or waitresses, like lots of the women in this place did.

'Go on, then. Back to work.'

I pointed at their ears. They each had a headset connected to their computer. I sat near the open window, observing. I was making them nervous, but what could they say? Tell me to go away? Number One started speaking first. She wasn't as good as Number Two, but it sounded like she'd been taking lessons. The list was split into three, and they had one third each. She slipped into her spiel easily, just like I'd taught her. I didn't know who she was talking to, and I didn't care. It was their own fault for being so gullible. If you were that easy to convince, you only had yourself to blame. There were several scenarios the women had to fall back on. This one was to do with a refund from their bank. Total and utter shite, but some people heard the word 'bank' and nothing else. Thank God for officialdom.

I blotted out what she was saying and thought of Sarah. Would she still be gullible? I didn't think so. Not anymore. But I bet she still had no idea I could hear every word she said in her flat, through the four-ways I put there, the ones with the sim cards in that recorded conversations. She hadn't spoken to Leanne much about me lately. Maybe she was getting over me. I did hope not.

I closed my eyes, massaging away the headache that was beginning to press at my temples. This life wasn't without its stresses, but it beat prison hands down. I'd tried to work out why I wanted to see Sarah again and what I might do when I set eyes on her. Surely, for us to pick up where we left off could never happen, no matter how much I wanted it to. But it could if she forgave me. For now, I'd be happy just to see her and know she was alright. Maybe she could go out with me not knowing it was me. Sounded far-fetched, but if I could change myself that much, would it be possible? Who knew? Anyway, for now, I'd keep an open mind. I had a lot to sort out before I even got that far. One step at a time.

5

'SO? WHAT DO YOU think?' I asked, sliding the plate across the counter.

Jenny picked it up and peered at the slice of cake on it. 'What is it again?'

'Lime and ginger drizzle, but I added a lime frosting with bits of dark chocolate in.'

She sniffed it and closed her eyes. 'It smells divine. I knew we shouldn't have offered you a job. I can't stop eating your cakes.'

I laughed as she put the plate down and broke a bit off with her fork. She made sure to get the extra squidgy lime buttercream from the back of the slice. There was no assuaging her sweet tooth, and she was the ideal guinea pig for anything new I tried.

She sighed and looked sadly at the plate. 'It's heavenly. I'm going to have to finish it now, aren't I?'

'Yep,' I said. 'Eat up like a good girl.'

She didn't need telling twice and was soon scraping the plate clean. 'Aren't you having any?'

'I've tasted it non-stop all afternoon. I'll be sick if I have any more. Do you think it's good enough to add to the repertoire, then?'

'Definitely. We'll have it as a special on the board as soon as you make more.'

'I'll do three tomorrow morning and have them on the counter before lunch.'

She put her fork down and picked up her tea. 'You need to start just giving me tiny bits to try instead of a whole slice. I've put nearly a stone on since you started working for us. I'm going to end up diabetic at this rate.'

'Okay. I can do that.'

She prodded her stomach and pulled a face. 'Maybe I should start jogging or something.'

I hid my smile behind my mug of tea. There was no way she would. Just the thought was cracking me up. We had this conversation at least twice a week.

'So, how's it going with the new cafe?' I asked.

She put her cup down and leaned on the counter. 'No hitches as yet. I keep waiting for something to go wrong, though.'

I stayed silent. It was a bit dicey, trying to weigh up the fact that she was able to pay cash for a cafe in York with the fact that the money had come from the sale of her beloved parents' house, due to their recent deaths. As she had no siblings, she'd got everything. She knew she was lucky to have had such a large inheritance, but she was so cut up about losing them so close together that it was hard to know what to say for the best. We'd talked about it endlessly, but she was still devastated. The new cafe had been the only good thing to come out of it for her.

'I still can't believe how much that house went for,' she said for the umpteenth time. 'It's ridiculous.'

'I know. It's nuts.'

Her parents had lived in the same tiny three-bed terraced house in Kensington that had been in her dad's family for generations, and investors had been circling it like sharks for years. Sometimes, her parents had found notes shoved through the letterbox from random property developers offering to buy it. Prime real estate, they called it. 'Ripe for development.' She'd showed me pictures of the house. It was very dated and small, but it had still gone for almost a million pounds. They had several interested parties after it. I think they called it 'potential'. I called it madness.

'Do you have much to organise?' she asked me now.

'No. I travel light these days. And the flat over the cafe will be a godsend. Are you sure you don't want me to pay the going rate of rent for it? I'm paying a pittance compared to down here.'

'No. Absolutely. I'm more than happy with our agreement. I'll own it outright and I'm just relieved to know it'll be in good hands. Although I'm so going to miss you here. And I know Sandra will, too. Are you absolutely definitely sure you want to go?'

'I am.'

In fact, I couldn't wait. I was really looking forward to it. Managing my own shop. It was a dream come true. And what I'd seen of York so far, it was absolutely beautiful. I told her so.

'I love York so much,' she said. 'I've got a bit of a soft spot for it. It's probably why I wanted the café when I saw it online.' She cupped her chin with her hand. 'Pete and I have had some great weekends away there when we've managed to palm the kids off with his mum. We stayed in some lovely hotels.' A wistful look came over her face.

'Yeah, I bet you never saw much of York, really. Did you even leave the room?' I said.

Her face flushed. 'We did. Sometimes,' she said, laughing. 'You have such a filthy mind, Sarah.'

'Yup. I do.'

'Any plans what you might do when you get there? In your free time, I mean?'

'I want to just wander around, soak it all in, and act like a proper sightseer. And I want to do that ghost walk I've seen online.'

'We meant to do that, but we ran out of time…'

I shook my head, and we both laughed. She and Pete were still loved up after two kids and fifteen years of marriage. It was heartening to see. Not that I'd ever find anyone like that. I only seemed to attract shits. Yet, Adam hadn't been a shit, so it wasn't fair to say that.

Jenny stood up and pushed her chair back, making me jump. 'I'd better be off. You okay locking up?'

'Yes, I'm fine. I'll see you in the morning.'

She put on her jacket, went to the door and stopped with her hand resting on the handle. I sighed inwardly, knowing what she was going to say yet again.

She turned. I held up my hand.

'You don't need to say it, Jen. Really. It's fine.'

'But I do. I feel so bad about making you go on that date with David. I had no idea…'

'You didn't make me go. You were trying to help. Please stop apologising.'

'I know but…'

I smiled. 'You might have done me a favour, in a way.'

'How come?'

'It confirmed that I'm not ready, and I really am happier on my own. Just promise me you won't set me up with anyone else.'

She nodded. 'I'd say 'Scout's Honour' but I wasn't a scout and I don't know that thing they do with their hands.' She waved her fingers around in the air in a useless fashion.

'Goodnight,' I said, hoping that would draw a line under it and neither she nor Sandra would bring it up again. They'd been mortified when I told them what he'd said and how he'd turned so nasty.

'Night,' she said, and left, the door banging behind her.

I breathed out slowly, put our dirty plates and cups in the dishwasher, then walked around slowly, trailing my hand over the gleaming kitchen surfaces. It was so quiet. I loved having this place to myself after a busy day. Everywhere was spotless. Jenny couldn't bear a dirty kitchen. Every day before closing, she cleaned it thoroughly. She couldn't leave until it was done to her standards. She did most of the work, to be honest, leaving me to tidy behind the counter and the cafe area.

It was going to be a wrench leaving this place, but when they'd asked me if I'd be interested in running the new venture in York, it was too good an opportunity to pass up. The more I thought about it, the more I wanted to get out of London and leave the last year behind. To think, twelve months ago I wasn't even seeing Chris. Such a lot had happened since Christmas. I needed to leave here to escape the ghost of him. Yet some days I missed him so much I couldn't think straight. But he was bad through and through, and that was all there was to it. And people saying 'You can't help who you love' didn't know the half of it.

I boxed up the leftover cake to take home for Leanne. It was a lovely stroll home in the sun, and I took my time, enjoying the buzz of Shepherd's Bush. I hoped she was at Sam's, like she said she would be, as I wanted the place to myself for a bit. Inside the flat, I dropped my bag in the hallway and listened. The TV wasn't on, so Lee definitely wasn't here.

I closed my bedroom door and took a deep breath, then walked over to my wardrobe. An old handbag was hidden at the back, and it slid out easily when I grabbed the handles and tugged at it. Laying it on the bed, I sat beside it and unzipped it, savouring the anticipation. Nestling inside, all in individual bags, were all the baby things I couldn't seem to stop buying. In the first one was a set of three vests, size newborn, and snowy-white. I hadn't ever taken them out of the packet they were neatly folded in, and I didn't now. Instead, I pulled the flap up that was now loose and slipped my hand inside. The softest cotton was cool to my touch. They were pure, unsoiled, like my baby would have been if it had been born full-term. The next packet contained a tiny babygro, printed with giraffes and elephants. It had the most cute tiny feet in it. It was still on the hanger. 0–3 months. I sniffed it. It smelled of nothing, certainly not of a baby.

I upended the last bag and a fluffy grey teddy, no longer than my hand, fell out. It wasn't the sort of thing you could leave in a cot, but would look gorgeous on the windowsill of a nursery. I felt wetness on my face and put my hand up. These days, I wasn't even aware I was crying, half the time. At least there was no one here to see.

I curled up on the bed, clutching my purchases to my stomach. No one in the world knew how bad I felt. My mum knew I wasn't right, but I couldn't tell her the extent of it. She'd worry herself sick, and so would my dad. They still hadn't really got over the shock of me being pregnant, being rushed into the hospital for emergency surgery, then learning that I'd been secretly dating a killer. But it wasn't like I'd known what he was. When I saw them, which was often, I pasted a smile on my face and told them everything was wonderful. But I could see the anxiety in their faces. Like Jenny, I was an only child, and all they had. I was well aware that I was their world.

The only person I'd ever talked about having a baby with was Chris, and look how that turned out. To take my mind off things, I thought about the new flat in York. I'd only seen it in pictures. It had two bedrooms, so it would be great for when Mum and Dad, or Leanne, came to stay. It was fully furnished, but the furniture wasn't my style. Jenny said I could sell anything I didn't like and buy whatever I wanted with the money.

There was no doubt that York looked like a great place to live, but the main reason I wanted to go is that I didn't see how Chris could find me there. I had no connection with it at all. I saw him everywhere in this flat, especially in my bedroom, and I needed to get away from that. The truth was, when I laid in bed with him, our fingers intertwined, I had never had such depth of feeling for anyone. I trusted him completely, and he ripped my heart out. But I struggled to accept that he had no feelings for me. I knew he was telling the truth when he told me he loved me.

I sat up fast when I heard the distinctive squeak of the front door opening. It must be Leanne.

'Sarah? Are you in?' she called out. She'd knock before opening my door.

'Just in my room. Give me a sec,' I shouted back. 'I thought you were going to Sam's.'

'I was.' She sounded like she was passing my door now. 'But he got called into the hospital on some emergency. He'll probably be gone for hours, so I came home.'

I scooped the baby things into bags as fast as I could and threw them back into the handbag.

'I've got an awful headache,' she called. I heard cupboard doors banging in the bathroom. 'Have we got any paracetamol in here?'

'No. I used the last ones this morning, so I bought some more. They're in my bag.'

I shoved the handbag back into my wardrobe and slid the door shut. Why was my heart banging so wildly? I wasn't doing anything wrong. I needed to calm down, so I sat at my dressing table and smoothed my hair down, running my fingers through it. In my eyes was a look of wild panic, like a terrified horse or something. I needed to get a grip.

It was then I remembered. The baby bootees were still in my bag. I'd been carrying them around, finding it oddly comforting just knowing they were there.

I wrenched open my bedroom door to see Lee going back into the bathroom, having been in my bag. She closed the door behind her and I picked up my handbag. The STORK bag was near the top and you could see straight in. I hadn't bothered closing it, I'd been looking at them so often. She must have seen it. There was no way she couldn't have. The packet of paracetamol was next to my bag, with the blister pack pulled out and two tablets removed.

The toilet flushed a minute later, and she came out. She looked at me for a second longer than normal.

'You alright?' she asked, her eyes searching my face.

'Yeah. I'm fine.' My face felt tight as I tried to smile.

She nodded, and as she went past me she squeezed my shoulder, but didn't say a word as she went into her bedroom. That was it, then. She'd seen them for sure. But my lovely, special friend knew exactly what I needed. And that was for her to keep her mouth shut.

6

I SHUFFLED ABOUT ON the creaking chair in my dingy motel room, with the stuffy air clogging my lungs. The air con was broken. It had never worked since I'd been here. Leanne looked up at me expectantly, her tail nearly wagging off. She jumped up in the air and caught the chicken I pulled out of my sandwich and tossed her way, gobbling it up in a second. Then she sat back down to wait again.

'You're not starving now, you know. You don't have to beg my stuff all the time,' I grumbled.

In return, she wagged her tail and her eyes moved from me to the bread and back again.

I threw her a tiny bit more. 'Now piss off.'

The tail stopped, but she didn't move. Instead, she barked.

'Shh!' I hissed. 'You know what'll happen if *she* finds you in here.'

Leanne barked again, quieter this time.

'Get under there!' I pointed at the bed and, amazingly, she got up and slunk away, creeping underneath it and pulling most of her tail in. I could see the tip of it still waving about.

I looked up from my laptop towards the door. No sound of footsteps yet, but the woman who ran this place missed nothing. I was convinced she worked on sonar. She was like a bloody bat.

'No dogs,' she always said whenever she saw me, followed by the inevitable finger wag in my face. 'NO DOGS!' Her life's work now was trying to catch me out.

She wouldn't chuck me out, though; she wanted my rent too much. I told her the dog stayed outside, under the bushes. Her usual answer was a narrowing of her eyes. She was one of those people who hate to lose. A bit like me.

Looking around the room, I couldn't see what the problem was with having a dog in there. It was hardly The Ritz. I could afford somewhere a lot better than this, but I was conserving my money as much as I could. No point wasting it on better digs when I could easily slum it.

Still no footsteps. She must be out, or she'd have been hammering on the door by now. She knew damn well the dog was in here, but she kept up the pretence just for show. Maybe she was fearful that if I was seen to be getting away with it, then what might the other residents bring in? It was basically a rooming house with short-term lets. Short-term as in by the week. All the other renters were men, too. No idea why.

Leanne scooted out from under the bed, then jumped up onto it and flopped down to sleep. She'd obviously forgotten about my lunch, so I finished it off and turned back to my laptop, where rows of different tattoo designs filled the screen. Should I have a real one or use those temporary things? I hated tattoos. I'd never wanted one, but it could be just what I needed. Something distinctive and superficial that drew attention to it and away from other areas. But where to have it? Not the neck; that's for yobs. Same went for the hands. The arms? Forearms or biceps? Somewhere it could be covered if need be, for a job interview or such like.

I laughed out loud at the thought of me going for a job interview. What the hell would my CV say these days? Skills: computer hacking and running scams. Do you have any criminal convictions? Well no, but that's because they haven't caught me yet. Hobbies: fuck all.

Back to the tattoos. Real was the only way. Those temporary things would keep coming off, wouldn't they? Surely the clue was in the name. I pulled my sleeve up and checked my bicep. These days, there was hardly anything there, compared to what I used to have. I'd let myself go, lost all my muscle tone. But I had to; I bulked up real fast, so it was better not to do any weight training at all. I'd look too much like the old me if I did, and then I'd fool nobody.

Hang about, there was one tattoo that didn't look *too* bad. It started at the shoulder and reached to the elbow. Looked like an eagle or some other bird of prey. It was pretty cool, actually. Its wings were high above it as if it was coming in to land to catch something in its sharp talons. I liked it. And for the other arm? There was a weird kind of Aztec design, down the inside of the forearm, like random symbols and squiggles. It wasn't as bad as some of the others. I leaned back in my chair, picked up a pen, and chewed the end, thinking. If I had them done, they'd be there forever. You could never properly get rid of them. The lasers left scarring, didn't they? But maybe it was a risk I had to take.

There were loads of tattoo parlours around here. Latinos seemed to love tattoos. Most of the women had them, too. Sarah never had a tattoo. She wouldn't deface her body like that, although she might find them sexy on a man. We never talked about it. It didn't come up. I tried to think back if that Adam guy had had any. She must have found him attractive in some way to go out with him in the first place. I couldn't remember him having any obvious ones, and I notice details like that. There again, on the few occasions I saw him, I think he had a coat or jacket on.

Adam. Just the name made me shudder. On paper, yeah, it looked like I killed him, but it wasn't like that. Not really. When I hit him, he'd attacked me. I can't claim it was self-defence; he barely landed a blow on me, but he tried. If he could have hurt me, he would. So when I lost my rag and jabbed him in the head with my elbow, yes, I thought it would slow him down. Put him down, even, but I didn't kill him. He died days later when they turned his life support off. Can't blame me for that, really. I'd thought about it in great depth since it happened and that's exactly how it went down. Trouble was, a good prosecution lawyer could argue anything, couldn't they?

The only one you could argue I meant to kill was Luisa, my disgusting neighbour. But she goaded me into it and tried to turn Sarah against me. That was unforgivable. I mean, you could only take so much. And I never meant to strangle her, not really. It was more like I lost control and when I came to, it was over. I couldn't remember doing it. She was just lying there, not moving. And as for the kid I ran over all those years ago, well, that was obviously a tragic accident. So that wasn't murder or manslaughter. I didn't even know the kid and certainly never set out to kill her. And I was only a kid myself when I nicked Dad's car. Tragedies happened sometimes. It was the way of the world.

So, yeah, my CV wouldn't be your average one. I suppose I was on my own again now. Me against the rest of the world. I closed the laptop lid, and the tattoos disappeared. Sod it! I'd just get them done. Maybe another one on my leg, so if I wore shorts, it would be the thing people noticed. Perhaps you didn't need an appointment at the parlours around here; it might be like having a haircut. You went in, sat down and waited, and came out with a massive, gaudy picture defacing your skin. Forever.

I opened my laptop up again. Something at the back of my mind was nagging to get out. The rows of tattoos stared out at me again. In one of them, a guy, a mean-looking dude, had a nasty scar on his face. Like someone had glassed him under the eye. When you looked at him, you barely saw the barbed wire tattoo around his neck. The scar hogged the limelight and refused to share it.

Leanne huffed softly to herself. She was stretched flat out on her side now, making cute little noises as she dreamed. Her paws twitched, along with her nose. She was completely relaxed. I wondered what it was like to dream like that and have no cares. After Adam died, I thought I'd never sleep again. Some nights I still didn't, but it wasn't through guilt. Shit happened, and you moved on. The reason I couldn't sleep was because Sarah wasn't there with me. I needed her. I thought I'd get some plan together to get her back, but now I wasn't sure. Her reaction, if she ever saw me again, was the unknown in all of this. I knew she loved me and probably still did, but could she get over the fact she thought I killed Adam to get her away from him? I saw first-hand the guilt she'd suffered when they turned his machine off. She tried to hide it, but I heard her over the four-ways telling Leanne (the real one) that she felt guilty over Adam because she'd made all those excuses not to see him anymore and had lied to him to spare his feelings. She hadn't told him she was seeing me, but he'd known anyway. That's what we'd argued about, him and me. He knew everything I'd done, from the hacking of her computer to the pictures I'd taken of her through her webcam and posted online. He'd tried to tell her, and that's why I'd had to stop him. I couldn't risk him spilling it. If he'd only taken the money I'd offered him to keep quiet, none of the rest would have happened and he'd still be alive. Yet, ironically, Sarah worked it all out on her own, in the end. I still wasn't sure how; everything was such chaos.

Leanne opened an eye and stared at me.

'So, what shall I do, girl? Have the tattoos?'

She wagged her tail. That could be a yes. When I sat forward, she stood up on the bed, ready for action.

'Tomorrow. I'll have them done then. They'll fit me in.'

I went onto Google and started to research cosmetic surgery, especially nose jobs. Most of the pictures were of ones where bad noses had been improved. I looked in the mirror on the wall. My nose was okay. I'd never really looked at it before. It didn't have a bump or a hook; it wasn't too big or too small, or too long, or wide, or short, or snub. It was just a nose. I flattened it with my finger, then pushed the tip up. How could you change a nose? What would I ask for? Maybe I should just run into a wall and see if I could bust it. That might do it. It seemed a bit drastic, having surgery to change your appearance, but that was the point of it in the end. Usually to improve something. Would a doctor do it just to change how I looked? Probably. They'd do anything for money around here. Plus, I could say I was in Witness Protection or something and I needed it doing to save my life. No one would argue with that.

No, there was an easier way. I looked at the man with the scar again. It was amazing. The scar really was all you noticed. It made him look tough, but how hard was it to have a bottle smashed in your face? Could you do it to yourself? I couldn't see it somehow. You'd flinch at the last moment or not do it hard enough. I bet there were plenty around here would do it to me for a fee. Or maybe for a drink, although it would be an odd request. I'd have to think about it, and I thought best when I was doing something.

I stood up abruptly and Leanne was on the floor next to me, ready for action.

'Time for our swim,' I told her. 'Come on.'

I pulled on my swim shorts, put my T-shirt back on, and grabbed a towel. My ground floor room had a door to the outside, so I didn't have to go through reception to leave. Weirdly though, it didn't have a handle on the outside, so I couldn't get back into the bloody room unless I went through reception. It made no sense. I opened the door and looked around outside. No one was about. We ventured out and Leanne crept past me, then shot into the bushes. A little gate led onto the dusty street.

As we rounded the corner of the building, the landlady was skulking about outside, watering some scrawny plants in tubs outside the front door. I waved to her, and she scowled at me when she saw the dog. Before she could shout 'NO DOG', we were walking down the road towards the sea.

Leanne trotted along beside me, gazing up at me.

'Later on, we're going into the office,' I told her.
She wagged her tail.
'To see if those silly bitches are pulling their weight.'

7

'SO WHEN IS THE job due to start?' My mum pasted a smile so bright on her face it was more blinding than the sun, but it didn't fool me for one second. Instead, I saw straight through to the misery below. But not once had she asked me not to go.

'The sale should have gone through in about a month, we think. But before I start, I'm taking two weeks off. Jenny and Sandra have insisted, with...' My voice tailed off and I swallowed.

'Everything you've been through,' she finished. 'Sounds like a good idea. Any plans?'

'Maybe. Ben keeps asking me to visit him and Katie in Inverness, so I'm thinking about going up there for a few days. I'll see if Lee fancies it.'

Dad came through the door with a newspaper tucked under his arm. His slippers scraped on the carpet as he shuffled. His stoop seemed more pronounced.

'I've been thinking,' he said. 'I reckon it'll do you good, you know, the new job. More responsibility.' He straightened his shoulders and sat further back in his chair. 'Manager, eh? They must have some faith in you to ask you to take it on.'

'I know. I can't believe all they've done for me. They're like my fairy godmothers. I'm so lucky.'

'So, what else have you been up to?' he asked.

'Just working. Every day in the deli is mad. There's no time to be bored. I love it.'

'She was just saying she's going up to see Ben,' my mum said, slowly and loudly, as if he'd gone a bit deaf. Had he? I hadn't noticed.

He frowned. 'Who's Ben, again?'

Mum shifted in her chair, trying to get more comfortable. Her arthritis was getting worse. Even though they were only in their early sixties, they both seemed to have aged recently. When did that happen? With a jolt, I realised some of it had been since my emergency surgery with the pregnancy. They were worried sick they were going to lose me. Dad's grey hair was noticeably whiter.

Mum rolled her eyes. 'He's that homeless man Sarah found. The soldier one. He used to sit outside the tube station. Remember? Our Sarah took him under her wing and found his family.'

'It was Lee that found his family,' I said.

Dad pursed his lips and scratched his ear. 'Oh, yeah. Ben. How is he doing these days? Scotch fella, isn't he? You going all the way up there?'

'I'm thinking about it. He lives in Inverness. Quickest way is to fly straight from Gatwick or Heathrow. Takes about one hour and forty. The train is over ten. I can't face that.'

'It's certainly a long way. We've never been past Newcastle,' he said.

Mum frowned. 'I have! I went to Edinburgh.'

'When was that?' He screwed his body round to look at her.

'Before I met you. I went with Betty for a weekend break.'

'Oh yes. Forgot about that.' He chuckled.

Mum winked at me. 'We had a wild girls' weekend, alright. Bars, men, nightclubs, men. I've never been so drunk. Learned all sorts on that trip, me and Betty did!'

Dad and I burst out laughing.

'Nothing wrong with your memory,' he said to her. 'Good job I snapped you up when I did or there's no telling where you might have ended up.'

'Yes, thank you so much for saving me, darling. So anyway, how is Ben?' Mum asked.

'I'm not sure, to be honest. From the tone of some of his emails, I don't think everything is hunky dory up there. But with what he's been through, how could it be? I feel so sorry for him. And Kate.'

'Why, what's he been saying?' asked Dad.

'It's more what he hasn't been saying. When I ask him how things are, or a more direct question, like about his counselling, it's like he glosses over it, and I don't find anything out. And I don't know Kate at all, although I've spoken to her briefly on the phone a few times. Only met her that one time in my flat. I'm slightly nervous about going. I haven't agreed to it yet, so I don't have to. What do you think?'

Dad leaned forward. 'Maybe you shouldn't go. You don't know him that well, either, do you? He could be a raving madman for all you know.'

'Oh, thanks, Dad! That's just great! Thanks for putting that in my head.'

'Well, I'm just saying. You don't.' He turned to Mum. 'Does she?'

'I suppose not. But he hasn't come across like that to me. It'll be fine. Stop worrying her!' She stood up slowly. 'I need the loo.'

As she went past the TV, she almost caught her foot on a cable that was trailing over the carpet.

'Careful,' I said, jumping up and pulling it out of her way. 'You need to do something about those. They're going to kill you if you're not careful.'

Mum left the room and trudged slowly upstairs. She wouldn't be back any time soon.

'Have you thought any more about getting a downstairs toilet put in, Dad?'

'Yes. We've got a couple of contractors coming round next week to give us quotes. Anyway, I'm gagging for a cuppa. Do you want one?'

'Yes. Please,' I said, still eying the cables.

'I'll go make us one.' He closed the door behind him.

The cables were making me think about Chris and his OCD ways. All the nice things he used to do for me. The monstrous side of him that was obviously there had been well hidden. He'd taken one look at all the wires tangled in our flat and brought some four-ways over to tidy everything up. By the time he'd gone, the place looked a million times neater. They were still there, but I barely even noticed them anymore. To be honest, I hadn't really paid much attention to the wires themselves, either. His place had been like a showhome, with not a thing out of place. Ever. Except for the time he'd had one wild night with his mates and messed it all up. It hadn't lasted long though, and the next time I'd seen it, everything was in its place again.

It didn't add up really: how could someone with such an aversion to dirt and mess actually choke a person to death? It had to be a messy business in some ways, surely. Murder was never sanitised and clean. It couldn't be. No matter how hard I tried, I just couldn't picture him doing it.

I let out a big sigh. I'd thought he and I were forever. How could I have been so stupid? I nudged the cable with my foot, then stepped behind the TV, where it was cramped and dusty. I crouched down and started to separate the cables to see where they were coming from, coiling up all the spare lengths. There was barely room to move, but it looked much better when I'd finished. Maybe I should buy a few multi-way plugs like Chris did, and do a more permanent job.

Dad came through the door with two mugs in one hand and one in the other. One mug was tipping slightly and dripping tea onto the carpet.

'Give it here before Mum sees,' I said, squeezing out from behind the TV and taking it from him.

He frowned. 'What the heck are you doing behind there? You're all dusty.'

I put the cup down and brushed my jeans off. 'It needs tidying up behind there. There are too many wires. I'll get something to make it neater?'

He looked at me, aghast. 'Neater? Who looks behind the telly?'

'You never know.' I heard the toilet flush upstairs. 'The Queen might drop round.'

'Well, she can take us as she finds us, then,' he said. 'Behind the bloody telly!' He tutted loudly, but his eyes twinkled. He tapped me sharply on the forehead.

'Ow! What was that for?'

'Just looking to see if our Sarah is still in there or if someone's stolen her. You're the messiest of all of us.'

'I used to be. Not anymore, I'm not.'

He wasn't convinced.

An hour later, I said goodbye to my parents and headed off home. Because of the cables, I thought about Chris all the way. Where in the world was he?

When I let myself into the flat, Leanne and Sam were watching some Sunday afternoon film, curled up on the sofa together. They pulled apart slightly when they saw me.

'How's your mum and dad?' Lee asked, swinging her feet out of Sam's lap and onto the floor.

'They're alright. Same old same old.'

Sam said 'Hi' before turning back to the film, where a man brandishing a gun was running down the street, chasing someone who seemed to be able to shin over twenty-foot fences with ease. Leanne gave me a brief smile.

I would always be grateful to Sam for restoring her trust in men. Ironic though, that I was now the one that didn't trust people. She had a rapist for an ex-boyfriend, and I had a murderer. And neither of us had a clue.

I sat down and my eyes went straight to the four-ways Chris put in. They had a liberal coating of dust. Maybe Chris's obsessively tidy ways didn't rub off on me as much as I thought. The portfolio he did for me, full of pictures of the wedding cakes I made, was tucked in at the side of the TV. I hadn't opened it in ages and it, too, was covered in dust. Since I started at the delis, I'd been too busy to do more than the odd cake and I wasn't after new business. But if it hadn't been for Chris, I wouldn't have started the business in the first place. He lent me the money for my first wedding fair.

I sat up straight. The repayments I made to him. They were still going on when he disappeared. I'd tried to pay him back in a lump sum after my first wedding cake sale, but he'd refused, so I'd been doing it in tiny instalments. I hadn't checked if they were still going out or not. If they were, maybe his bank account was still open and the police could use it to track him down.

I leaped off the sofa, startling Sam and Leanne, and rushed into my room. I lifted the lid of my laptop and waited while it fired up, then logged onto the bank. Damn! The last two payments had been returned after the date of my ectopic surgery and I'd never noticed. Maybe his bank account was closed then. I still owed him a hundred pounds, although he'd insisted I didn't have to pay any of it back. He'd said he was just glad to help.

I ran my finger over the tape that was firmly in place over my webcam. The webcam he used to watch me through. How many times had I sat there not knowing he was watching? And why was he watching when he was sleeping with me, anyway? He'd insisted, when I confronted him, that he'd stopped after we started going out, but I didn't know what was lies and what was the truth. Most of what came out of his mouth was probably a lie. It was easier to think that than try to decide what he really felt for me.

A soft knock on the door and Lee called out, 'Are you okay?'

I opened the door. 'Yes. Just something I thought of. I'm fine.'

I followed her back to the living room as she said, 'You scared the living daylights out of me, jumping up like that.'

'Sorry. It was nothing.'

In the living room, I made a snap decision. 'I have two weeks off before I start the new job. I'm going to go up to see Ben and have a little break? Fancy coming?'

Lee pulled a face. 'I would love to, but I can't have any holidays until Christmas. Because of that surprise break in Tenerife Sam took me on.'

'Ah. Yeah. Forgot about that.'

'Sorry,' said Sam, looking put out. 'I thought you'd like it.'

'I did. It was brilliant,' Lee said. 'I didn't mean that.'

It must have been good. She'd gushed about it for weeks after they got back. And all the time she'd been gone, I'd crept around the flat, jumping at every little noise and checking the doors were locked. And the windows. Never mind the fact we were three floors up.

'I can fly to Inverness. Ben emailed the details just last week. He and Kate are keen for me to visit. It'll be a nice break, and September can be a lovely month up there, so he tells me.'

'You might as well go,' said Lee. 'Wish I could come. Maybe next time.'

'I'll email him back later. Tell him I'll go. Then it'll be time to pack for York.'

I sat back in my seat, staring at but not seeing the film. I didn't know if going to Inverness was a good idea or not. But there was only one way to find out.

8

I MANAGED TO BOOK an easyJet flight from Gatwick to Inverness for under fifty pounds, so I was well chuffed as I boarded the plane and settled into my seat. For the first time in what seemed like forever, I didn't keep scanning the faces of everyone within a twenty metre radius, and I relaxed back with a magazine and a gin and tonic for the flight.

As we got nearer to Inverness, a gathering of butterflies stirred in my stomach. I didn't know what it would be like to see Ben again, never mind stay in his house with his family. It was a bit of a gamble to stay in close proximity to people you didn't know very well, and I'd committed to doing it for five whole days.

Ben was due to pick me up from the airport and as I went straight through, having taken only cabin baggage, he was the first person I saw. He was standing alone, almost a head taller than anyone else, with his hands shoved deep into the pockets of his jeans. At first, he looked right past me, then his eyes swung back to mine. A huge smile spread across his face and he waved. I breathed out in relief. His smile was genuine, at least.

He walked up to me, stopped, looked me up and down, then enveloped me in a bear hug that almost knocked me over.

'You look well,' he said.

'So do you,' I told him, as we fell into step together and made for the exit.

'I can't tell you how pleased I am that you're here. We weren't sure you'd come. And Kate is so looking forward to you being here and getting to know you better.'

'Thank God for that! I've been thinking 'What if she doesn't like me or we don't get on?''

'Not a chance. She talks about you like you're her new best friend.'

'What? You're making her sound like a stalker, Ben!'

He laughed. 'I know. I didn't mean it like that. It came out wrong.'

'Never mind. How long is the drive to yours?'

'Twenty minutes or so. Not far.'

Just as we left the airport terminal, a flash of dark hair made me glance round, and I stumbled into Ben as my heart started to race. The man strode straight past me, not even glancing my way. It wasn't him. It looked nothing like him. Even the hair, now I had a good look, was all wrong. I needed to stop doing this. How and why would Chris be in Inverness airport?

'You alright?' Ben asked, steadying my arm.

'Yes. Sorry. Tripped over my own feet.'

Outside, it was blustery but bright, and he pointed to the short stay sign.

'Over there,' he said, reaching over and taking my case.

'It's okay, it's not heavy. I've packed light,' I said, laughing. 'Bet you thought I'd be one of those women that packed everything but the kitchen sink, didn't you?'

'I did, aye. And it's nae bother carrying it. After all you did for me.'

'Look, you need to stop this gratitude thing or it's really going to get on my nerves. We're friends. Equals. Not you in debt to me. Okay?'

He looked at me, startled, and pretended to hand me back the case. 'It's only a bag,' he said.

'I know. But you know what I mean, don't you?'

A smile played at the corners of his mouth. 'I do, aye. I'll try, alright?'

'Good. So, tell me, what is there to do in your neck of the woods?'

'Let's see: well, there's the castle, the cathedral, the city. Plenty of shops. All the usual stuff, I suppose. But lots of people come for the scenery, and to get away from it all. It's quite something, even if I do say so myself.'

'Sounds great. I'm looking forward to exploring.'

Ben was a naturally fast walker, and I was almost running to keep up with him.

'Your knee seems a lot better,' I huffed.

'Aye, it is much better. The doctor's given me some pills for it and they've taken a lot of the pain away. Living on the streets aggravated it, I think. You know, the constant cold.'

'I can imagine it wouldn't have helped.'

He never told me that much about the injury to his knee that he got in Afghanistan, and I didn't like to ask him. Other than the shrapnel lodged in it that they couldn't remove, I didn't know what else might be wrong with it. It never seemed the right time, back in London, to quiz him about it. With the issues regarding his mental state and his PTSD, his knee seemed the least of his worries.

We reached a blue Fiesta, and he popped the locks with a key fob.

'Jump in. Excuse the mess. Sofia leaves stuff everywhere.'

I climbed in and closed the door. Despite the kiddie's toys strewn everywhere, it was clean and smelled of the orange air freshener that hung from the rear-view mirror.

'So what are you doing with yourself these days?' I asked him as he started the car.

We pulled away, and he glanced at me, smiling. 'You won't believe it.'

'Try me. I'm intrigued.'

'I'm working at Asda. On security at the entrance. I wait for the alarm to go off.'

I burst out laughing. 'Really? Do they know you can't chase anyone with that knee?'

He laughed. 'I might not have told them that. Well, it's stress free, with the exception of the odd teenage gobshite. And that's fine for now. But it is boring. It gets me out from under Kate's feet, though.'

'Is she working this week?'

'No, she's taken the week off, in honour of your visit. She's drawn up a list of places to take you, including dragging you round the shops and doing girly things. I'll be like a spare part.'

'Sounds great to me. And I can't wait to see Inverness.'

'I think you'll like it. You won't be bored.'

'So, whereabouts do you live?'

'Near Raigmore. It's between the airport and the city. I can take you into the city tomorrow, if you want. I'm allowed. It's on the itinerary.' He smirked.

'I'd love that. And how is Sofia? I can't wait to see her.'

'She's grand, aye. Changes every day, it seems. She has very strong opinions. You'll see.'

I took a deep breath in. Enough with the chitchat. 'How has it been for all of you since you got back? It can't have been easy.'

'It has and it hasn't,' he said, stopping to insert a ticket into the barrier, which lifted up to let us out.

I inhaled sharply as we drove through. My fingers curled around the door handle.

'What are you doing?' he said, looking at me sideways.

'I always feel like those barriers are going to come crashing down on top of the car. Don't you?'

He frowned. 'No. I don't, you daft bat!'

We left the airport behind and, within minutes, were in open countryside. He put the front windows down an inch.

'Is this your car?'

'No, it's Kate's. I haven't got around to getting one yet. She works from home a lot now, and I use it when it's there.'

'What is it she does again?'

'She's a business consultant. Works for herself. I don't know what she does in great detail, but she's in demand and gets well paid for it.'

'It sounds ideal, to be able to work from home. And she must be good at it. Is that what she did at uni? Some sort of business degree?'

'Aye, she did. Got a first, too. She's got a good brain on her. No' like me.'

'Don't be silly. And don't put yourself down. Not everyone could do what you did.'

'Go off to fight? You just do as you're told. If you can't follow orders, you won't last.'

I wanted to say 'look where following orders got you— almost killed', but I didn't. He might not like it.

'Are you having counselling again?' I turned in my seat to look at him.

Aye.' His face was impassive.

'Is it helping?'

He shrugged. 'I don't know. Maybe. How do you tell? Everything feels the same. In here.' He touched his chest.

'I'd imagine there's only you could answer that. You know how you feel.'

'The funny thing is, in a way, I miss London. I never thought I would. It was rough there, sleeping on the streets. But I felt free. Does that make sense?'

'I don't know. Depends what you were running from, I suppose.'

'I was running from people who loved me because I didn't feel worthy of them. I think that's why I thought they'd be better off without me.' He sighed. 'It's gonnae be a long road, but at least I've started up it now.'

I smiled and touched his arm. 'I think you're doing incredibly well, from what you've told me in your emails.'

'Sometimes I feel like running away again, though. Just a bit of me.'

I looked at him in alarm. 'But you're not going to, are you?'

He shook his head. 'No. I'm not going to. I'm not risking losing them again.'

'It's bound to take time, Ben. And you can't beat yourself up about every little thing.'

'I know. And you're right.'

'Are you happy?'

He thought for a bit. 'I'm getting there,' he said, eventually. 'I just worry that I'm not making other people happy.'

'In what way?'

'Kate worries all the time that I'm going to disappear again. I can see it in her face. It must be so stressful for her.'

'But you're not going to. You just said so.'

'Aye, I know.'

'Maybe it's the responsibility you want to run away from. Not the actual people.'

'Maybe. I've never considered that. You could be right.'

I settled more into my seat and looked at the blur of scenery passing by the window. 'It's so green and fresh here. How the hell could you prefer dirty old London to this?'

'I know. It's mad. So, are you looking forward to moving to York?'

'God, yes. Even more so now I'm here, funnily enough. I think it's just being out of London. I haven't been gone for twenty-four hours yet and already I don't want to go back. Just looking at all these fields is making me want to buy a farm with chickens and a pony. And some dogs.'

He gave an exaggerated gasp. 'My God! Where's Sarah gone? The lass who couldn't stop internet shopping and impulse buying? Who's kidnapped her?'

'That's what my dad says, but I think she has gone, in some ways. And she's not coming back. This is the new older and wiser me.'

He was silent. Then he said, 'Is it because of him?'

I looked out of the window at the green, open space, with the Moray Firth beyond. 'I think so, yeah,' I said.

It was his turn to touch my arm.

'Leanne told me what he did to you. I know you've sort of glossed over it in our emails. What sort of shit does that?'

'Him. That sort of shit.' I turned my head to look at him. 'You know, when you think you know someone...'

'Aye. You can talk to me if it'll help, you know. I'm here if you want a man's perspective. Although that's probably the last thing you want, right?' Then he threw his head back and laughed. 'Look at us. The two lost causes.'

I smiled, but the words stung. Was that me? A lost cause? I didn't want people to think that.

We chatted for the rest of the way to his house, and he pulled up outside a semi on a newish housing estate. It was on a cul-de-sac, with fields on both sides.

'Oh, this is lovely,' I said, opening the door.

I got out of the car and stood on the drive, breathing in the air. It was fresh, and I could imagine my lungs being cleansed with each breath. The front door opened, a voice shrieked, 'Daddy!' followed by, 'Aunty Sarah!' and a small figure hurtled down the path towards us.

'Hi, Princess,' Ben said, swinging Sofia into the air. She put her arms around his neck, eyed me, and said defiantly, 'Daddy says I can call you Aunty Sarah. And I will.'

'You can. I like it,' I said.

She wriggled, and he put her down, then got my case out of the boot. She grabbed my hand and dragged me into the house, straight past Kate, who was in the hallway, and into a lovely, pale blue kitchen.

'Steady, Sofia,' Kate said. Sofia ignored her.

'I've made you a cake,' she said.

57

'Oh, fantastic.' I sat down at the table in front of a small empty plate made from red plastic.

She cut me an imaginary piece, and I pretended to eat it, rolling my eyes. 'It's delicious. You're a very good cake maker.'

She sat down next to me, satisfied, and pretended to eat some herself. 'I'm better than you,' she declared.

'Sofia!' Kate said from somewhere behind me. 'Hi, Sarah. Sorry you got dragged in.'

I turned, stood up, and she hugged me. It wasn't awkward, and I hugged her back. 'It's no problem,' I said. 'I liked it. It was fun.'

'Welcome to our home,' she said. 'I'm so glad you're here. We're going to have the best week. I've got an itinerary.' She bit her bottom lip. 'Hope you don't mind; I'm such an organiser'

'I don't mind,' I said.

Behind me, Ben gave a soft snort.

9

THE TATTOO PARLOUR I decided on was a small one down a dusty side street. I'd picked it because it wasn't too busy but looked the cleanest: a one-man-band kind of set-up. Also, there was a sign in English in the window that read *Tourists Welcome*. The main problem with it, though, was it rarely seemed to be open. On my fourth visit, someone was there. About time.

The tattooist, a lean, hairy guy with one of those stupid man-bun things, glared at Leanne when I walked through the door with her at my side, at one o'clock in the afternoon. He rattled off something in Portuguese.

I shook my head. 'Sorry. Do you speak English, mate?'

He scowled. Not the welcome this tourist was expecting.

'I am closing,' he said.' No dog.' He shook his head vigorously.

'No dog? Why not?'

'No dog,' he said again, his frown deepening.

He paused while inking a woman who was face down on a bed, his tattoo pen pointing at the ceiling.

'She won't be any bother. She'll just sit here with me,' I said.

Before he had time to answer, I went to the corner near the window and sat down on a hard plastic chair. When I snapped my fingers under the seat, Leanne crawled underneath and lay down.

'See. Like I said, no bother.'

The tattooist glowered at me again, then went back to his latest victim.

The woman was having a flower of some sort etched into her back, next to a large butterfly. What was it with women and this shit? Butterflies and flowers? They'd look better if they left themselves alone.

They were speaking in Portuguese, the woman's voice muffled by the bed, and I couldn't understand a word. They could have been saying all sorts of shit about me and I'd never know. Not that I was bothered, anyway. They could say what they liked.

I leaned back in my seat and studied the rows of pictures on the wall. The prices were displayed underneath in Brazilian dollars, and it was considerably more expensive than I was expecting. A fraction of the price of plastic surgery, though. In some of the pictures, there was hardly any skin left to see through all the dark blue and black ink. They looked awful. I really didn't want to do this, but I didn't have a choice. It was for a greater good.

From under the chair, Leanne growled, but the man didn't hear her over his tattooing pen, which was whining like a dentist's drill. Maybe the noise hurt her ears. I didn't like it either. It sent a shudder through me. I once had a filling and when the dentist was drilling, he must have hit a nerve or something. Whatever he did, I almost leaped out of the chair. For that brief second, I'd never known pain like it. After that, I had to find a new dentist, but I didn't trust any of them now. He'd apologised, of course, but it left me traumatised about dentists for years, not surprisingly; sadistic bastards, the lot of them.

I watched the tattooist at work. If I craned my neck, I could see him filling in the colours on the flower's petals. It was very intricate, and I realised how much of an artist he must be, although that wasn't the first thing that sprung to mind when you looked at him. With his creased and grubby vest and shorts, he looked like he'd just crawled out from a sleeping bag in a shop doorway. The shop looked much cleaner than him. My heart sank. I hoped he didn't smell when he was doing my tattoo. It was so hot in the shop and if he was sweating, it would be hard for me to sit there for as long as it was going to take. Maybe I should just go.

The woman was smiling now and attempting to sit up. She was wearing a low-backed vest, and she pulled a thin shirt over her new design. Before the shirt covered it up, I noticed that the skin all around and underneath it was bright red. Bet that would hurt for days. I grimaced inwardly at the thought. For people to do this just for the look of it was lunacy. Yet here I was, doing the same thing. At least I had a better reason.

She handed him some notes and left the shop. He shoved the money in his pocket and lit up a cigarette before glancing over at me. Great! Now I was going to stink of smoke! But cigs were everywhere here. It was more usual to smoke than not, or at least in the bits of Brazil I'd been in so far. But I had to do this, stink or not.

The tattooist looked over. 'I am closing,' he said with a shake of his head. 'I already tell you this. I close every day at one.' His voice was deep and resonated around the space.

'I'll pay double,' I said.

'No.' He turned away and fiddled with his tools.

'Triple.'

He turned back, looking puzzled, and I held up three fingers, as if he was an idiot. Which he may well have been.

He paused, then his body softened, and he beckoned me over. Leanne darted out from under the chair as I got up, but returned when I told her to. Her eyes followed me all the way to where the tattooist waited for me. He pointed to a chair by the bed and I sat.

'Okay. What are you want doing?' he asked me.

I pulled out my phone and showed him the bird design I didn't hate. There was a similar one on his display wall and I pointed to it.

'Something like that.' I pointed to my left upper arm. 'On here.'

He sucked some more smoke down. My eyes watered and I coughed.

'Which one? That one or that one?' he pointed between the two pictures.

'Any. I'm not bothered.'

He blinked and scratched his beard. 'Not bothered? What you mean?'

'I don't care. Whichever is the quickest to do. How long will it take?'

He studied the bird one on his wall. 'That one? Ten hours. Or more.'

Ten hours? For one tattoo? Fuck! I scrolled to the Aztec design on my phone and touched my right forearm from the elbow to the wrist, above where a watch would sit. I wanted it covered if I need to wear a proper shirt. 'And this one here? Or something like it.'

He shook his head and tutted, rolling his eyes. 'Something like it! So, not exactly? What about this?'

He pointed to a picture I hadn't noticed on his wall. It looked more like Celtic symbols than Aztec. It wasn't bad.

I nodded. 'Yeah. That'll do. How long will that one take?'

He narrowed his eyes at me. 'It is simpler. Two, maybe three hours. But you take the piss or something, yes?'

'What? No. Why?'

'Because most people want exact thing. I think you don't want tattoo really.'

'Not really,' I agreed. 'But let's just get on with it, shall we?' I touched my arms again. 'Bird.' I tapped the left arm. 'Whatever that squiggle is.' I touched my right. 'And I might want one on my leg here.'

I touched the calf on my right leg.

'What of?'

'Dunno. What do you suggest?'

He breathed out slowly. 'I suggest you go away and think about it. All of it. And come back when you are sure. I close up shop now.'

'I said I'd pay triple if you do them both now.'

He glared at me. 'I can't do both now. It takes long time.'

'Please?' I glared back. For God's sake! What happened to the customer is always right?

He glanced up at the ceiling, probably working out the maths. 'I start bird one now. You come back every afternoon at one this week when I close. For three hours. Five days. For this money.' He held up three fingers, grinning. *Holy shit!*

I nodded. 'Okay. Great. Thanks.'

'What colours?' he asked, walking over to the door. He locked it and pulled a blind down over the glass, casting a gloom over the interior. Leanne wagged her tail as he went by, but he ignored her. What a wanker! I disliked him even more.

'Surprise me,' I said. 'Er, does it hurt?' Maybe I should have asked this first before I antagonised him. What if there was a way for him to make it extra painful? 'I don't like needles. I might faint.'

He eyed me up and down. 'You don't look like you will faint.'

'Trust me. I might. If you're rough with me.'

His face relaxed, and he tried not to smile.

'Okay, I will be gentle, if you insist.'

He lifted my left arm onto the armrest of the chair. 'Stay relaxed and don't move,' he instructed, his eyes roaming over the picture of the eagle on his wall.

He leaned over me and cleaned the area with something on a wipe. I breathed out gratefully; if I ignored the cig smoke, he only smelled of aftershave. I cranked one eye open as the pen started up. Leanne lifted her head and cocked her ears forward, the left one swivelling like a radar. But she stayed where she was. Just as well she didn't rush out from under the chair and bite the guy on the ankle just as the needle touched my skin.

At the thought of the needle, I went hot, then cold. The whine of the pen got worse, and I squeezed my eyes shut, feeling dizzy. A sudden flush of anxiety had me gripping both armrests.

'Just relax,' he said. When I looked, the bastard was smirking.

'Easy for you to say.' It came out in a strangled tone. Then I remembered tattoos covered his arms, so it wasn't easy for him to say. He liked it. He must be one of those masochistic fuckers that got off on pain. Shit!

The pen stopped.

'Are you absolutely sure you want this? No one is forcing you.' Now he had a big grin on his face.

'They are forcing me,' I said through clenched teeth. 'My girlfriend loves tattoos. She wants me to get loads of them.'

He chuckled, turned a radio up loud, started the pen and got to work.

In the end, the pain wasn't as bad as I was expecting. What was worse was the shit Portuguese radio station that blared out crap music, and his awful singing that went with it. I was convinced he was doing it to prolong the torture. But it took bloody ages, and I was bored stupid. If he'd offered me a general anaesthetic I'd have taken it. I'd been in the damn chair for over three hours, like he said, pausing only twice: once to let Leanne out in the small yard at the back of the shop, and once for me to use the loo myself.

But watching him at work, I got the feeling he took real pride in what he did, and the eagle taking shape in front of me was mesmerising to see. At long last, he switched the pen off and straightened up with a groan, causing his back to crack violently. Leanne, who had been curled up asleep on a chair, opened her eyes, yawned, and jumped to the floor.

'Your dog is good dog,' he said as I stood up.

'Yep. She is.' A sharp stab of pain in my lower back made me wince.

Leanne came creeping over and the next thing, he was bending down and stroking her under the chin. She was in raptures, like he was her new BFF.

'Thought you didn't like dogs,' I said.

'I love dogs. Just don't want them in shop. Everyone will bring them in if I am not careful. Place will be like zoo.'

My arm felt hot and I hung it over the side of the chair towards the floor. Leanne sniffed it for a second before losing interest.

'How was it? You did not faint,' he said, casting a critical eye over the image.

'It was okay. A lot better than the dentist.'

He laughed. 'That is glowing recommendation. How it feels now? Sore, uh?'

'A bit.'

'That is usual. Keep it clean, yes?'

'I will. Can I swim in the sea? I usually swim every day.'

'Yes, that will be good. The salt, you know.'

I opened my wallet and took out an exorbitant amount of money for the three hours' work he'd just done. He patted me on the back as he took it from me and pocketed it with a big grin.

'I am Miguel,' he said.

'I'm Carl.'

See you tomorrow, Carl. One o'clock.'

'Can't wait,' I deadpanned.

***

For the rest of the week, I went back to the tattoo shop every day after lunch to find Miguel waiting. On the second day, he worked on the eagle again, then started the other arm the day after, to 'give the first one to rest.'

The time spent in the chair dragged on, but gradually he began to talk more each afternoon, and I began to relax and enjoy his company. He was more of a laugh than he'd seemed at first. He should be, considering all the money I was giving him. On the last day, he seemed happier than ever. I wondered if he'd got laid last night or something.

'You know the pub near the harbour? With the flags outside?' he said. He put his tattooing pen down, dipped a cotton wool pad in some disinfectant, and dabbed my arm with it.

I hissed through my teeth. 'Yeah.'

'I go there most nights,' he said. 'You come. For drink.' He mimed lifting a glass to his mouth, as if I didn't know how to drink.

'Okay,' I said, thinking, 'No way.' I was suddenly uneasy. Was he hitting on me? Didn't seem gay. And I'd told him I had a girlfriend; I'd been lying about her for days, mainly describing Sarah. In the end, I decided he wasn't. He was just being friendly. Then, at last, he stood up and nodded. Thank God; it was finished.

I sat up in the chair, my back killing me. If mine was this painful, I dreaded to think what his must be like. But he was lithe and supple as he leaned over to inspect his handiwork.

'I have a boat in the harbour. I am always there,' he said, turning my right arm this way and that, checking the design. Several interlinking Celtic bands now wrapped around my forearm. Much less intricate than the eagle.

'A boat?'

'A little pleasure cruiser. We have parties on there. Lots of women and drink, if you fancy. Bring your girlfriend.'

'Sounds good. I'll come down.'

'The boat is *Santa Lina*,' he said.

'Santa Lina. Okay.'

He pointed at my new tattoos. 'So, what do you think? You like?'

'Mmm. They're good, actually. Better than I was expecting.'

'Praise indeed, then.'

'Thank you. No, seriously. I'm grateful. You're good.'

He gave a small bow. 'See you soon then, Carl,' he said.

I hesitated. I hadn't made any friends since I came here and it would be good to pal around with someone. I never expected him to be on the same wavelength as me, but people surprise you, don't they? And the mention of boats had piqued my interest.

'Alright, I will,' I said. 'Sounds good, mate.'

I paid him the final instalment and told him I'd come back for the leg doing. If he still thought I was strange, he didn't let on.

'So I will see you at the bar or at harbour sometime? It will be fun. I like you English.'

'Yeah, I'll come down. I'll look forward to it, Miguel.'

'Call me Mig.'

I smiled. 'Okay. See you soon.'

Leanne shot out of the doorway in front of me and danced in circles around my feet. I stood in the sun, resisting the urge to scratch the red-hot skin on both my arms. I'd better not get an infection in this damn place. When I thought about it, I had no idea why I'd even picked Brazil to flee to. I'd just plucked it out of thin air, as it seemed far enough away.

There was a bar near the tattoo place that I'd never been in, with a few rickety-looking tables outside. Although it wasn't yet lunchtime, I made my way over to a table and sat down. Leanne lapped loudly from a bowl of water on the floor outside, then sat by my feet. Before long, a woman came over and asked me what I wanted. I ordered a double tequila. For what I was about to do next, I needed a dose of strong stuff, both to give me courage and to dull the pain that was coming. It would be much worse than the tattoos.

10

INVERNESS WAS BRILLIANT, AND Kate had whisked me off to see the sights. We'd been to the castle, sitting atop its hill overlooking the city, all red brick walls and round turrets. It was spectacular. Same with the cathedral, and we'd shopped and pampered ourselves in beauty salons. But my favourite part was just walking along the river, watching Sofia and Ben chasing pigeons and squirrels. We'd done this every morning, after Sofia had come back from nursery, and it felt like a comfortable old routine. I'd miss it when I left.

Kate's gaze was never far from Ben. Sometimes, the tension around her mouth was clear. My chest tightened at what it must feel like to have your partner just up and leave like he did. She must feel he never loved her enough to fight, but that wasn't true. It wasn't that simple. In a funny kind of way, I think it was because he loved her too much. He couldn't stand the thought of hurting her in any way or seeing any disappointment at him in her eyes.

'It's so beautiful, this city. Have you always lived here?' I asked her, as we watched Sofia race along the river's edge.

'Aye. I've never lived anywhere else. I'm settled here. Wish I could say the same for him, though.' She nodded at Ben, who was running with Sofia.

'Why? What do you mean?'

'He seems unsettled sometimes. Like a caged animal. I can't describe it any other way. I live with the constant fear he'll disappear again.' Her eyes met mine. They were loaded with anxiety.

'That must be so awful. But I'm sure he won't. He's getting better, isn't he? I mean, the counselling is helping. He told me it was when he picked me up at the airport.'

'Did he? I'm not sure. He clams up when I talk to him about it. I don't know what to do.'

'Maybe you don't need to do anything. Just let him get on with things in his own way.'

She shrugged. 'I suppose. But it's like walking on eggshells.'

'I can imagine.' My phone pinged with a text. It was from Leanne, asking if I was having a nice time, followed by a pouty-face emoji.

'She's so annoyed she couldn't come,' I told Kate, trying to lighten the mood a bit. 'I think she'll be up here first chance she gets. If not with me, then probably with Sam.'

'I hope so. That would be great. I hope you both can come and see us often, separately or together. I'd love for Sofia to really get to know you.'

'I will, if I can. And you three will have to come and see me in York after I'm settled.'

We left the path and headed back towards the shops and the car parks. Sofia had been promised ice cream, and there was no way she would forget. She tugged Ben's hand all the way to the cafe where she'd seen the tubs of ice cream lined up behind a counter. She turned to us, a delighted grin splitting her face.

'I'm having Tutti Frutti. What are you having?'

'Um, Fudge, I think,' I said. 'Or toffee.'

'Strawberry for me,' said Kate.

Sofia pulled a face. 'You always have strawberry.' She rolled her eyes, and I tried not to laugh.

'What's wrong with strawberry?' Kate asked.

As Sofia dragged Ben off, Kate turned to me. 'I'm going to take Sofia to my parents later. Leave you and Ben to catch up and have a proper chat without madam keep interrupting.'

'Okay. Maybe we'll go for a walk.'

I hoped she wasn't expecting me to quiz him and report back to her. That wouldn't feel right at all.

***

After lunch, a massive sugar rush hit me, and I had to go for a lie down. The spare bedroom was cosy and comfortable, and as soon as I stretched out, I dozed off. When I woke, the house was deathly quiet. I looked at the bedside clock; I'd been asleep almost an hour. Kate must have gone to her parents, like she said. It was odd, the house being so still. I hadn't realised kids made so much noise. Sofia shouted everything, despite her mum and dad constantly telling her not to. The quiet was a welcome change.

Where was Ben? I sat up and scooted off the bed.

'Ben?' I opened the bedroom door and listened. No sound came from anywhere.

I went down the stairs and stopped at the bottom. The living room was empty, as were the kitchen and dining room. I stepped outside into the back garden. He wasn't out there either. I stood as still as I could, listening hard. A soft noise came from behind me. The only door I hadn't checked was the one into the garage. Another sound, a shuffle this time.

I put my hand on the door and hesitated, not knowing what I might find inside. If Ben was more depressed than he'd been letting on, anything could be behind that door. Desperate people did desperate things, didn't they? I didn't want to go in, but I had to. What if…?

I pushed the door open and rushed through it with my heart slamming, then stopped dead at the sight of Ben, curled up in the corner and not hanging from the rafters, as my imagination had suggested.

'Ben? What on earth?'

He was sitting on the dusty floor with his back against the wall, holding his head in his hands, and his shoulders were shaking from his sobbing.

'Ben? Hey, it's okay.' I sat beside him and wrapped my arms around his unyielding body, holding him while he cried. He wrapped his arms tighter around his head and couldn't seem to stop. There was nothing I could do but hold him. The sound of someone's heart breaking was a sound like no other, and before long, my face was wet with my own tears.

It took a long while before his body stilled and his sobbing eased. After wiping his face on his sleeve, he looked up at me with red eyes.

'Sorry,' he said, sniffling. 'I'm so sorry.'

'You don't have to apologise to me.'

I shifted position, trying to get comfortable on the hard floor. Ben didn't move. I thought I understood it then.

'Is this what you do? Wait for them to go out, then come in here and fall apart?'

He sniffed harder and cleared his throat. 'Aye. Sometimes.'

'Waiting until the coast is clear?'

'Something like that.'

'I get it. I've done a similar thing myself when Leanne's gone out. It's like you can kind of completely let go, the first chance you get, and you take it. Right?'

'I thought you were asleep. I just couldn't hold it in. I… I tried…' He gripped both sides of his head and squeezed tightly, his knuckles going white, until I prised his fingers off and brought them to his lap.

'I get it. I really do.' I spoke softly, like he was a wounded animal that could bolt at any second. It reminded me of when he was in London, and someone dropped some plates in a cafe. He'd leaped out of his chair, petrified at the noise. It was sharp and sudden, like a gunshot. 'Now, let's get out of here and go inside. My back is killing me,'

I groaned, making a show of getting up like an old woman, and held my hand out to him. He grabbed it and got up, one of his knees making a loud popping sound.

'Aargh!' he shouted. It made me laugh and then I couldn't stop, which made him start.

We were still giggling five minutes later, sitting in the garden after brushing dust off our clothes. I shivered. In the distance, from the direction of the river, dirty black rain clouds were billowing up.

'I'll make us some coffee, shall I?' I said.

'Thanks.'

He was sitting quietly now, in a garden chair, staring down at his hands. I wondered what he was thinking, but maybe I wouldn't understand. I didn't ask. Every time I tried to imagine the horrors of what he must have seen and lived through, it was as if a part of my brain shut down and refused to contemplate it. But his couldn't do that. Perhaps it was like someone kept hitting rewind and play, and he couldn't stop it.

I stood inside and watched him through the window while I waited for the kettle to boil. If there was something more I could do to help him, I didn't know what. Maybe some things were just too broken for others to fix. I hoped he could find the solution to fix himself. Whatever I'd been through, he'd been through much worse.

When I made the coffee, I took it outside and put it on the table. Ben eyed the cups then got up.

'Leave it. We'll go for a walk instead. I'd rather be out when they come back. Just to pull myself together a bit more.'

'Alright. Let me put some trainers on first.'

I tipped the coffee down the sink. If we left two full cups untouched, it might look a bit odd.

We went out of a small gate in his back garden, which led to a footpath that cut straight through the field.

Neither of us spoke for a while until I said, 'I think you should just tell Kate exactly how you're feeling and stop trying to hide it from her. It's probably making her worry more that she has to try and guess what's going through your head all the time.'

He didn't respond, but sped up slightly as we neared a stand of trees. I caught him up and put a hand on his arm. He stopped.

'What is it you're afraid of, Ben? Surely the worst has already happened. How can it get worse than what you've already been through?'

His eyes searched mine. He was really listening to me. Should I plough on or back off? I was beginning to understand what it must be like for Kate, afraid to say the wrong thing in case he took off again. I didn't know if he would let himself be found a second time.

His shoulders slumped. 'I know what you're saying is right. It's just, she wouldn't be able to handle me talking about what it was like over there, the things I've seen. And I'm done talking about all that.'

'You don't know she wouldn't. But she doesn't need to know the gory details, anyway, does she? You haven't told me that stuff, but I can see you're still hurting. Stop shutting her out. She loves you. Let her help you.'

His gaze wandered the horizon, but I didn't think he was seeing it.

'What I think is that unless you've lived that life and been to those places, you probably can never understand. Isn't that why Army people say their colleagues become like their family?' I ask.

'Exactly. Aye. But Kate and Sofia, they're precious, kind of unsullied, if you like. I feel like I'll contaminate them if I bring it into our lives here.'

'I don't think you will. Kate is stronger than that and she loves you so much. Just give her a chance. She won't let you down.'

'How come I can talk to you about it more easily than her?'

I laughed, and he frowned. 'What?'

73

'That's exactly what I've been asking myself. I can't talk to my mum or Leanne about what happened with Chris, but if a stranger walked up here now and said 'spill, and I'll never see you again', I probably would. It's understandable. So either talk to her or your therapist. But the worst is over. Don't let the past destroy what you have left in front of you. It's just not worth it.'

He turned to face me. 'And are you going to follow your own advice in that?'

'What do you mean?'

'York.'

'Yes. I bloody well am. That's what York is for me. A fresh start. I've wondered if I was running away, moving to York, but I've decided I'm not.'

I turned away so he couldn't see the uncertainty that must be written all over my face. To my relief, he said nothing, but I didn't know if he believed it. I didn't know if I believed it myself.

11

'AUNTY SARAH? WHAT TIME are we making this cake? I've been waiting forever.'

Sofia sat on the stool she'd spent ages dragging over to the worktop, slumped down theatrically, and let out an enormous sigh. She cast her eye over the mixing bowls, cake tins and other baking paraphernalia that were lined up ready.

'When your daddy gets back from the shops with everything we need. We can't make a cake without all the right ingredients, can we?' That must be the tenth time I'd explained it. In five minutes, she'd no doubt ask again.

She glared at the empty weighing scales, her face hostile. I looked away so she couldn't see me dying to laugh. She had one hell of a personality, alright.

'He won't be much longer.'

'But he's been gone ages,' she whined, poking at a half-full bag of caster sugar.

'Well, it probably isn't easy to find purple food colouring around here. Or blue. Or red. He has to get the things you specifically asked for.'

'Sofia, please stop moaning,' said Kate from her seat at the kitchen table. 'Or Aunty Sarah won't want to bake with you at all. She might change her mind and decide not to do it if you're going to whinge like a brat all the time.'

Sofia sat bolt upright. 'You won't, will you, Aunty Sarah? Please say you won't!' Her eyes went wide, and she looked at me imploringly.

I glanced at Kate, who shook her head and tried not to laugh.

'I might,' I said, 'If you can't be patient. Baking is all about patience. How are you going to wait for it to cook if you have no patience?'

'Good answer!' muttered Kate, flipping over a page in her magazine. 'You're good at this.'

I sat down to wait. I'd been walking on eggshells ever since Ben's meltdown. He hadn't said a word about it. When we got back from our walk, Kate and Sofia were back, and he acted as if nothing was wrong. His acting skills were top notch, I'd give him that. I couldn't say anything to Kate, as it wasn't my place. But I was going to make sure they got some time alone, so he could bring it up if he wanted to. I thought he should. It was why I suggested I bake a cake with Sofia in the first place, so they could go out on their own. Now I just had to persuade them.

Just then, the front door opened, and Ben stepped through, clutching a very full carrier bag.

'Daddy!' Sofia screeched, flipping round on her stool until she was on her tummy, then sliding down so her feet touched the floor. 'Did you get everything on the list?'

He put the carrier bag on the worktop. 'I hope so. Or my interpretation of the list, anyway.'

'What does that mean?' she asked.

'Never mind,' I said. 'Right; let's have a look.'

There was self-raising flour, two blocks of butter, eggs, cocoa powder and strawberry jam. Small bottles of different food colouring were at the bottom, along with a bottle of vanilla extract and a packet of white fondant icing. Some of this wasn't supermarket stuff. I raised my eyebrows at him.

'The supermarket was rubbish. There's a kitchen shop in town that sells specialist stuff. Like bloody purple food colouring! It's taken me forever.'

I flashed him a smile. 'Great. Now why don't you two go for a walk or something while us girls do the important stuff. Get out from under our feet.' I stared at him meaningfully from under my eyebrows and he blinked.

'Oh. Okay. Good idea. Kate? Are you coming?'

She was already on her feet, pulling on a jacket that was on the back of her chair. 'I don't need asking twice. Sounds fab to me. We can go to that coffee shop I like.'

She went into the hallway to find some shoes and I whispered to Ben, 'Don't waste this opportunity, and don't come back in under two hours. Preferably three. Make the most of me babysitting.'

He looked terrified. 'I won't. And thanks.'

Sofia was laughing, repeating 'get out from under our feet' in her sternest voice, as her parents went through the front door.

'So,' I said to her. 'Are you absolutely sure about this? You can still change your mind.'

'I don't want a stupid unicorn. I want a Catalina cake.' Catalina, the hideous troll doll with bright purple hair, a blue face, a red dress and red shoes, was clamped tightly to her chest. 'Hate stupid unicorns. They're stupid.'

'So I gather. Okay, then. Prop her up over there, away from the flour, so I can look at her when I need to, and we can get started.'

She did as she was told, and I switched the oven on. I showed her how to grease the cake tins and weigh out all the ingredients. It was a joy to work with her. I wondered if my baby had been a girl, is this how if might have been? Of course it would.

'You have to help with the washing up, don't forget. And there'll be a lot of it,' I reminded her.

She nodded her head so vigorously it was a miracle it didn't come off. 'I will. Anyway, I know where everything goes.'

I let her take the lead for the next hour, fighting against my instincts to take over if she didn't do it right. It was her first time. Baking wasn't Kate's thing. After a few days away from the deli, I was dying to get stuck in, and doing it with Sofia was even better. Despite the kitchen looking like a bomb had exploded in it, it was the most relaxed I'd been in ages.

We washed up while the four sponges were in the oven, and by the time they came out, the kitchen was mostly clean again.

'We need to leave them to cool, now,' I said.

'Then we can decorate them?' She was gazing at them on their wire racks as if they were the most exquisite things she'd ever seen. Like Chris had, when he'd once made a cake for me. By my standards, they were a bit on the flat side.

'Yep. You got it.'

'Yep. You got it,' she parroted. 'How long does it take?'

'About an hour. They have to be fully cold.'

'Why?'

'Because the frosting or icing would melt otherwise and run off the cake. So if there's something else you want to do, now would be a good time.'

'Can I go and watch TV?'

'Would Mummy let you?'

She nodded. 'I'm allowed to watch cartoons on Cartoon Network. I know how to put them on.'

'Alright then. Off you go.'

She ran out of the kitchen and I soon heard raucous music and cartoon sounds coming from the living room, along with her loud peals of laughter.

I sat at the table. Alone at last. I hoped Ben and Kate were making the most of their time together to clear the air. What if pushing them together in this way wasn't the right thing to do? But I was going home soon and I had to try. Ben was in such a state yesterday, I didn't know how long he could go on. He couldn't keep shutting her out for the rest of their lives.

I slid my tablet out of my handbag and switched it on. Funny how I hardly ever went on social media anymore, yet not so long ago I was rarely off it. I was like a junkie, always looking for the next fix. Now I hated it. Since I closed down my Facebook profile, I rarely went on Instagram either. I'd been so busy with the delis that my baking business had taken a back seat. I wasn't unhappy about it. It'd be there when I wanted to take it up again.

I Googled the cafe in York. It was called *The Pantry*, but we intended to change it to *Delish*, like the other two in London. It was smack in the city centre, and the customers were a mix of shoppers and workmen. From what Jenny said, the menu seemed very basic. The two waitresses who worked there full time had agreed to stay on, so I wouldn't be looking for staff, which suited me. I'd never interviewed anyone, and the thought of firing someone terrified me. I'd probably be the one who ended up crying. There again, if they were totally useless or nasty, I might be glad to do it.

It wasn't a big shop and the cafe only had eight tables. I'd be kept busy as I'd be making most of the stuff to sell myself, except for the bread, which would be delivered fresh every day. Bread's never been my thing. I've always been more a cakes and desserts kind of girl.

Before I realised, I was googling *Christopher Gillespie*, my fingers glancing over the keys on muscle memory. I'd googled it so many times, and it brought up all the usual results. I scrolled to the one I wanted, a picture from the London Evening Standard, in a report after what happened with Luisa and Adam. He looked decidedly dodgy in it: he'd been caught mid-blink, so his eyes were half-closed, and he was unshaven. And his hair was tousled. Apart from the eyes, he looked gorgeous, and I felt the familiar kick in my stomach at the sight of him. Try as I might, I couldn't stop this reaction. What was wrong with me? Something must be, I knew that much. I pressed my fingers hard into my eye sockets to stop the prickling there.

Another round of screeching laughter came from the living room, and I checked the clock on the oven. I was good for time. When I changed my phone, I didn't copy the pictures of him from my old one onto my new one. I didn't see the point, but God, how I missed them now. There weren't that many, but I loved the ones of us together. Looking at him should have made my skin crawl, and when I thought about what he'd done, it did. But also, when I thought of the way he was with me, tender and loving, all I felt was the loss of him; keen, sharp, and deep.

What the hell had possessed him to do such horrible things, though? Hacking my webcam? I still couldn't get my head around it, even six months on. And where was he? The thought I might never see him again brought me relief, but also terrified me. How would I live my life without him in it? Whenever I thought about it, I'd go panicky. But I had to. He was a monster. If I could just turn off my feelings for him and never think of him again, then I just might be alright. The only hope I had was that I wouldn't always feel this way, time being a great healer and all that.

His LinkedIn account was still there. That had the best picture of all. He was staring straight at the camera, about to smile. That picture of him was the one that could bring me to my knees. I studied his eyes, intense and expressive. His full-lipped mouth. I'd always loved his mouth. He could make me laugh in an instant, but his remarks could also be cutting, crude, and cruel. But they were never directed at me. He could be hurtful, but never at my expense. And I knew, beyond a doubt, that he would have stuck up for me in any situation, even if he thought I was wrong. Would our baby have looked more like him or me?

I stared deep into his eyes. If he was the Devil himself, then what did that make me? The Devil's advocate?

I was lost in that photo for such a long time, I jumped when Sofia came flying in.

'Aunty Sarah, are they cool yet?'

I switched off the tablet. 'Wash your hands, then touch them very gently and see.'

Her hands barely got wet before she poked a finger in the top of one of them, leaving a dent at least a centimetre deep.

'I said gently! You've squashed it in, look.'

She put a finger to her mouth, her eyes wide, and said, 'Oops!'

'Never mind. We can fill it with icing.'

She looked relieved.

'Let me cut them. The knife is very sharp.'

She nodded solemnly while I did it. 'They're a different colour inside!' she breathed in awe.

'Test the sponge with your finger,' I said, pressing it very lightly with the pad of my middle finger.

She copied me, the tip of her tongue poking put in concentration. 'Why?'

I laughed. 'Because it feels nice.'

She giggled, her shoulders rising up to her ears.

'You spread the jam on two of them, GENTLY, and I'll think about how to make a doll shape.'

She spread strawberry jam liberally over the cut sponges, as well as the boards they were standing on and half the work surface, until the jar was empty.

'I don't think you can help with the next bit, but you can watch me.'

'Okay,' she said, seemingly happy to sit there.

I divided the fondant, colouring it blue, purple, red, and black, using Catalina herself to give me the right shades. It wasn't far off.

'Are you happy with those colours?' I presented them for examination.

'Yes, yes, yes.' She nodded eagerly, barely looking at them.

I cut the sponges up to form the body and head into roughly the shape of Catalina, the ugliest doll in the world.

'The head's not right. It's too square,' Sofia said.

I stared at her. 'Who's the professional here?'

'You are.'

'Well, let me do it then. Without criticising, if you don't mind.'

'Without what? What's that?'

I thought about it, then said, 'Never mind.' She was putting me off my stride. I couldn't be giving her an English lesson when I had this troll to finish.

She didn't interrupt anymore and by the time I was almost done, Catalina the Cake Girl was scarily like Catalina, the original version. There was only her hair to finish.

It wasn't easy, with most of my professional tools missing. I'd just have to improvise.

'Do you want to help put her hair on? I can cut it and you can help stick the strips to her head. I'll do the first one to show you.'

'Yes, yes, yes,' she said, clapping her hands.

I rolled out the purple fondant thinly, then cut it into inch-long strips, just like the real Catalina's. About forty should do it. I stuck one to her head and twisted it into a spike, pressing it onto her head at about a forty-five degree angle. It stuck straight up. Sofia and I did the rest together, and I mostly resisted tweaking hers. Not everything had to be perfect. What else about my life was?

I was just putting the finishing touches to her nose, mouth, and eyes when the front door opened. I looked up to see Ben and Kate's linked hands separate.

'How's it going?' Kate's eyes were bright, and her cheeks had a healthy flush. 'Oh, wow! Sarah, that's amazing. How have you done that?'

She walked around Catalina, taking her in from every angle, looking from the cake version to the doll version and back again. 'You should be on one of those cake making shows on the telly. You'd walk all over them.'

I shrugged. 'Thanks. We've just about finished.'

Ben said, 'It looks great. Can we eat some?'

Sofia looked shocked. 'No! We can't cut her up.'

'Oh! Isn't that the point?' He looked at me. So did Sofia.

'Well, it is a cake, I suppose. Daddy's right, but it's your cake, so it's up to you.'

'No, then. We can't eat Catalina. It would hurt her. She's coming to bed with me.'

'Er, no, she isn't, young lady! Now, who's for a nice cup of tea? And some biscuits, seeing as we won't be having cake,' Ben said, rolling his eyes.

As he put the kettle on, Kate slipped off upstairs. Sofia had her elbows on the worktop and was gazing at the cake, singing softly to it.

'So?' I said quietly to Ben. 'Any good?'

His eyes slid to the stairs and back. 'I think so. You were right. About everything. We had a good talk, cleared the air. It was good.' He smiled. 'Thanks for kicking me up the arse. I am trying, you know.'

I touched his arm. 'Brilliant.'

I left it at that. I'd done all I could.

12

I'D CHICKENED OUT REPEATEDLY over the last few days, and now I'd whiled away the whole afternoon sitting in the shade outside the bar. I'd had too many for Dutch courage and I couldn't have any more. If I didn't have a steady hand for what I was about to do, it could be even more catastrophic.

'Come on, Leanne,' I said, draining my last tequila. I stood, still holding the glass in my hand, then put it in my pocket. At least I hadn't brought the moped. I wasn't sure I'd be in a fit state to drive.

At the thought of that, a deep shudder ran right through me. The last time I wasn't fit to drive, I ran over that kid. Even though it was half my lifetime ago, it was as fresh as yesterday. As well as only being fifteen and not having a licence, I shouldn't have been driving because I was coked up.

I hadn't touched coke since I'd been over here. I never thought I'd do it again after that night all those years ago, but I'd fallen back into it since meeting Sarah. Something else I'd had to work hard to hide from her. It wasn't hard to get drugs around here. I'd been offered them openly by little kids in the street, but no way was I going back to that mug's game. Besides, I needed all my money to get back home. Living this frugally was only bearable because I was doing it for a higher purpose. It made me think about the unnecessary trappings of the life I had before.

Leanne trotted beside me as I set off back down the street. We were walking parallel to the beach, and it was quieter back here. Suddenly, Leanne stopped dead, right next to me.

'What? What's up, girl?'

I looked to where she was gazing down the street, her fur standing up at the back of her neck and shoulders. Wise move. There was a mean-looking bastard of a dog, a huge beast, outside a gate, and it was eyeballing her in a way I didn't like. Thankfully, a thick chain was around its neck.

I picked her up and tucked her under my arm before crossing the road to put plenty of distance between us. That thing could eat us both alive. Leanne trembled in my arms, still watching the dog. When we got level with it, it growled and lunged forward. The chain tightened with a snap, and for a horrible second I thought it was going to break. Leanne barked at it before hiding her head under my arm.

A man came stalking out of the gate and shouted at the dog, which ignored him. When it carried on barking, he dragged it back inside on its chain and, before closing the gate, rattled off something to me. I didn't understand a word of it, of course. Why the dumb bastard didn't just keep the gate closed in the first place was beyond me. Some people! No brains, that was the problem.

I felt a massive surge of homesickness for the UK. I didn't belong here, and right now, I'd rather be anywhere else. Even the Leeds shithole I came from would be preferable to this.

For the first time in months, I thought of my sister, Shay, the only living family I had left (I wasn't including the old man in this analogy. Even if he was still alive and in jail, my dad was dead to me). Just recently, Sarah was the only thing I had that felt like family. My sister hadn't felt like family for a long time.

I remembered the track marks on Shay's body the last time I saw her before our darling Mummy croaked. I didn't know for sure when she decided heroin was worth it, but it looked like she'd been hitting it hard. When I did go home to England, would it be too much risk to see Shay? She'd gladly shop me to the police the first chance she got. But I had unfinished business with her. She was responsible for a lot of the things leading up to Sarah finding out about me. She sent Sarah the letter my mother had written that said she saw me driving that night, all those years ago. But before that, she'd given Sarah the old scrapbook I'd kept from childhood, documenting my old identity, the one I'd worked so hard to leave behind. There was no need for her to do that. She did it purely for spite. But if I knew my sister at all, my answer to the problem she posed would be easy to solve.

A few more back roads and the motel came into view. When we got there, we went through the whole rigmarole—through the small gate, Leanne running to hide under the bushes while I had to go through reception to my room. Once inside, I opened the outside door for her and she darted inside. I sighed again at the lack of a door handle on the outside. I could strangle whoever thought that was a good idea. Strangle? Oops, no; maybe that wasn't the best example, not after Luisa.

I listened at the inner door, the one that led to reception. No footsteps, so we were in the clear. I changed the water in Leanne's bowl and placed it on the bathroom floor behind the door. I used to pick it up every time I went out, but I didn't bother now. The landlady knew fine well the dog was in here. One of these days, I thought I might walk straight through reception with Leanne in my arms. But, for now, I couldn't be arsed with the hassle.

I stood in front of the mirror, my hands resting on the small basin. My brown eyes were now a wishy-washy blue, thanks to the coloured contact lenses. They took ages to get used to and even now, sometimes my eyes felt gritty and sore with them. I was going to get some green ones. They'd look better; more distinctive.

I washed my hands and removed the contacts, blinking away the tears as I put them into the little box they came in. When my vision cleared, I ran my hand over the small beard. I kept it bleached, like my short hair. The difference was amazing. I looked nothing like the old me.

It was no good; I couldn't put off what I needed to do any longer, and I took a deep breath in. I washed my face and looked at myself in the mirror, turning my head left, then right. Which side? Did it even matter? Probably the right side; as I was right-handed, it might be easier. I slid the glass from the bar from my pocket and rinsed it under the tap before closing the bathroom door to keep the dog out. Before I could think too much about it, I brought the glass down sharply on the edge of the sink with one swift strike. It shattered, sending shards all over, leaving only the thicker base of it in my hand. Already, a bead of blood was running down my arm, tracking a scarlet path over my wrist. A felt a sharp, stabbing pain in my hand; there was a sliver of glass between my finger and thumb. I eased it out, then looked down at my feet, wishing I'd put trainers on before I'd broken the glass, rather than my flip-flops. I daren't move or I'd probably slice my feet open.

I kept my feet firmly planted, picked up the biggest piece of jagged glass and pressed it as hard as I dared into my face, jamming into the puffier flesh under my right eye and onto my nose. Watching in the mirror didn't make it any easier as everything was back to front. Nothing much was happening, so I pulled it sharply outwards, pressing harder. That did it. A thin red line opened up under my eye. It wasn't anywhere near big or nasty enough. Fuck! It was stinging now, as well, but the cut was too clean. I needed a decent scar or it wouldn't be worth it. Holding my breath, I repeated the move several times, each time moving the glass a millimetre or so either way. I tried to pull on the skin to open it up, and the blood flowed faster. I wet the corner of a towel and blotted the blood away to see the cut better. It still wasn't jagged enough. It would have been better to get one of the local thugs to do it (I'm sure one of them would have been happy to for a small fee), but I'd been worried they might enjoy it too much and take my eye too. So, better this way. Several slashes later, and the pain was getting more than I could bear. The anaesthetic effect I wanted the tequila to have wasn't working too well. It'd have to do for now. It had been well sliced open. I'd know soon enough if it was the first thing you noticed about my face.

Outside the bathroom door, Leanne scratched at the wood and whined.

'Just a minute,' I called to her. There was no dustpan and brush anywhere in this room. Why the bloody hell didn't I think to buy one? I scraped up as much broken glass as I could with the towel and dropped it into the bathroom litter bin, cutting my hand further in the process. The cut under my eye was red hot and bleeding freely. It stung like a bastard. I took two paracetamol to take the edge off and held a wet flannel under my eye. The flannel quickly turned bright red, and I felt a bit woozy at the sight of it. The blood on my arm had started to dry, and I wiped it hard with the flannel, holding it under the tap as best I could. Nausea made me dizzy, and I grabbed the edges of the sink, swaying until it passed.

After making sure there were no glass splinters in my feet or flip-flops, I went into the bedroom and closed the bathroom door behind me. I'd have to get a dustpan and brush later, to clean up properly. For now, I needed to lie down.

Leanne was on the bed, and her tail wagged at the sight of me. My head was spinning as I lay down. My face hurt, and both my newly tattooed arms were itching. She tried to lick the cut on my face.

'Fuck off! I don't want your dog germs infecting me.'

I shoved her away, and she slunk off the bed at my harsh tone, curled up on the floor, and glared at me from under her white, bushy eyebrows. The flannel under my eye was bright red and soaked through now. I sat back up and stripped a pillowcase off one of the pillows, balled it up and pressed it to my face. It would have to do. I hoped I never got glassed for real; it fuckin killed.

The paracetamol did fuck all for the pain and I lay there, every second feeling like an hour. Maybe a dip in the sea would take my mind off it, as well as dulling down the pain. The salt was supposed to be good for healing, or so they said. I swung my legs off the bed, pulled on my swim shorts, called Leanne, and left.

13

'HERE WE ARE,' SAID Kate, coming out of the of the French doors and into the garden.

I looked up to see her carrying a tray with a pot of fresh coffee, two mugs, and a plate piled with croissants. I'd been out here on my own for the last hour, feeling like a spare part when they wouldn't let me help clear up after breakfast. They hadn't let me lift a finger to help them all week, despite my attempts.

She smiled when she saw me and held the tray higher. 'I'm sure these aren't a patch on yours, but they're pretty nice. They're from an artisan bakery around the corner.'

'They look delicious,' I said as she put the tray down on the glass top of the rattan garden table. 'It's so peaceful out here. I'd be outside all the time if I lived here, even in the snow!' I turned my head back to look at the open fields beyond the garden hedge, most likely kept low to make the most of the view. That's what I would do if I lived here.

She laughed, tucking her hair behind her ears, where it fell in a shiny blonde curtain. 'You've obviously never been in the snow this far north. But aye, it's one of the reasons we bought the house.' She sat down opposite me. 'I bet you're finding it a lot different to the chaos of London.'

'You can say that again.'

Scotland was in the grip of an Indian summer, and I slipped my thin cardigan off my shoulders, onto the back of the chair. I suddenly realised the house was quiet. 'Where's Ben and Sofia?'

'He's taken her to the park to give us some peace. She'll be pestering him to push her on the swings. She can't get enough of them just lately.'

'She's a gorgeous little girl. You must be so proud of her.'

'I am, aye. What can I say? She's my life. Well, her and Ben, obviously.'

'Obviously. He's doing well overall, isn't he?'

'Yes.' She poured us both some coffee. 'It was always going to be a long road. But if a thing's good, it's worth fighting for. That's what I think, anyway.' She pushed a mug towards me and I added cream from a little jug on the tray.

'Thanks,' I said, bringing the cup to my nose. I inhaled deeply, savouring the rich aroma. 'And thanks for making me feel so welcome here. I was a bit apprehensive about coming, actually.'

'I know exactly what you mean, especially with us only having met the one time. We didn't really get to talk much when we came to collect Ben, did we? But I knew we'd be fine. We kind of just clicked, didn't we?'

I relaxed my shoulders in the sun and considered what she'd said. 'Yeah, we did. I feel like we could talk for hours, like old friends would, who haven't seen each other in a while. Does that sound silly?'

'No, it doesn't at all.' She bit into a croissant and pushed the plate towards me. 'Try one and give me the verdict. Are they as nice as I think they are, or do I just have no discerning palate or taste?'

I took one, and the sweet, crumbly pastry melted on my tongue. Deep inside was a dark chocolate centre that hit a second later. I rolled my eyes. 'No, it's fantastic. Could give mine a run for their money, but I can't say they're better, of course. But I'd buy them every weekend if I lived here.'

'We do. I'm addicted to them. My waistline is going to suffer before much longer. I have to compensate in the week with salad.'

'Yeah, I do that, too.'

We sat munching our croissants, then she shuffled back into her chair, settling into the plump cushions. I got the feeling she was building up to something.

'So, how are things with you? I understand you've had a rough few months,' she said.

What exactly had Ben told her? I hadn't told him much myself, but that didn't mean Lee hadn't blabbed her mouth off. They emailed each other, too.

'What's Ben said?' I asked.

'We haven't been gossiping, if that's what you're worried about. He's only told me the bare bones.'

'It's okay. He only knows the bare bones unless Leanne's talked to him. So what has he told you, and we'll take it from there?'

I had a powerful urge to offload onto her in a way I hadn't with anyone else.

'He said you got mixed up with a bad fella, got pregnant, and lost a baby. That's pretty much all I know.'

I blew on my coffee and sipped it. She wouldn't judge me, I felt sure. She was looking at me expectantly now. There was no one here to interrupt us and I'd like her take on what happened.

'Well, I met Chris at work. He was hot, sexy, all the cliches, really. But there was something that massively drew me to him. Do you know what I mean? Something I've always thought about as a once in a lifetime thing.'

She nodded. 'Oh, aye. I know that feeling.'

Did she mean Ben? I hoped so. 'So, anyway, we get talking at the Christmas party and he kisses me. It blew my socks off. I think I knew I was going to fall in love with him even then.'

Somewhere off to one side, a bird trilled loudly. Had I even heard a bird in London? Not as a rule, other than in a park, and even then I wasn't sure.

'We started to meet up at lunchtime outside of work and he offered to lend me money to get my cake-making business off the ground, you know.' She nodded. 'Anyway, I kind of felt beholden to him, which I didn't like, but I needed his money to progress. He introduced me to a friend of his in the restaurant business and I started to make desserts for him.

'Chris went out of his way to do nice things for me. He did a website and made a portfolio for me to show prospective clients. Soon, we were going out together properly, but Leanne didn't like him. Couldn't stand him. He didn't like her either.' I sipped more coffee. The thought unsettled me that I liked talking about him so much.

'I was seeing another guy before, but we only went out a couple of times. Adam. He was so lovely, but I just didn't feel the same about him. If I'd fallen for Adam the same as I did Chris, things would have been different. Anyway, to cut a long story short, Chris wasn't all he was cracked up to be. He had some dark secrets in his past. I found out later he'd knocked a kid over, joyriding in his dad's car when he was only fifteen. The child died and Chris let his dad go to prison for it. Although, by all accounts, his dad was a horrible person, but that doesn't make it alright.'

Kate's eyes were wide, her mouth open. 'Oh, my God! I had no idea.'

'No one did. It was his best kept secret. But his sister found a letter from their mother after she died, when she was clearing out her things. She'd seen the whole thing and known Chris was driving from the start, and had made a written account of it. But she hadn't gone to the police. She was happy to see her ex-husband go to prison and to protect her son—'

'What?' Kate said. 'Why would she write that down?'

93

'She said something about wanting it being documented 'in the event of her death'. Weird, isn't it?'

'Yes. Anyway, sorry for interrupting. Carry on. I'm all ears.'

'So, Chris had a rough upbringing, but he escaped from it. He did really well for himself after he left home. Turned his life around, at least, that's what it looked like. But he was up to some bad stuff as well. He hacked my webcam and laptop. Watched me through it and took photos of me. He could see everything on my computer: read my emails, go through my bank. I mean... everything.'

Kate shook her head. 'I never knew that was even a thing until recently. All those scams you read about.' She shuddered, despite the warmth of the sun.

'Nor did I. That was my problem. Little Miss Naive, wasn't I? But not anymore. I've learned so much. Maybe Adam discovered what he was up to and challenged him, or something. I don't know exactly what happened, but he attacked Adam and he died. There was proof.' I lifted my chin up sharply and sniffed, blinking the tears away before they could fall. It was amazing there were any left.

Kate was absolutely still. 'I... God! I... I'm so sorry.'

'Do you know the worst thing? Adam wouldn't be dead if it wasn't for me. His brother and sister told me that he'd said he was in love with me. He was gutted when I told him I only wanted to be friends. Do you have any idea what that sort of guilt feels like, that someone is dead because of you?'

'No, I can't begin to imagine. But I don't agree it's your fault, Sarah. You didn't kill him.' Her voice was soft and gentle, and it only made things worse.

My tears fell freely now. 'I feel so guilty, though.' I blotted my eyes with the sleeve of my cardigan. 'Sorry. I never meant to do this.'

Kate laid a hand on my arm. 'I'd like to help you. You've done so much for me and Ben. If it helps to talk it out, carry on. I'm a good listener, Ben says.'

'You are. This is more than I've told anyone. Even Leanne and my mum.'

'Hang on a sec.' Kate went into the kitchen and returned with the box of tissues that were next to the half-eaten Catalina cake. I blew my nose and wiped my eyes.

'Thanks. Right. So, anyway, one evening, Leanne got an email from an unknown sender. It had a picture attached she thought she'd deleted off her laptop ages before. A naked one of her, but don't tell her I told you. She freaked out, and I took both our laptops to Adam's business partner for him to look at. He discovered the extent of the hacking. I worked out it could only have been Chris.'

Kate blew out a slow breath. 'Bloody hell! So what did you do?'

'I stormed round to his flat to confront him with it all. Only, I didn't know about Adam then. I only twigged later, after I got there.'

She leaned forward, craning her neck and frowning. 'How come?'

'There'd been a jacket hanging up in his flat that went missing. I didn't realise it wasn't there at first. But I saw an appeal on TV to find Adam's attacker. It was a grainy CCTV image of a man running away in a jacket with a logo on it. Blurry, but distinctive enough. It clicked in my brain it was him. His jacket. But not until I was confronting him about hacking me.'

I paused to sip my coffee. The images in my head were as plain as day. Me screaming at him about him hacking my computer, him denying everything and crying and saying he loved me and would never do such a thing. Then me tripping over the doormat, reaching for the jacket to break my fall and it not being there, and all of a sudden, everything making sense.

'What happened then? Did you tell him you knew?'

'I told him I knew he had attacked Adam, and we argued. I can't remember much after that because I collapsed. My fallopian tube had ruptured. I hadn't even known I was pregnant.'

I gazed into the distance over the fields. This had got to be the worst bit. My tears had started again. I wouldn't be able to stop them now. The baby did this to me every time. Kate squeezed my hand.

'You poor thing,' she said. 'I had no idea it had been that bad.'

I gripped her hand as I cried, hoping Ben wouldn't come back yet, until I'd got myself together. I felt a massive burden had been lifted as I told Kate everything, but grief still weighed heavily. Grief for Adam. For my lost baby.

'That's not the end of it,' I said, trying to stop my hitching breaths. 'There's more.'

She handed me a tissue, and I blotted at my face and eyes. I couldn't stop now. I had to get it all out there.

'His neighbour, Luisa—she was a bit weird, to be honest—he was coming out of her flat when I arrived at his. He looked guilty, and all dishevelled. He always said how much he disliked her. I thought he'd just slept with her, so we argued about that, too. But the truth was much worse.'

I shook my head as I wiped my eyes. 'He'd strangled her. Because she'd seen him burning the jacket and clothes he wore when he attacked Adam that night, the ones from the appeal on TV. She'd asked me about it. Said it was suspicious. He hit the roof when I told him. Then, that day I found out, he'd just killed her.'

Kate put her hands over her mouth, horrified.

'So that's another death I have on my conscience. He killed her because of me, too. Because I told him what she'd seen.' I blew my nose hard. 'So that's it. The whole sordid tale.'

I looked at her, and her eyes were kind. They were glistening with unshed tears that threatened to fall.

'I'm sorry. I didn't mean to upset you,' I said. Maybe I shouldn't have told her all that. It was a lot to take in, and she'd been through enough sadness and worry of her own.

'You haven't. I'm just so upset for you.'

At a loss to know what to do or say, I picked up another croissant and nibbled it. 'I eat when I'm stressed,' I said, forcing a smile. At least if my mouth was full, I wouldn't blab any more.

'It's good to talk,' she said. 'Although I'm not sure Ben would agree. I think he's sick of me saying that.' She side-eyed me. 'Although, as you're aware, we talked after you engineered that little stunt yesterday. Thank you for that, by the way.'

'You're welcome. I don't think Ben is a natural talker, though. I don't think it comes easy to him. Maybe things will get better now you've both cleared the air.'

'I hope so. Anyway, how do you feel now? About everything?'

I pulled a face. 'I'm really mixed up about lots of things, I suppose. Mainly the baby...' I inhaled deeply. 'Funny, really, but I hadn't ever thought of being a mum. Now, most days, it's all I can think about.'

'It must have been awful for you.'

'What I can't understand is why I took it so hard. It wasn't a proper baby at just a few weeks, was it? More just a cluster of cells. Yet to me, it was.'

'Of course it was. They're babies from conception. Each one is special.'

'I've been going into this shop and buying baby things, then hiding them when I get home. Small things I can squirrel away easily, where no one will find them. But I can't work out why I'm doing it.' The words were out before I realised. And I couldn't take them back. I bit my lip.

Kate blinked. 'I can. It's obvious.'

'Why?'

'You're grieving, Sarah. That's what grief is. And if it brings you some comfort, then why not?'

'I'm not sure it does, though.'

'Well, you're certainly not hurting anyone by doing it, are you?'

'Hang on.' I jumped up from my chair and grabbed my handbag from the kitchen. I hurried back outside with it, dug around in it for the STORK bag, and pulled out the bootees.

'I'm even carrying these around everywhere I go.'

She took them from me and sat them in her palm. 'I totally get it, you know. I had a stillbirth two years before we had Sofia.'

'Oh, I'm sorry. I didn't know that.' Ben had never mentioned it. Maybe she did understand a bit, then.

'I couldn't even look at a baby. If I so much as saw a pram coming, I'd run the other way.'

'How far along were you?'

Her shoulders slumped, and she looked at the floor. 'Twenty-one weeks. I had to go through with the birth, knowing the baby had died.'

Horror pinned me back in my seat, and I could feel myself about to start snivelling again.

'I don't know what to say.'

'These things sometimes just happen.' She sounded like a robot speaking, and I wondered if that's what she'd been told over and over. I could imagine the doctors saying it.

'And now you have Sofia,' I said, trying to warm up the chill that'd crept in.

'Yes. We do. And she was worth the wait. And all the heartache. I'm sure it'll be the same for you when you're ready.'

'I hope so. Even with one fallopian tube, it can still happen, or so I'm told. The scary thing is that if it happens again on the other side, I'll be looking at other options.' My fingers shifted to the area where my tube burst.

'You can cross that bridge when you come to it, though, can't you?'

'Yeah. I'm missing something major first, though.'

'What's that?'

'A man to have one with.'

She smiled. 'And you will, one day.'

'I don't know. I'm off them for now.'

'That's understandable. So, how do you feel now about Chris and what he did?'

That was the six-million-dollar question. My eyes swept across the open landscape beyond, then back to Kate.

I shrugged. 'That's the hard part. I'm so mixed up. I loved him so much, but what he did was so hateful. Sometimes, though, I can't say for sure that I've stopped loving him, no matter how hard I've tried. And I can't believe I'm saying that out loud. I bet you think I'm totally mad.'

'I don't at all. Feelings aren't something you can just turn on and off like a tap. He must have good qualities, too; the things that made you love him.'

'But he's a monster. And part of me hates him, for sure.'

'But you weren't to know what he'd done years ago or what he was capable of doing now, were you?'

'No.'

'So is this fresh start in York the right thing for you, or are you just running away?'

The blatantly put question shocked me for a moment. 'Bit of both, probably, if I'm being honest.'

She nodded, slowly. 'Are you scared he'll find you?'

'In a way, I am. Although he could have killed me back there, on that day, if he'd wanted. He had enough opportunity. Instead, he called an ambulance to save my life. I probably would have died if he hadn't done that. I was writhing around the floor, covered in blood. It was horrific. He'd talked to the paramedics at his flat and told them he'd follow in his car. Of course, he didn't. He'd cleared out by the time the police got there after I reported him the next day. Despite that, I've found myself looking over my shoulder every day since it happened. Some days, I think I see him everywhere. My brain tells my eyes I'm seeing him and that's it. And it terrifies me. He could come back and kill me if he wanted to.'

'And you have no clue where might be?'

'No. Nor do the police. He took his passport. Whether he ever left the country, who knows? I don't. And people can change how they look, can't they? The only thing they can't change is their DNA. And his must be on record now.'

Kate squeezed my hand again. 'For what it's worth, I think you're incredibly brave.'

'Me? I haven't done anything. That's the last thing I feel.'

'No, you definitely are. You're an inspirational woman.'

'You really think that? In what way?'

'You're fighting back and forging on ahead. You're starting a completely new chapter. That's admirable.'

'Or, like you said, I'm running away.'

'I don't really think you are, though. I just wanted to know if you thought you might be. If I was him, I wouldn't want to come face to face with you. Look up 'feisty' in the dictionary and there's probably a picture of you there.'

I laughed. 'I don't think I've ever been as angry as I was that day I went to confront him. I didn't run away from him then. Mind you, I didn't know he'd killed Luisa and Adam. I might have thought twice otherwise.'

Just then, the front door slammed and Sofia came flying through the house and into the garden, clambering onto Kate's knee.

'Sorry,' Ben said, following her. 'I tried to keep her out for longer, but she kept saying she wanted to see Sarah.'

'Sarah!' Sofia yelled, sliding off Kate's knee and climbing onto mine. She put her arms around me and I sniffed her silky hair. Her little-girl smell was scrumptious.

'I love you Aunty Sarah!' she whispered into my face, squeezing my cheeks too hard. I tickled her under her arms until she let go, squealing.

'Ooh. Is this the real reason you sent me out?' Ben said, reaching for a croissant. 'Sneaky! I should have known you were keeping them to yourselves.'

Sofia grabbed one and bit into it, and a shower of crumbs exploded all over me.

'I don't want you to go home tomorrow, Aunty Sarah. Can she stay here with us, Daddy, please?'

'She can for me, but she has to start an exciting new job. Making scrummy buns for people like us to eat.'

Sofia scowled at Ben. 'Horrible Daddy! I want her to stay!'

'Hey, don't blame me. It's not my fault. I've said she can.'

They bickered until Sofia slipped off my knees and pretended to wrestle him on the grass until he was on the ground, begging for mercy.

Kate winked at me, and I laughed. At that moment, I was so relaxed I didn't ever want to leave here.

Here, I felt safe.

14

WHEN I WOKE THE next morning, I couldn't move my head or open my eyes without pain. A lot of it. What the hell was wrong with me?

I put my hand up to my face, where it hurt the most. Was someone jabbing me in the cheek with a red-hot needle? I forced my eyes open and looked at my fingers. They were all sticky and bright red. It was only then I remembered the cut on my face. It had taken ages to stop bleeding yesterday, despite going swimming. Sometime in the night, it must have started again.

I sat up slowly, and the pain in my head got worse. That would be the tequila. I'd only drank it once before and it made me ill. How could I have forgotten that and drank it again yesterday?

Leanne was stretched out on the bed next to me. She sat up, wagged her tail, and whined. My watch was on the bedside table and I picked it up. Two hours past her breakfast. No wonder she was desperate.

I swung my legs out of bed and put my feet on the floor. My head got worse, and I felt a bit sick, but stood up nonetheless. I opened the door for Leanne and she trotted outside to do her business. Thankfully, she had never messed in the room, not once. I'd be sick if I had to clear that up.

While she was outside, I opened her dog food and scraped it into a bowl. The smell made me gag, and I swallowed down acid. When I put the bowl down outside, she was on it before I'd even straightened up.

I left the door open for her and went into the bathroom, dreading looking at my face. I put it off by peeing and making myself a cup of tea first, but then it was time. In the harsh electric light of the bathroom, the cut was jagged, very red and also weeping a clear fluid, as well as blood. Shit! I must have been more heavy-handed than I thought. Why did I go over it so many times? It looked very deep. For a brief second, I was worried it might need stitching. I didn't fancy going to a hospital or doctors around here; I might come out with something worse than I went in with. If I kept it clean and dry, it might be enough.

I washed it the best I could and applied some antiseptic ointment I had kicking around. Then, not knowing whether I was doing the right thing, I stuck the largest plaster I had over the whole area. At least it would keep dirt out, if nothing else, and there was always plenty of that around here, mainly a fine dust with sand mixed in it from the beach. It could do with more rain at this time of year to wash it away.

Blood was leaking from behind the plaster. For the first time, I worried about what I'd done to my face. Sarah had initially been attracted to me because of my looks. The sexual attraction between us was the strongest bit of our relationship. Just say, against all the odds, that we met again, she forgave me everything, knew who I was and kept my secret, and we were together again. It could happen (maybe on another planet)—a man had to have some hope. Anyway, how could I expect her to fancy me with my face cut open and scarred? Just how stupid was I?

As rage boiled up inside me, I looked around for something to throw. Something that wouldn't make a noise and have the landlady banging on the door inside of ten seconds. There was nothing except towels, and most of them had blood on from yesterday. I'd have to wait it out. I couldn't afford for the red rages to take over, anyway. The loss of control that came with them was something I couldn't handle. That's how I strangled Luisa, even if it was her own fault. I needed to have more self-control. Just reacting and losing it was what the young version of me, Colin, would have done, and I wasn't him anymore. He was a loser.

I gripped the edges of the sink, my knuckles so white it looked like there was no skin, just bone, and clung on, counting to ten slowly. In the end, I counted to fifty before my breathing slowed even the slightest bit.

Afterwards, I shuffled back into the bedroom and lay on the bed. The breeze from the open door was nice, and no one was able to see in. Leanne was free to go in and out as she wanted, and I could sleep again. Maybe I'd feel better when I woke up.

I didn't. If anything, I felt worse. I'd been asleep for three hours and when I woke this time, my arms were sore and itching too. The fuckin tattoos! I'd never even looked at them earlier. My head felt like a full marching band was rehearsing in there. I swallowed four paracetamol tablets and some ibuprofen. Anything to feel better. There would be no swimming today. I wouldn't make it down to the beach if I tried.

All there was to eat in the room was dry bread and some biscuits, so I made do with them. At least I wasn't sick. All I wanted to do was sleep and feel better. I leaned back and closed my eyes as nausea hit me hard. And then the pain returned.

15

THE DAY AFTER I got back from Inverness, I visited Adam's grave one last time. As I entered the crematorium where he was interred, a strong autumn breeze kicked up stray leaves around my feet. The last time I'd visited his parents had been there, and I'd waited around the corner until they'd gone, not wanting to intrude on their grief. Also, what could I have said to them? They didn't know Adam had been killed by my boyfriend. Nor did his sister, Debbie. So few people had known we were a couple, it had seemed easier just to keep it that way. So I took the coward's way out and kept out of their way.

There was no one at his grave now but, judging by the overflowing fresh flowers in the small brass urn, someone had recently been here. His mum and Debbie kept the flowers fresh. Debbie had postponed her forthcoming wedding to Andy. She said she couldn't face it without Adam, and she was right; it wouldn't be the same without him. He was going to be Andy's best man. I recalled the trepidation in his voice as he asked me what his speech should be about. I'd told him to work on it nearer the time, to keep it fresh. What a joke! He didn't have the time, did he?

My throat tightened as I walked over to Adam's grave, marked by a plaque that was set in a tiny square of immaculate grass. They weren't really graves as such. They didn't need to be body-sized. Row upon row of plaques lined the path, like squat sentinels.

His plaque was bronze. His name, and birth and death dates, along with 'Our Beloved Son' in gold script were engraved on it. 'ADAM WARNER' was twice the size of the other letters. I traced my fingers over his name, unable to shake off the guilt that I shouldn't be here. After all, I didn't kill him. I loved him as a friend—just not the way he loved me, as it turned out. And you couldn't help or change the love you have for someone. If I could have loved him that way, he would have been the way better choice. I knew that now. But at the time, the lure of Chris had just been too strong for me.

It was quiet in the cemetery, with just one other person at the far end, sweeping fallen leaves and petals from the grass. They were changing the flowers. They stood and walked over to the tap to refill the vase. I looked back at Adam's name, my eyes so blurred with tears I could barely make it out.

There was no one around me, so I squatted down and began.

'I'm leaving London, Adam. It's time for a fresh start.'

I cleared my throat, feeling stupid, but less stupid than the first time I spoke aloud to him. And who knew—maybe he was listening. There were no secrets between us now. He knew damn well it was Chris who hit him.

'Jenny's bought a cafe in York and I'm going to manage it.' I picked at the grass with my fingers, plucking out a few blades, then let them fall. 'Don't think because I'm moving away that I've forgotten you. I never could and I never will.'

Trees lined the perimeter and my head jerked up as I thought I saw something. Had someone moved just then, beyond the tree line, in the shadows?

I studied each trunk and the spaces in between them for some time. Apart from a squirrel that leaped from one tree to another, and a blackbird, nothing moved. The hairs on my arms stood to attention, and I scanned the area more quickly, staring hard at the dark shadows.

It must have been the birds or something. Whatever else it might have been didn't seem to be there now. My legs hurt from being hunkered down, so I sat properly on the grass and stretched them out before cramp could set in. Then I worried it looked disrespectful, so I stood up again. I glanced at the trees once more, but all was still.

'I need to get away from here, Adam. He's everywhere, you know. And I can't forgive myself. If it hadn't been for him, you'd have been...' I wiped away a stray tear, determined there wouldn't be any more. I'd even told Adam about the baby and apologised so many times I'd lost count.

I'd give anything to hear his voice say to me, 'It's okay, Sarah. I forgive you. It wasn't your fault.' But that was impossible, of course.

'If I could have loved you like that, I would have. You were such a great person, Adam.' I looked up at the sky. Thin white clouds covered the face of the sun, but some heat was still getting through. The branches and leaves on the trees stirred violently as a gust of wind blew up from nowhere, sending my hair flying all over my face. I pulled strands out of my mouth.

'Is that you joking around? What are you trying to say?'

I shook my head. If only I believed in such things as messages from the grave. I stood for a long time, in quiet contemplation. It was time to leave the cemetery. Maybe one day I'd come back, but I didn't know. Adam wasn't going anywhere, was he?

'Goodbye,' I whispered as I turned to go. 'I love you, my friend. I'm so, so sorry.'

Then I walked out of the gates for the last time.

I didn't want to go home and sit in an empty flat. There was something else I'd rather do. I imagined the feel of downy soft velour in my hands, the only thing that could soothe the ache deep inside me. For once, I didn't have to rush; I had all day. I didn't want to go back to the baby shop where Janice worked. I'd find a new one instead. I walked through Shepherd's Bush to the end furthest away from where I lived, finding a few new baby shops on the way. The one I liked best was called 'Tots'. A beautiful crib was in the window, draped with lace to create a sumptuous tented ceiling effect. My heart constricted at the sight of it. I wanted it so badly. Of course, I couldn't have it. Couldn't hide that in the wardrobe, could I?

The shop had two floors. An assistant smiled at me from her position behind the counter and called a cheery 'Hello'. It was so serene in there, like a soothing balm on inflamed, itchy skin. The yearning inside me dulled a little. I went up the stairs, hoping there was no one up there, and onto a large, open floor consisting mainly of cots and pushchairs. It was beautiful. I trailed my hand over the wooden rails of the cots and placed my other hand on my tummy. I'd have had a huge bump by now. Maybe I wouldn't have even managed the stairs, or I'd have had to waddle up them. I'd asked myself many times over if I would have kept the baby and I know I would have, despite who its father was. At the time, it was conceived in love. I just didn't think I could ever go through with aborting one. It seemed too much like fate that a life, against all the odds of conception, could take root there in the first place.

One cot in particular caught my eye. It was made from silver-grey wood, with hand-painted small animals, stars, and rainbows on it in pastel colours. I loved it. It was what I'd have chosen if—

'Hello there. Is there anything in particular you're looking for today?'

I gasped and jumped, my hand clutching at my throat. A tall, balding man stood just behind me. I hadn't realised there was anyone else up here. To the side of me, a door slowly swung closed. He must have come out of it.

'I'm so sorry, I didn't mean to startle you,' he said.

I couldn't speak for the hammering of my heart. I really needed to stop jumping all the damn time.

'It's alright. I didn't see you, that's all. I was miles away.' My eyes returned to the cot and skimmed over the rainbows.

A bright red badge was pinned to his black shirt: it read *Kevin*. His eyes dropped fleetingly to the hand still resting protectively on my stomach, then back to my face. He must have noticed my non-existent baby bump. 'Is it a cot you were looking for?'

'Um, yes, actually,' I said, to see how it felt. It wasn't like he was ever going to know, after all.

'Oh, congratulations. How far along are you?'

I wanted to say, 'Well, I would have been almost eight months by now.' Instead, I just said, 'It's very early days. Not three months yet. We haven't told anyone. I've just sneaked in here for a look on my own, to see what sort of thing I like.'

He smiled, a co-conspirator. 'There's nothing wrong with that. In fact, I hear it all the time. Let me know if you have any questions or need any help.'

'I will. Thank you.'

He went to stand behind the counter and began doing something on a computer. Had I given him 'go away' vibes? Nevertheless, I was grateful he'd gone. I didn't much go in for small talk anymore.

Fortunately, for the next twenty minutes or so, he gave me a wide berth, and I lost myself wandering through the baby paraphernalia. I decided I would have had the silver-grey cot. There was a pram that was very similar that I'd have, too. I picked up what looked like a backpack for a baby. You kind of strapped it to your back with the baby in, and you could go around that way. Or maybe you strapped it to your front. Either way, that would be much easier than a pram or pushchair, especially for a baby that was still tiny. If worn on the front, its little head would be right under your chin, surely the ideal proximity for kissing.

I could go walking in parks with this, pretend I'm hiking like a proper Mother Earth. I ran my fingers over it. It was navy blue, made of soft cord, probably so you could wash it when the baby puked or dribbled on it. There was a matching bag, because you'd still need to take nappies and things, wouldn't you?

The image of me striding up Primrose Hill or Hampstead Heath, or feeding the ducks in Regent's Park, was vivid. It looked right. It felt right. Then I was brought back to reality with a bump. I wasn't pregnant. There was no baby. I was just having an over-emotional day after visiting Adam's grave to say goodbye.

I needed to get out of London fast. It was driving me insane, and this shop wasn't helping.

As I got to the top of the stairs to leave, I saw a woman about to come up. I recognised her straightaway. Desperately hoping she wouldn't glance up and see me, I backed away. Kevin, the man behind the till was staring at me. I walked backwards into a hanging crib, causing it to sway alarmingly.

Before he could say anything, I hurried to the back of the shop, into the furthest corner away from the stairs, where the woman was coming up them. It wasn't that I didn't like her, in fact she'd been one of my closest friends at the solicitors' where I used to work, before leaving to work at the delis. It was Donna. She was lovely, but I hadn't kept in touch all that well since I'd left, despite her texting and emailing me. I didn't know how much she knew of what happened with Chris and me, if anything at all. It had been easier to avoid her than see her. Shame, really. We were once so close. But what the hell was she doing around here? I thought she lived over in Ealing. Or was it Battersea?

She must be pregnant. She and her bloke had been trying for a baby while I still worked with her. I'd have loved to chat to her, but what could I say about why I hadn't been in touch for the last few months?

I peered out from behind a child's wardrobe, my knees bent and my fingers clutching the sides. Kevin's eyes were following me around the shop, but I didn't care what he thought. All I cared about was getting out of here without Donna seeing me.

At the top of the stairs, Donna turned left, away from me. An older woman was with her. Maybe it was her mum. My mum would love to go baby shopping with me for her first grandchild. The thought she may never get to do that made my eyes sting.

When Donna turned to the side and her coat fell open, I saw a decent-sized bump. Maybe five months. I was pleased for her, I really was, but my eyes were blurring now. I had to get out of there. Raging jealousy consumed me at the thought of her having a baby of her own to hold in just a few short months.

I skirted around the edge of the shop floor until I reached the top of the stairs. I raised my hand in a wave to Kevin. He must think me deranged. Looking bemused, he gave me a half-wave back before I rushed down the stairs, through the rest of the shop and into the street, feeling like an interloper. I shouldn't have been in there. I shouldn't be in London. I shouldn't be anywhere. Maybe I should be dead, like Adam.

A little voice in my head said that maybe I shouldn't be in York, either. I could run, but nowhere would ever be far enough. I didn't fit in anywhere anymore.

16

AFTER THE INFECTION SET in, it was a good job I
didn't know then what was to come. The cut on my face
got steadily worse until a yellow-green goo oozed out of it
continually. Day after day of me tossing and turning in bed,
bathed in sweat, followed. I had vague memories of the
landlady calling a doctor and getting me some antibiotics.
At first, Leanne hid outside under the bush, scooting
through the open door every time the landlady came into
the room. Then, at one point, I opened my eyes to see her
sitting in a chair on the landlady's lap. The landlady
brought me food and water, and she must have fed the
dog, as well.

I don't know exactly how many days of hell passed
before I felt anything like my normal self. In all the time I
was ill, I couldn't think straight for the burning in my brain
and body. But the pain in my face was pure agony, like the
flames of hell were burning in the flesh there.

Then finally, I felt able to sit up then then get out of
bed. When I looked at my face in the mirror, it was far
worse than I'd been expecting. The wound under my eye
was thick, still very red, and deep. Scabs crusted the
surface, while raw bits still oozed liquid. At least the liquid
was clear now. I turned my head one way, then the other,
my fingers pressing as near to the wound as I dared. By the
look of it, I'd really done a number on myself. The sight
sent me scuttling back under the bedcovers. No woman

would look at me now, let alone Sarah. But maybe some attractions were more than skin deep, and they couldn't be denied, no matter what the surface appeared like.

Eventually, after some bread and cheese the landlady had thoughtfully left by the side of my bed, I felt strong enough to go to the beach, perhaps try a swim.

Leanne waited for me on the bed while I showered and changed. She was first to the door and stayed by my side as we left, but walking down to the beach was exhausting. In my weakened state, I had to stop several times along the way. As I tried to get my breath back, Leanne looked up at me, puzzled. Her tail wagged when I looked at her.

'This is harder than I thought. It's okay for you. All you've done is sleep for days. It's me that's been battling infection.'

Her tail wagged harder.

'Come on, then.'

At the beach, the waves were higher than normal and it was blustery, blowing my hair into my eyes. It wasn't a good idea to swim to the rock. There was no way I'd make it. It looked further away somehow.

'We'll just have to paddle instead,' I told Leanne.

It was freezing cold around my ankles, making me gasp at the icy fingers stroking my skin. By the time I was up to my knees, I couldn't feel the lower half of my legs. After days feeling ill and red hot, though, it was good. Refreshing.

I turned around to head back the few feet I'd come and bumped into a white straggly thing struggling to keep afloat.

'Leanne!' I grabbed her, hauled her out of the water, and tucked her under my arm, soaking my T-shirt. Then I placed her gently back into the sea. She stayed afloat, paddling like crazy, her nose just above the waves. But her lips were pulled back and her mouth was open; she looked like she was having the time of her life.

'Hey. Look at you. I didn't know you could swim.'

113

She followed me back to the shallower water and onto the sand, then shook vigorously all over it and me. Then she belted round like a demented thing, kicking up sand in her wake.

Despite the gusting wind, it wasn't cold, and I sat on the beach while the sun warmed my legs up and dried my T-shirt. It was quiet, with some kids in the distance kicking a ball, and a few dog walkers about. A couple of families were sitting around on beach towels, their kids running around or building sandcastles. To say it wasn't that far to Rio, which would most likely be heaving, it was like a world away here. Although, it would be easier to hide and stay lost in Rio if it came to it.

I lay back on my elbows, looking out to sea. There were several ships in the distance, one of them an old-fashioned galleon, the sort you could hire for a cruise if you could afford it. The strong wind was billowing out the sails, and it was really moving. I wondered where it was going. Part of me wished I was on it, going anywhere, but I needed to spend the next few days getting my strength back and taking it easy.

My stomach rumbled. I could murder a steak and some chips. There was a place around the corner that opened in an hour for lunch, but steak and chips wouldn't be on the menu around here. The empadas, mini chicken pies, they did were really good, though.

'Let's head back,' I told Leanne. She was almost dry now and was up in a second, prancing from foot to foot. She shook herself again, this time showering sand all over me.

We ambled back to the digs, and I stopped outside. Did I need to still go through the rigmarole of pretending Leanne wasn't in my room, or should I just stroll past reception with her? I opted to stop all the bollocks and went in with Leanne close behind. The landlady raised her hand, waved to both of us and said not a word. I stopped in front of the desk and she stopped her scrawling in a ledger.

'Thank you. For everything you did,' I said.

She nodded, her mouth softening. 'All better now?'

'Yes. Much.'

'Let me know if you are needing of anything.' She smiled at the dog. Seemed all the games in the past were now forgotten. 'What her name is?

'Leanne. And thank you for feeding her.'

Her skin was like parchment, crinkled and ruckled, and it creased more as she smiled and lit up a cigarette. 'Ah,' is all she said as she waved me away.

In my room I made a coffee, wincingly bitter, but better than nothing. I sat on the bed, leaned back into the pillows and made myself comfy, anticipation driving away the remaining dregs of tiredness. I'd missed too many days and was out of touch with what was going on back in London.

Leanne jumped onto the bed.

'Off,' I said. 'You're covered in sand.'

She jumped onto the floor, glanced dejectedly my way, and disappeared under the bed. I picked up my phone and dialled the most important numbers saved in it, the ones for the four-ways with the listening devices in. When I heard Sarah's voice on the recording, all those thousands of miles away, my heart clenched up tight. She sounded so clear she could be in the room right next to me. I wished to God she was.

I closed my eyes and let her voice wash over me, like a gentle tidal swell, soothing and healing me. She was speaking to Leanne, of course. Who else had that high-pitched, nasally whine, the one that jolted and jarred on the nerves? A lot of their conversation was small talk, but I could tell just by Sarah's voice that she wasn't right. How could Leanne not pick up on it? She was supposed to be her best friend. To me, she sounded lost, lonely and frightened, not the confident, vibrant woman I fell in love with. The one I was still in love with and always would be.

My only ever ten out of ten. They were talking about their respective days at work. Nothing of any interest.

A different day and time now. It was Leanne and that dickhead boyfriend of hers—what was his name again? Oh, yeah—Sam. The doctor who was too useless to even learn to drive. Although he must have had some guts about him to still be with flat-chested Leanne. The thought that dog-Leanne here had bigger tits after her litter of pups than human-Leanne back in London made me laugh and lifted my spirits a bit. When did I last even laugh? I couldn't remember. Although I did enjoy chatting to Miguel as he was defacing my skin. I was definitely going to hook up with him now I was better, and get to know him a bit more. He could be useful. I'd like a hermit since I came to Brazil, and it wasn't good. People need people, right?

I checked the skin around the tattoos, and was relieved to find it was no longer red or itchy. They actually looked better than I thought they would; Mig did a good job on the designs. I twisted my arms this way and that, taking in the tattoos from different angles. I kept noticing intricacies in the design that I never saw before. My God, he was a bloody craftsman!

I focused my attention back on what I was listening to. Sarah's voice again. I closed my eyes again and pictured her leaning over me, bending down to kiss me. God! I had everything. Everything. And I lost it all with my own stupidity. I was so close, too. She would have done anything for me. No one had ever loved me like that before. When Adam looked through my window and saw the pictures of Sarah I'd taken through her webcam, I'd already stopped. I wasn't doing it anymore. Instead, I was doing the right thing and taking them down. If he hadn't followed me home when he saw me leaving her flat, I'd have been home and dry. That's what started the whole thing, and everything that followed on from then just became a juggernaut rolling ever faster, until it was out of control, and the crash and carnage were inevitable.

Then Leanne said, 'I'm so going to miss you. But I won't say I wish you weren't going. It'd be selfish of me. I know it's what you want to do.'

I sat bolt upright, my coffee slopping onto the bedcovers, leaving an ugly brown stain. What? Sarah was leaving? When? Where was she going? If she left London for good, I might never find her again. She could slip off the face of the earth and I wouldn't know where to look. I listened hard now as Sarah spoke.

'I know. I'll miss you, too. But, like I keep telling you, you can come and visit all the time.'

Her voice was getting further away now, like she was walking out of the room. It seemed the conversation was over. I tried to relax, but my heart was knocking against my ribcage as if trying to get out. But if Leanne could visit, then it couldn't be that far away.

If they didn't mention where she was going, and she had no Facebook page now to blab her life on, I could be in trouble here. I sipped my coffee, thinking. Leanne landed beside me on the bed and I stroked her as she settled down, barely noticing she was there. Sarah was no longer big on any of her other social media platforms and certainly didn't update them much. I grabbed my iPad and checked them all. Nothing on any of them about her moving anywhere. I needed to be rational about this and not panic. It was the only way that would get results.

A germ of an idea popped into my head. A long shot, but it might just work. I couldn't believe she'd leave that job of hers she loved so much. What was the name of that place she worked again? The deli? Oh yeah, of course: Delish. Maybe they had a Facebook page or a website or something? In all this time, I'd never thought to look. I typed it into Google and bingo! They had both, plus they were on LinkedIn, too. The website was okay, but was mainly pictures and info about the products, the cafes and the outside catering services they run.

Facebook, as usual, was my saviour. Hallelujah! The first post was about a cafe they'd bought in York. It even gave the address and a handy photo of the outside. And guess who was going to run it? Yup! It was all there, in black and white.

My mind was on overdrive at the news. This was brilliant. She was leaving London, and I didn't know anyone in York, so no one could ever recognise me there. This was the best news ever. I read everything again, more slowly this time, in case I missed anything before. They said it should be about a month or so until the cafe was up and running. Sarah would be living in York in a month. I didn't know where, but that wasn't a major problem. I knew where she'd be spending her days.

Visions of the two of us strolling hand in hand down the Shambles and round York Minster filled my head. The vision turned into one of us in bed, her beautiful body beneath mine, while she stroked me and played with my hair, and told me how much she loved me. Just like it used to be. I groaned; all I had in my bed was a curly, white mutt.

York, though; why York? She had no ties to the place that she'd ever mentioned to me. Dunno, but it was good news. I could go and see my dearest sister in Leeds while I was there. We had unfinished business, her and me. This meant I could finally finish it.

I had some serious planning to do, none of it clear at this stage. Each thing I thought of had flaws and would never work. I needed to give it time. These things had a way of sorting themselves out. But, like I said, I knew where she was headed now. And I had all the time in the world. It sounded like she was relocating for the long haul. And so would I be. A rush of feel-good chemicals flooded my system, energising me.

LOOK AGAIN

I got off the bed, calling Leanne. 'Come on, girl. Those empadas won't eat themselves, now, will they?'

17

'DAD, YOU DON'T NEED to drive me all that way. I've booked a train ticket. I'll get everything I'm taking in one suitcase.'

Dad's eyes flicked towards the kitchen, where Mum was making tea, then back at me. He lowered his voice.

'She won't hear of it. I know you've got a train ticket, but she went mad. *I'm not letting my only daughter pack up her life and move there all on her own,*' she said.'

I tried not to laugh. It wasn't the best impersonation of Mum I'd ever heard, but I got the gist.

'I think she really wants to check out the flat, you know,' he said. 'Make sure you're settled in. You know what she's like.' His voice had dropped to a whisper.

I chewed my bottom lip. 'But it's such a long drive for you both. You can't possibly do it there and back in a day. And the beds there won't be made up or anything. The place could be damp for all I know. I don't think anyone's lived in the flat for a while. I think they just use it for storing stuff.'

He leaned forward so our knees almost touched. 'Between you and me, she's looking at hotels in York for an overnight stay. Somewhere nice, you know, not Travelodge! She's looking forward to it. Don't take that away from her. She wants to help you.'

'In that case, why don't you stay for longer than a night? A couple of nights in a hotel, then more at my new place, if it's suitable.'

'Can you get a refund on your train?'

'I'm not sure. I'll look into it.'

He settled back into the sofa, more relaxed, and I realised he'd been stressing about telling me in case I dug my heels in and insisted on going on my own. I was worried about how much pain Mum could be in on a five-hour car journey with her arthritis, but ultimately it was her decision. And I'd love to not be going up on my own. For the last few nights, I'd been waking really early, thinking about it.

Starting afresh in York would be the first time I'd ever done anything truly on my own. In London, Mum and Dad had always been there, ready for me to run back to if ever I needed. I certainly did that after the Chris debacle, and they were great. They were never judgmental, although they were shocked at the pregnancy. Mum was disappointed I never confided in her about my relationship with him, but it all happened so fast, and I'd still been trying to work out if we had a proper future together or not. Dad, understandably, wanted to hit him.

'Just give me five minutes alone in a room with him,' I heard him mutter to Mum after I'd been discharged from hospital.

Mum came back in, her crooked fingers gripping the tray surprisingly well. Dad took it from her and put it on the coffee table. She'd cut up the Bakewell tart I'd made and brought over. Her eyes darted to Dad's, and I knew she was wondering if he'd mentioned anything to me yet. I could read the pair of them like a book. Might as well put her out of her misery.

'Okay,' I said, passing Dad his piece of Bakewell as she sat down.

She glanced at Dad again, more hopefully this time.

'I told her,' he said. 'And she says it's fine.'

'So we can come with you? Oh, love, that's brilliant.' She put her hands to her mouth but couldn't hide her smile.

'I was just saying to Dad, you may as well stay for a few days. You can help me clean the flat.'

I was joking, but she said, 'I definitely can. We don't really know what state it's in, do we? There might be curtains to wash and things. Ooh, there is a washer, isn't there?'

'I imagine so. I haven't asked.'

'You'd better check. If there isn't, you'll have to get one. You don't want to be messing about with laundrettes, do you?'

'Mum, I'm sure there will be a washer. It has a fully equipped kitchen, Jenny says.'

Mum slid her hand under a newspaper and pulled out the sales brochure for the flat and shop. She must have swiped it from my flat. I'd been looking for it everywhere. I thought Lee must have thrown it away.

She peered at the kitchen photo. 'Ah, yes. I think that's the corner of a washer just there. It's cut off on the picture. What do you think?' She handed it to me.

'Yep. It's a washer, alright.'

I tried not to laugh at the look of satisfaction on her face at such a simple thing. My mum washed all the time. The bed covers were barely back on the bed before she had Dad whipping them off so she could wash them again. The thought of cleaning the flat was satisfying lots of different needs in her, not least her maternal one. If I said I could do it, she'd only feel side-lined and miserable, so it was easier just to let her.

'Better look at hotels then,' I said.

She opened the ancient laptop they shared, but Dad rarely used. 'I've, er, seen some nice ones already. On Booking.com.'

'Of course you have,' I said, laughing.

She looked anxiously at me. 'We're not interfering, are we? Just say if we are.'

I picked up her hand, straightening out her bent fingers on my thigh. 'Look, I'm really glad you thought of it. I didn't like to ask, as it's so far away. It'll be great having you there. I know I'm a big girl, old enough to stand on my own two feet and all that, but I've been really nervous about going up there and not knowing anybody. It's a bit daunting, even though I'm excited about it. Are you sure about coming, though? Hotels aren't cheap, are they?'

'We have a bit set aside I was going to spend on a new sofa,' said Mum. 'I'd really rather spend it on this.'

I swallowed hard to take away the lump in my throat. Never had I doubted how much my parents loved me, but sometimes it still pulled me up short. Mum's hand was still in mine, and I gave it a squeeze.

'We'll have a lovely few days,' I told her. 'Like a mini holiday. Just don't start blubbing when it's time for you to tear yourself away and leave me there or you'll set me off.'

'Of course I will. You know that.' She squeezed my hand back, then lapsed into silence. The look on her face changed and my stomach plummeted.

'So, you haven't heard anything, then? About you-know-who, I mean?' she asked.

I let go of her hand and scratched my nose. She couldn't seem to let it go, despite Dad telling her to drop it.

'No. No news. I don't know where he is.'

Her pinched face tightened more.

'Stella,' Dad warned quietly. Mum shot him a look and he shook his head, his eyes holding hers.

'It's no good ignoring it,' Mum said defiantly, tilting her chin up. 'We need to talk about it. About *him*.'

My mum may be a softy, but she's always had a core of steel running through her, buried deep inside. You couldn't tell her what to do.

'It's okay, Dad,' I said. 'We all know he's still out there somewhere.'

123

'I want to know how you're coping with it, Sarah. And don't just tell me what you think I want to hear, like you have been doing since it happened. I'll know if you're lying,' Mum said. 'And you can be quiet,' she said as Dad was about to butt in.

'Charming,' he muttered, looking out of the window at the neat back garden, where his bedding plants were still going strong, thanks to the mild weather. 'Might as well be off to my shed then, eh?'

I could tell he was hurt by her brusqueness. He didn't move, though.

'If you want,' she said. She turned back to me. 'So, how are you, really?'

I couldn't tell her the truth: that I jumped at shadows and had a sensation of being watched all the time; that I feared he may come for me in the dead of night, to get me out of the way. He was good at eliminating people who could shop him, and I was now firmly in that category. He could get rid of me in a few minutes if he decided to. Snap my neck as easily as breaking a biscuit. How could I tell her that? But I wasn't her daughter for nothing. The same core of steel ran through me, too, and I'd do whatever I had to to protect her. Even if it did mean lying to her.

I cleared my throat. Dad turned to look at me, his petunias forgotten. 'The one thing you're forgetting is that I'm not the same person now that I was back then. I've learned a lot. I'm not vulnerable and ignorant anymore. And I was. I definitely was, in many ways. I've finally had to grow up.'

I resisted the urge to touch my tummy, knowing it would never get past her. She didn't miss anything where I was concerned. The baby was something else we didn't talk about. Or, rather, I didn't.

'I'm not scared of him, and I'm not running away. Far from it: I'm getting on with my life. Anyway, I don't think he'll come back. Why would he? To go to prison? Plus, the one thing you're forgetting is that if he wanted to kill me, he would have done it that day, in his flat. Instead, he saved my life. He had the opportunity, and he didn't do it, so what would he gain from doing it now? It's easier for him to stay away. He's escaped, remember? Why would he risk his freedom and come back?'

It was the longest, frankest exchange we'd had since it happened. I'd avoided it, not wanting to address it with them, and they'd avoided it, not wanting to upset me. So now it was out in the open.

'Don't worry, Mum. It's over and done with. And I'm alright.'

She stared at me, as if seeing right into me. *Don't look away*, I told myself. *Or she'll know you're lying.*

Okay, so I was scared. I didn't believe a word of what I'd just said. I'd told the police everything and Chris surely wouldn't forgive or forget that. The only truth I spoke was that he did have the opportunity to kill me then, and he didn't do it. Mum was still watching me. I didn't blink or avert my eyes, and I tilted my chin to match hers. Eventually, she nodded, satisfied.

'Well, I'm proud of you,' she said. 'You'll always be my little girl. I'll never stop wanting to protect you, though.'

'I know. You're a tiger-mum,' I said.

'Damn right I am.'

'Well, if I ever see him, I'll rip his bollocks off,' said my dad, before taking a large bite of his Bakewell tart.

'Peter!' said Mum, shocked. Whether by the language or the violence, I didn't know. I stifled the urge to laugh. I'd never heard my dad say 'bollocks' before. He wasn't given to what he called 'coarse talk'. Seemed that with Chris he was willing to make an exception.

He glared at us, chewing fiercely. 'What? I will,' he said and shrugged. 'It's true.'

'Why don't we all calm down and finish our tea?' I said, desperate to change the subject. 'Before I go home and start sorting out what I'm taking.'

'I'll just watch the headlines,' said Dad, picking up the remote and switching on the TV. That, if nothing else, signified that all was well in his world. He went back to his Bakewell, eyes glued to the telly.

Except it wasn't all well and good in mine. Deep down, I thought Chris may well come back. I'd just have to keep watch and wait. And hope that when he did, I'd be ready.

18

YORK. IT WAS ALL I'd thought about for days now. Suddenly, everything had become more real and achievable. I quite liked the idea of living in York. It was more my neck of the woods, not quite my old stomping ground, but much nearer to it. Who would have thought it—Chris Gillespie going back to Yorkshire?

The more I thought about it, the more it felt right. I was getting carried away, but I couldn't help it. Besides, I was enjoying it. The thought of getting out of this room, this place, this country, and into the fresh Yorkshire air was tantalising, as I sat on the bed, sweating in the heat.

I turned on the little TV in the corner with the remote, and whizzed up and down the channels to find the English-speaking ones. It sounded daft, but they showed a few Irish programmes, mainly comedies, and I'd made a decent stab at an Irish accent. I'd also tried Scottish, Scouse, Geordie and Brummie, and Irish sounded best. Most Brits probably couldn't differentiate between Belfast, Londonderry and Dublin, so I picked Father Ted and Derry Girls, of all things, to be my new coaches. They were on a fair bit and I reckoned if I watched them long enough, they'd use most words I could ever need, and I could make up the rest.

For the last few days, I'd only spoken and thought in that accent. I needed to immerse myself in it, let it take over. I changed my voice to be softer and deeper. Most things become second nature if you did them long enough. I'd reinvented myself before; I could do it again.

One thing that bothered me, though, was the way I walked. I didn't know what, if anything, might be distinctive about it, but something probably was. Sarah could probably identify me from that alone. But could you change the way you moved? It was ingrained in everything you did, even more so than speaking.

I spent a lot of hours sitting down at the beach and in the town, just watching how people moved, the way they held themselves. Some shuffled, some strode out, others stooped, as if wanting to make themselves smaller. It was fascinating, and not something I'd ever focused on before. The first time I walked into town, I was conscious of every movement of my body, concentrating hard on just putting one foot in front of the other. How did I hold my shoulders, my head, did my feet turn in, point straight, or turn out? I'd discovered I strutted in what some would describe as an arrogant, perhaps over-confident way, which made sense—I'd never been one to hide in a corner. Not my style at all. I'd walk into a room and want to own it. People would notice me and I'd want them to. I was never the invisible man. Now, I was going to turn into him, blend in, be part of the wallpaper. It went against the grain, so I'd have to get new grain. The old me was gone. Again.

I was sitting on a bench in town, sipping a decent Brazilian coffee and eating a pastry. Leanne was at my feet, and every few bites, I threw her a morsel. Her attention was on me, but I was watching a man over the other side of the square. The fascinating thing about him was the way he walked. He spent the whole time leaning forward slightly, as if braced to walk into a strong headwind that was constantly pushing him backwards. He was stocky and short, the opposite of me, but it was so alien to the way I moved, I was mesmerised.

The man was moving slowly now, browsing in various shop windows as he waited for his woman to come back out of one of them. He stood, bent forward like a taut bow, with his hands in his front pockets. His elbows were bent and his arms arched away from his body. He reminded me of one of those carved animals on the prow of a ship, curving out over the water.

I gave the last bite of pastry to Leanne, my eyes still on the man. His woman joined him and they went up the street together, her arm linked through his. He was moving faster now, but still shoving his way through the atmosphere, barging his way through the world. For someone who was as into weight training as me, it was against everything I'd ever learned: straight back, chin up, shoulders back and down, stomach in, backside tucked under. Interesting. Sarah would never recognise me with a gait like that. I'd have to practise, though. I reckoned it must lead to chronic back, neck, and shoulder problems in the long run.

The thought that if I was ever caught, my posture would be the last of my worries in prison brought me out in a sharp, cold sweat, despite the mid-twenties temperature. I shivered, and the woman beside me on the bench turned sharply to look at me. I ignored her and gazed straight ahead, my thoughts returning to the man, who had now disappeared around a corner. The woman was still looking at me and I realised she was staring at the scar on my face. She couldn't tear her eyes away from it. It was working, then. It was still a livid red, jagged cut that dominated my face. I turned my head slowly to stare at her, summoning up a cold, hard feeling inside that I hoped transferred to my eyes. She got up quickly and hurried away. I watched her go—she didn't look back.

I scanned the street both ways, to see if there was anyone else moving notably. There wasn't. My back was stiffening up from sitting here for so long. I got up, stretched, and looked around. The beach would be quieter. Maybe I could work on my new posture there. I couldn't force my way through the air like that bloke, but perhaps I could channel some of that. Think *slump*. Perhaps I could walk as if my bones were dissolving.

Leanne was at my feet as I started to move. My head was up, my shoulders back, and I was walking normally. I let them go and rolled my spine forward, my head going with it. I felt like an ape! If I carried on like this, I'd be dragging my knuckles. *Stick with it; come on!* I parted my legs wider as my feet touched the floor, feeling my hips grind with the effort. My feet turned out ever so slightly in my natural gait, so I changed the angle so they turned in. Pigeon-toed. Instantly, my knees and ankles hurt. How the hell did anyone walk like this? I modified things so they weren't so pronounced.

The beach was ten minutes away. I slowed down, focusing intently on each and every bit of my body. Leanne hugged my leg, looking up at me like one of those performing dogs on Britain's Got Talent. Ignoring her, I imagined there was a strong wind pushing me back, and I braced the upper half of my body. I probably looked like a question mark. Two lads on bikes were just up ahead and as I passed, one lad nudged his friend and sniggered, pointing at me. When I lifted my head and stopped, he saw my face and stopped laughing.

'Fuck off!' I said, speaking a universal language. They fucked off.

Now I concentrated on making my feet adjust to their unnatural position. Leanne ran a circle around my legs, almost tripping me up.

'Stop it. Heel!'

It was like she was already trained as she fell back into a slow step by my side.

It would take weeks at this rate, for any of this to become second nature. Well, I had weeks. I couldn't contemplate going back until I was convinced I could be someone else.

On the way to the beach, I stopped at a tourist shop and bought a paperback thriller, the first book written in

English that my hand rested on as I twirled the wire rack around. I opened it, still walking down the street, and began to read the story aloud in a quiet mutter. Every word was spoken with an Irish accent I channelled from Father Ted. It was laughable really, but if it got the job done... And when I'd finished the book, I'd start over with another. Any book would do. It could be a car manual or the Bible for all I cared.

As I read, I kept on pushing through the air, my chin down and my shoulders rolled forward. Toes turned in. By the time I got to the beach, I was worn out with the effort of it all. It was a relief to stop, put the book down and step into the sea. Today would be the first time I'd attempted to swim all the way to the rock since I got the infection. The sea was choppy. Maybe I wouldn't make it.

'Stay there,' I told Leanne, sternly. 'It's too rough for you.'

She ran after me into the shallow waters. I sent her back.

'Guard the book.' She ignored me and barked, still standing at the water's edge.

I waded deeper in and pushed off, gliding further out. The salt water burned my lips. It felt good to be swimming again, and the ache in my shoulders from walking hunched over began to ease. When I glanced behind me, thankfully, Leanne had returned to the beach and was running back and forth, barking.

It seemed to take longer to reach the rock than when I first started, and I hauled myself out, flopping on my back like a fish. Exhaustion weakened my muscles, and all I could lift was my head. I looked back towards the beach. Where was the dog? I couldn't see her anywhere.

I narrowed my eyes and scanned the area. Small white breakers looked like a tiny dog's white fur.

Shit! I pushed off the rock. If she swam after me this far out, she'd drown for sure. She couldn't fight waves like this. I swam back as hard as I could, the salt water stinging my eyes as I kept them open to search for the dog. The shore got nearer and still I couldn't see her. Where was she? By the time I got to the shallows, I'd swallowed a ton of water and scanned every white bit of foam I could see, my heart sinking at the thought of finding a lifeless, tiny body. Why did I leave her? She came after me last time. I should have known she'd do it again.

I stumbled, coughing, out of the shallows, fell to my knees, and shouted for her. Still nothing. I pulled myself to my feet and looked up and down the beach, frantic for a sign of her. Had someone taken her? The beach was busier today than it had been for a while. She was so friendly, anyone could pick her up, and she'd just lick them.

There was a bark in the distance, but I couldn't work out where it was coming from, or if it was even her. I shaded my eyes from the sun. Another bark. It seemed to come from the direction of several large rocks. I ran over to the first one. Nothing. I tried the next one. Same. Then, a third one—a white tail was sticking out from behind it. She barked again.

'Leanne!' And there she was, barking and scrabbling at... a half-submerged crab! It was stranded until the sea came back in, only a shallow pool of water keeping it from frying in the sun. She wagged her tail when she saw me.

I dropped to my knees, and she pawed at the crab again. It waved its claws at her, and I pulled her away. She twisted and wriggled to get back to the crab as I snuggled her tiny body into me, my heart clattering madly. She licked my face. I could bloody kill her!

'Leave the crab. It's naughty!'

I didn't dare put her down yet. She'd just go straight back. At this rate, I'd have to get her a collar and lead, yet she was usually no bother. She'd really scared me this time, though.

A voice in the back of my head kept pushing its way in—*What will you do when you go back to England? You can't take her.* But I wasn't sure I could leave her, either. I couldn't think about it now.

I got back to where my book was lying abandoned on the sand and sat down. Leanne settled by my side, the crab now forgotten. I started reading again, the accent feeling stilted and forced, but I couldn't get into it. Instead, I kept stealing glances at the dog to reassure myself she really was okay. And I couldn't hush that damned voice up either.

19

WE'D MADE IT TO York! We were actually here! Lendal, the street the café was on, was only a few minutes' walk away from York Minster. I couldn't stop the excitement that fluttered in my belly as I unlocked the door to the cafe and pushed it open. *My* cafe, to run as I saw fit. Jenny had given me carte blanche to change what I liked as long as I ran it by her first and kept to the business model of the other delis.

I put Mum and Dad's small suitcase down on the floor after stepping inside. It had been a trek from the train station, dragging it behind me with it banging into my legs all the time, but it was a lot lighter than the one Dad had carried, that was crammed with all my things. In the end, Mum had decided it would be easier on Dad if we all got the train instead of him driving 'all that way'. I think he was a bit relieved. He didn't argue about it, anyway. Thank God I hadn't cancelled my ticket. It had taken us ages to walk, though, what with the amount of times I'd got us lost with Google maps. I never knew which way up the map was supposed to be.

I stood, looking at the counter. The old menu was written on a chalkboard on the wall behind it. I wasn't keen on what was on it: *pie and peas, sausage and mash, burger and chips.* It was a lot more greasy spoon than I was expecting. Typical workmen's fare. And it smelled like it, although everything looked clean. There was no shortage of cheap cafes around here, so I didn't think this one would be missed. Jenny had done a recce of the area when she was here, to see where we would fit into the market, and she was happy we would get enough custom if the workmen stopped coming. And there was no doubt they would. But I thought we could offer something a bit more refined.

Behind me, Mum put down the carrier bag of cleaning products she'd insisted on bringing, despite me saying we could get it all here. She'd even brought two old toothbrushes 'for the hard to reach bits'.

'Ooh, it's lovely, isn't it?' she said, her eyes shining in the gloom. She looked tired, but happy.

I opened the blinds on the front window and sunlight flooded in, illuminating the counter area and the shop floor, with its tables and chairs. It was a good size, but it needed a much stronger identity. Before I came in, I noticed there was room outside for at least four tables, two either side of the door, which was an option I could explore later. The outside definitely needed doing to match the interior, too. And I couldn't wait to redo the signage.

Dad closed the door behind him and dumped my huge suitcase down, grunting at the effort.

'Which way is the flat?' asked Mum, her eyes shooting in all directions.

'Through there, I think.' I pointed to a door with a lock, right at the back of the shop, next to the toilets. It had a 'Private' sign on it.

I sorted through the keys in my hand. There was only one Yale.

'Must be this one.'

I locked the street door behind us and we trooped through the shop, past the rounded glass cabinet on the counter, along which I trailed my fingers, imagining how my cakes and desserts would look lined up in there. Jenny had allocated some money for the cafe for me to spend how I liked. The kitchen behind the counter was an area I'd have to leave until tomorrow to explore. If I went in there now, nothing else would get done. Jenny had said it was well equipped. I caught a glimpse of shiny stainless steel beyond the open doorway. My heartbeat quickened and my fingers actually twitched.

I unlocked the door, and a narrow staircase was revealed. With no natural light, it was dark and poky, and, for a moment, I didn't want to go up there.

'Come on, then. What are we waiting for?' said Dad, pushing past me. He hefted my suitcase up and rested it on the bottom stair. 'Want me to go first?'

Yes, I thought. 'Course not, don't be daft.' But my feet felt stuck to the floor.

Light flooded the staircase when Mum found the switch and flicked it on. The stairs creaked badly as we went up them, the cheap carpet worn thin on the edges of the treads. My first thought was that I'd hear anyone creeping up them a mile off, so that was a good thing.

'Do you have to go through the shop to get up here?' asked Dad. 'Not very convenient when it's closed, is it?'

'No, you don't. There's an outside staircase at the back that leads right into the kitchen, I think Jenny said.'

We were at the top now. Suddenly, faced with three closed doors, I didn't want to go through any of them. What if it was in a disgusting state? But with Mum and Dad breathing down my neck, I had to. They couldn't know how anxious I was. I'd been worried sick since packing all my things that I was doing the right thing. 'Cold feet,' Mum would call it if she knew. Thank God they'd insisted on coming with me.

I opened the door right in front of me. It was a small bedroom, or at least I thought it was. All I could see were boxes piled everywhere, blocking out the light from the small window. Jenny had told me the owner had assured her they would be removed. So that was a great start, then!

None of us commented on the unassuming space. Dad went through another door, straight into a small bathroom.

'This is alright, isn't it? Shower over the bath, so you have the option. What else do you need?' he said optimistically, pulling the string to turn on the light.

There was no window though, which was a bugbear of mine. At least the suite was white. So were the tiles.

'This grout will come up lovely. I've got some bleach. And a toothbrush,' Mum said. 'Peter, that's a job for you.'

'I thought it might be,' Dad said.

The walls around the bath were tiled, but the others had been painted a horrid dark green colour that sucked even more light from the room.

'We can easily change this,' said Dad, noticing my face at the sight of it. 'It's just a bit of paint.'

'True. I'll get some colour charts. And this is awful.' I touched the shower curtain. It was stiff and orange at the bottom, with old soap scum, and spots of black mould. 'It's going.'

'You can get some lovely fancy shower curtains these days,' said Mum. 'We can have a look for some.'

The floor just needed a good scrub, being a black vinyl, best described as 'durable'. I didn't want to look down the toilet, but Dad wanged the seat up. I had to say it looked better than I was expecting, but there was a faint ring of brown around the waterline.

'We need some denture tablets,' Mum said. 'It'll sort out that limescale in no time. And my old toothbrush and some Viakal will get it off those taps. They'll shine like new by the time I'm through with them.' She sniffed, satisfied, her examination of the basin taps done.

'If you say so.' I led us through the next door, which took us into the compact living room. There was a sofa, a TV, a small dining table with two chairs, and a sideboard, all Ikea by the look of it, which was modern enough, so it could be worse. The sofa looked clean, too.

'At least it has a laminate floor. There's nothing worse than inheriting someone else's grotty old carpet. Do you know how much dirt carpets harbour?' Mum asked.

Dad and I shook our heads.

'Yuk! I can imagine,' I said.

Dad was over by the window. 'Great location,' he said, peering through the slats in a white vertical blind. 'Right in the city. They could get a lot of rent for this flat. I wonder why they never rented it out.'

I looked out at the street. An art gallery was opposite, and there were quite a few eating places near here. We'd passed some cool clothes shops on our walk from the train station, and it hadn't escaped my notice that you could see Betty's Tea Rooms on St Helen's Square from here. The city was bustling with shoppers, even at two o'clock on a Monday afternoon. It had an amazing vibe and I couldn't wait to explore it. I already loved it. And I was going to live here for four hundred pounds a month rent. It was crazy!

Dad grunted. 'I expect it'll be dripping with Christmas lights soon. Why do they have to start so early? They get earlier every year. It's still September. Until tomorrow, at least.'

'Oh, Sarah,' Mum said, her voice full of wonder like a child's. 'Can you imagine Christmas here? It'll be absolutely magical. They have a light show on the Minster, don't they?'

She'd been on Google again. 'I think so. And there's a Christmas market on Parliament Street that's supposed to be good.'

She was right. It would be fabulous to spend Christmas here. I could picture a tree laden with lights in the living room, the narrow street outside strung with Christmas decorations, carol singers and late-night Christmas shoppers. I could extend the cafe's opening hours to take advantage of them, even if it meant extra staff. Hot mince pies would go down a treat. So would mulled wine, but we didn't have a license for alcohol. Yet. Perhaps I should mention it to Jenny.

There were two doors off the living room, one to the left and one straight on. The one to the left led into a well-fitted kitchen, not much smaller than the one I shared with Lee in Shepherd's Bush. It'd more than do nicely for just me.

'Oh, this is nice,' Mum said, bumping into me from behind as I stopped to examine the cooker. It was gas, and I was used to electric. 'I've always liked white units,' she said, opening the nearest cupboard. 'Oh, for goodness' sake! They could have wiped these out for you.'

Apart from a few crumbs and dirty rings, they could have been a lot worse. For a brief second, I thought of Chris's kitchen. That'd had white units too, but they were glossy with no handles. No crumb or dirty ring would have dared to take up residence in them. These white cupboards were laminate and slightly dated, with wood-effect worktop. To me, though, the kitchen in Buckingham Palace wouldn't top this. This was mine, all mine. To be as messy or as tidy in as I liked.

I tried to shake away thoughts of Chris, but a powerful image of him lifting me effortlessly onto the vast kitchen island at his immaculate flat, stripping off my clothes, and exquisitely pushing himself into me as we both lost control came unbidden into my mind. I turned away from Mum before she clocked the flush of heat rising in my face. A pang of longing so intense hit me like a kick in the guts.

'This must be the other bedroom, then,' Dad said, opening the other door off the living room. Mum was right behind him. I hadn't seen her move so fast in years.

'It's a good size,' Mum called back.

By the time I got there, Dad had opened the curtains to let light in. It wasn't a bad room, actually. It had wide, bare floorboards instead of a grotty carpet, and the double bed was in good nick. There was a large wardrobe, more than enough for my things. Since I started selling the stuff I didn't wear, my wardrobe was more than pared down. There was a small dressing table too, with a little stool. I didn't really need anything else. Like the rest of it, it was a bit dated, but I could sort that out with a bit of decorating.

Some of these furniture items would look great painted up, which would save me having to replace them. I could paint the floorboards too, so they looked whitewashed. I'd been watching YouTube videos on what you could do with a tin of paint. It was amazing. It was how I'd probably be spending my free time for the first few weeks or months. I wouldn't be going out with friends, would I? I'd have to make some new ones first.

Mum touched the curtains and pulled a face. 'These have seen better days. You need new ones.'

I looked at them. They were thin and brown, and hung crookedly from the pole.

'You're not wrong, Mum. It's not a big window, though. New ones wouldn't cost much. Some nice, thick, lined ones. And the pole looks sturdy enough.'

'We can go looking for some tomorrow,' she says. 'And some nice bedding.'

I look at the bed. The duvet was thin and as for the pillows—well, no way was I sleeping on those stains. Looked like sweat.

'I want a thick mattress protector, a new duvet and pillows. I'm throwing this lot,' I told her.

'We can get those in Argos,' she said, beaming. 'There must be one around here.'

'There's bound to be. There'll be loads of places we can get them.'

Dad was looking out of the window. Like the kitchen, it looked onto a small back area that was just concrete. It wasn't much to look at, but it was the outside space for the bins. The backs of other premises crowded onto it, with narrow alleys that ran higgledy-piggledy in places, just one car wide. I didn't like alleys. They always struck me as dark and lonely, with too many hiding places. On second thoughts, it might be better to go through the shop to enter the flat. I'd have to see.

'It must be about time for lunch,' Dad said. 'Where shall we go?'

I looked at Mum. I knew what she was thinking, that Betty's Tea Rooms weren't far away from here. We'd already walked past them, although she was looking the other way at the time. She hadn't noticed the throng of people queuing around the corner to get in, and I wasn't about to mention it. She'd heard all about them, had never been, and thought they were my competition. I didn't think they were at all; we'd never get away with charging what they did. And I couldn't see the allure myself. I once went to Harrogate for the weekend with Leanne and Emma, queued up for forty minutes to get in the Betty's there and was bitterly disappointed at the fare once we did finally get a table. But Mum was dying to go. She kept slipping it into the conversation. She probably thought my goal was to work there. It *so* wasn't.

'We passed a sandwich shop around the corner. I can just go there, if you like,' I said. 'We can book for Betty's another time, Mum, when we can make an afternoon of it.' I smiled. 'My treat. Maybe at Christmas.'

'Ooh, yes. That would be lovely,' she said. 'Something to look forward to.'

Oh yeah. Can't wait! I tried not to feel insulted. I knew she didn't mean it. Dad shot me a look out of the corner of his eye and shook his head very slightly. He was trying not to laugh.

I hurried to the sandwich place, determined to not get distracted by the variety of shops along the way, then headed back to the cafe, where we ate them at a table at the back. I was right, at least, about the cafe being spotlessly clean, despite the smell of old grease.

After lunch, we got busy scrubbing and tidying the flat upstairs. Dad took all the boxes, which were mainly empty or full of things I didn't want, out of the spare bedroom, and piled them in the yard at the back. In the process, we discovered they were piled on a single bed, which looked in decent nick. Looking around at the space, minus all the boxes, I reckoned you could probably get a double in here, at a push. I'd get new bedding for this bed, too, while I was at it. The view from this window was nicer too, with it being at the front, and there was a wooden vertical blind at the window that didn't need replacing.

'Mum,' I called, looking at the inch-thick layer of dust and fluff on the slats. 'There's a job for you in here, with your toothbrush.'

She came in, slightly out of breath. 'I need the vacuum first,' she said, inspecting it. 'Is there one?'

'Yes. I've seen one in a cupboard somewhere.'

I hoped she didn't do too much and knock herself up with all the jobs she had planned. But I wasn't about to say that to her face. I didn't have a death wish.

Before the shops closed, Mum and I went to Brown's, a department store I'd never heard of, to get new bedding for my first night here. We returned with a new duvet, four new pillows, a dove-grey duvet cover and pillowcases, a fitted bottom sheet, a mattress protector, a white shower curtain with silver sparkles on it, and some new curtains for my bedroom. It cost a bit more than I was planning on spending, but the quality was exceptional. It was nice to put the linen on new stuff, and the mattress itself looked quite new when we stripped the old bedding off. I was still glad of the new mattress protector, though. As I put it on, it hit me that I'd be alone here tonight, when Mum and Dad had gone to their hotel. I felt a frisson of apprehension.

This place didn't feel like mine yet but, with a few updates, it would. It was just strange and new, I told myself.

At ten o'clock, when I'd finished hanging the new curtains, Mum and Dad left for the hotel just a few minutes' walk away, I had an urge to go with them, and shout 'don't leave me here'. Of course, I didn't. I couldn't. I wanted to stand on my own two feet, and I had to.

I locked the door behind them and went back through the dark cafe, every shadow and dark corner unnerving me. What if I'd made the wrong decision and I couldn't do this? And I couldn't forget the fact that Jenny was relying on me to make money.

I locked the door up to the flat behind me and hurried back up the stairs, wishing there was a lockable door at the top.

In the now-cleaner bathroom with its new shower curtain, I took a hot shower, feeling better for washing off the day's grime. I'd closed all the curtains and blinds in the flat earlier, and no one could get in, yet my ears strained in the silence, taking in all the unfamiliar noises. I was in the living room in my dressing gown, combing my wet hair, when a loud bang came from somewhere out the back. Startled, I squealed and peeked out of the window, my heart lodged somewhere in my mouth. Because of a high wall, I couldn't see anything, and there were no more noises. Maybe it was a fox or something, scrabbling around in some bins. Isn't that what they did? I knew what Adam would say: get some cameras put up here. He'd be right. When I got some spare cash, which shouldn't be long given the small amount of rent I was paying, I'd get CCTV installed as my first priority.

After drying my hair and having a cup of tea, I got into my strange bed and, despite the pristine new bedding, the mattress felt cold and damp. But I may have been just imagining it as the flat hadn't been heated in months, and it wasn't cold enough to put the radiators on. Thankfully, Dad had checked the heating worked. I lay down, pulled the duvet up high under my chin, and closed my eyes, listening to the unfamiliar sounds of the night.

When Mum and Dad arrived early the next morning at eight thirty, I hadn't slept a wink.

20

MIGUEL RECOGNISED ME STRAIGHT away when I pulled up on the moped at the harbour, having called at the shop first and found it locked up. I'd suspected this was where he'd be if he wasn't tattooing someone. He straightened up on the deck of a small boat, stopped fiddling with a coil of rope, and waved to me.

The *Santa Lina* was much shitter than I'd expected. It was one up from a wreck. It looked like it used to be blue, but the paint was so faded and peeling it was hard to be sure. Mostly, it was wood-coloured. It was moored alongside some much bigger, better looking specimens, which made it look even worse. I got off the bike and put Leanne on the floor. Mig watched us walk towards him, his hair tied up in his man-bun. Funny, but it no longer annoyed me as much.

'Ah, I know I was be seeing you, but not when. Welcome aboard, my friend,' he said.

He waved me towards him. Leanne pulled back, maybe not sure of the feel of the warm wood of the jetty under her paws. When I went forward, she followed me, and jumped onto the boat first.

Mig rubbed her ears and tickled her under the chin as she fussed around him. Another person she'd charmed, after him not even wanting her in his shop. She was good at this. Perhaps she could work on Sarah for me. If only.

I stepped onto the boat as it rose and fell gently with the swell of the sea, hoping it didn't wobble. It did, alarmingly, and I clutched the side.

'Alright, mate? Shiver me timbers,' I said, staggering and spreading my feet as I tried to adjust.

Mig stood there rock solid, looked confused, and frowned at me. 'What?'

'Never mind.' I straightened up slowly. There was no point doing my Irish accent. He'd heard me talk before, so I might as well speak normally and have a day off.

'Ah. Hello. Yes. Alright mate. How you are doing anyway? The arms they are good?'

He squinted at my tattoos and nodded at his own handiwork. 'They look good, yes? You like?'

'I fuckin love 'em.'

'Yes. Good.' He missed my sarcasm entirely. 'What happens here?' He pointed at my scar, still red and angry.

'Accident.'

'Bottle?'

'Yeah. You should see the other guy.'

He frowned again and cocked his head to one side.

'Never mind.' I pointed at the boat. 'So, this is her?'

He nodded, and I couldn't help noticing how proud of her he looked. Bloody hell! Had he not seen the others along here lately?

'I am taking her out if you wish to come right now,' he said. 'Not far.'

'Okay. Sounds good. As long as I don't get seasick.'

'Seasick, hmmm.' He mimed puking, and I nodded. 'Is gentle boat. You not be sick.'

'If you say so.'

He tossed me a life jacket like his, and I put it on.

'What about the dog? She needs one.' I pointed at Leanne.

'Dog jacket? I not have.'

He rooted around in a box before pulling something out and tossing it over. It was a life jacket that looked made for a baby. It was still too big, but maybe I could make it fit her. While I got busy with the buckles and straps of my life jacket, then Leanne's, he started the engine, and we pulled away from the jetty. The boat was surprisingly quiet, and the low throbbing of the engine under my feet felt good. As we increased speed, Leanne freaked out and jumped up onto me, trying to wrap herself around my neck. The life jacket I'd just fashioned fell off, and her claws raked my thighs as she panicked.

I pulled her down and onto my lap while she got used to it. No matter how I tried, the life jacket wouldn't stay on. Mig watched me, amused, then dug around in a wooden box and threw me a child's inflatable rubber ring in fluorescent orange.

'Try,' he said, shrugging.

It was better than nothing so I blew it up, and put it on the floor, next to my feet.

After a bit, she settled down and seemed to enjoy the wind ruffling her ears as she sniffed the air. Mig lit a spliff, took a drag, then handed it to me.

We headed out to open sea much faster than I expected from the old wreck. The spliff filled me with a relaxing calm after I took a deep drag on it, so I had another. The sea wasn't too choppy the further from the shore we got and the swaying of the boat was soothing. I put Leanne down in the bottom of the boat, where she couldn't fall overboard. Mig handled the boat like a pro, adjusting the steering smoothly.

'Where are we going?' I shouted above the engine noise.

He shrugged. 'Wherever. Free, like is the bird.'

He pointed at my eagle tattoo and smiled. In the distance, I saw the galleon again, the one rigged out for cruises. Maybe there were a few of them that looked the same. Either that, or it didn't do long voyages and stayed around here instead. Ships of all sizes dotted the ocean: some looked like cruise ships, some smaller pleasure boats, others could be fishing trawlers. I wasn't up on boats, but I could definitely get used to this life. Massive tankers that didn't seem to move dotted the horizon. God knows what they were for. Maybe something to do with oil. They looked industrial, anyway. I lay down on one of the side benches and squinted up at a near cloudless sky, taking the occasional pull on the spliff.

After about thirty minutes, Mig pointed to where a large rock face jutted out from the beach, a few miles out to sea. I couldn't see what was around the other side.

He began to turn the boat toward it, and we slowed down, cruising around the rocks. A small sandy cove revealed itself the further around we got. It looked deserted.

As we approached the shore, I realised rocks jutted out of the sea all around us. Mig skilfully steered the boat around them, avoiding them all. I was impressed. He was a much better sailor than I'd given him credit for. He cut the engine, and we drifted into a pocket that seemed just made for the boat as he tucked the nose into a crevice. The beach was still a few hundred yards away. He dropped the anchor.

'Swim?' he asked, pointing to the beach.

'Sure.' I pulled the rubber ring over Leanne's head and eased her front legs through so it was around her middle. It was on the large side, and she looked at me anxiously, trying to wriggle free. She couldn't get out of it, though, if I held onto her.

Mig picked up a backpack that looked waterproof.

'Phone?' he said. 'Keep dry.'

I passed him my phone to put in it and he went over the side, onto a ladder. I followed, with Leanne tucked under my arm, the rubber ring squeaking against my own life jacket. Mig pushed away from the boat and began to swim away. I stepped off the ladder and shivered. The sea was freezing, and I couldn't feel the bottom. I stretched my legs out and could just touch the rocky bottom with my toes. I let Leanne go, and she paddled hard, her lips pulled back and her tongue lolling to one side. Her flotation device was working a treat!

'Good girl,' I said to encourage her. 'Keep kicking.'

Her little legs moved like mad and we swam slowly to the shore. The water was crystal clear and calm, just the odd ripple sending her up and over it, then back down again. Still she kicked out, her little legs going like the clappers.

Mig reached the beach and strode out of the water, letting his hair loose and shaking it like a dog, and stripping off his life jacket. I followed in his wake, careful not to deviate for fear of the rocks. The floor came up suddenly in a sandy shelf, and I stood up. Leanne sounded knackered now, and I tucked her under my arm, feeling her ribs heave as she got her breath back. Her bony little body was soaked and shivering, yet she'd never looked happier. She was enjoying our jaunt as much as me.

On the sand, I took her out of the rubber ring and she ran madly in circles, barking at nothing.

'What is this place?' I asked Mig, looking around. The cove was small but really private, with white sand strewn with damp seaweed. The rocks behind us were huge, and I realised they were caves.

Mig didn't answer but shrugged off his backpack, then his T-shirt, and stretched out on a flat piece of rock. His skin was a deep-golden brown, smooth, except for a large scar that ran the length of his torso, jagged and raised. It looked old, pale and silvery.

'What happened?' I said, sitting on another rock next to him.

He opened his eyes to see me pointing at the scar.

'Jealous husband and big, big knife.'

'Christ! Really?'

He laughed and said nothing, but his fingers traced the scar then dropped to the side. His eyes flickered briefly over my scar before he closed them. Was he joking about the knife or not? He made it clear he wasn't bothered about talking by going to sleep. Before long, he was snoring fit to wake the dead.

I walked around the edge of the rocks, going in and out of the caves with Leanne. They were much taller inside than I thought they'd be. Water dripped from the roofs and cascaded down the walls. The enclosed spaces muffled sound, and the claustrophobia was horrible. I imagined smugglers centuries ago dragging things here from ships that had beached on the bigger, nastier rocks further out to sea. There were twenty caves altogether, and I went in all of them. A couple of them had paths cut into the rock that went way back into the darkness. When I went down one of them, the walls narrowed and the claustrophobia grew as the darkness deepened. I wished I had my phone so I could turn the torch on, but it was in the backpack. I turned back and rushed towards the shaft of light, back onto the beach. Leanne, the wiseass, had stayed outside after only venturing in a few steps. She barked the whole time I was in there.

We wandered back to Mig, who was awake now and digging around in his pack. He threw me a wrapped package, and I ripped it open to find pastels nestled inside. I broke open the fried pastry, hoping for a filling of chicken. Bingo! I hadn't realised I was so hungry. The swimming and walking had made me ravenous. Leanne too, it seemed, as she never took her eyes off my food. I tossed her a bit of meat and she swallowed it whole, then waited for the next bit.

Mig removed the tops of two beers with a small bottle opener on his keyring and scooted down to sit on the sand, still chewing his own pastels. I realised he'd just given me half his lunch.

'This place is amazing,' I said, accepting the beer he held out to me.

He nodded. 'Yes, I come here lots, alone. For to relax and do thinking. I like it. Not many come here.'

He had a laid back air about him that was infectious. I hadn't felt this relaxed in years. I could really go for this life, but this wasn't my home. Why couldn't I just stay here and make a new life? I knew why. Because of Sarah. I just couldn't go the rest of my life without seeing her again. It was that simple.

I sat on the rock and watched the boats drift by as the sun heated my skin. Mig talked about all the ships. By the sound of it, he knew a lot of the crews and what all the boats were. I listened to him, getting the breadth of what he knew, and it was astonishing. His knowledge of the area was immense. I couldn't have found out this much by any amount of research on the internet.

Sitting on the rock, looking out to sea and listening to Mig, the cogs of my mind began to turn, shucking off the rust and dust of the previous months. It was about time.

21

MUM AND DAD RETURNED to London after three days of helping me clean the flat and shop. At the station, with tears clogging my throat and a knot in my chest that was so tight I couldn't breathe, I saw them onto the train, Mum's movements slow and painful as she climbed into the carriage with Dad's help. I knew she'd done too much, but she just wouldn't stop. I could see from their posture how much it hurt them to be leaving me here, and it killed me.

Then it hit me properly that for the first time ever I was going to be truly coping on my own. I stood on the platform until the train disappeared around the bend in the track, waving even though they could no longer see me. Mum had said they were coming back up in a few weeks. I wished they hadn't left.

I turned to go and ran smack into a man standing only a foot away. He was over six feet tall, had black hair, and his eyes were the darkest chocolate. It was him! My heart plummeted, landing somewhere around my feet while he glared at me. I'd knocked his coffee, and it slopped onto his shoes.

'Bloody hell! Watch where you're going!' he snapped.

'I'm so sorry,' I muttered as he brushed some dregs off his jeans.

He looked nothing like Chris, but for a split second, I could have sworn it was him. I turned away, feeling his eyes still burning into me, and left the train station, almost running. Chris couldn't be here, anyway. How would he know I was here? It wasn't possible.

My heart calmed down as I walked back towards the city centre. In the few days exploring since I'd been here, I'd fallen utterly in love with the place. From what I could tell, the change of scene was exactly what I needed. If only I wasn't so alone. I stopped on a stone bridge over the River Ouse and looked down. The water was dark, almost black, like oil. To the left of the river bank was a tall building, four storeys. The ground floor was a pub, The Engine Room, with a beer garden on the banks. Almost all the tables were taken, and my eyes landed on one table where a couple sat with a pram next to them. The man picked up his beer while the woman rocked the pram gently. They looked happy. She sipped her orange juice, then reached into the pram and lifted a baby out. If it was crying, I couldn't hear it. I couldn't tear my eyes away from the tiny body, helpless as a newly hatched chick. The mother confidently changed the baby's position whilst never letting the little head drop back. The man unfolded something and handed it to her. I watched, mesmerised, as she somehow tucked the baby under her top while remaining completely covered up. The man draped and adjusted the shawl around her, then resumed drinking his beer. The tiny hole in my chest opened into a yawning cavern, but still I couldn't look away until the woman looked up and caught me staring. Then the spell was broken.

Fighting the urge to call Leanne just to hear a familiar voice, I left the bridge, not stopping until a second-hand shop caught my eye. This end of town seemed to be brimming with them. An antique lamp with an ornately carved wooden base stood in pride of place in the window. I loved everything about it. The shade was grubby but intact; it would look beautiful on my little dressing table, if I could clean it up enough. There was no price tag on it, but I pushed open the door, went in, and after a bit of haggling, it was mine for just fifteen pounds. Bargain.

The rest of the day was mine, to adjust to being alone, and the next few days until the grand reopening on Monday, would be taken up with redecorating the cafe itself. The two waitresses who worked here before were staying on and Jenny was paying them to help me decorate, but one of them, Rebecca, had made it known she wasn't keen on what she called 'slave labour'. 'If I'd wanted to be a painter and decorator, I'd have become one, wouldn't I?' she'd informed me when I'd met them the day after I moved in.

Mum had been shocked, then outraged, as had Dad.

'I wouldn't be putting up with that if I were you,' Dad had remarked.

I'd been a bit stunned, unsure how to react. I was going to be her boss, after all. The other one, Claire, had looked embarrassed at Rebecca's outburst, and assured me she'd love to help.

I needed to watch Rebecca. If she thought I was a pushover, then she could think again. I thought I couldn't sack anybody, but the way she spoke to me and made me feel that day made me realise it would be a pleasure to get rid of her, just to see the look on her face.

As I walked back to the flat, replaying the incident with Rebecca in my head yet again, the anger I felt then flared up once more. Waiting-on staff couldn't be that hard to find in a place like York. University cities usually had no shortage of applicants for casual jobs like that. Rebecca should be careful. The old me might not have said boo to a goose, but that wasn't the case now.

I polished up my hard exterior (going through possible ways to get rid of her) as I unlocked the flat and went upstairs to place my new lamp in the bedroom.

On the spur of the moment, I called her. When she didn't answer the phone, I left a voicemail, saying she needed to come in tomorrow to help Claire and I, as she was getting paid for it, after all.

I just managed not to add, 'And if you don't like it, you can bloody well look for another job,' at the end.

With a few hours to kill and not wanting to dwell on the fact that I'd be alone tonight, without my parents a few minutes' walk away in their hotel, I did the only thing that would soothe me. I went into the cafe kitchen, put a podcast on and started to bake.

***

In the end, I slept better than I was expecting to, thanks to a herbal Nytol and a large glass of wine. The next morning, Claire burst through the door at nine o'clock prompt, as arranged, dressed in clothes already spattered with paint. Her long, blonde hair was tied up in a scarf and she carried a small toolbox.

'Right, then,' she said. 'Where do you want me?'

She was so eager to get started, I couldn't help laughing.

'You're keen,' I said.

'To tell you the truth, I've been dying to give this place a revamp since I started working here. Just give me a paintbrush and point me in the right direction. I can't flippin' wait.'

Her broad Yorkshire accent reminded me so strongly of Chris, and how he'd sometimes lapse into Leeds-speak without thinking. And his sister, although I'd struggled to understand a word she said.

'First, elevenses,' I said.

She frowned. 'It's nine o'clock.'

I shrugged. 'And?'

Her eyes lit up. 'Is there cake?'

I pulled a face. 'Is there cake? Did my reputation not precede me?'

She sniffed the air and went into the kitchen, where she saw the three cakes I'd made the night before lined up on the side.

'Oh my God!' she called back. 'Is that lemon drizzle?'

'Yup! And chocolate orange cake with fudgy buttercream, and date and walnut. Help yourself.'

I lined up three tins of paint on the counter and peered at the labels.

'Oh man! These look awesome,' she shouted back.

'I'm not running the coffee machine today, but there's a small kettle I've brought down from the flat. Stick it on, will you, and I'll make us some tea,' I said. By the time I got into the kitchen, she was already filling it under the tap.

Rebecca hadn't shown up yet, despite being given the same start time as Claire. Surely she wouldn't do a no show, would she?

Over tea and cake, Claire and I bonded. She was a year younger than me, and doing an Open University History course in her spare time. She was so likeable and bubbly it was impossible not to get on with her. It reminded me that people used to say I was bubbly at one time. I wasn't sure they did any more.

'Ooh, is this what we're using?' she said, noticing the paint. She tipped each can back in turn, looking at the colour labels. 'Oh, I love them, especially this dark grey. Which wall is it for?'

'This long one, opposite the counter. The back wall is going to be pink, and that one mauve. Sounds a bit awful, saying it like that.'

Claire pushed all three tins together. 'No, I think it's going to look great. I can't wait to get rid of this yellow and orange scheme. It's so gaudy and bright. I don't think it's been decorated in about ten years.'

'Have you done much painting before?' I asked her.

'Loads. When I lived at home, I wanted a different colour so often, my dad refused to do it and said I'd better learn. Have you?'

'No. Hardly any. You can show me your techniques then. I'm a willing student.'

'No problems.' She rummaged in her toolbox for a screwdriver and prised the lids off the paint.

I'd already covered the tiled floor in old dust sheets I found under the bed in the small bedroom and bought a couple of small stepladders, so we started to get some paint on the walls, Claire taking the largest wall of grey.

'Just copy me,' she said, wielding her paint roller like a pro. 'There's nothing to it.'

But it took me a while to get the hang of it. In the end, she showed me how to minimise drips and get it nice and smooth without overspreading it. And there was no way I could do the cutting in against the white ceiling, like she could. I'd leave that to her. I checked my watch and glanced at the door. Still no Rebecca.

'Problem?' asked Claire, watching me out of the corner of her eye.

'Yes. I told Rebecca to get here at nine. And it's half past ten now. I think she's taking the piss.' I walked over to the window. Plenty of people were passing, but none of them were her.

Claire lowered her roller and climbed down the stepladder. 'She texted me yesterday morning. Said she's not coming in. I thought she would have told you.'

'What? Really?'

The damn cheek of her! How many chances were you supposed to give people when they acted like her? Then I remembered I'd left her the voicemail since then.

'What's her problem?' I asked Claire. 'She was off with me from the second we met.'

'Well, you know the manager before you?'

I shook my head. 'I thought the owner was the manager.'

'No. We hardly saw her, the owner; Gail. The manager was Vanessa. Her and Rebecca were like that.' She twisted her middle and forefinger together and held them up.

'Obviously, she got the shove when your mate bought the cafe because you were taking over and she wasn't needed.'

'Oh! I didn't know that. No one told me.'

So that was it! She blamed me for her friend losing her job. For a second I felt bad, but it wasn't my fault. I didn't even know.

'Right, well, thanks for telling me that. I wish someone had before now. I feel bad for this Vanessa woman.'

Claire shrugged. 'It's not your fault. Um, so what are you going to do about Rebecca?' She loaded up her paintbrush, eyed the ceiling, and went back up the ladder.

'I don't know yet. Tell me, what's she like? Is it worth giving her another chance, do you think, or is this typically how she's going to perform, because I'm not putting up with that.'

'Well, I don't want to badmouth her, but I've always found her lazy. She never puts herself out for the customers at all.'

She wasn't comfortable talking about her colleague like this, but I needed to know the truth.

'Go on. Lazy how?' I loaded the roller with the mauve paint and continued on the wall around the window at the front of the café, not painting right into the corner where it met the grey. That was Claire's job. Next to the grey, the mauve looked good; fresh but kind of moody.

'It's like, if there was a table to clear, she'd walk right by it and leave it for me. She'd rather stand behind the counter, playing on her phone. And Vanessa never told her off for it. In fact, sometimes they'd both stand there gossiping while I ran around like a blue-arse fly. And she wouldn't ask customers if they wanted more drinks, even when their cups or glasses were empty. I think that's a missed opportunity, you know, the whole upselling thing.' She got down from the stepladder, reloaded her brush, and climbed back up it in one swift motion. 'I should have brought a small paint kettle for this,' she chided herself. 'Anyway, my parents had a restaurant. We lived above it. I worked evenings there from being thirteen and I had it drilled into me: 'Claire, an empty glass is money that could be in our pocket.' And it's true. Half the time if you ask someone if they want another drink, they say yes.'

'I'm glad to hear you say that. That's exactly what I'd be expecting you to do, without having to be reminded.'

I chewed my lip. If Rebecca was lazy, I couldn't keep her. None of this looked good for her, if Claire was telling the truth, and I had no reason to think she wasn't. She seemed genuine to me.

Just then, the door opened and Rebecca came in, frowning as she stepped onto the ruckled dust sheet. She pointedly checked her shoes, then looked at my mauve paint and pulled a face like I'd just smeared dog crap over the walls.

'Glad you could join us,' I said, looking at my watch and only narrowly avoiding painting a stripe down myself in the process. 'You got my message then?'

'Obviously.'

I took a deep breath, holding onto my temper. No way was I going to be able to work with her for long. She was bloody awful.

'You don't appear to be dressed for painting,' I said, glancing up and down at her pale pink skinny jeans, white jumper, and black denim jacket. The jumper was really nice, fluffy and soft-looking. I wondered if it was mohair, then pushed the distraction away.

She scrunched her nose up. 'I already told you, I don't paint. I don't do manual jobs.' She looked at her nails, which were they're very long and perfectly manicured. She didn't consider waiting tables manual labour? It was hardly brain surgery or rocket science.

'So what are you going to do to help today, then?' I asked her. *With those totally impractical nails?*

'Actually, I'm not staying.'

I blinked. 'What do you mean?'

'What I said.' She rolled her eyes like I was an idiot or something.

I couldn't believe her attitude. Maybe Jenny didn't meet her. She surely wouldn't have thought I'd be happy to work with her. The thing was, could I sack her just like that, without a proper reason, other than I didn't like her? I was clueless about that sort of thing. Could she take me to a tribunal or something?

Before I could think of what to say next, she pushed her bag further onto her shoulder, gave me a smug smile, and said, 'I just popped by to hand in my notice. I'm leaving. As of right now. So I won't be here on Monday for your *grand opening*. Soz!'

I tried and failed to find any words as she spun around, flipped her hair over her shoulder and flounced out, slamming the door behind her. I looked at Claire, who was halfway up her stepladder, mouth gaping open.

'The cheeky bloody cow!' she said.

I shook my head, unable to believe what had just happened, and put my paint roller in the tray. I needed to sit down. Rebecca had just left me with a huge problem.

'What am I supposed to do now? Much as I didn't like her, I needed her, at least until I could find a replacement.'

I sat down heavily on the nearest chair and dropped my head into my hands as Claire clattered down the ladder.

'It'll be okay,' she said, trying to reassure me.

I felt like crying. I hadn't even opened up, and it was going wrong.

'How will it be okay? It's a disaster. I'll be in the kitchen fifty percent of the time, and you can't do everything else on your own.'

I realised too late that paint coated my hands, and I'd just smeared it all over my hair and face. Fantastic!

'I can't believe she's dropped me in it,' I muttered. 'And she loved it, didn't she? Did you notice?'

'Oh, I noticed, alright. The smug cow!'

All the doubts I'd been holding back were set free and came flooding out of captivity with a vengeance. I couldn't run this place. Why did I think I could?

Claire pulled out the chair and sat opposite me. She said something, but I was barely listening. I'd failed before I'd even begun. What was I going to tell Jenny? She'd put all her faith in me. My fledgling panic was about to go into full flight. I couldn't breathe.

'Even if I put an ad up in the window or the job centre or somewhere, I'll never find anyone in time. At least Rebecca knew what she was doing. She was better than nothing.'

Claire sighed and gave a loud tut.

I looked up. 'What?'

'I think I may be able to sort it.'

'What? How?'

'I just said! My friend, Ellie, is looking for a job and I think it would suit her.'

'Has she done this sort of thing before?' I clung on to the tiny lifeline Claire had thrown me.

To my surprise, Claire laughed. 'I'll say. She's done more than waiting on and serving; she's fully qualified. Went to catering college and everything. In fact, she's like you, but with savoury stuff.'

A glimmer of daylight cut through the gloom. 'Really?'

'Yep, and she packed her job in a few weeks ago. Said the place she worked in didn't give her any freedom or input to create her own stuff. She's not desperate for the money, so she's been waiting for the right thing. With Rebecca leaving, this changes things. Shall I ring her?'

'Er, I don't know. I can't think straight. Do you think she'd be interested?'

'I think she would be. There's only one way to find out, isn't there?' she said, taking out her phone.

22

MIG LIVED AROUND THE corner from the tattoo shop, above a laundromat. I'd been there a few times now, but this time was different. It was make or break for me. I climbed the stairs to his apartment, with Leanne running up ahead of me, completely at ease with the place.

'Hey,' said Mig as I came through the door at the top. 'Come. We are ready for you.'

A rugged, barrel-chested guy, unsmiling and dark-skinned, stood up as I entered the small living room. He was around fifty, although he could have been in his thirties and just have had a hard life. He looked me up and down for a long time. Probably wondering if I was a lying bastard. I was thinking the same about him. An unlit cig was jammed between his lips, and his eyes swivelled back to Mig. He gave Mig a brief nod. It seemed that whatever test I'd just been through, I may have passed. How did I know if I could trust him, though? This guy could be about to rip me off for everything I had, and I only had Mig's word to say otherwise. And I only had instinct to go on to trust Mig enough to even get this far.

Leanne, the little traitor, was sitting on Mig's lap and licking his face. Would he look after her for me if it came to it?

'Sit, please. Beer?' Mig asked. He seemed a bit jittery. Not surprising.

I nodded, and he passed me a bottle of ice-cold beer. Condensation dripped down my hand as I took a swig.

'This is Zico,' Mig said, nodding at the man, who was still scrutinising me. 'He is willing to help you.'

'How much do you have?' Zico asked. His voice was gruff, no doubt after a lifetime of cigarettes, but his English was clear and easy to understand. Conversations would definitely be easier with him. If I did this.

Might as well level with him from the start and cut the shit. 'Ten thousand English pounds,' I tell him. 'That's the limit.' I spread my hands palms upwards and shrugged to hammer home the finality.

Zico lit his cig, took a deep drag, and narrowed his eyes as he looked at me through the smoke.

Mig glanced between us, looking hopeful. He'd be getting a cut of whatever Zico charged me. It was zero risk for him, but whatever he got it would be a bonus for five minutes of his time and an introduction. It was *my* money, *my* life, *my* decision ultimately. But I'd be putting my life literally in Zico's hands.

'That will do it,' Zico said without hesitation.

Fuck! Mig had said Zico would probably want fifteen thousand minimum. If I'd known he'd accept ten, I'd have suggested five and gone up. Had Mig played me? It was too late now.

'Can you pull it off, though?' I asked.

Zico waved his hand around dismissively. 'It's not a problem.'

'Not for you, no. But I could die. So, I'll ask you again. Are you sure you can do it?'

Zico shrugged. 'I can do it. There is no one better than me. But it's up to you, in the end. Can you do your bit?'

Mig said, 'You can trust him, Carl. Zico is closest thing I have to brother. I trust him with my life.'

'You might do,' I said. 'But I don't know him, do I?'

I stood there, biting my bottom lip. If there was one thing I'd learned in life, it was that sometimes you just had to trust people. Not everyone was going to let you down. It wasn't a foregone conclusion.

'You can take your time and think about it,' Zico said. 'If you miss the deadline in two weeks, you will have to wait a full eight weeks after that until the next one. But maybe waiting is not so bad. It is a big decision for you, I understand.' He shrugged and pulled a face. I got the feeling he wasn't desperate for my money, which was good. So maybe he wouldn't have done it for five. It was still a risk for him.

'How long have you been doing this run?' I asked.

Zico smiled, showing broken, black stumps. I preferred it when he didn't bother.

'Ten years now.' He tutted and rolled his eyes. 'You English and your sugar. I only do sugar, see? No contraband. The UK ports know me. They trust me.'

Did they though? I had another slug of beer. No contraband? What was I, then? I was hardly a few hundred black market cigarettes or even an illegal white powder.

'Have you done this before?' I asked.

He laughed and shook his head. 'I can't possibly answer that.'

That could be a yes, then. 'How sure are you we can get close enough?'

'Positive. If we do it how you said. I get you to UK and you do the rest. Whatever that is.'

I still wasn't one hundred percent sure. At least here I was alive. Did I risk it or not? The very thought of it scared me shitless, but for now, it was the best chance I'd got. Let's face it, it was the only chance I'd got. If I didn't take it, I could be stuck here for the rest of my life. And life had to be about chances. One thing I was sure of was that I wasn't going to prison. If it ever came to it, I'd do myself in first. That wasn't a life I could contemplate. Was two weeks long enough, or should I wait and prepare for longer? But what else, really, did I need to do? Waiting weeks would only add to the anxiety, and I'd be in a worse state at the end of it. No, it was now or never.

'Alright,' I said, looking Zico squarely in the eye. 'Two weeks. Let's do it.'

'You will not regret it,' he said. 'If anyone can help you, it is me.'

Leanne jumped down from Mig's lap and onto mine, where she turned around once and settled down with a contented huff. It was then I knew for sure.

'One other thing,' I said, fluffing her ears.

'What?'

'The dog. She'll be coming with me.'

He frowned. 'You must be joking. She will die.'

'Carl? You cannot take her,' Mig said.

'She won't die. She'll be fine with me.'

Zico opened his mouth and closed it again, then shook his head and tapped a yellow-stained forefinger to his temple. Then he leaned towards Mig and said, 'You're right. This guy? He is fuckin crazy.'

23

CLAIRE AND I FINISHED the decorating in the cafe two days before we were due to open. I could never have got it all done without her. As well as being so good at painting, she was also a brilliant visionary, not only sharing my insight for the cafe, but improving on it with her own suggestions, things I would never have thought of. Turned out we had similar tastes, and after many brainstorming sessions on Pinterest, we set out about achieving it. Thanks to Jenny's money, and all the second-hand shops around here, we were able to fill the cafe with quirky, one-off pieces that had given it a vintage-but-still-modern feel. A set of shelves at the back of the shop had, with a fresh coat of purple paint, become a brilliant area to display our newfound treasures: teapots, cups and saucers, glass vases and the like. The whole interior was now warm and inviting when you walked through the door, instead of being assaulted with the garish, eye-watering colours of before. It had gone from harsh and too-bright to soft and warm, a place to sit and relax with friends. Exactly what I set out to achieve. More importantly, the space felt like mine.

I waited at a table in the window of the cafe for Claire's friend Ellie to arrive. When I spoke to her on the phone, she'd seemed keen enough. If this interview didn't go well, though, we'd be opening short-staffed. Claire had informed me that wouldn't be the case. I desperately wanted to believe her.

165

Claire, from her place in the kitchen, called out to me. 'She's just texted. The bus was late, but she's on her way. She'll be ten minutes. Stop fretting.'

'Brilliant. I thought she might not be coming.'

'Nah,' said Claire. 'She's not like that.'

When I went into the kitchen, she was poring over the new menus I'd laid out on the pastry prep space.

'So, what do you think?' I asked.

'I definitely agree with the direction you're going in. Offering simple, hot food that's quick for us to prepare but has also got a good mark-up on it is a no-brainer. Like you, I'm all for getting rid of the greasy spoon, all-day-breakfast image and going a bit more upmarket. More ladies-who-lunch.'

'Absolutely. I'm going to have the scrambled or poached eggs on toast available all day, but scrap the fry-ups. It's just not us. They do fry-ups around the corner, anyway. Any other jacket potato fillings you can suggest? And I want to do a couple of salads. Although, with the amount of cake that'll be on offer, I can't claim we're a health food place.'

She scanned down the menu. 'No, these fillings look great. Lots of variety.'

'I really want to push the cakes and desserts, though. Get more people ordering them at the tables and also boxing them up to take home if they're full. I want them to come here especially for the cakes, because they've heard how good they are. I've thought of a new slogan: *Better than Betty's*; what do you reckon?'

Claire laughed so hard she snorted. 'Not round here. You'll get lynched. What about *Betty Who?* But people will come when word about your cakes gets around, I'm sure. I rang the paper up, like we said, and they said they might come and do a feature next week, but I wouldn't hold your breath. I don't think they were too happy to give the place free advertising without something in return, to be honest, but if it's a slow news day, they may.'

I paused. Claire told me her dad knew the editor. But I didn't want to be in the local rag or any other paper.

'And I heard back from the Lord Mayor's office,' Claire continued. 'He's coming too. His department is big on upcoming new business, apparently, so he can put his money where his mouth is. He'll probably turn up with a film crew for the local news to do a piece. He's all about publicity, especially furthering his own.'

'What?' My pulse began to gallop in alarm. I didn't want to be on TV. I was trying to keep a low profile. Although the chances of Chris watching a local Yorkshire TV station were probably nil. There again, he was from Yorkshire. He could have come back here to hide, and I'd never know.

'I don't really want to be on the TV or in the paper,' I said. 'You can take centre stage if that happens.'

She looked at me closely. 'Why? This place is your baby, not mine. Your name above the door, as it were.'

What could I tell her? She wasn't stupid. And I probably looked like a rabbit caught in the headlights.

'Sarah? What's wrong?' she asked me, her voice wavering.

'Nothing's wrong. I'm just not comfortable at the thought of being on TV, that's all.'

She gave a mock gasp and put her hand to her chest. 'You're not in witness protection, are you? Did you see a gangland execution or something? Is the Mafia after you?'

'No! Don't be daft. Of course not. I just like to keep a low profile, that's all.'

'Hmmm. Well. I'd have thought you'd have been shouting about this place from the rooftops.'

'I will be. Just not on telly. Or social media.'

She nodded. 'Okay. Well, I'm sure you'll tell me all about it when you're ready.'

I sighed. 'There's nothing to tell.'

'You're not in danger or anything? Seriously, I mean?'

'No. Look, I'm just trying to put a bad relationship behind me, that's all. Nothing half as dramatic as what you're imagining.'

She looked at me now with sympathy. Her phone pinged, and she swiped at it. 'Ellie's nearly here. Is the door unlocked?'

'Yes.' I hurried out of the kitchen, smoothing down my clothes. Anyone would think it was me being interviewed. I was probably more nervous than Ellie was. But I needed for this to go well.

A minute later, a woman with short, bright-blue hair, a nose stud and the most eccentric dress sense I'd ever seen came through the door. She looked far better in yellow and black striped tights, orange shorts, and a black biker jacket than I ever would. It sounded an awful get up, but it really suited her. She towered over me. My fleeting thought was I hoped she didn't scare the customers away with her thick, black eyeliner and outlandish dress sense.

'Hiya,' she said, smiling, closing the door quietly behind her.

'Hi. I'm Sarah. You must be Ellie. It's so nice to meet you.'

'You, too, Sarah. I've heard an awful lot about you from Claire.'

We shook hands awkwardly, then Claire came out of the kitchen and enveloped her in a big hug. I stood like a spare part, watching.

My first interview. I needed to be the boss. Be businesslike but friendly. I was wrong-footed when Claire put her coat on and zipped it up.

'Where are you going?' I said. 'I thought you were staying.'

'Things to do.' She tapped her nose. 'I'll leave you two to get acquainted.'

After she'd gone, I took charge and showed Ellie to a table at the back.

'This place looks great. A definite improvement,' she said, looking at the new décor.

She sat down and placed her hands in her lap. I didn't know what to do with mine, so I copied what she did.

'Claire's told me a lot about you,' I began. 'You know the position here was originally for someone to wait tables, clear up, that sort of thing, but I'm absolutely open to someone with your skills joining us. In fact, I'm quite excited about it.'

Did bosses say things like that, or did I sound desperate? Well, it was too late. All I could do was be myself.

Ellie leaned forward now. 'Claire says you like input from your staff, as in ideas and things.'

'I do. Definitely. I'm happy to discuss new ideas for the place, as long as they fit in with my general plan to go a bit more upmarket.'

'Well, I know you do cakes, and I do pastries, mostly savouries, so you've doubled the repertoire already. And I also make my own yogurt and ice cream. All organic.'

I pulled my seat closer to the edge of the table. 'Organic? I like the sound of that. Although there are some organic and vegan places around here. There's a lot of competition. I do the odd vegan cake, but that's it. I can't help feeling it's a token, though.'

'Most of those other places, and I know them all, are exclusively organic or vegan. I think, if we mix my stuff in with yours, we could serve a much broader range of customers. The other cafes can stay in their niche and we won't be competing directly. You see, I'm vegan and my boyfriend is an out-and-out carnivore. I feel he's short-changed in a vegan place (he calls it rabbit food!), and I have nothing to eat in a steak house, his favourite place. You could do the best of both worlds and combine them?'

My mind was racing ahead at the possibilities. 'I really like that idea. I think it could work.'

'Good. I hoped you would.'

I was warming up now. 'Ellie, how good are you at managing yourself? I don't see myself as a micro-manager, to be honest. I want people who don't need telling what to do every five minutes.'

'I work best that way. I'm more than capable of producing my stuff right here. In fact, I have quite a few people who came to the place I last worked, mainly for my things. They all say they'll come here, if I do. It's very flattering.'

I paused. This could be the sticking point. Inwardly, I was cringing as I said, 'Claire told me you've already left your last job because of creative differences?'

She sniffed. 'It's true. They just wanted me to serve the rubbish they bought in instead of letting me make my own, which is much better. It was about cost cutting really. But I'm not a demanding diva or anything like that. I just had a different vision to them.'

I believed her. I wouldn't have wanted to work at the delis in London if they hadn't given me a certain amount of freedom.

I relaxed a bit into my seat, and the talk turned to pay and hours. I thought she'd lose interest as I couldn't pay her a great deal more than I would a server, but she didn't.

'The better the café does, the more we can all get paid,' I said.

'Absolutely. I'm all for incentives. Um, did Claire tell you I have a child?'

That could have been another grey area. What was I supposed to say? I was nervous about saying anything discriminatory. 'Yes, she did.'

'Darcey's five. I have a great support system in place. My boyfriend, Jeb, works nights, so he's around in the day, and I'm back in the evenings. And my mum helps a lot. She idolises Darcey and can't get enough of her. She's on her own since my dad died. And she only lives next-door-but-one. Darcey's just started full-time school, so it's a godsend, and Mum's more than happy to step in at the last minute. My last job was full time, and I never had any issues.'

That put my mind at rest. I thought of a boss-type question. 'So what makes you want to work here, in particular?'

'Claire has told me all about what you want to do here. She also said we'd get on, and I think we will, which is really important to me. And I think we have the same goals and direction about what we want from our work life.'

She couldn't have given me a better answer. 'Why don't we give it a go?' I said. 'You'll have a lot of freedom here to create what you want. And I can't wait to taste your ice cream.'

'Brilliant. What time do you want me here? Jeb gets in at seven, but Mum does the school run if I need her to.'

We spent the next ten minutes finishing up the finer points and Claire came back, holding a bottle of fizzy wine, which she plonked down on the table between us. 'Am I to open this, then? Or has it all gone to shit while I was out, and she's already sacked?'

I snorted with laughter. 'No, it hasn't. And there's nothing wrong with drinking in the day. Crack it open, quick, before she changes her mind.'

'No chance of that. I can't wait to start,' Ellie said.

I got up to find a bottle opener. It seemed my employee problem may have been solved, as Claire had said it would be.

We made a toast to working together, and, after a glass each, they left, laughing and chatting. I locked the door behind them, feeling a lot more hopeful than I did this morning. Upstairs, in the flat with the remainder of the wine, I googled CCTV firms in the area and emailed some to give me a quote. Since that first night, dosed up on Nytol and wine, I hadn't slept too well. I was up and looking out of the window at every noise. And there were a lot of noises. Almost as many as in Shepherd's Bush, but I had Leanne with me there in the flat. I used to sleep with

171

no bother back there. A car bomb could have gone off and I wouldn't have got out of bed. But here, on my own, it was different, and I didn't want to rely on sleeping tablets.

I lifted my laptop screen and logged in to the Mumsnet account I'd made two days ago, in the middle of the night when I was wide awake. The forums were full of questions from new mums.

My newborn won't sleep longer than forty minutes; what can I do?

I'm having trouble getting the baby to latch on. Help! My nipples are bleeding and cracked. It's agony.

My partner isn't supportive, now our baby is three months' old he's back in the pub with his mates three times a week. Any suggestions?

I scanned all the comments, feeling a bit like a fraud, eavesdropping on private conversations. But I also felt like I belonged here. Or I would, if I had a baby.

I began to type under the name I set up yesterday: Cakemom. It was stupid, but I didn't care. Everyone else hid behind a fake persona these days. Why shouldn't I?

Help, I typed. *My daughter is three weeks old and I feel like I don't trust my OH to look after her as well as I can. I think he'll drop her, as he's always been clumsy. He thinks I need to calm down and relax. It's causing arguments between us. What should I do?*

Maybe one day, I could have this issue for real, anyway. I didn't feel so much a sham now. I sat back, running my hands on a soft babygro in my lap while I waited for the replies to come in. I didn't have long to wait.

24

ON THE FIRST DAY of opening, I got up at five after being awake for most of the night, partly through nerves, still listening to the unfamiliar noises all around, and partly excitement. Instead of being exhausted, though, I was absolutely buzzing. I pulled on sweatpants and a sweatshirt and headed downstairs.

There were no windows in the café kitchen, so there was no fear of being watched or overlooked. It was heaven. All my ingredients, having been delivered in batches over the last few days, had been removed from their paper packets or sacks, and were now stored in the various new containers I'd bought, mainly plastic with airtight lids. I ran my hand over them, all labelled and lined up neatly on shelves. It struck me that Chris would approve of the organisation, which immediately made me want to mess them up, but I didn't. It was different when it was work.

I put on a podcast while I got busy. I'd found a few I liked lately, and I lost myself in listening to other people talk. It helped take my mind off the negative thoughts. Every time I felt uneasy about being alone in a new city, or that I couldn't do this on my own and make it work, or any other of the hundreds of negative thoughts that plagued me in dark moments, despite me constantly telling myself I was as good as anyone else, I still had a little niggle of doubt. And I couldn't deny there was a lot at stake here; it wasn't a game. I had to get this right. It might take practise and no end of perseverance, but I would. Too many people were depending on me to succeed. And I had to say, their faith in me spurred me on. Did it matter if you didn't believe in yourself enough as long as others believed in you? They thought I could do it, therefore I could.

By six o'clock, the cakes were in the oven and I'd made some sweet pastry for tartlet cases, which was resting in the fridge. I was rolling out some scone dough, my hands coated with flour. I sometimes wondered why baking made me feel so good, so relaxed and soothed. The short answer was I didn't know. It just did. The podcast I was listening to finished, and another loaded on autoplay. One more hour on my own until Claire and Ellie arrived.

When my phone rang at six thirty, my heart sank. What if it was one of them ringing in sick, or changing their minds about working here? The thought was too awful to contemplate. It would be totally disastrous. While I was hurriedly scrubbing the sticky dough off my hands, an even worse thought hit me: what if something was wrong with Mum or Dad, and I was here, miles away? Instead, when I looked at the phone, it was Jenny. Thank God!

'Hi,' I said. 'Are you checking I'm not still in bed?'

She laughed. 'No. I know there's no chance of that. What time did you start?'

'Five,' I admitted.

'I knew you'd be up. I just wanted to wish you luck one more time.'

We'd had a good chat last night after I'd come off the forums, and I'd updated her on everything. 'I'd had a bad feeling about that Rebecca girl, but I'd thought it was just me,' she'd said. 'Thank God you found Ellie.'

'I know,' I'd said, not letting on just how worried I'd actually been.

'So,' she said now, after I told her what I was making, 'Send me some pictures of your first batches, and how the shop looks now you've decorated it, and I'll pop them on the Facebook page.'

My blood suddenly felt icy. 'What Facebook page? I didn't know we had one.'

'Didn't I tell you? We set one up for the delis ages ago. You'd stopped doing social media, so my sons helped me with it. They know how useless I am with all that. But all I have to do now is the actual posts, which I find okay. It's easier than I thought.'

I was swiping on my phone now, as fast as I could. 'What's it called? The page?'

'Delish,' she said, sounding bemused. 'What else would it be called?'

As I finished typing *Facebook* in, one of the oven timers went off.

'Can I ring you later? I've got to get the cakes out,' I said.

She'd barely said goodbye before I cut her off. The cakes were done, and I removed them from the ovens, leaving them on top to cool, almost dropping one of them in my haste to get back to my phone.

It was all there, on the Delish Facebook page. The new cafe was a pinned post, with a picture of the shop itself and also one of me, in one of the London cafes. I looked really happy in it. I would do; it was taken in better times, before my world imploded.

Sarah is going to be taking command of our new project, it said, as plain as day. I sat down heavily on a stool as blood rushed through my head, making me dizzy. Jenny had announced to the world weeks ago every last detail. Most of all where I was moving, and I had no idea. Along with a photo of the cafe, there was a full address. The only thing it didn't say was that I'd be living above the place. It might as well have done. It said everything else.

The horror was still sinking in that if Chris was looking for me, he wouldn't find it hard now. With his computer skills, it would take him less than a second. They'd announced to the entire world where I was.

I dropped my phone on the worktop and held my head in my hands, feeling sick and shaky. I'd thought I was doing the right thing, keeping my personal problems to myself and not telling Jenny and Sandra the extent of it. And now it had backfired spectacularly. If I'd told them the truth, they would have been horrified but supportive. Most of all, they would have known not to do what they'd done. I only had myself to blame. Me and my idiotic insistence on secrecy. Mum begged me to tell them so they could understand, and I wouldn't hear of it. I didn't want them to know how much of a loser I was when it came to picking partners.

Here, alone at dawn in York, with no friends or family, no CCTV, and minimal security, I'd never felt more vulnerable.

Then something stirred in me: common sense, and the need to keep things in perspective. I looked around me, my heart still pumping way too fiercely. But really, what had changed in the last few minutes other than I'd discovered something I hadn't known? Was I now expecting him to burst through the door to the cafe, leap into the kitchen and kill me, because I'd learned some new information? I was being ridiculous. It had been more than six months since I'd seen him. Maybe he'd forgotten all about me, and not given me a second thought, rather than obsessing and fixating on me, like I'd done with him.

If I didn't pull myself together, this day, and all the rest to follow, would be a disaster. The only person who could change things was me. I stood up. It was time to get changed before my staff arrived. *My staff.* I wouldn't let him ruin my fresh start. I couldn't.

But by the time Ellie and Claire arrived soon after, I'd never been so glad to see anyone in my entire life.

25

'YOU HAVE EVERYTHING?' MIG asked as I pulled up at the jetty. He frowned when Leanne's head popped up in the basket on the front.

'You not see sense, then?' he said. 'I take her.'

'No, she's coming with me. We had a long discussion about it last night, me and her. It's what she wants. She said so.'

He shook his head and gave a loud sigh.

'She's a good little swimmer. And she has her life jacket.' I held up the proper dog one I bought.

And she'd be the best distraction I'd got. More so than tattoos, coloured lenses, accents, or scars. Anyway, she'd only die if I did, and I wasn't going to let that happen. So we were fine. She was coming. She'd think I'd abandoned her if I left her, and I didn't want her thinking that, even though I knew that was stupid.

Mig eyed my small, waterproof backpack. Zico would have everything else I needed on the ship, and it still wouldn't amount to much. In the backpack were my fake passports, minimal clothing, some cash, and my new green contact lenses. I handed him the keys to the moped. He'd agreed to return it to the hire place for me.

As I climbed onto his boat, I wondered about the women in the office still working my business. I'd considered shutting it down. Instead, I'd told them I was going away for a month and I needed them to continue as normal. It had been going really well as they'd got better at it, and I had little money left, so they might as well carry on. I could access the funds from anywhere and I was going to need something to help me in the UK. While it was making money, I was going to leave it. It practically ran itself anyway now the women compiled their own lists of targets. Once I was settled in the UK, if I'd got something better set up, I'd shut it down. Yeah, they'd turn up for work one day and find nothing was working, but that was their problem.

If Mig was sorry to be losing his new friend, he didn't show it. But he had given me his phone number. I hadn't given him mine.

The only person I might get in touch with back home was Alex, my old uni mate, who taught me scams in the first place; if I needed him for anything, that was. I already owed him for getting me out of the country six months ago, though. If anything, he should be the one calling in favours. But he was probably the nearest thing I had to a friend right now. Other than Mig, of course, who seemed happy enough now to see me go, having made some considerable money out of me. I think he'd got ten percent of the ten grand, or 73,000 Brazilian Reals I was giving to Zico for my passage. He and Zico weren't aware that I'd caught the word *dez* several times in their conversations. I might not have picked up much Portuguese, but I knew enough to count to fuckin ten. So he was 7,300 Reals richer for doing literally nothing other than giving my name to Zico and setting up the meeting in his flat. Zico and I did the rest.

Zico was waiting out to sea for us, in his small cargo ship, packed with sugar cane bound for the UK, his regular run. Ten grand for my safe passage back to UK waters for all of four weeks' work for him seemed like a good deal to me. Although it wasn't quite that straightforward.

I groaned at the thought of up to four weeks at sea. Compared to a twelve-hour flight. But it was the only way I could think of to get back.

I put on my life jacket, then Leanne's, as Mig started the boat and we accelerated quickly away. We were going much faster than when we went to the deserted cove. I watched as the coastline of Brazil got further and further away. Leanne was more than happy on board now and wagged her tail as she looked up at me. A vision of a small, white, lifeless, soaked body sprang to mind, and I put it in a box and locked it away. She wouldn't die. And neither would I. We were infallible.

I sat down and faced out to sea, looking for the first sign of Zico's boat. The first step towards my new life. Or, really, my old one.

26

THE LAST FOUR WEEKS had been hell. The worst of my life, and that was saying something. Zico's boat was much bigger than I thought it was going to be, which wasn't a problem in itself. The issue was it was a cargo vessel, a lot smaller than a large commercial one, but an awful lot bigger than Mig's boat, and there was nothing luxurious about it at all. It was about as far removed from the smoothness of a cruise liner as you could get. Consequently, I'd been sick just about every day. The constant swelling and rolling of the ocean was easily matched by the lurching of my guts. And Zico and his crew seemed to think it was funny and had spent most of the time at sea sniggering at me.

There were three crew members plus Zico, two of them his sons. They looked just like younger versions of him, but with better teeth, so their future didn't bode well. They were still ugly bastards, like their dad. The other bloke, Luis, barely spoke to any of them, let alone me. He was a good sailor though, and he did a lot of the technical stuff, so I guess that was why he was here. But he didn't like Leanne, so I didn't like him. He'd shoved her out of the way with his foot once, really roughly, while I was being sick again. She now cowered away from him. If I wasn't puking so much, he'd be the one I'd hit first, no question. They hadn't spoken a word of English to each other, only to me, so I had no idea what they'd said about me in

Portuguese. I could guess, though, and it wouldn't be complimentary. They probably thought I was a rich, spoiled bastard buying his passage back to the UK. Only the last part of that was true. Rich and spoiled? Moi? No way.

Early this morning, Zico woke me and told me it was time to leave the cargo vessel. He launched a small boat that had been attached to the side of the cargo vessel, and we clambered aboard, him with the ease of a seasoned seaman, and me, gripping Leanne tightly, stumbling around like I'd been on all-night bender. But my heart was bumping in excitement: this was what I'd been waiting for.

The route from Brazil was South Atlantic, North Atlantic, Bay of Biscay, then English Channel until they docked at Southampton with their legal cargo of sugar cane. But the plan was that I would leave in a much smaller boat somewhere in the middle of nowhere and we would sail around the coast of the UK until we came to Newquay in north Cornwall. It was my plan, and I hadn't known whether it would work, but Zico considered it at length and said he could do it. Turned out he was a lot more thorough than I gave him credit for. When I mentioned coastguards and shipping lanes and stuff, he just shrugged and said to leave it to him.

So I did. That was why I was paying him everything I had. It was nice, for once in my life, to hand over control to someone else. But the next bit was going to be the trickiest and most dangerous part for me and Leanne. It was daring and brazen, but in this instance I believed there was something to be had about hiding in plain sight.

When I first got onto the cargo ship, Zico had brought the few things I'd asked for: a wetsuit, a surfboard, and a paddle.

We'd travelled through the night and had been anchored out at sea now for a while. Zico said we were waiting for the tide to come in. According to him, it wouldn't be long now. Amazingly, the motion of this boat was more like Mig's, gentle and enjoyable, and my stomach was feeling much more settled. Consequently, I was feeling stronger than I had in weeks, my belly was nicely full, and my enthusiasm was high. It didn't last, however.

I glanced at Zico's face. His jaw was set, and he looked serious as he glanced up at the sun. I'd waited for this day for a long time now, but suddenly I was petrified. I'd never been this frightened. The shore looked so far away.

I was sitting here in a wetsuit in October. Thankfully, Britain was having an Indian summer, and the beach in the distance had plenty of people on it. Suited me fine. Who'd notice another surfer or swimmer coming out of the sea? And loads of surfers had dogs on their boards, too. That was why I'd done so much swimming in Brazil, in case the need ever arose. I had a hunch, long before I formulated the plan, that water would be my only option. I couldn't fly back to the UK, or go by train or plane. Formal borders were a no go. Places with eye scanners were out, too, either with or without the contact lenses that changed my eye colour. I couldn't take any risks. As a wanted man, I'd be on more systems over here than I could even think of. As would my DNA.

The sea must be cold though. No matter how warm the sun, it was still October in the Atlantic. My balls were shrivelling at the thought of it. I checked my pack again, even though I only did it ten minutes ago. Everything in there was wrapped securely in waterproof coverings, including the few clothes I'd change into when I took off my wetsuit.

'It's time,' Zico said, squinting up at the sun. I couldn't wait to see the back of him. It was probably the easiest ten grand he'd ever make. But Sarah was worth every penny. The thought I'd be in the same country as her and would see her in the near future made my heart swell bigger than the waves I was about to dive into.

Leanne had her life jacket on and so did I. I could pop her in the backpack, hitch it high up, and she should be fine; no swimming needed.

Zico started the engine, and my heart did a double flip. This was it. From now on, I'd have to second guess everything I did and think things through thoroughly. I had to bring my A-game.

The coastline was coming closer now. Zico's boat wasn't big enough to warrant any attention. There were tons of boats out here just like it. I didn't know or care how he knew where rocks were, or about currents and riptides, I just trusted that he did. There was equipment he checked on a regular basis, stuff I couldn't even hazard a guess at what its purpose was.

When we were closer to the shore, he shut the engine off again and dropped the anchor. He looked around constantly, his eyes skittering over the horizon. I don't know what he was looking for, but no one was paying us the slightest bit of attention, from what I could gather.

He helped me on with the backpack, shortening the straps to their minimum.

'Okay?' he asked.

I tested them and rolled my shoulders. 'Good, yeah.'

'This is it, then. Good luck, my friend.' He clasped my hand with his and pumped it up and down. Friend? That was a bit rich. I'd been mostly ignored for the last month, although he had made more effort to talk to me than the others, to be fair.

'I didn't know you cared,' I quipped.

He grinned, exposing his awful teeth, and pointed at the ladder that disappeared into the sea. My legs shook badly at the sight of it. What if it gave way? He glanced down at it.

'You can do this. Everything will be okay,' he said, his voice rattling in his chest. He nodded, and it gave me some extra strength from somewhere.

I passed Leanne to him while I got into the water. As I thought, it was freezing, and the wetsuit offered little insulation. It pulled the air right out of my lungs. Could the dog get hypothermia before I reached the beach?

I flailed around in the water, trying to warm my muscles up after four weeks of half-hearted lunges and squats on the ship, in between bouts of puking and lying down with the most horrendous headache. The shape I used to be in seemed a lifetime away now.

The cold sapped strength from me by the second and snatched my breath. I was expecting cold, but not to that degree. Leanne wouldn't survive that, and Luis wouldn't think twice about throwing her overboard if I asked him to take her back. Into the bag for her it was, then.

I went back up the ladder, shaking like mad now, my teeth chattering together.

'Put her in here,' I said. 'It's too cold for her.'

He nodded, removed the backpack from me and took my stuff out, put her in, then packed everything back around her. He left the cover that came down over the top to one side and just tightened the drawstring around the neck instead. She whined and struggled to get out.

'Stop it,' I said sharply, to make her listen. Amazingly, she quietened. I got back in the water, which didn't feel as cold now my legs were so numb. I could barely feel her weight. Zico leaned over and handed me the surfboard, attaching it to my ankle as I grabbed onto the ladder and lifted my leg as high as I could. Then he handed me the paddle, which I clipped to the board through a metal hoop I fixed to it when we first set sail. That left both my hands free. I checked over my shoulder. Leanne was level with my head and bone dry. Safe enough, hopefully. But anything could happen from here to the shore. At least the tide was going that way, so I'd be pushed in that direction, regardless. My biggest fear, though, was undercurrents dragging me down. If that happened, I'd be a goner for sure. And, despite me researching them before I left Brazil, I still didn't know much about them or how to predict where they were, other than what I could find on the internet. *Wiki-fuckin-pedia, don't fail me now*. Everything I knew about them was from there. They couldn't hold you under if you didn't panic. *If you find yourself in one, swim or paddle parallel to the shore*, said one website about Fistral Beach, the popular surfers' beach, which was where I was trying to get.

The board was tugging away from me now, straining to take me with it. Time to get going. I turned to Zico, who raised a hand.

'Good luck,' he said again.

I managed to turn my body to face the beach and a powerful wave swept me up in its swell with frightening ferocity. When I came down the other side, I was further away from the boat than I would have thought possible. I heard Zico start the engine. Taking a deep breath, I hauled my body onto the board and lay on my stomach, pulling hard with my arms towards the shore. Salt water smacked me hard in the face, going up my nose and down my throat, and I spluttered as it burned. I could barely see. Should have brought some goggles. How could I not have thought of them? Not much I could do about it now, though.

I narrowed my eyes and strained to look at the beach, blinking the stinging water away. Now I was in the sea itself, it seemed further away than before. I risked a look back. Zico was still there on the boat, watching me. I didn't know where he was meeting up with the cargo ship. I hadn't asked.

I couldn't see any flags or lifeguards on the beach, despite it being quite busy; maybe because it was now out of season, despite the warm weather. I was hoping to see flags and swim between them. Maybe they were there and I just couldn't see them from this far out.

As my heart began to pound at the enormity of what I was attempting to do, I lowered my head, gritted my teeth, and got on with it. Every metre nearer the shore felt like a metre nearer to safety, rip currents or not. The waves were fierce, battering my body. I felt like a tiny ant, about to be crushed at any moment. It was a horrible thought, and panic crept nearer the surface with every breath. After another mouthful of water that went straight to my lungs, I took shallower breaths and not the deep lungfuls I'd been gasping in. My arms and shoulders burned like crazy and I tried to glide for a bit on the board, but was thrown up and down like a ragdoll. It was like the craziest, most dangerous theme park ride I'd ever been on, with no safety equipment or checks.

I was tossed high into the air on the crest of one wave and the board threatened to topple over when it hit the water again. I clung to it, hauling my body back into position. From somewhere behind me, Leanne whined. I could feel her moving about on my shoulder and her scrabbling unbalanced me as I turned my head to look at her. Before I knew it, I was tipped in the water and my head was under. I couldn't breathe. Which way was up? This was it. I was going to die. Zico was right when he first met me and said I was crazy. Just now, when he'd said I could do it, he was lying. Just saying it to be nice. And now he'd gone, got out before he could watch me drown and be implicated in anything.

My head broke the surface without me doing anything, and I gulped air, panting hard. *Leanne. Did she go under?* I trod water as the board knocked into me and looked over my shoulder. She was there, but she was wet through. She shook her head and whined, eying me anxiously. One more like that and that could be it.

I pulled myself onto the board again. What went wrong? What could I do if it happened again? It was the looking over my shoulder that had sent me off balance. As long as my shoulders were above water, so was her head. So get on with it.

I was relieved to see the beach was a lot closer now. In fact, I couldn't believe the speed at which I was being pushed towards the shore. A few metres more and I wouldn't be the furthest person out to sea. Surfers were just in front of me. That must mean something. I stared at the beach and didn't let my eyes move. Focus. Concentrate. I lowered my head and shoulders, and pulled as hard as I could until my arms felt dead and wouldn't move.

As soon as the lactic acid went, I was away again. Now I could see flags flying on the beach, but I was outside of them, not a good place to be. I pulled harder with my right arm to turn that way. I was level with other figures on boards now. Maybe I should have learned to surf in Brazil instead of just swimming. Another oversight?

I wondered how far below me the ocean floor was. Maybe I could roll off the board and see if my toes could touch it, but I didn't think I'd have the strength left to get back on it if I did. I pulled harder and faster now, desperate to feel solid earth beneath my feet. A swell of a massive wave threw me forward, and I struggled to stay on the board, but managed somehow to cling on. All I could think about was getting to the sand as fast as possible. Everything else could wait.

I got into a rhythm, and the waves propelled me to the shore faster and faster. People to both sides of me were standing on surf boards now and riding back in. I started to relax, and that was when I felt it; a tug from below that made the board jolt alarmingly. *Shit! What was happening?* When it happened again, I tried to be ready for it, but I wasn't. And my leg was tensing up with a pain I'd felt a million times before. I was getting cramp at the same time as a rip current was tearing the board out from under me. My right leg went rigid with intense pain and my muscles started to spasm. When I used to get cramp in the gym, it could floor me. I really couldn't get it now. I tried to kick and bend my leg, but nothing happened. Another spasm hit me and the board was sucked away, plunging me into the icy water and pulling me down. The backpack was tugged off one shoulder and I swallowed a great mouthful of water, which ended up in my lungs. In my panic, I found from somewhere the strength to kick upwards as the urge to take a deep breath in and cough became too much. My head broke above the waves and I spluttered and coughed until my ribs hurt.

Leanne? Treading water and bobbing up and down like mad, I finally swung the backpack off my shoulder. There was no dog in it. I looked around, frantic, and tried to turn 360 degrees, scanning the waves, which were white-topped, so it didn't help. Every burst of foam looked like her fur. I finished the circle and the horrible truth hit me. Leanne was nowhere to be seen.

27

I COULDN'T BELIEVE IT! The cheeky git! When the mayor eventually did us the massive favour of gracing our establishment with his presence, he seemed to think he was getting a freebie. We'd been open almost a month now, and everything had gone great, but I'd been dreading his visit after what Claire said about him perhaps bringing a TV news crew with him. Thankfully, though, he hadn't. By the way he was acting, maybe the local news people couldn't stand him, either. I bet he'd asked them and they'd said no.

So, he'd arrived about two hours ago, with four hangers-on, ordered afternoon tea for the five of them, scoffed everything while treating us like serving wenches from a bygone era, and was now getting ready to leave. None of them had asked for the bill or anything. He didn't seem to know the words *please* or *thank you*, and had insisted on being referred to as *Mr Mayor* for the duration. I wasn't calling him 'Mr bloody Mayor' any longer. His name was Richard Hancock, and his cronies had been calling him 'Dickie' all afternoon. Dick was about right.

I printed off his bill and gave it to Claire. 'Can you take this to the mayor's table?'

'Sure.'

I just had a feeling he was going to try not to pay. Afternoon tea was seventeen pounds per person, and they'd had extra drinks that weren't included in the set menu price. I watched him out of the corner of my eye from behind the counter.

His head jerked up as Claire put the bill in front of him and walked away. He frowned and pushed it away with one finger, then stood up and put his jacket back on, pulling it tight over his belly to fasten it. He soon gave up when it didn't meet. I hid a smirk. He needed a bigger jacket.

They were going. *I knew it!* It was time I started acting like the boss. I couldn't expect Claire or Ellie to do it. Moving faster than I thought I could, I got to the door before him and blocked his way, a copy of his bill in my hand.

'Excuse me, *Dick*,' I said, planting my feet and pulling my shoulders back.

His eyes narrowed, and a weird noise escaped the back of his throat as he tilted his head to look down at me. He actually had the gall to try to wave me aside, but I didn't budge.

'You seem to have forgotten to pay.'

I handed him a copy. He took it and frowned. 'I was under the impression it was free gratis,' he said.

'Whatever gave you that impression?' I said, matching his frown with my own. 'We're a new business, sir. Not a charity. That's ninety-five pounds and thirty pence to pay, please.'

'Can't you take it up with my office? It's on my expense account.'

'I'm afraid not. You pay us, then claim it back. That's how expenses normally work, isn't it?'

His lackeys were shuffling their feet now, eager to go. The mayor and I stared at each other.

'The till is this way,' I said, ushering him from behind. He had no choice but to lead the way, as other diners were now looking at him with curiosity.

He didn't look too pleased as he extracted his wallet from his inside pocket. It was a wonder he could remember where he kept it.

'I hope you enjoyed your meal this afternoon,' I said, taking the credit card he begrudgingly handed me.

'Yes. Although it's not my sort of thing, really, afternoon tea. I'm more of a cooked meal person. I don't find a bit of bread or cake particularly fills me up for long. It's just stodge.'

Stodge, was it? I eyed his ample belly pointedly. Well, seeing as he'd fired the shot across my bow... 'We do salads, too. And lots of healthy options. Maybe you could try one of those next time.'

He made a weird harrumphing noise as he put his card away, and turned to go back to his lackeys.

'Hope to see you again soon,' I called after him for the benefit of the other diners. His reply was the door slamming behind him.

'People like him shouldn't be in civic positions,' I muttered to Ellie as I squeezed past her behind the counter. 'He's a freeloader. I don't think he'll be back. Does he look like he can't afford his own food, for God's sake? I think not.'

Ellie giggled and whispered behind her hand, 'Good for you. I bet he gets away with that trick on a regular basis, just because people are too embarrassed to stand up to him like you just did.'

'More fool them, then. I'm not running a bloody charity to feed greedy pigs like him. They didn't leave a scrap, did you notice? I thought they were going to lick their plates at one bit. No compliments to the chefs, though. No tips either. People like him make me sick. I hope he doesn't come back.'

I switched on a smile as an old lady shuffled to the counter, leaning heavily on a stick while she paid her bill. She had a wide smile on her face.

'That was wonderful, dear,' she said. 'Both the food, and your standing up to the mayor.'

I felt my face going red.

'My food was delicious. I won't need anything until breakfast tomorrow, that's for sure.' She leaned in in a conspiratorial fashion. 'Cheaper than Betty's and much nicer,' she whispered loudly, putting two pound coins in a glass jar I'd put on the counter for tips.

I laughed and clapped my hands together. 'Thank you so much. You have no idea how much that means.'

Instead of leaving, she stood there, then said, 'I don't know if you've thought about running any promotions, but OAP discounts go down extremely well around here. I'd bring all my friends in. I'm President of the local Women's Institute, and we're always looking for new places we can visit. It would put quite a bit of money your way.'

I tapped my finger on the counter, thinking. 'I hadn't thought of that. And thank you, I'll certainly do that. Any tips on when?'

She shuffled her feet and leaned on her stick. 'Tuesdays and Thursdays are best. Not *every* lunchtime, as it's not special then, is it? Keep the exclusivity. That's my tip.'

I narrowed my eyes, taking in her immaculate appearance—her stylish clothes, and her grey hair swept back and twisted into an intricate knot. 'Did you used to be in business, by any chance?'

She nodded, beaming. 'I used to be high up in the local Chamber of Commerce before I retired.'

'It shows,' I said. 'I'll see you Tuesdays and Thursdays, then. Bring any menu suggestions you have, too.'

'Your menu doesn't need changing. Do you know, I used to walk straight past this place every week? Never came in, as it didn't appeal. I'm glad I did, now.'

'I'm glad you did, too.'

'I'll see you next week.'

'Brilliant. I'm Sarah, by the way.'

'Olwyn. See you soon.'

Her friend was waiting for her by the door and they left together, after giving me a little wave.

'Can you believe the difference in people? Compare her to the mayor,' I said, shaking my head. 'They never cease to amaze me.'

Ellie agreed before going to take her last batch of pastries out of the oven. She'd been as good as her word, and her old customers were coming in especially for her food.

I went outside to check the three tables I'd put there. Only one was occupied, by a couple having coffee and cake. I looked up at the sign above the shop. The new *Delish* sign was due to be fitted next week, along with a board for outside, and I couldn't wait. It'd match the new menus.

Before I went back in, I checked the street both ways, scanning male faces and body shapes. If I saw him in the distance, would I recognise him? What if I wouldn't? Ever since I found out about the Delish Facebook page, I'd been more creeped out than ever. Maybe I should change my appearance, go blonde and have my hair different or something. But what good would that do? It had already been announced on Facebook that I was working here, so there was no point. Perhaps I was destined to spend the rest of my life looking over my shoulder and that was all there was to it. If he came, I'd just have to be prepared. Thoughts of the alley at the back of the shop, with all its gloomy corners and shadows, filled my mind. Looked like I wouldn't be sleeping well again.

28

THE CRAMP IN MY leg was making it impossible to kick against the waves. The rip current tugged at me again as I struggled to remember what to do. Was it wade or swim parallel to the beach, or towards it? I pushed down with my good leg and my toes touched something—a beautifully firm and sandy seabed. Thank God. I could almost stand. Where was Leanne? She couldn't be far.

I tried to calm down and rationalise the situation. She had a life jacket on, so she would pop up to the top. But could the rip current hold down a body as small as hers?

Stress was making my throat close up, and it was harder to breathe. I had to find her. The board was butting against my hip, and I dragged myself onto it and onto my knees as it wobbled and threatened to tip me off again. Despite my leg, I managed to stand half upright and scan around. It was then I saw it; a scrap of something white with the orange life jacket surrounding it. About ten metres away. It wasn't moving. I got on my belly and sculled hard before she could drift away. It was definitely her. I grabbed the handle on the top of the life jacket and yanked her out of the water, laying her on the board in front of me. She still didn't move, and her eyes were closed. My scalp prickled with fear at the thought she may be dead. It was all my fault! I should have left her with Mig in Brazil when he'd offered to take her. I brought her because of my own selfishness.

But I didn't know she was dead for certain. What if she wasn't? I needed to get to land right now. Despite the people around me, no one was paying me any attention, which was the idea in the first place. I was on my own with this. They wouldn't risk their life to save a dog's anyway. Why should they? The old me wouldn't have done.

'Leanne,' I said urgently, poking at the body on the board. 'Wake up. Come on.' My breathing was a harsh, ragged mess that hurt my chest. I rubbed her hard, but nothing happened. Could you give a dog mouth to mouth? I didn't even know. It may already be too late.

I was out of the rip current and I carried on pulling towards the shore, the sun now warming me as the water got rapidly shallower. Thankfully, the pain in my leg was starting to ease off a bit and was turning to more of an ache. But I was frozen to the bone, and Leanne was even worse. Several people nearby were standing in the water and it only came up to their waists, so I rolled off the board and started to wade with the biggest strides I could, tucking Leanne under my arm. Her head lolled horribly, and she still didn't move. When a large wave tugged the board away, I brought my elbow in hard to drag it back and it squeezed Leanne's ribcage through the bulk of her life jacket. Water burst from her mouth and she snuffled, coughed, then sneezed. It was the best sound ever. She did it again, and the water was now only up to my knees. I hauled the board out of the sea and ran on the damp sand away from the waves. I dropped down and placed her on my lap, rubbing her body furiously to warm her up. She moved her head and blinked as I slipped the life jacket off her, my fingers trembling so bad I could barely grip anything. My backpack hung limply from my shoulder, and I swung it onto the sand and tipped it up. Water spewed out but my documents and money were in zipped up compartments so were safe. By the look of it, nothing was missing. My clothes and a towel were also in various waterproof containers and I got out the towel, wrapped her in it and hugged her to me, desperate to warm her up. I was freezing and shivering, but I had to warm her up first. Only her little face was sticking out of the towel. She tried to shake her head, but the towel was too tight.

Her body lurched, and she was sick on my legs, spewing out more water.

'That's it, get it all out,' I said, rubbing her belly. Whether it helped, I hadn't a clue. But it couldn't hurt.

'Is she okay? Poor little thing.'

I looked up to see a woman and two kids peering over my shoulder.

'Oh, Mummy, she's so cute,' said the girl, who looked maybe ten.

'She is,' the woman agreed.

The boy with them, who was smaller than the girl, said nothing, just sucked ice cream out of his cornet and looked at Leanne with cold, curious eyes. Hard-hearted little fucker! Couldn't he see she nearly died?

'She's alright, yeah, thanks,' I said in my best Irish, as Leanne shivered under the towel. I tried out my new smile on her, the one where I strove to make both sides of my mouth turn up at the same time instead of one side dragging slightly behind the other, my natural way. It'd been one of the hardest things to change about myself. 'We had a bit of a mishap, that's all. Capsized when a rip current grabbed the board.' I had no idea if what I was saying made sense but, from my years of experience, I knew that if you said any old bullshit with confidence, people would think you knew what you were on about.

The woman was nodding. 'Yes, they can be bad around here.' Her eyes snagged on the still-livid scar on my face. 'Well, I'm glad she's okay. Come on,' she said to the kids.

The girl followed her, saying, 'Can I have my pop now?' as they hurried away.

The boy hung around, still eyeballing Leanne. What a little ghoul. He looked almost excited that something nearly died. A psychopath in the making, I reckoned.

'Fuck off!' I said to him. 'Stop gawping! It isn't polite.'

His eyes slid away from Leanne to me as he straightened up.

'You fuck off!' he said before running to catch his family up. What a little bastard! What were they teaching kids these days?

I was getting colder, and my teeth chattered together as I shivered. With trembling fingers, I took my T-shirt and a fleece-lined hoodie from their waterproof bags, and lay them on the sand. Still sitting, I managed to unzip the wetsuit to my waist, wrangle my arms out, and pull them on. When I zipped up the hoodie, I was instantly warmer. I slid my arms through the backpack after putting the scattered contents back in and looked around to find somewhere to change my bottom half.

A loud squelching sound accompanied me when I got up, still holding Leanne tight to my chest, and unclipped the surf board from my leg. The board could stay here; I wouldn't be needing it anymore. The paddle I didn't use was still fastened to it. I'd had a vision of me standing on it, paddling in on a calm sea, with Leanne at the front edge as the beach got closer. Stupid now, I realised. What had been a daydream had turned into a nightmare we were both lucky to come out of alive. For as long as I lived, I'd never forget the power of the sea and how tiny and weak it made me feel. I didn't care if I never saw an ocean again. Thankfully, York was inland, so no bother there. But I couldn't help the grin from spreading over my face. We were here! We'd made it! I was home.

I picked up Leanne's life jacket, tempted to leave it with the board and paddle on the sand, but kept it at the last minute. If nothing else, it could serve as a reminder of what had happened today should I ever want to scare myself shitless.

There were some changing rooms and toilets off to my left, near the ramp leading down to the beach. I hoped they were open. They must be. The beach was fairly busy.

Before I got there, I removed the towel from Leanne and set her down on the sand. She shook herself, stumbled, and almost fell over. She was half-dry but still shivering, whether from cold or shock, I didn't know, so I scooped her up, wrapped her up again and went into the men's toilet block. There were three showers, all empty, plus some separate changing cubicles, again unoccupied. Someone had thoughtfully left a stray towel hanging up on a peg, and it was dry.

I turned one of the showers on and waited for it to run warm. Leanne wouldn't like it, but it was the fastest way to warm us both up. When I thought it was warm but not too hot, I stripped off my T-shirt and hoodie, and stood underneath it, making sure most of her body was in the flow too. She wasn't happy and scrabbled about, her claws raking my bare stomach.

'Keep still. It's what you need,' I told her.

Soon enough, we were both warm. I grabbed the dry towel that had been left there and went into one of the cubicles. A small slatted bench ran along the back, and I placed Leanne on it. Her tail wagged feebly when I wrapped her in the dry towel, and she seemed happy to just sit there; she was probably exhausted, like me. Now the adrenalin was wearing off and the shock of what we'd been through was sinking in, I felt weak and drained.

I pulled the wetsuit off my legs and put on boxers, socks and thick jogging bottoms. All I'd been able to fit in the bag was some canvas deck shoes, so they'd have to do. They'd look a dick with socks, though. I'd get some boots first thing tomorrow. October in Britain and summer shoes were not going to go well.

The backpack was empty now, apart from money and documents. I left the wetsuit hanging in the cubicle and put Leanne, still wrapped in the towel, back in the backpack. Her head stuck out of the top, but she seemed settled enough. I carried it in front of my body so I could keep an eye on her.

I needed to buy a coat of some sorts and a new sim card for my phone, but right now, finding lodgings was more important. Before I'd left Brazil, I'd looked up some places that took dogs, but I didn't know if they were open this late in the year. I hoped to God one of them was. I'd memorised their positions from Google maps and written their addresses down on a scrap of paper that was tucked into my wallet. First, though, I wanted to check something.

Back outside, I made for the lifeguards' station. Was there one on duty? There was. He was sitting inside, scanning outside much more infrequently than he should. A pretty young girl sat opposite him and they were flirting like mad. By the look of it, he'd be slipping it into the back of the net tonight. So, it didn't matter how many people could drown on his watch today, as long as he got to dip his wick later. Fuck me! Some people. He should be sacked.

Yet, if he was doing his job properly and saw me get off the boat, would he do anything? Border controls on an island like ours are just a joke. I'd long suspected you could get back in this way and I'd just proved it. If I sounded British, then who would think anything of it?

I walked right past his window, and his eyes passed straight over me. Clueless bastard!

Now to find a place to stay, at least for tonight. I took out the piece of paper with the hotel addresses on it, along with Mig's scribbled phone number. I threw the number in the first bin I passed.

'Come on, Leanne,' I said. 'Time for an adventure. Tomorrow, we're going to York to sort out a place to live. Then Leeds.'

She licked my face. She approved.

29

I STOOD OUTSIDE GRANFORD Towers in Leeds, my baseball cap pulled low over my eyes and my coat collar turned up. The wind cut straight into me. It was gone three in the afternoon, and it would be dark in an hour or two. Leanne was tucked out of sight in my backpack and quiet for once. She'd spent a lot of time in there recently, out of sight of some of the truck drivers I'd hitched lifts from all the way from Newquay to York. After I got from the A30 to the M5, it wasn't too bad, but I was so sick of sitting in a truck, listening to one foreign lorry driver after another telling me their life story. At what point did they take the hint that YOU'RE NOT FUCKIN INTERESTED?

I scratched my chin. My beard itched from all the peroxide I'd been dying it with for the last few months to make it blonde, even though I hadn't done it in weeks. A tuft came away in my fingers and I looked at it with dismay. There again, if it became a defining feature, it wouldn't be a bad thing. But I hoped it was a one off. I looked freakish enough with the damn scar!

There was no sign of Shay, my beloved sister, as I looked up at the window of our old flat. The minging net curtain was as yellow as ever. She hadn't bothered to wash it since our dear old ma passed away, by the look of it. The smell of the place from last time I was here, of unwashed bodies, cig smoke and decay, rushed back to me and made my stomach heave, even though I was still outside.

Memory was a powerful thing. And when I thought of the memories I had from living here, none of them were good. Not a single one.

I patted the bulging envelope in my pocket. There were two things I could do now: post it through her door and walk away, trusting I knew her well enough to actually do what I needed her to do, or get her to open the door, let me in and watch while she actually did it. Even with how much I hated her, I wasn't sure I wanted to see her stick the needle in, and watch the ensuing aftermath. It was a messy business, an overdose. The problem with the first option was I didn't know how I'd find out whether she'd actually done it or not. I could hardly knock on doors and ask the neighbours, or check the local papers. Did they even do death notices anymore? It wasn't like anyone would care enough to pay for one.

Maybe sticking around to make sure would be best. At the thought, though, a wave of nausea rushed up, bringing burning bile into my throat. All that rolling about and wailing? I just didn't fancy it, even though I wanted her gone. I swallowed the acid down again, feeling the burn all the way.

No, it'd have to be the cut and run. She'd do it, I was sure. It'd be her dream, heroin in that quantity? A no-brainer. And I'd get out of here much quicker, so that suited me.

I hurried up the concrete stairs and pushed open the door at the top. The dimly lit walkway stretched before me. Our door was halfway down on the left. On the right was the low wall that looked over the estate. The view was no better up here than it was down there. I reached the door and stopped. The telly inside was blasting out some crap or other, so she was in. The shouting and cheering and clapping of the TV was only slightly muffled through the thin, council-approved door. It was probably only equivalent to a few layers of cardboard.

The concrete walkway was deserted. Before anyone saw me, I pushed the envelope through the letterbox, trying not to breathe in any stench that might seep out. Despite the screeching coming from the telly, there was a loud thud as it hit the mat. Shay wasn't one to look a gift horse in the mouth, so there was no way she'd question where that amount of cash might have come from. She'd just ram it into her veins and be glad. Not like Sarah, who questioned *everything* I sent her anonymously, when I'd got her things she'd liked online. They were like chalk and cheese, Sarah and Shay. They barely even looked like the same species; one gorgeous, heavenly creature and one hellbound, hideous crone.

As I turned to go, a nasty thought hit me: what if she'd moved since Ma died? From what I knew, she'd never lived anywhere else, but nothing was impossible. She could have. And I'd just put a grand in cash through her door. For all I knew, it could be some other loser in there, and I'd just given them beer money for the next God-knows-how-long. I couldn't leave now. *Fuck!* I was going to have to go in.

The key I'd carried all these years, never knowing when or if I might need it, was on my keyring. It slotted straight in the lock and turned easily. I pushed the door open and a rush of warm air greeted me, along with the blast of the TV. At least whoever was in there wouldn't hear me coming over the racket. One bedroom was on the left, one on the right. The living room was straight ahead. Both bedroom doors were open, and I peeked inside them as I went by. They were both dirty and messy. Nothing in them had changed other than Ma's old bed had no covers on. The stench of decades-old burnt cooking fat and cigarettes singed the tiny hairs inside my nostrils, even though I was trying not to breathe in.

The living room door was partly open, and I peered through the crack on the hinge side. I could see her, asleep in the chair, her head tipped to one side and her mouth open. Not a pretty sight. Right. That was it. I could go.

I left fast, the money still on the doormat. When I got back outside, I still hadn't seen anyone. No matter. No one would ask anything, anyway. Round here, no one gave a shit about anyone but themselves. And no one was looking for me, I was sure. But what to do now? It didn't feel right to leave and not know for sure if she'd done it, no matter how much I'd have liked to. Even though there was zero chance of her sticking the money into an ISA, I needed to hang around.

I tucked myself into a doorway right at the other side of the estate, where I could still see our old flat and the entrance to the block. It had got a good view of the car park, as well. The doorway I was in now led to some flats that had looked derelict last time I came. They were still boarded up. Suited me. No one would be coming in and out then. It reeked of piss and I pulled my T-shirt over my nose and mouth. Leanne stirred and shuffled. I took the backpack down, lifted up the flap, and she poked her head out.

'It's okay,' I told her, rubbing her ears. 'Go back to sleep.'

She wouldn't need the toilet as she'd gone half an hour ago, and she was fed and warm. She seemed happy sitting up now she could see out. At least she wasn't cold, like me, as she was wearing a little fleecy coat I got her in Newquay. I hadn't got myself a coat yet, so I'd still only got my hoodie.

I shivered and thought of the place in York I'd found to rent. God, I wished I was there. It was obviously not a patch on my old place in Fulham, but there was no point in crying over losing that. It was long gone, as was all the stuff I'd left behind in it. I loved that place. It was as far away from Granford Towers as you could get. The place in York was okay, though. Six months' rent paid in cash and no questions asked.

'I've just returned from overseas so I can't give you my last landlord's details for a reference, I'm afraid,' I'd told the landlady. I'd found the place in a private advert, so no lettings agents were involved.

She'd cast a glance over me, obviously not bothered by the scar, and Leanne had won her over, as I'd known she would.

'And who is this little beauty?' she'd purred, stroking Leanne's head.

She'd not been bothered about references when she saw the cash in my hand. She'd run her tongue over her lips, counted it, stuffed it in her bag, and handed me the keys.

Two nights I'd spent there before coming here on the train. The money to kill my sister, and the six months' rent, was the last of the cash I'd brought in my backpack from Brazil, all snug and dry in its zipped-up pocket. I had just a few hundred left now, so I was hoping my Brazilian ladies did a bit of overtime and had a good month, as I'd hardly got any clothes to wear. They were still doing well. There again, they'd been taught by the best. They knew the harder they worked, the more they could make. And they wanted as much as they could get. Suited me. They'd be paying for my new life in York, at least in the short term.

Leaning on the cold wall in the dank entrance, I shivered again. Why hadn't I bought a coat? It was warm back in Newquay, yet now it felt like winter. But, cold or not, I'd stand here all night if I had to. If I'd gained one thing, it was patience. I was much better at waiting now than I'd ever been. If Shay woke up and found the money, though, it would speed things along no end.

Two hours later, at five PM, a bloke pulled up in a black heap-of-shit car and got out, looked around, and set off up to our flat. I could see him again once he got on the walkway outside. Our door opened, he went in, and ten minutes later he came out again. I melted back into the shadows as he looked all around him. For a second, I considered smashing him over the head and taking my money back. It galled me to give my hard-earned cash, slaved over by three poor Brazilian women, to him. But I was supposed to be keeping a low profile. Coshing a drug dealer over the head and nicking his cash didn't really fit with that, but I was itching to do it.

As he drove away, Leanne began to squirm, and I let her out of the bag.

'Go back there,' I told her, stopping her from going outside.

She ran to the back of the lobby and immediately squatted down. It couldn't make it smell any worse in here, so I left it. Poor thing must have been desperate. She added a piss to the side of the dump and started to sniff about.

How long did these things take? I googled 'death by heroin overdose' on my phone, but couldn't find out how long it took to die. Surely, a few hours would do it, though, especially in the quantity she was likely to ram in.

At eight o'clock, stiff with cold, I trudged to the shop on the corner, bought a sandwich for me and a foil packet of dog food for Leanne, and took it back to the flats for us to eat. The sandwich was dry, but it was better than nothing.

'Come on,' I said to the dog, as she chased the empty foil container around the floor for the third time, trying to get her tongue into every corner. 'I can't stand this anymore. I'm gonna freeze to death.'

I put her back into the bag and lifted it onto my shoulder. As I walked across what should have been grass but was more litter and dog shit towards Granford Towers, my legs felt heavy. What might I find when I went in? What would she look like? It was horrible, but sometimes you just had to grit your teeth and get on with the unpleasant tasks.

There were a few people around, but none of them gave me a second glance, just like I knew they wouldn't. It was easy to be invisible around here. I'd certainly managed it for my entire childhood. I went back up to the flat and stood outside the door, listening. Nothing. I knocked softly. Still nothing. The TV noise had gone. Probably a good thing. Who wanted their death throes to be accompanied by EastEnders or some other shite soap? It was better that she turned the TV off. It seemed more respectful somehow. A nice, dignified heroin overdose!

I let myself in. If she came out of the bathroom or something and saw me, I had no Plan B. Could I do to her what I did to Luisa? Yeah, but it would involve touching her and I'd rather not.

The living room door was pulled to, and I crept towards it. Suddenly, my heart was beating so hard it felt like it was in my mouth. I stopped as I reached the doorway, my hand going for the handle before I imagined all the germs crawling on it, and pushed it gently with my shoulder instead. The room before me revealed itself. It was empty. Where the hell was she? It was such a small flat, there weren't many places left to hide. The only time I wasn't watching the place was when I went to get food. Could she have gone out?

No. I'd gone past the bedrooms. I knew without a doubt that she'd have retired to her bed to have the trip of a lifetime. Why not? It was the most comfortable place.

I whirled around and rushed to her bedroom. The curtains were drawn, but I could see her on the bed. I flicked on the light to see her lying flat on her back, a small, withered shape. The room was a nightmare: bedcovers thrown on the floor, clothes strewn everywhere, the sheet she was lying on stained and wet, and disgusting puddles of vomit all over. She was wearing a T-shirt and tracksuit pants, also dirty and crumpled. I dragged my eyes up to her face, needing but not wanting to see. Her lips were blue, her face white. Her eyes were wide open, unblinking, and staring at the ceiling. There was no doubt she was dead. But I needed to be sure. There was no way I was touching that to check for a pulse. Instead, I put my hand under her nose, as close as I dared. Nothing came out. The more I looked at her, the easier it got, and my own pulse calmed a bit. It wasn't like I hadn't seen dead people before. Did she look better or worse than Luisa? Hmmm? Just different, really. Mind you, neither of them looked that great while they were still alive. That thought made me chuckle, and I choked it down as a hysterical urge to laugh got stronger.

Anyway, she was definitely dead. I didn't need to be a doctor to determine that. No need to hang around. I wouldn't be coming back here ever again. Was there anything here of mine from years back that I wanted? I already knew the answer to that. Nothing of my life was here. It was time to go. If I left now, there was a train due back to York within the hour. I could be relaxing back in my new place soon, close to Sarah. The longing to be there was an ache I couldn't ignore.

I couldn't stand to be in this place a second longer, but I forced myself back into the living room, where I pulled my sleeve over my hand and picked up the TV remote to turn it on. I turned it down when it blasted out, so it was more dull background noise. She always had it on a lot as I remembered, so it might be more suspicious if there was no noise coming from the flat. The longer it was before she was found, the better. I doubted anyone other than her dealer would be knocking on her door any time soon, and he probably waited for an invitation. Time for me to fuck off.

I left the flat, pulling the door closed using my sleeve again, and got the hell off the estate, eager to be as far from here as I could. It was time to get the bus to the train station.

Thanks to Carl Frost's bank account that I set up before I left Brazil, I now had a contactless card I could use and it all checked out. It was a proper account, just on a fake ID. It made me a real citizen, to all intents and purposes. One swipe of it and I'd be on the train to York. From there, it was a twenty-minute walk to my new flat, and I'd be walking through the door. Home at last.

30

I WOKE UP ENERGISED after getting home late last night from visiting the old flat in Leeds. Shay was gone, and there was nothing left of my old life, other than my dad, Joe, and he was still languishing in prison (or he was the last time I checked). He would have been out by now if he didn't keep getting time added for shit he did in there; violence against other inmates and drug offences, to name but two. His initial sentence was the maximum fourteen years. And if he ever got out, there was no way he'd find me. He took so little interest in me, he probably couldn't even remember my name, or any other details about me. So, yep, I felt fantastic.

I sat up and Leanne, in a new furry dog bed on the floor, opened her eyes, looked at me and raised her head. Amazingly, she'd suffered no ill effects after what had happened in the sea. The flat was on the ground floor with a little back garden that was for our use only. It was straight off the kitchen, so she could go out whenever she wanted. Just like in Brazil.

I pulled on sweatpants and a hoodie as she yawned and stretched. She followed me to the kitchen, and I let her out while I opened a tin of Chappie for her breakfast. She adored it, and, as usual, it was gone in seconds. After coffee and toast, I was raring to go, but it was way too early for me to make a move yet. Although the cafe did breakfast, I didn't want to hang around before shoppers got there. The lunch hour rush would be soon enough. That gave me time for a shower and a nice, leisurely morning.

This place was cleaner now than when I moved in. I think it had had a damp cloth run over it but nothing more. Why people didn't use bleach more I couldn't fathom. Cheap, easy, and nice-smelling, at least you knew things were clean when you'd used it. The kitchen grime had cleaned off nicely with it, and I was happy to eat here now. I'd have loved to have docked some of the advance rent I paid, but it was no use rocking the boat. I needed a place and this would do fine.

I turned the shower on and stripped off while the water got hot. The bathroom was basic but functional, and the grout was now white again after my bleach, not that horrible grey colour it was when I'd moved in. I took my time in the shower; the anticipation of this being the first time I might actually see Sarah in the flesh was building nicely. Through the shower screen, I could see Leanne sitting on the new bath mat, waiting for me. She liked to lick my legs when I got out, for some reason known only to her. Must be a dog thing.

I ran my hands over my body, lathering on some fruit-scented shower gel, regretting I was still a bit on the skinny side, even more so after puking for four weeks on Zico's boat. With all the carb-laden rubbish I'd been eating non-stop since I'd got back, I'd soon put some back on. I thought of the gym-toned body I once had, the one that had captivated Sarah and lured her in. She used to tell me my body had a way with hers and it could get her to do all kinds of things, even if she wasn't in the mood. *Her body betrayed her,* was how she'd once put it. To prove her point, I'd stopped her getting out of bed even though it made her late for work. Point proved.

I turned off the shower and shooed Leanne away as I stepped out, sending her out of the room and closing the door. She could keep her damn tongue to herself. After I'd dressed, I scratched my chin again and more hair came out.

209

Maybe I should shave the beard off or just have a break from dyeing it. Would it be so bad if it grew back dark and my hair was still blonde? And how come the peroxide I still put on my hair didn't make my scalp dry or itchy anymore, like it had at first? It seemed to me I'd never had so many questions about my appearance as I had now. I might have no choice to stop dyeing the beard as I couldn't stand this itching. I'd have no skin left at this rate. Perhaps if I dyed it light brown or something else that didn't have peroxide in, it would be better.

In the living room, with its beige carpet, cheap pine furniture and scuffed magnolia walls, I booted up my laptop and logged on to see the money situation of the scammers in Brazil. Wow! It was better than I was expecting. My fears that when I was away, they'd start slacking had been completely unfounded. I could draw a bit of cash out of the bank and get myself some new togs, something the old Chris wouldn't have been seen dead in. Something that didn't draw attention. Something I could be invisible in. So, like what? I wasn't that interested in clothes before, but I was even less so now. My main criteria was that they were cheap. Maybe a supermarket would be the best place. Bargain price jeans and T-shirts, boxers and socks. There was a big Tesco within walking distance. Maybe that would do. I'd have time to get there and back before lunchtime.

Leanne immediately started to whine when I told her to stay. I could hardly tie her up outside a Tesco. She'd be gone when I got out, but she hated being left behind. She had separation anxiety, according to the internet. In Brazil, she'd just gone everywhere with me.

'You're just bloody spoilt,' I told her. She sat down and scratched at the collar around her neck, another thing she didn't like. 'You'll have to get used to it,' I said, getting a dog biscuit out of the box in the kitchen and tossing it to her. It landed at her front paws, and she ignored it, glaring at me instead.

'Whatever,' I muttered, closing the door behind me. Her howls followed me as I walked up the short front path to the street. No doubt she'd be curled up on the sofa before I reached the end of the road.

The flat was just outside the city walls, on the ring road. It must be well sound-proofed, as you could barely hear the road noise when you were inside. I set off to the Tesco, zipping up my hoodie. Maybe they'd have a thick winter coat. As I got near the supermarket, it started to rain, and I ducked inside just as it got worse. Black, angry-looking rain clouds now covered most of the sky. That wasn't good. It was much harder to blend in in the rain, as no one else would be standing around in the street near Sarah's cafe. With a bit of luck, it would have stopped before I got there.

I whizzed around Tesco, grabbing the first things I saw. Black jeans, various T-shirts, socks and underwear, jumpers and fleeces, and a navy padded jacket. It wasn't that bad, to be honest. A quick scan in the pet section and I picked up some dog treats, a brush (for the knots she kept getting in her coat), and some poo bags. I couldn't have her shitting all over the city, even though scooping it up made me retch. Five minutes at the checkout and I was done. It was raining harder when I got outside, so I ripped the labels off the coat and put it on. It wasn't a bad fit.

There was no howling coming from the flat when I got back. That was good, at least. I didn't want the landlady kicking me out because of the dog. It seemed I was forgiven as she ran to greet me at the door. I was more than forgiven when she discovered the chew sticks.

The rain didn't last long so, after a quick cup of coffee and a sandwich, I bundled Leanne into the backpack. She must have thought it was better than being left behind, as she settled down quite happily. She'd have been better off walking, but I didn't want her to be seen yet, not until I was ready. Today was an eyes-on-only mission. I was incognito, gathering evidence until I had a plan. I smiled at the thought that I was on military manoeuvres. Might as well be, if I didn't want to get exposed. I was going to have to plan everything with near-military precision. Shoddy planning would mean it'd be over before it had properly begun.

We walked into the city centre, which didn't take long, and I lingered in the area around Low Petergate, taking in the more-expensive shops along the way. I wouldn't have batted an eyelid at one time about spending obscene amounts of money in them, mainly because I'd earned obscene amounts of money. I'd been struggling to think, if the scams stopped generating income, what else I could actually do here. Nothing with a CRB or any other type of police check, so that was a lot of decent jobs ruled out. As good as I thought Carl Frost's ID and documents were, I couldn't see any point in subjecting them to unnecessary levels of scrutiny. So what job could I get instead? Every time I thought about it, I drew a blank, which was unusual for me. But I would need money. I didn't see myself doing any type of labouring job, like on a building site. Maybe I'd be better off doing some kind of tech-based start-up, like design. But web design probably wasn't that lucrative these days, with so many others at it.

I decided to leave it for now, as it was making my brain hurt. On St Helen's Square, I stopped, my feet suddenly feeling glued to the pavement. Lendal, the street her shop was on, was a stone's throw from here, and she'd be right there. A few steps more and I would be at the corner where St Helen's Square and Lendal met. I had to be careful. Too blasé and overconfident, and I'd blow it. Months of planning would be up the Swanee. Leanne started to squirm, as she always did when I stopped, wanting to get out and have a run around. There were some damp benches nearby, and I went to sit on one, next to a middle-aged woman eating a waffle smothered in cream. I moved away from the cloying smell, right to the edge. By the looks of her, it would have done her good to give that shit a miss.

I put the backpack on my knee, and Leanne popped her head out. She didn't share the same view as me about the waffle and stretched her neck to sniff it. I stroked the top of her head, her silky fur soothing my nerves, which were feeling more shredded by the second. What would I do if Sarah walked by right now? She could do, for all I know. I imagined I could see her right now, coming down the street, her shoulders slumped and her eyes sorrowful and heavy with the loss of me. My stomach churned at the thought, and the ache and longing to see and touch her turned into something almost tangible, it was so strong. I closed my eyes for a second, letting the feelings wash over me. It was invigorating.

A horrid thought came next; something I'd not considered as a possibility, but it could well be after all this time: what if she had someone else? How could I not have thought about it? The image of her walking by hand-in-hand with some bloke, some wanker that got to hold her and undress her at night, and kiss the intimate parts of her that I used to kiss, replaced the lonely picture of her from before, and my gut clenched hard. I gripped the edge of the bench with one hand and Leanne's ear with the other, not realising I was squeezing until she let out a whimper. Next to me, the waffle-eating hag turned to look at me sharply.

'Sorry,' I whispered to Leanne, letting go and resuming the gentle rubbing I'd been doing earlier.

The woman was still glaring at me and I had to resist the urge to stuff the waffle right in her face. I was still stroking Leanne when I turned full-on, exposing the scar on my face.

'Yeah? Did you want something?' I asked in my best Irish, glaring at her.

Her eyes widened briefly. 'Um, no. I was just going.' She got up from the bench, one hand grabbing her bags and the other still gripping her carb-laden treat. I noticed she took it with her, so the fear of losing that was greater than the fear of a thug like me starting something.

I breathed in deeply to calm myself. There was no point putting it off any longer. At the top of Lendal, I scanned both sides of the street until I saw the cafe on the left. There was no missing it. It had a sign outside, in exactly the same colours and font as the cafes in London. *Delish* written in black on a pink background, in a delicate cursive font. Simple, appealing to women (cake eaters) and really effective. If they'd asked me to design it, I'd have gone for something similar. Even just seeing the name again affected me. It was so familiar; so *her*. As I stood looking at it, it was like I could feel her nearby.

Before I could change my mind and bottle it, I pulled my cap low, adjusted my tinted glasses, and walked past, concentrating hard on my new, lumbering gait. I glanced out of the corner of my eye at the cafe as I passed by, but didn't turn my head to look at it. Every little detail imprinted itself on my brain. The inside was dark and moody, stylish, and there was a woman with blue hair doing something behind the counter. The tables inside all seemed to be taken, although it was hard to see right to the back from this angle. Three tables were outside. A lone man sat smoking at one of them and the others were empty, probably due to the chill. And then I was past and I couldn't see anything else.

I didn't realise my heart had been slamming so hard against my ribs until I turned the corner at the top. Sweat dotted my hairline. I couldn't believe what a state I was in. I stopped, leaning my shoulder up against a wall separating two shops. Leanne squirmed in the backpack. What now? I didn't think it would be a good idea to walk by again. It might arouse some suspicion. I noticed things like that even if most people didn't. There again, being observant wasn't Sarah's strong point before. Maybe she wasn't that person anymore, though. She had to have learned something from what had happened to her. She may be wary or on her guard now. I was going to have to be careful.

With nothing to do and a long afternoon stretching ahead, I made for the small park over the road. Leanne could have a run off, and I could start training her to get used to the lead, based on the YouTube videos I'd watched.

It was going to take a lot more thought to figure out what to do next regarding Sarah.

31

SO, WE'D PUT UP the new *Delish* sign and decorated the café for Christmas. It was late November, and all the shops around here were done. We'd chosen a black Christmas tree that was now laden with pink baubles and dripping with lights, right in the centre of the window, flanked by pyramids of mince pies on either side. We were getting more regulars all the time. Olwyn had been as good as her word and was bringing in her Women's Institute pals. Word had spread and a few more clubs like hers were choosing to lunch with us on a regular basis. I'd settled in, done a bit of decorating in my flat, and was busy experimenting with dessert and cake ideas. Things really couldn't be better.

And yet, if I wasn't busy, I was miserable. The evenings were long, as it was dark before we closed up. Every sound had me jumping and running to peer out of the windows, my palms clammy and my pulse racing, despite the CCTV cameras I'd had installed. And there were so many unfamiliar noises, especially in the back alley. Lids clattered, cats fought, even foxes shrieked regularly, their piercing cries going right through me. And I saw a rat the other day, emerging from a wheelie bin, and I had to rush back inside and barricade myself in. I hadn't seen the biggest rat of all, though, so that was a good thing.

Him. I knew he was a rat, but some nights I just couldn't stop myself from thinking about him. On particularly bad nights, I imagined I could feel him, smell him, hear him, and every bit of me ached to have him here, to touch him, despite what he did to me. I should hate him, and some days I did, but I'd recently admitted to myself that I still loved him, too. I just couldn't help it.

Then there was the baby I lost that consumed my thoughts. The one I scoured baby shops buying things for. Sometimes I thought I must be going mad. Back in London, I had everything. *We* had everything, and he'd thrown it all away. There was a good chance we would have been together until the end, until we were old, wrinkly, and toothless. A love like that doesn't come along very often. And, deep down, I didn't believe I'd ever find it again, either. That was my one chance, our one chance, and he blew it.

I logged out of Mumsnet after another evening spent pretending I was a mum, turned off my computer, checked the locks on the doors and the windows, and turned in for the night. The second I got into bed, images of him and what we used to do to each other filled my mind. I longed for him to come through the door, rip off my clothes and possess me, like he used to. I knew I needed to stop being his, and I was really trying hard, but it was just not working.

I sighed and turned over, but sleep was a long way off. Instead of fighting thoughts of him, I gave into them, remembering the ways he'd make love to me and how I always, always wanted more of him. It was easier to remember and indulge than keep fighting. The morning would no doubt see me getting up exhausted once more, applying more make-up to conceal the dark circles around my eyes.

***

After a busy lunchtime in the cafe, I was taking payment from another happy customer when Claire, having cleared a table, put the crockery on the counter and just stood there.

'Thank you. Hope to see you again soon,' I said, smiling at the woman who was just putting her purse away.

'Oh, you definitely will. I'm already looking forward to it,' she said before leaving.

'What?' I said to Claire. She had her back to the shop and was facing me over the counter, her hands still gripping the tray stacked with dirty plates.

'Over there… don't look now…' she hissed, as my eyes sought out what she was going on about. 'You see that woman in the pink coat?'

'Er, yes. Why?'

It's her. My old boss. Vanessa. From here.'

'Oh. Right. What the hell is she doing in here?' I whispered. I'd have thought giving us her money would have been the last thing she'd have wanted to do.

I lowered my head and studied her from under my brows. Vanessa was a mean-looking woman with small eyes, a thin nose and even thinner lips. She picked up a menu and studied it with a face like she'd just sucked a lemon. This wasn't good. She wasn't reading the menu anymore—her eyes weren't moving. More like she was trying to listen to what Claire and I were saying.

'What shall we do?' Claire asked. 'I can hardly pretend I don't know her, can I? She used to bloody work here.'

'What are we whispering about?' Ellie asked quietly, making me jump as she came up behind me.

'Ssh,' Claire hissed, picking up her tray and coming round to the back of the counter. She jerked her head at Ellie, who followed her into the kitchen to get filled in, leaving me standing at the counter alone.

I lifted my chin. So what if she'd come in here? She'd get treated like anyone else, as far as I was concerned. I wouldn't be nasty, but I wouldn't be apologetic, either. It wasn't me who sacked her. Maybe it was because of me she'd lost her job, but it wasn't that simple. She must have some front, though, coming in and sitting herself down. Maybe she was meeting Rebecca, and I'd have the pair of them to contend with. Great! She knew Claire still worked here, so she was hardly incognito while checking us out. But I really hoped she wasn't going to create a scene. The cafe was still full and a handful of people had just come in for takeaway stuff.

'Hi, what can I get you?' I asked the couple first in the queue.

While I served them, my eyes kept sliding to Vanessa, who hadn't made a move to get up and order. We didn't do table service; it was order at the counter. It said so quite clearly on the new menu. If she wanted to wait, she'd be there a long time. But I really needed the table back if she wasn't going to order.

Just then, Ellie came back out, carrying a large tray of her vegan pastries, which she started to stack behind the counter. It was her last batch of the day and they'd all be gone by the time we closed.

She leaned forward to reach the front and as she did, she said to me, 'I'll go and tell her it's counter service only, if you like.'

I should do it. I was the boss. There again, I was serving. I felt cowardly relief as I nodded. 'Thanks.'

Ellie went off, her blue hair sticking to her head from the heat of the kitchen. I couldn't stop myself from glancing over as Ellie smiled, nodded her head, and pointed to the counter. Vanessa didn't look pleased, but stood up and joined the back of the queue, still clutching a menu. All three of us worked to get the queue down, and she was soon standing in front of me. Claire had gone into the back to make some sandwiches.

I pretended I didn't know who she was. 'Hello there. What can I get for you?'

She didn't return my smile as she said, 'A pot of tea and some carrot cake.' No 'please' or 'thank you'.

'I'll bring them right over.' I held the contactless machine out for her to pay.

Well, that wasn't too hard, but I'd be glad when she'd gone. She was making me edgy. She was going to be judging me on my cakes; I could feel it.

I got on with making her tea and cutting her cake, and when I turned back, she'd returned to her table.

'Shall I take them over?' asked Claire, who was beside me once more.

'I don't mind. I can do it, if you like.'

'I should, really. I do know her, after all.'

I shrugged, annoyed at how relieved I was. 'Okay. Maybe you're right.'

She grabbed the tray, grimaced at me, turned around, and walked over to Vanessa's table.

'A hot chocolate please, with marshmallows and sprinkles, to take out,' said a small voice. I hadn't even noticed the young boy standing in front of me with his mother.

'Coming right up,' I said, smiling at him. He was cute, maybe about six, and had freckles and a pale complexion. I took the five-pound note he held out and looked at his mum. 'Anything else?'

'Um, I'll think I'll try one of those brownies. They look scrummy. Josh likes brownies as well, so make that two. And another hot chocolate,' she said, glancing at the boy and adding a ten to the five. She smiled guiltily, before patting her stomach. 'I shouldn't really but…'

'Why not? Treat yourself. I would.' I got her change and handed it over.

She eyed my flat tummy. 'You don't look as if you do,' she said.

'I do, though. All the time. I taste everything I make.'

She sighed. 'How do you stay so slim, though? I'll have to starve before my Slimming World class for the rest of the week now.'

'Good genes, I guess,' I said. 'But you look great. You don't need to lose weight, anyway.'

My eyes flicked to Vanessa, who was still standing next to Claire. What were they talking about? Claire wasn't her usual smiley self and now had her hand on her hip.

'It's since I had him,' the woman in front of me said. 'I used to be able to eat what I liked and stay the same. I can't anymore.'

I gave her my full attention. It was what she deserved. What did I care about Vanessa, anyway?

'Eat the damn brownie and enjoy it!' I said with a laugh. 'Life's too short not to eat a brownie.'

'Well, when you put it like that.' She laughed, and I made their hot chocolates then bagged up two brownies. They left happily, two more satisfied customers.

Maybe I should put that somewhere, on a banner or something: *Life's too short not to eat a brownie.* I liked it, although I preferred *Just Eat The Friggin' Brownie!!* It probably wasn't a good idea to go with that one. I snatched a pen and wrote it on an order pad, then ripped it off and put it in my pocket. A neon sign in the window might look good. Or maybe it was too many letters. I could put it on a plaque instead.

'Claire's coming back,' Ellie said, pretending to fiddle with something in the cabinet.

Claire rolled her eyes as she reached the counter.

'What did she say?' Ellie asked, adjusting a label that said *Herby Vegan Sausage Rolls.*

Claire pulled a face. 'She said there wasn't much on the menu she liked.'

'But she somehow managed to find something to order,' I remarked.

'Yep. She said she'd have the carrot cake as, 'You can't go wrong with that, can you?''

Bloody hell! The cheeky cow! If she was going to criticise my cake, then all bets were off.

'What else? You were gone too long just for that?'

'She doesn't care for the decor. It's too dark and gloomy.'

I thought of the hours Claire and I had spent painting and wanted to chuck her out. No one asked her to come in. There were plenty of other cafes she could give her custom to. I stifled a laugh as the words '*Of all the cafes in all the towns in all the world, she walks into mine*' played in my mind in a Humphrey Bogart voice. You couldn't beat Casablanca. I'd watched it again last Sunday, huddled up under a blanket, alone in the flat in the afternoon with nothing else to do.

'What's funny?' Ellie asked, looking at me closely.

I shook my head. 'Nothing. I hope she's not going to kick up a stink in front of all these,' I said, nodding at the rest of our customers.

'I'll frogmarch her out if she does,' said Ellie.

I got the feeling she'd look forward to it.

Vanessa sipped her tea and grimaced at the taste. Half the carrot cake was gone.

'Look at that! She might as well be drinking gnat's piss!' Ellie grumbled.

'I wish that's what I'd given her,' I muttered. 'Just ignore her. She'll be gone soon.'

Claire just said, 'Hmmm.'

'Hmmm what? You don't think she will?'

She shook her head. 'Nah! She'll find something else to complain about, if I know her.'

'Well, it'd better not be about my cake,' I said. 'If she disses that, she's out. Banned.'

The other two laughed, but they knew I wasn't joking. I poured my heart and soul into everything I made. You could taste it. But she probably couldn't. I just wished she'd leave.

With no one immediately needing to be served, I fiddled around with items in the cabinet, arranging them to be displayed at their best. Ellie was in the kitchen and Claire flitted around the tables, checking everyone was okay. Just five minutes later, Vanessa got up, her chair legs screeching loudly on the tiled floor. People cringed. One woman shuddered and pulled a face. Vanessa must have done it on purpose. I got the impression Claire wasn't wrong, and she was a bitch to work for. At least she was going, so good riddance.

As she went by the counter, I called out, 'Thank you, hope everything was to your satisfaction' to her. No reason not to be polite.

She stopped and in a loud voice announced, 'It wasn't, actually, seeing as you're asking. I don't normally complain but I wasn't happy, so I won't be coming back.'

I tilted my head on one side. 'Oh, I'm sorry,' I shot back, aiming for not sounding sorry at all.

She glared at me. 'I should ask for my money back for that muck you're serving.'

My hackles, along with the hairs on the back of my neck, stood right up. The nerve of her! 'I beg your pardon?' I hated her so much right now I wanted to shove her out of the cafe. 'What didn't you like?'

'The cake. It was soggy. Not for me, I'm afraid.'

I wasn't going to bite. It wasn't soggy. Carrot cake should be moist, but Claire said they used to buy everything in when she ran the place, so what would she know, anyway?

I shook my head, scratching around for some cutting one liner, when another customer, a woman whose face I recognised from her numerous visits, piped up, 'I just had the carrot cake. It was really tasty. Everything I've had here is top-notch. I love it.'

'So do I. We come here all the time,' said someone else, and people all over nodded and murmured in agreement.

'Best cafe in town,' said an old man in a tweed flat cap, who'd been here a few times before.

'Maybe you'd be better in a different cafe, more to your liking,' I said with a broad smile. 'Everyone else seems to like it here. We make everything fresh, right here on the premises. This place has picked up no end since we took it over. Business is booming.'

Her lip curled at one side and her eye twitched before she turned on her heel and marched out. The door slammed shut behind her, making people jump once more. I stood there, really embarrassed, but also proud.

'Good bloody riddance!' someone shouted, and laughter broke the silence.

A relieved breath escaped me. 'Thank you all for your support.' I could feel myself blushing. 'I really appreciate it.'

'Don't listen to her, love. It's just sour grapes because she used to work here,' the old man said. 'I remember her. Right sour puss, she was. And the food was nothing to write home about. Not like now.'

People went back to eating and, to cool my face down, I went outside. There was a man out there that Claire had served half an hour ago. I'd forgotten about him.

I opened the door to find him still sitting there, bunched up in his coat against the cold. At least it wasn't raining today like it had been all week, even though it looked like it might start. A little white dog in a fleecy jumper was scooting around under his chair, hoovering up crumbs. He bent over one side of his chair, untangling the dog lead from around his legs. She wagged her tail when she saw me.

'Anything else I can get for you?' I asked him.

He pushed himself higher up in his chair, his eyes hidden behind tinted glasses. He was sitting side on, facing down the street to the park. His baseball cap was pulled down low, and a navy padded coat had fresh crumbs all down the front. He brushed them off. No doubt the dog would gobble them up. He scratched a patchy-looking, light-brown beard and covered his mouth with his hand as he cleared his throat. I got the feeling he was testing his words in his head before he spoke them.

'Ah, I'm okay, thanks. That was really nice.' He had a strong Irish accent, and his voice was surprisingly soft. He picked up his glass of coke and drained it before standing up. 'I'd better be off. It's freezing out here.'

I stepped back to let him out. 'Your dog is cute. What's her name?'

He paused, looking down at her. 'Um, Lulu.'

I didn't expect that. 'Bye Lulu.' I bent down to pat her, and her tail started wagging again.

'Bye,' he said as he began to walk away, towards the park.

I put his used cutlery on his empty plate, stood the glass on top of it, and walked out of the cold, back into the warm shop, just as it started to rain again.

32

THE MAN WITH THE white dog was here again, sitting outside, looking at the menu. He'd been here several times now, always sitting at the same table while the dog settled down either on his knee or under the chair. I'd seen him take the dog out of a backpack he always carried as he got to the table. He picked up the menu, although he must know it off by heart now. I watched him from inside.

I didn't normally go outside to take orders, but it was better than him having to leave the dog on its own again, as he had been doing. Someone might steal her. There was a sticker saying 'no dogs except for guide dogs' in our front window. It was there before we took over. I wondered if I should take it out and allow dogs inside. There again, I didn't think some of our customers would be too keen to eat a nice afternoon tea with a dog under the next table. I'd probably lose more in existing customers than I'd gain in attracting new ones with dogs. Dog owners were still free to sit outside, so we still served them, anyway.

I picked up the card reader from the counter and went outside.

'I'll take your order out here today, save you coming in and leaving Lulu out here on her own,' I said.

He jumped and dropped the menu as if he hadn't realised I was there.

'Oh, great, if you're sure,' he said in his soft Irish voice.

'Have you decided, or shall I come back in a bit?' I bent down and stroked Lulu, who jumped up at me, wanting to be fussed.

'Get down, Lu,' he said to her. 'I can order now. I know what I want.'

I took his order and watched as he took his wallet out and held the card to the reader.

Back inside, Ellie was busy behind the counter. She looked up at me.

'I think we should take orders outside from people who have dogs,' I said to her as I washed my hands. 'If they're on their own, I mean. They can't leave their dogs tied up in this day and age. They'd be pinched when they get back. Have you seen the news on dog thefts? There was an item on last night. It's rife, apparently.'

'No, I haven't seen it. The problem with doing it for people with dogs is that everyone will expect it. It can get a bit confusing, one rule for some and a different one for others.'

'Yes, that's true. I just took his order, though.'

She looked out of the window. 'Oh, it's him again. Scarface. He's not bad looking though, is he? I think the scar is quite appealing. I wonder how he got it.'

I shrugged and went to get his order of coffee and a toasted sandwich, thinking about his scar. The first time I'd seen him, he'd been he'd been side-on, and I hadn't noticed it. I'd tried not to react to it when I did see it. It looked quite fresh, but it wasn't that big. It was under one eye. Looked like a typical glass in the face to me. Had someone glassed him? If so, what happened to the other guy? Or woman?

When I took his food out, he was just zipping his coat up. Lulu whined when she saw the plate. She was wearing her stripy fleece again.

'Oh, she's so cute in that.' I couldn't help myself, and I bent down to scoop her up. 'Are you cold out here, you poor little thing?' I jerked my head away as she tried to lick my face. 'How old is she?'

'I'm not sure. She was a stray. Under two, though, I think. She's had puppies before, you can tell.'

I put her down on the floor, and he wrapped the lead around his leg.

'Enjoy your food,' I said, going back inside.

As I washed my hands, a large group of eight came through the door, wanting a table. By the time they'd been seated and served, when I next looked out of the window, the man outside had gone. Claire was clearing and wiping his table.

The next time I saw him was three days later. I'd been watching out for him, hoping to see him again. He was much later today than usual. We were due to close up in half an hour and our last customers were down to a trickle. It was the quietest time of day, with people coming in mainly for takeout drinks and snacks. As he was about to sit down outside, I opened the door and stood in the doorway.

'You can sit inside if you like. Out of the cold. It's empty in here. Apart from us, of course.'

He hesitated. 'Are you sure?'

'Yep. I'm the boss. It's up to me. Of course, if it was busy, then...'

'Oh, absolutely. But it is freezing out here. That's the problem with having a dog. And she hates being left. Creates merry hell with her barking and whining. Thank you.'

He followed me inside and I pointed to a table right at the back, away from the window. Lulu was still in the backpack; I could just make out the top of her fluffy head. He smiled at me when he caught me looking.

Ellie came out of the kitchen with a stack of clean plates that she piled behind the counter. She scanned around the shop and stopped when she saw him. 'Ooh, is he back again? Where's the dog?'

228

'In the bag. I'll just take his order.'

'No, it's okay. I'll go. I can't resist that dog, you know. She's so cute.'

'I know. I can't, either.'

'Darcey's been pestering us like mad for one,' she said as she walked over to him.

He took his coat off and put it on the seat behind him. He was wearing a T-shirt, and a large tattoo ran from his elbow down the inside of his right forearm. I couldn't make out what it was of. Another peeked out from under the left sleeve of his T-shirt, but it was mostly obscured.

Ellie had her back to me at his table, jotting down his order. Sometimes I wondered if we'd be better with a new electronic point of sale system that did everything from orders to payments to stock inventory. There again, we didn't have that many tables. It was hardly the Ivy we were running.

Ellie came back, ripped the order off the pad and stuck it to a corkboard I'd put there. 'He's just having coffee and some cake. I've told him we're closing in half an hour and it was too late to order anything hot.'

'Right. No problem. I'll do it if you make a start sweeping the floor over near the window.'

'Okay,' said Ellie.

While Claire was cleaning up in the kitchen and Ellie was doing the shop, I took his order over, then started clearing up behind the counter. He'd taken his glasses off and placed them next to his plate.

'Is everything alright? More coffee?'

He fixed me with startlingly green eyes. It was the first time I'd seen them.

He nodded. 'Everything's great, thanks. As always. That's why I keep coming back.'

'I'm glad to hear it,' I said, picking up his empty plate and glancing at his arm. The tattoo looked to be Celtic symbols or something similar. I wondered what the significance was, if there was any.

It was fifteen minutes to closing. Fifteen minutes until another evening alone in the flat upstairs. Some evenings I went across to the little park at the end of the road. It was well-lit and there were always plenty of dog walkers in there. It blew away the cobwebs after a busy day.

After the man had left, Claire, Ellie and I sat in the kitchen as we did every day, with a cup of something warm.

'What's it like here at Christmas?' I asked, slipping my shoes off and flexing my feet. Sometimes, by the end of the day, my feet felt twice the size they should be. I wished I could work in soft, furry slippers.

'It's magical. Sometimes there's a light display projected onto the Minster that's really spectacular,' said Claire. 'I'll take you to see it, if you like. We can go for a drink afterwards. You've hardly been out since you've been here.'

'Yeah, my mum mentioned it. Let me know when it's on.'

'Do you miss London at all?' asked Ellie, refilling her tea.

I paused. 'Do you know, I don't think I do. I've barely had time to think about it, so I can't do, can I?'

'I think London's alright for a weekend but I wouldn't want to live there,' said Claire. 'I don't think you can beat York. And Leeds is lovely too. And Liverpool and Newcastle and Manchester. There are so many great places up here.'

'I haven't been to any of those,' I said. Then I remembered I had been to Leeds. To see Chris's sister that day. It was so awful I'd blocked it out of my mind. I didn't bother to correct myself. They didn't need to know all that, although Claire sometimes still tried to get me to open up. She'd convinced herself I was running from heartbreak in some big romantic story. She was half right, I suppose. The less I told her, the more convinced she was that I had a big secret or some tragic past.

I stood up and followed them out, locking the door behind them. The windows were bare, as I'd thrown the old, stained blinds away, and I felt exposed standing there with the lights on when it was pitch dark outside. At least the new blinds I'd ordered were due to be fitted in the next couple of days, so I wouldn't have long to wait.

On the spur of the moment, I decided to go straight over to the park before fixing something to eat. If I went upstairs and got comfortable, I'd probably not bother to go back out, and I could do with the exercise. I got my coat and stepped out of the shop, locking the door behind me. With just the Christmas tree lights on, and some fairy lights at the back, it really looked beautiful inside, all dark and moody. I still couldn't believe it was mine to run as I saw fit.

I made my way to the park, crossing the busy road at the end of Lendal. The Minster, in all its glory, was down to the right. I loved the building and often went in on the weekend. It was so peaceful inside and I always came out feeling better.

The small park was overrun with squirrels, their antics fabulously funny as they fought over food and pinched whatever was going. People fed them all the time, and they scampered around the grass, darting out of the way of dogs and kids. Over the other side, I thought I recognised a small white dog. I made my way over. It was Lulu. The man hadn't got far when he left the cafe, then. He was throwing a ball for her when he turned and saw me.

'Hi,' he said. 'Finished for the day, then?' He had a thick scarf wound around his neck.

'Yes. I often pop over here when I've done. Recharges the old batteries.'

'It certainly does today,' he said, hanging onto his cap as a gust of wind threatened to lift it off his head.

'So you live around here?' I asked.

'About a fifteen-minute walk. Just outside the city walls.'

'What is it you do?' I asked, thinking of the odd hours he was free to visit the cafe.

His eyes followed the dog as she chased after a squirrel, barking at it. Had he heard me? Then he said, 'I'm between jobs at the moment.'

Shit! Trust me to ask a sensitive question. Me and my big mouth.

'I'm a graphic designer,' he said. Behind his tinted glasses, a tear escaped from his eye, a consequence of the biting wind. It dropped down towards his scar and I looked away. 'I'm thinking of setting up on my own.'

'Sounds interesting,' I said. 'I had my own business not long ago. I made cakes. Wedding cakes and things like that.'

'Oh, right. I bet you were good at it, judging by the cakes in your shop. Do you make them?'

'Yeah. Up early every morning, ovens on by five. I love it. Means I'm falling asleep by nine PM, though, so I'm not much fun.'

Lulu ran up to him, then noticed me and jumped up my legs. He pointed to a bench under the shelter of a tree.

'Want to sit out of this wind?' he asked.

'Yeah. Sure.'

I followed him there. Lulu sat at his feet and immediately began scratching at the collar around her neck.

'Something else she doesn't like. The collar and lead. She's a free spirit, you see.'

I laughed. 'I've been wondering about something. You can give me your opinion.'

'On what?'

'Do you think an awning would help? Outside the shop. I mean. I've seen you sitting there in the wind and the rain. It would keep the rain off at least, for anyone sitting outside. Lot of other places around here have them.'

'Yeah. I think it's a good idea.'

'I don't know anything about them, cost-wise and stuff. Do you? Being a designer, I mean?'

'No, actually. I could have a look. Can't be that hard, can it?'

232

'I wouldn't have thought so. Nothing's hard with Google, is it?'

He laughed. 'Correct. That's what I do these days.'

'I bet you can get them to match your signage,' I said, imagining it pink or black. Both would look nice. 'It'd be a good idea, if it's not too expensive.'

He nodded. 'Probably, yeah.'

'What sort of designs do you do? I've got some ideas for the shop. Well, one, mainly. Kind of a slogan I thought of.'

He turned his head, the darkness making his scar almost invisible on the far side of his face. 'What slogan?'

'It's daft, really. I told a woman in the cafe the other week that life is too short not to eat brownies. I've been thinking about it since, and I think it would look good painted in large letters on the wall. But I'm not sure how to do it. It's not my area of expertise, although I have hand-painted some cakes before. Is it something you would be able to do?'

'There are a few ways you could do it. I'd have to have a look and see. Do you want it painting directly on the wall, because I'm more computer-based design than free hand? I don't think I'd be very good at that.'

'Why don't you come by the cafe at closing tomorrow, if you're not busy? We could chat about it some more. And it could be a commission for you while you're not working. I'd pay, of course. I'd be looking at it as sort of individual artwork. You could tell me what's possible.'

He was quiet for a moment. He wasn't going to come. Then he said, 'Alright, yeah. I'll have a think about what we could do.'

'Brilliant.' I stood up as the cold seeped into my bones. It was time to head home. 'I'll see you tomorrow, then. Oh, I'm Sarah, by the way.'

He smiled and gave me a small wave. 'I'm Carl. See you tomorrow.'

33

THE FOLLOWING NIGHT, JUST as we were closing, he came through the door, Lulu's head sticking out of the pack on his back. Claire and Ellie, who were just leaving, glanced at each other and smirked. They knew he was coming, but were somehow convinced I'd got him here because I fancied him.

'Are you sure you'll be alright on your own with him?' Claire had said earlier when I told her he was coming round. 'You don't know anything about him.'

'I'll be fine. I have a good nose for these things and I'll be perfectly safe with him.'

'I can stay on, though. It's no bother.'

'Look, I wasn't scared before, but now you're freaking me out. We'll be in the shop with the lights on. What, you think he's going to murder me in full view? There's always somebody walking past here, as well you know.'

She couldn't argue with that, so she just muttered something under her breath before saying, 'Well, if you're sure.'

'I'll keep my phone in my pocket and ring you if I have any problems.'

'Alright,' she'd said, eventually. 'Be sure you do.'

'Hi,' he said now, as he stood in the doorway. 'Okay if I come in?'

'Of course. I've made a fresh pot of coffee if you want some.'

'Great. I never turn down free coffee or tea.'

He went through to the back of the shop and took off his coat and glasses while I brought the pot over. He kept his cap on as if he'd forgotten he was wearing it. I'd never seen him without it, but there was no hair sticking out from underneath it. If he had any, it was very short.

'I was thinking about painting it in this area here.' I pointed to the dark grey expanse of wall. 'Do you think it would look good written here in white? Or maybe something else bright?'

'It would. I can see it,' he said. He pulled an envelope out of his pocket and took out some sheets of A4. The words were printed on them in various fonts and colours. I sat down opposite him.

'Just to give me an idea of what kind of thing you're interested in. Just one thing to mention, though. If it's going to be big and take up a lot of this space, I'd have to work on it here. There's no room to swing a cat in my flat, especially for a project of this physical size.'

'No problem.' I shrugged. 'I'm always here, anyway.'

'Do you live around here?' he asked.

I pointed at the ceiling, realising he wouldn't know where I lived. 'Up there.'

'Oh, wow! That's handy for work. And you're right in the centre.' He smiled and Lulu whined and wriggled in the bag. 'Is it alright if she comes out?'

'Yes. If she's house trained,' I mock-scolded. 'And she's not allowed in the kitchen. Health and safety and all that.'

'Understood. And she won't embarrass herself by doing anything like that. She's a lady! And if she did, I'd clean it up.'

He lifted her out of the bag and placed her on the floor. I wasn't keen on her running around in here with it being food premises, but what could I say? Maybe she'd curl up on one of the banquette seats and go to sleep.

235

I picked her up and sat her on my knee so she couldn't pee on the floor. She seemed happy enough as she tried to lick my face.

'Oh, I just remembered.' I took a business card out of my pocket and slid it across the table to him. It was one of the embossed cards that Chris did for me at the wedding fair as a surprise. 'I like the fonts and design on this. I'm thinking about getting some done for the counter for people to pick up. Maybe the slogan could tie in with it in some way.'

'Okay. Can I keep this one?'

'Course.'

He put it in his pocket and flipped through the designs. 'I like this one.' He swivelled the paper around to face me. It was nice, but nothing like what I was after. It was too masculine and blocky.

'I was thinking something more scripty, if that's a word. Like the signage outside.'

He plucked a different one out of the middle of the pile. 'More like this?'

'Ooh, yes. I like that one. How would you do it?'

'Like I said, not straight onto the wall. I'm not that sort of artist. But I could possibly do it onto a large canvas or piece of board. That's what I meant about keeping something large here, on site.'

'That might actually look better. More like a proper piece of art.'

He took a sip of his coffee, his eyes still fixed on the paper. His eyes rarely settled on me for long before flitting away. He seemed shy. My eyes went to the tattoo on his arm, and I wondered if he had any others anywhere.

'I like your tattoo,' I said. 'It's really decorative. Does it mean anything?'

He glanced at his arm as if just remembering it was there. 'Oh, no. I just liked the design, that's all.' His fingers touched the scar on his face and he stroked it, but didn't seem aware he was doing it.

'How did you get that, if you don't mind me asking?' I said. 'God, sorry—I'm so nosy. Just ignore me.'

'No, it's fine. Bar fight back home. I got caught in the middle.'

'So you weren't in a fight yourself then?'

'God, no. I was scared to death, to tell you the truth. I'm a lover, not a fighter.' He flashed a self-conscious smile.

'I would have been petrified.' I fiddled with Lulu's ears before saying, 'There's never any need for violence, if you ask me.'

'I know. But some people seem to think it's the answer. It's beyond me why.' He dropped his head, shaking it, as if deep in thought.

'So, where is that, anyway? Home. I mean, Ireland, obviously,' I said.

'Erm, Derry.'

'I've never been to Ireland. I hear it's beautiful. Is Derry where you grew up?'

'It is, yeah. But I haven't lived there for a long time.'

'Don't you miss it?'

'Sometimes.' His eyes flitted to mine before glancing away, then back, holding my gaze for longer. 'But other places have benefits too.'

Was he coming onto me?

'Whereabouts in Ireland is Derry?'

'Far north. Above Belfast and to the west.'

'Where have you been living since you left Ireland, then?'

'All over. I've lived everywhere.'

He got out a tape measure and asked me to hold one end. I scooped Lulu up and placed her onto the banquette. She glared at me before flopping back down on the cushion.

'About to here?' he asked, holding his end of the tape measure against the wall.

I nodded.

'And how high?'

'What do you think would look best? I think it should start just above the chairs and go almost to the ceiling, for maximum impact.'

I held the tape measure while he measured the space and jotted down the measurements.

'We should talk about money,' I said.

'What's your budget?'

'I'm not sure. How long do you think it'll take? I don't know what the going rate is for something like this.'

'I could do it for a fixed fee of two hundred and fifty. How does that sound? Then if it takes me longer, I'll be working for free. Give me an incentive to get it done.'

'I can manage that. Thanks.' I was probably getting a good deal there for something custom. Although I hadn't seen any of his work yet. What if it was awful?

'A week should be enough, based on two or three hours every evening after you close. Do you have anywhere to store it in the day so I can just get it out and work on it on an evening?'

'Yes. No problem.'

He glanced around at the wall. 'Do you have any more of this paint? So I can paint the board the same colour?'

'Yeah. There's loads left. But I was thinking of a different background colour. Perhaps that mauve over there, to tie it together.'

'Yeah. I think that would work really well. When do you want me to start?'

'Whenever you like.'

'I'll order a big piece of ply tomorrow. Is it alright if I have it delivered straight here? There's no room at mine.'

'Yes, of course. I'll find somewhere for it.'

He scribbled a phone number down and handed it to me. 'Give me a ring when it comes. Might be a few days.'

I folded the paper and put it into the back pocket of my jeans. His green eyes followed the movement of my body, but not in a creepy or lecherous way. Lulu woke up, and I played with the top of her head. She yawned.

'She's absolutely gorgeous. I'm smitten.'

He looked at her. 'I know she is. We've been through a lot together, me and her.'

What did he mean by that? What had they been through since he rescued her?

'Sounds ominous,' I said, fishing once more.

'Have you ever had a dog?' he asked.

Nice swerve. I didn't push it. 'No. We had two cats when I was growing up. Plus two budgies, a ferret and several guinea pigs. But never a dog. My parents always said it was a big commitment, as if I wouldn't look after it or something. But I would have. My cats were lovely, though. The last one only died a few months ago.'

'Aw, poor thing. Lu is my first dog. I've never been much of an animal person. But now…' His eyes went back to Lu. 'I'm smitten with her, too.'

I offered him more coffee, and he shook his head. 'I'd best get off. Let me know when the ply arrives, and we can take it from there.'

He looked at me, a brief but searching, intense look, and I felt something tug at my pelvis. That hadn't happened in a long time.

He stood up and pulled his coat on, zipping it up right under his chin. Lulu was on her feet right away, determined not to be left behind.

'I'll leave these here,' he said, indicating the printouts on the table. 'Have a good look through them and get a feel for any you like. If you don't like any of them, we can start from scratch.'

I wanted to say, ' I like you,' but I stood up and grabbed the coffeepot, holding it as a shield between us. 'I'm happy to go with that one. Consider it picked.' I pointed to the one I liked from earlier.

He put it back in his pocket. 'Great.'

As he walked to the door, Lulu, now off the banquette, gambolled around his feet. He stooped and clipped her lead on. She immediately sat down, and he sighed.

'See?' he said. 'She hates it.' To the dog he said, 'You are walking home, young lady. I'm not carrying you everywhere.'

Lulu didn't move as he tugged at the lead.

'It's just something she'll have to get used to,' I said. 'Dogs are like us, really. They don't like change.'

'S'pose, yeah.'

Lulu got up reluctantly and allowed herself to be dragged to the door.

'Carl?' I said as he reached for the handle.

He didn't respond for a second and then turned around, blinking.

'Thanks for this,' I said. 'I really appreciate it.'

'Glad to help. See you soon.'

That night, I slept better than I had in months.

34

I HAD TO GET out of there before I lost control, stripped her bare and did all the things to her I'd been dreaming about for so long. When she got that business card out that I'd made for her, I was so surprised I could have fainted. She'd hung onto it all this time. That must mean something. Instead, I managed to not bat an eyelid. Everything so far had run like clockwork. From the first time I saw her, I knew I wasn't wrong to come back.

It surprised me how easy I found it to speak with my Irish accent all the time, even though it was a really bad attempt. An Irish person would suss me straight away. Thankfully, Sarah knew nothing of Irish accents. I only said I was from Derry because of watching Derry Girls. Got to laugh, hadn't you? Where else could I say I was from? Craggy Island like Father Ted? Even though she probably would have believed it and asked me where it was.

Leanne looked up at me sharply as I cracked out laughing, walking home. Excitement was causing adrenalin to run amok, and I felt overcome with giddiness.

'Come on, *Lulu!*' I said. She pulled on the lead and shook her head, hating the collar. 'You have to leave it on. Even Sarah said. I'm not picking you up. You need the exercise.'

My mind turned to the project I'd agreed to do for Sarah. Making the business card, and doing her website and portfolio, were easy, but I couldn't draw to save my life.

My only hope was to try and make some sort of stencil from thick card and hope for the best. Sarah was so impressed with the business card I did back then, but it had taken two minutes to knock up with Canva.

Looked like I'd be staying up all night trying to work out what the hell I was going to do, although I had a few days' grace until the plywood arrived. I'd think of something. I always did.

35

I STOPPED THE FOOD mixer and glared at Claire whilst also trying not to laugh.

'I've never met anyone as nosy as you,' I said.

'It's a fair question.' She took a tray of quiches out of the oven while Ellie put another batch in. 'Isn't it? What do *you* think?' She looked over at Ellie.

'Keep me out of it.' Ellie closed the oven door. 'But, yeah, I'd quite like to know if you fancy him, too.'

I tutted. 'You two are always ganging up on me. Why is it so important whether or not I have a man in my life? Last time I looked, you were single, too, Claire. Why don't we pick on you for once and leave me alone?'

'For your information, I'm thinking of becoming gay. I'm off men since that last tosser I went out with.'

'You can't just decide to be gay. You either are or you aren't. It's not something you get to choose,' I said, laughing.

I split the chocolate cake mix between three tins and banged them down hard on the worktop to get rid of any air. Claire opened the oven door for me to slide them straight in.

'God, we're like a well-oiled machine,' she said, closing the door as I turned away, my face flushed from the rush of heat that had escaped. I set the timer and wiped my hands on my apron, one of the new black ones with the pink *Delish* logo I'd got for us. Jenny liked them so much

I'd ordered some for her and Sandra, and the rest of the staff in London.

'Well?' Claire asked, her hands on her hips. 'Do you fancy him or not?'

'You're like a dog with a bloody bone! Have you got nothing else to do because I'm sure I can find you something?'

'I'm just interested, that's all. Because I care,' she said, kissing the air and blowing it my way.

Ellie checked her ice cream in the ice cream maker. 'Half an hour,' she said to herself.

'So he's starting tonight, then? Just you and him alone in here together?' Claire pulled a lascivious face and Ellie laughed.

The big sheet of ply came yesterday, and I'd stashed it in the kitchen, propped up against a fridge.

'Looks like it,' I said, testing a cold lemon traybake with my finger. It sprang back nicely. I knocked it out of the tin, onto a board, ready to drizzle.

'She does like him. I can tell,' Claire said, nudging Ellie.

'Leave her alone. If she wants to turn into an old spinster, it's her business,' Ellie said.

'Exactly,' I replied, then frowned at the barb. 'Hey, I'm not an old spinster.'

'Yet,' said Claire.

'So what about your love life, then? I think you're the one who fancies him. I've seen you sneaking glances at him as you walk away. Checking to see if he's watching your arse?'

Claire burst out laughing. 'What if I did fancy him? Even with his scar and his weird, scratty beard, he is attractive, don't you think? There's just something about him. And I adore that dog. I want to run off with her.'

I shrugged. 'I can't say I've noticed if he's attractive or not. Although I do like the dog.'

'Would you sleep with him if he came onto you?' she asked. Behind her, Ellie snorted.

'Oi! What's funny? I have had sex, you know!' I said to Ellie, indignantly.

'Not as innocent as you seem, then?' she said. A bit of pinned-up blue hair fell down around her face and she blew it out of the way.

'I don't come across as innocent. Do I? Wow! I've never been called that before.'

I shook my head. I loved the banter between us; these two were fast becoming the sisters I never had. At the thought of how close we were, I felt a pang of guilt. Leanne rang last night, and I never rang her back. I was always so tired after work it was all I could do to stay awake until nine. She sent a text this morning, asking if I was okay. I wished she wouldn't worry so much. She wanted to come up for a visit soon and I couldn't wait to see her. Ellie and Claire would love her.

But she was the one who knew the true me, and everything about me. Claire and Ellie still knew nothing. of any importance Did that make me a true friend when I hid so much from them? Maybe not, but here, where no one knew me, I felt I could truly breathe and relax.

I mixed up the drizzle for the lemon traybake. The cafe would be open for breakfast in fifteen minutes, although no one would be buying cake. The croissants and bagels were what people came in for.

I was looking forward to Carl starting the project. I just had to get a work day out of the way first. Claire and Ellie's banter carried on over my head, but I was thinking about the design now. I didn't know how he was going to do it. What would I say to him if it was crap? But it was done now, and in a few hours, he'd be here.

***

He arrived half an hour before I shut up shop and I noticed Claire's eyes sparkled at the sight of him. My God! Did she really like him? I was just joking before.

245

'Hi,' he said, coming through the door. He was carrying a toolbox and a carrier bag, his customary cap on his head. No glasses this time. Lulu must be in the backpack, as usual. She'd have to stay in there as the cafe still had customers lingering over coffee. He made straight for the back, hung his coat up, and sat down at the table in the corner. Then he pulled a large envelope out of the carrier bag and tipped it up. As he spread sheets of paper out, I watched him. He was hunched over them, engrossed in what he was doing.

'Want me to stay and help?' Claire asked, wiggling her eyebrows. 'If you don't want him, I'll have a crack.'

'Ssh! He'll hear you! Stay if you want, yeah. I don't mind.'

She frowned. 'Oops, no, I can't. Forgot. Got a date.'

I gaped at her. 'A date? Who with? Male or female? After all you said earlier!'

She laughed and sauntered away, her hands full of empty crockery. What a bloody dark horse! I'd get all the juicy details out of her tomorrow, by nagging her, like she did me. I doubted it'd take much nagging, though.

I followed her into the kitchen to make Carl a coffee. It was the least I could do. As Claire walked past me, she said, 'I may be a little late in the morning. If I've been up all night. You never know. This one is proper hot.'

'I'll dock your wages a pound for every minute you're late.'

'God! Slave driver! He might be worth it.'

I pulled a face at her as I went back out. Ellie had finished mopping the floor and opened the door for the last customers to go out into the dark afternoon.

'Look, is it alright if I get off now? Darcey has a birthday party she needs picking up from and she wanted me to do it, not Mum. I don't know why.'

'Of course. You get off. We're just about done here, anyway. See you tomorrow.'

Claire had finished up in the kitchen and was also eager to leave. Typical, after all the ribbing this morning. I thought she was going to stay and play gooseberry. Not that there'd be anything to see.

'Enjoy your hot date,' I said, as she put the dishcloth down and dried her hands.

'I will. Enjoy yours!' she said in a loud whisper.

'Just go,' I whispered back. 'And be in bright and early.'

'Yes, Mum!' She laughed, and I went to make Carl's coffee. The shop door caught in a gust of wind and slammed as she left. Now it was just me and him. When I took it through, he was still engrossed in his sketchings or etchings or whatever the hell they were. A little shiver passed through me like a jolt of electricity at the thought of us alone together, but I ignored it.

'Oh, thanks,' he said as I put his coffee down.

'Anything to eat? There's a bit of cake left over.'

'Oh, ta. I wouldn't say no.'

'I'll just get it.'

My hand trembled as I placed the leftover piece of coffee and walnut cake on a plate for him. *Get a grip!* When I got back out, Lulu was trotting around. I hated myself, but my first thought was 'What if she needs to pee?'

'She's just been to the loo, in case you were wondering. I had her in the park first,' he called out, still not looking up.

It was uncanny. I wasn't going there.

'I trust her,' I said, sitting at the opposite side of the table. 'So, what's the plan?'

'I need the piece of ply. Where is it?'

'Ooh, I forgot about that. I'll get it. It's just in here.'

I hurried into the kitchen and was just pulling it out when I felt him close behind me.

'Here, I can take it,' he said, reaching around me to grab it. His hand brushed my stomach.

My pulse galloped, and I just stopped myself from flinching. I needed to stop acting like a nervous wreck. He'd think I was mad.

'Sorry,' he said, hauling it away. 'I didn't mean to scare you just then.'

I tried to calm my ragged breathing. 'It's okay.'

'Are you alright? You seem a bit jumpy, if you don't mind me saying.'

'I'm fine, thanks. You just startled me, that's all.'

He took another step back and put the board down. 'Would you rather do this with someone else here? You don't really know me, after all. I should have thought of that before saying I'd come here after work. It was a bit stupid of me.'

'You don't know me, either, do you? What if I'm some mad, murdering axe-woman?'

His eyebrows shot up. 'Sounds interesting. I might like it.'

We both laughed, and it relieved some of the tension. He carried the plywood board out of the kitchen and pulled four tables together. Then he lay the board on top of them and removed out what looked like bits of a cardboard stencil from the carrier bag.

'Looks interesting. What is it?' I asked.

He shuffled them into some sort of order. 'I made stencils. It was the only thing I could think of. I hope it works.'

I sat down and watched him as he concentrated. There was something about a man deep in thought that was mesmerising to watch. Did I look the same when I was making or planning something new to bake? Maybe I did.

He wore a short-sleeved T-shirt, and I studied the Celtic tattoo on his arm. It was so well-defined and dark. When was it done?

'Is that new?' I asked. 'Your tattoo?'

'Nah, had it ages,' he said, and continued arranging the stencils. He tapped the board. 'I need to paint this first.'

'What's your other tattoo of?' I asked, nodding at the one on his left bicep that had been half-hidden every time I'd tried to see what it was.

'Oh. That.' He lifted up his sleeve to expose what looked to be an eagle with outstretched wings coming in to land. It covered his bicep and went up to his shoulder. His skin was golden, even under his sleeve.

'Is it an eagle?'

'Yeah.'

'It's good. Where did you get it done?'

'Some parlour in the arse-end of nowhere. He was a good tattooist, though.' He laughed, releasing his sleeve.

'I can paint the board now, if it'll help,' I said.

'Yeah, that would help. Good.' He stood in front of the wall, where the board was going to go, looking up at it, measuring the space with his eyes.

There was a small cleaning cupboard at the back of the kitchen, where I put the leftover paint from decorating, along with rollers, trays and brushes. I went to fetch them, switching on the radio as I came back. Heart FM played softly in the background.

'What sort of music do you like?' I said, placing the mauve tin of paint onto the board.

'Oh, anything really. I'm not that much of a music buff. This'll do nicely.' He leaned over the table again.

My eyes traced the curve of his lower body in his well-fitting jeans. The background noise of the radio hopefully muffled the loud crashing of my heart against my ribs.

'Damn,' I said. 'Forgotten the screwdriver for the lid.'

He reached into his toolbox and passed one over, then went back to studying the wall. I prised the lid off the paint and stirred it with the old wooden spoon I'd used before.

He moved the stencils off the board and onto another table while I poured some paint into a small tray. Just a year ago, I wouldn't have had a clue how to decorate anything; nor would I have cared to learn. Internet shopping, baking, and setting up my business were my only interests. Now, with my business on hold for the moment, baking was the only one that remained. I left the internet shopping habit behind ages ago. It had proved too dangerous.

It took only a few minutes for me to roller the board.

'It dries really fast. I can probably do another coat in half an hour,' I said.

'Come and look at this and tell me what you think,' he said. Lulu began scratting at something over by the door.

I put the paint roller into a plastic bag to keep it from drying out and went over to him. I felt like a small child at the side of him. He could crush the life out of me anytime he wanted. And I could smell his body, masculine and strong, but also fresh sweat mingled in there. Was he nervous too? He appeared so composed, but his shyness was evident. I swallowed hard and concentrated.

He arranged the stencils in the right order, and I read the words.

Life's too short not to eat the brownie!

The letters were in a fancy script, not too dissimilar to our brand name. Angled slightly upwards, it was stunning. It must have taken him ages to cut out the letters.

'Hope you don't mind. I changed 'a brownie' to 'the brownie'. I thought it sounded better,' he said.

I couldn't tell the difference.

'It's great,' I said. 'I really like it. Are you going to draw inside the letters or outside?' I noticed he'd cut out the middle of the letters, so he could trace inside if he wanted. Or probably if I wanted.

'What do you think would be best?' He straightened up and stared straight into me with his piercing green eyes.

My heart gave a fierce slam. It had been such a long time since I'd felt like this.

'I wasn't sure. Doing it this way gives us both options,' he continued, his voice sounding far away in my ears.

I leaned forward for a better look, trying to gauge whether it would look better with chunky or fine lettering.

At the door, Lulu was still scratting the floor. I hoped it wasn't a rat or mouse she could smell. I turned back to the stencils.

'Hmm. I think outside, so the lettering is bigger. Really make it stand out, so people can see it when they come in,' I said.

He nodded. 'I'll do it like that, then.' He took a step away from me and I breathed out. 'Lu!' he said sharply. 'Come and lie down. You're making Sarah nervous.'

It wasn't the dog making me nervous. He patted the banquette seat, and she ran over, leaping onto it. Then she settled down.

I looked from her to him. 'When you said you'd been through a lot together, you and Lulu, what did you mean?'

His body stilled completely, and I wondered if I'd said the wrong thing. He was frozen like stone. Goosebumps covered his arms. Then he thawed, smiled at me and said, 'We've been through some stormy seas together. That's all I can say.'

Mysterious. But if he didn't want to tell me, I couldn't force him. Was he speaking literally or figuratively? Must be figuratively, surely?

Something about him felt like it had shut down. I'd asked far too many questions, but I couldn't help it. It was like poking a snake with a stick to see how far you could go before it struck.

While we waited for the paint to dry, I made us some hot chocolate, more for something to do than anything else. My attempts at conversation were fast drying up. I asked him questions, but he was guarded, and it was like pulling teeth. In the end, the board turned out to be too wet to put another coat of paint on. I'd stupidly put too thick a coat on it the first time. Despite that, it was patchy, with poor coverage in other places. It would have been better if Claire had done it.

'Damn. I think I need more practise at this painting lark,' I said, staring down at it. 'I wanted to get cracking on the main bit, transferring the letters.'

'I don't think we can get much else done tonight,' he said, running a forefinger lightly over a damp patch of paint. It came off mauve. 'Looks like we'll have to leave this overnight. How about you put another coat on tomorrow and I'll come over the night after that, to start with the letters?' He drank the last of his chocolate and put his mug on the table, his tongue darting out to run across his top lip.

'Okay. We'll do that.' I tried not to show how disappointed I was, either that tonight was going to be cut short or that he wouldn't be coming tomorrow, as previously planned.

With nothing more we could do, he clipped Lulu's lead on and bid me goodnight. For a second, I thought he might linger by the door and I'd get a feeling one way or the other if anything else was on the cards. But he didn't.

'Night,' he said, disappearing through the door.

When he'd gone, I went upstairs, locked the door and checked the windows were locked, even though I hadn't opened any in weeks.

With nothing else to do, I poured a glass of wine and went onto the internet, spending two hours as Cakemom, outlining issues I was having with my make-believe family. I'd invented a partner or OH (Other Half), as they were referred to, who did little to help me with the chores or looking after the baby. I said I was emotionally and physically drained, and a barrage of vitriol towards him, and support for me, came straight back.

You can do this
You are worth more
You are strong
Make him change

What a load of crap! For a while, my fictitious problems were worse than my real ones, and that made me feel better. Maybe worrying about problems that weren't real was a sign of cracking up. Perhaps I was going mad, and that was all there was to it.

As I climbed into bed, I realised I'd forgotten to ring Leanne again. I texted her to apologise, and the phone rang straight away.

'Sarah! Where've you been hiding? It's like getting hold of the Scarlet Pimpernel!'

'I'm so sorry, Lee; I've been so busy. I'm up at five and in bed by nine. Most days, I'm so tired I can't even remember my own name.'

'God! Are you okay? It sounds awful.'

I laughed. 'But that's the thing, you see. I'm loving it. Every single second.'

A sigh came down the line. 'Well, thank God for that! I thought you were going to tell me you'd made the wrong decision and was regretting it.'

'No way. And I can't wait for you and Sam to come up. I'm dying to show you around. I've planned an itinerary.'

I thought of how Ben had laughed at Kate for doing the exact same thing.

'That's another thing; Sam can't come now. He's got some extra training to do, some discipline I can't pronounce.'

'Lol! I bet it's gynaecology,' I said, laughing. 'He'll use you as a subject when you get back.'

'Stop it! That's not funny. I'll never want to sleep with him again.'

'Oh, well, it's a shame he can't make it. But it'll be like old times, just the two of us.' I liked Sam, he was great, but now we could do girly things without worrying about him being bored.

'So what else is going on up there? Anything important to note?' she asked in a measured voice.

I read straight between her ill-drawn lines; she was really asking, '*Have you met anyone you like?*' I thought of Carl. Of his smell, his scar, his tattoos. His intense green eyes. And I thought of what Lee would say if she knew.

'No,' I said. 'Nothing important to note here. Anyway, tell me if you fancy doing anything in particular when you come up. There's something called *The Chocolate Story* I forgot to tell you about.'

Usually quick to spot a misdirection, surprisingly Leanne missed it.

Or perhaps I was just getting better at lying.

36

IT WAS OFFICIAL. I was shit at painting. I'd been up half the night, trying to keep inside the lines with a stupid paintbrush that had a mind of its own. The whole thing looked dire, and my tiredness and tetchiness was only making it worse.

I hurled the brush across the room and it narrowly missed Leanne, who leaped from her bed in fright and looked at me with accusing eyes. A small splodge of black paint slowly ran down the wall. I'd have to fuckin well clean the mess up now.

'Sorry,' I said to the dog, as she gave me a wide berth to jump on the settee. 'It just looks crap. What am I gonna do?' I eyed the hateful letters on the table before me.

She turned around and presented me with her arse, before flopping down on a cushion.

I got a damp cloth and wiped the wall, then picked up the brush and ran it under the tap. Good job the floor was laminate. I wiped that too. A sample of wallpaper was rolled out on the small dining table and the reverse side of it was covered in my mess of black paint. I wished Sarah had chosen a one-word slogan instead of a whole phrase. I could draw round the stencil in pencil okay, then I messed it up every time trying to paint a fine outline.

I leaned closer to it, studying the outline. It was patchy, sort of splotchy-looking, like a five-year-old had done it. I wouldn't want to pay good money for it on the wall of *my* shop, if I had one. My fingers drummed on the table as I thought what to do. There must be something. At this rate, I'd run out of time. I was due back at the cafe, to make a start on it. The mess mocked me.

But one pleasant thought hit me. Sarah, despite acting like a frightened animal at times, liked me. She was attracted to me, I could tell. But how far should I go in reciprocating? If I pounced on her, she'd likely run a mile. My shy act was getting to me, too. How did chronically shy people ever get laid? The whole thing was like walking on landmines with no equipment for detecting them. One false move and I'd be blown up.

I'd been so restrained whenever I'd been with her. All I wanted to do was shout, 'But it's me!' and kiss her. I could never do that and it was driving me crazy. I could barely think straight or look her in the eye when we were together, for fear of what she might see. There had still been no hint of recognition from her, but it made me sweat thinking about it. I'd had to get some stronger deodorant. But there was something between us still, even with me no longer being me. There was no denying it, and it just strengthened my knowledge that we belonged together. I was right all along. Not for one second had I regretted coming back.

I had to be careful, though. She kept firing questions at me, and I was having to think carefully about everything I said. One slip and the game would be up. I leaned back and closed my eyes, letting my imagination go wild, thinking about her naked. It was horny as hell. But my thoughts were interrupted when, suddenly, the answer to the stencil problem hit me. It was bloody obvious and so easy I couldn't believe I hadn't thought of it before.

I got up and reached for my coat. Leanne jumped up and wagged her tail. Seemed I was forgiven, then.

'Come on, dog,' I said. 'We're off to the shops.'

37

'I NEED TO NIP out at half four,' I said.

'No problem,' Ellie lifted the bulging bag out of the bin in the kitchen and tied the top. 'Will you be back before five?'

'Oh, yeah. I'll only be ten minutes.'

I noticed Claire, busy loading the dishwasher at the other end of the kitchen, didn't ask me where I was going. She was in a bad mood because her hot date hadn't shown the other night. She hadn't said a lot, but it had really knocked her confidence. I think she really liked him. Or, at least, she really fancied him. She wasn't looking for love or commitment, but she was still upset. It had definitely hurt her pride. She closed the dishwasher and went back into the cafe.

'Do you think she'll be okay?' I asked Ellie. 'She's awfully quiet.'

'Yeah. She's coming to us for tea tonight; Jeb's cooking. Then, no doubt, we'll crack open some wine. I'm sure I'll hear all about it then.'

I forgot sometimes that Ellie and Claire were close friends outside of work. And I knew that, to them, despite us getting on well together, I was still their boss. If anyone could pull Claire out of her sulk, it was Ellie. I'd leave her to it.

At half past four, I pulled my coat on and squeezed past the man who was fitting the new grey Roman blinds to the front windows and door. I'd had to drag the Christmas tree out of his way. He was almost done, and they looked amazing. He smiled as I went past.

'I just need to nip out for five minutes. Will you still be here when I get back?' I asked.

'Yes. I'm just about to start packing up now,' he said. 'I'll be about fifteen minutes. What do you think?'

'I love them. You've done a brilliant job. Thank you so much.'

He turned away and started to gather his things up as I left. Ellie and Claire were more than capable of coping with any last-minute customers that might come in. Sometimes it scared me that without those two, I couldn't run the business. The thought of either of them leaving made me break out in a sweat.

It was drizzling, so I pulled my hood up. I scoped all around in every direction before I moved off. I didn't seem to be able to break the habit of checking I wasn't being watched or followed. Perhaps I never would, and I'd just have to get used to it.

I hurried down the road and around the corner to Boots Chemist, which took all of three minutes, and closed the door behind me. The shop was empty, and I scoured the shelves while the assistant behind the counter was busy doing something. He smiled at me, then disappeared into the back. I found what I wanted and took it to the counter, feeling self-conscious about my purchase. The assistant, however, didn't bat an eyelid as he dropped the ovulation testing kit into a bag and handed it to me.

'Thanks,' I said, tucking it into my handbag and zipping it up.

On the way back, I glanced into a few shop windows, but nothing caught my eye. I'd barely been in any shops since I'd got here. I hadn't had the time. But, deep down, I didn't really care about possessions like I used to. I passed Humpty Dumpty, my favourite shop that sold baby things, and ignored it. I needed to get back, as Carl was coming round to work on the project. Once again, at the thought of him, my heart speeded up. I'd hoped it would have passed by now, but it hadn't. I was still like a cat on hot bricks whenever he was around. Tonight, I was going to play it cool.

When I got back to the cafe, I nipped upstairs to my flat and refreshed my make up. Then I wiped my underarms with a cleansing wipe, changed my top and put on fresh jeans. Back downstairs, I mucked in with the cleaning up and waited for him to come.

He was late, and Claire and Ellie had left long before he arrived.

'I thought you'd changed your mind,' I said, opening the door for him when he finally knocked.

A gust of wind entered the cafe along with him, and I forced the door shut against it, then locked it.

'Where's Lulu?' I asked. His backpack was flat and empty.

'She's in training. Learning to stay on her own. Sorry I'm late; we fell asleep.' He held his hands up.

'I'll forgive you. Just this once. Are you ready to start work, then?'

He slipped off his coat, and I watched the muscles in his shoulder blades flex and release as he hung it up on the hooks on the back wall. His beard seemed less patchy today. And thicker and darker.

'So,' he said, adjusting his baseball cap before turning to me and rubbing his hands together. 'Let's get started.'

I'd already got the board laid out, and I'd painted it again. It was a good, solid colour now, and ready to work on. He ran his hand over it and nodded. 'Nice job.'

He arranged the stencils on it and asked if I was happy. I leaned over, close to him, our bodies almost touching, and studied the board. The words were on two lines and pointed upwards at a jaunty angle, like Santa's sleigh in a Christmas night sky.

'Yes! I love it!' I said.

He stepped back and snapped a picture of it with his phone. 'For future reference,' he said, sliding it back into his pocket.

'You could have brought Lulu,' I said. 'I don't mind.'

'She's got to learn to share me.' He broke into a grin.

It took me aback. It was the most I'd seen him smile. He seemed more relaxed and less shy. In turn, it relaxed me.

I went to the front windows of the cafe and pulled down all the new blinds, cocooning us in our own private world. He looked at me and smiled as I walked back over to him. It made my heart thud once, hard, before settling back down. I could do this. I could show him I was interested. I was in control.

'The new blinds look great, by the way,' he said.

'Thanks. I agree.'

I sat on the tabletop next to him, a tiny bit too close, as he rummaged around in his rucksack.

'Ta da!' he said, pulling out a black marker pen.

'What?'

'You wouldn't believe the trouble I've had, trying to get a good edge on the letters with a paintbrush. I just can't do it. But with this…' he waved it around in front of me, 'I can get a good, thick outline. I'm filling it in with black paint, anyhow, so you'll never see it.'

'Sounds like a good idea. How long have you spent trying the other way?'

'Oh! You do *not* want to know.'

Maybe I wouldn't ask, then. He looked a bit tired. I hoped he hadn't been up half the night trying to get it right.

I shuffled around on the table, noting the way his eyes travelled up my legs before returning to the board. He was now applying spray mount to stick the letters to the board before drawing around them, first in pencil, then in black marker. I flicked my hair over one shoulder and angled my body towards him to see what he would do. His drawing hand stopped, then resumed, leaving a tiny, barely there break in the smooth line.

'I'll make us some coffee. Anything to eat?' I said, pushing myself off the table.

'No, I'm fine, thanks.'

I turned around to find he'd stopped drawing and was watching me.

'I've put four pounds on since I've been coming here. You're a bad influence,' he said.

The sleeve of his T-shirt was shorter than normal, exposing half the eagle. I wondered if it would take both my hands to encircle his bicep. A longing to trace the outline of the eagle with my fingertips filled me. I dragged my eyes up to his face, and his right hand, holding the pen, dropped down by his side. His eyes were fixed on mine.

'Am I?' I said. I looked his body up and down, slowly and deliberately. 'Sorry.'

With that, I turned back and went into the kitchen. I doubted he'd follow me and try anything. He wasn't sure enough of how I'd react. Also, it was too early. I'd done the test, and I wasn't ovulating yet, even though I'd been sure I was. I would be soon, though; all the signs were there. After all the research about ovulating and getting pregnant after an ectopic, I felt like an expert. Another thing the forums had been brilliant for. So, hopefully, this time, my body wouldn't betray me. I couldn't hold onto a baby last time, could I?

By the end of the evening, all the words on the board were in place and we'd both filled them in with black paint, him from the bottom and me from the top. He was leaning back in his chair, his legs apart, running his eye over the board. The air still crackled with sexual tension from our earlier exchange.

'Have you thought how you want to finish it off?' he asked.

'I've had some ideas. I want to add some silver, some pink, and a slight amount of glitter in the right places, to highlight and add a bit of shadow. Not too much. I'm more into subtle. I don't do brash.'

I caught his eye as I said it, and held it. Then I picked up my phone, surprised to see it was gone ten o'clock. I stretched my arms above my head as I yawned, my early start catching up with me. A draught of cold air hit my stomach, and I glanced down to see a large expanse of skin had been revealed where my top had ridden up. I yanked it back down, but his eyes were glued to where my skin had been seconds earlier. They slowly rose to meet my face, and he shifted in his seat.

'Well,' I said, getting up. 'Sorry. I'm completely knackered. Would you mind if we pack in for tonight? I'm up at five.'

'Course, yeah.' His voice was low, sexy, and rasping. He coughed, clearing his throat, and got up to go. 'Sorry. I forgot. I don't have to be up at the crack of dawn like you do. I'll be off and let you get to bed.'

The questing, probing looks of earlier were gone. I could practically see his feelers withdrawing and the shy persona was back. Good. Kept me in charge.

I opened the door to let him out, keeping my body well away from his. An awkwardness had developed between us. It suited me for the moment.

'Can we leave it a day or two?' I asked. 'I need to think about what I want to do with it next and I don't have much time in the day. You've seen how full on we are, with Christmas and everything.'

'Of course, yes. Ring me when you're ready, if you want.'

'Okay. Thank you. I'll see you soon.'

I locked up behind him and went upstairs. After a long, hot bath and a glass of wine, I sat in front of my laptop and ran my fingers over the tape covering my webcam. In one swift movement, I ripped it away, like a plaster off a cut.

'Come on, then, you bastard,' I said.

Not long after, I fell into a long, refreshing sleep, troubled by no monsters at all.

38

SHE'D BEEN FLIRTING WITH me like crazy. It wasn't like me, but I didn't know what to do. Should I take her up on it or let her do the running? The old me would have had no trouble diving in, taking what he wanted, then leaving. A few hours of pleasure then thanks, see you around. But not this time. Never with her.

Leanne jumped onto the bed from nowhere, knocking the cup of tea in my hand. It almost slopped over.

'Bloody hell, dog! Watch it!'

She wagged her tail. She didn't do repentant. I never used to either, until I met Sarah, but now, I was sorry for a lot of things. I was especially sorry for how everything had turned out, namely me having to pretend to be someone else in order to spend time with her. And if we did go to bed, how far did I take it? I hadn't really thought about that until now. Should I make different moves, go faster or slower, try to sound different? It was all instinctive, so how did you change that? Or would she be so into it she wouldn't notice?

The board project we'd been working on was almost finished, and that threw up another problem: how did I continue seeing her with no excuse to go round? Especially if she decided to leave it at that. I could be a customer, sure, but I couldn't live with just that. I had no job, an unstable income, a temporary home; it could all end tomorrow. Thankfully, the women back in Brazil were still bringing money in, but I worried constantly that it could end. If the scam was uncovered, and most were eventually, that'd be it. I wasn't there to keep on top of things and I didn't like not being one step ahead. It unnerved me. The women in Brazil thought I was still over there, and that I'd been seriously ill in hospital and was recuperating. No doubt they'd be expecting me to walk through the door at any time.

I sighed, tired of thinking about it, and Leanne whined for her breakfast.

'Alright, alright, slave driver,' I grumbled, getting out of bed and going to feed her.

She hadn't properly forgiven me for leaving her alone in the flat the other night when I went to the cafe. When I got back, she was wet through all down her chest. I think it was slaver and spit from anxiety. It was so bad I had to put her in the shower and give her a good wash, and it had taken her ages to stop trembling. I'd better not risk leaving her again. What if she whined or barked for hours? No one had complained, though. I think the old boy upstairs was deaf, judging by the volume he had his telly, so he'd be a fine one to talk if he collared me about it. If I mentioned his telly, he wouldn't have a leg to stand on, but I'd rather it didn't become an issue.

I opened a tin of dog food into her bowl and put it on the floor. She dived on it and I leaned back against the worktop, watching her, scratching my beard. It was due for trimming, but it did look and feel better since I'd stopped with the dye. I still bleached my hair, though, and kept it brutally short with some hair clippers I brought back from Brazil. If I stopped that, I might look too much like my old self.

I picked up the permanent marker pen from the worktop, took off the cap, then replaced it. Outlining the stencil with this had been a good idea. It had worked well, even if some purists would consider it cheating. She'd texted me yesterday and asked if I could come tonight. It had been four long days since I'd seen her. Tonight, we would finish the board. I think she was planning on doing most of the work, by what she'd said. That suited me. I wasn't faffing about with glitter and such like. It'd end up a right mess; I was far too heavy-handed for anything like that. Besides, I was more than happy to sit and watch her.

I got back into bed and scoured job websites on my laptop. Still nothing jumped out at me, but I was going to have to get something soon. I leaned back on the pillows and turned on the TV. With nothing interesting to do until tea-time, it was going to be a long afternoon.

It turned out to be just that. At five thirty sharp, I was at the door to the café, after wandering the streets for the last forty minutes. The other two were still there, just walking back into the kitchen. Damn! Should have left it a bit longer until they'd left. I kept forgetting about them. They were all meaningful glances and nudges. I didn't know why. Had Sarah said she liked me or something? God! That would be fantastic, and it would take all the guesswork out of it for me. One minute she was hot, then the next, lukewarm. I didn't know where I was with her, but it was definitely keeping me on my toes. As soon as I felt it would be safe to kiss her, she turned away, and I'd be left wondering if I'd imagined it.

One thing I was absolutely positive about now, though, was that she didn't have the foggiest idea who I was. The tattoos, the scar, and the beard had all done their job, along with my new accent, eye colour, the different aftershave I used even though I no longer shaved, and my new way of walking. The way I moved had been the hardest thing of all to keep consistent when I was around her. Thankfully, I'd got used to the contact lenses now, and most of the time I forgot they were there. I had to take them out overnight, though. I'd tried sleeping with them in and it didn't work. But if I ever spent the night with Sarah, I'd just have to put up with the itching and the redness. She couldn't ever see me without them.

When I opened the cafe door, Sarah looked up and smiled at me. She looked fantastic with her long, wavy black hair flowing down over one shoulder. I used to wrap her hair around my hand when I was fucking her. She loved it, just that little bit of restraint. She was wearing a tight, lowish top and skinny jeans. A frilly, little cardigan thing covered her bare arms. I imagined ripping it off. It would take very little effort on my part. It was taking a lot more not to. My hands twitched at the thought of twining them in her hair and pulling, firm but not too hard. The way she liked it. Just enough to expose her neck and throat to my lips. Then I'd move further down.

'Hi,' she said.

'Hey.'

'Oh, Lulu's here. Good. I missed her the other night.'

'She certainly missed coming here,' I said. 'She was in a right state when I got home. Shivering and slobbering. It was awful.'

'Oh, you poor little thing.' Sarah took the bag from me and lifted Leanne out of it. Leanne milked the moment, glaring at me as Sarah kissed the top of her head. 'It's like cuddling a real-life teddy bear,' she said.

The other women reappeared, coats buttoned up.

'We'll get off, then. Bye Carl,' the blue-haired lass said.

'Bye,' I said.

The other smiled and nodded, but didn't say anything. She looked a bit miserable, if anything. Then the door closed behind them, and it was just me and her. The blinds were already down. They were thick, good quality. No one could see through them from outside. I'd checked. We could shag right here on a table and no one would see. The thought of someone's scone sitting right where her arse could have been made me stifle a smile.

'What?' she asked.

'Nothing. I'm just happy to be here.'

She laughed, and I fought to keep my eyes above her neck. It was going to be a losing battle with her wearing that top. Unless she'd done it deliberately. Had she done it deliberately? If she had, the signs would be loud and clear. Please God, let her have worn it on purpose!

'Oh, do you want anything to eat or drink before we get started?' she said.

'Coffee would be good. And I'm a bit peckish, to tell you the truth, if there's anything going.'

'Coming right up. You eat anything, don't you?' she said with a laugh.

Fuuuuck! I'd screwed up. The old me ate anything. I should have been pickier when she'd fed me before.

'Um, I don't, actually.'

She was halfway to the kitchen when she stopped and turned, raising her eyebrows. Her arms were crossed underneath her boobs, pushing them up deliciously. 'Oh? What don't you like?'

She must be doing this on purpose. *Don't look at them!* She walked into the kitchen and I followed her.

'I don't like dates. Or prunes. Or liver. God, I hate liver. And all kinds of, what do you call it—offal. Tripe and all that stuff. Urgh. Makes me sick.'

'Urgh, yeah. I can't eat that either. I didn't know you don't like dates, though. You've had sticky toffee pudding here before now.' She bent over, with her head in the fridge, looking for something. She straightened up, holding milk.

'Has that got dates in? I didn't know.'

'It's full of them,' she said.

I shrugged in a 'I'm just a helpless man' type of way. 'Ah, I don't like them on their own, though,' I said. Not true. I'd just blurted out the first thing that came into my mind. I loved them. At Christmas, I could eat boxes of them.

'Try a juicy, fresh Medjool date and you'll change your mind,' she said.

'Alright. I will.'

I watched as she made me coffee, and a tea for herself.

'What don't you like?' I asked, getting with the game. 'Food-wise, I mean.'

She stirred the drinks, her upper body swaying gently with each rotation of the spoon. It was hypnotic, like a snake charming a mongoose. I was the mongoose. Christ, I just wished she'd bite me and get it over with. One of these days, I was going to explode.

'Um, let's see. I don't like cheap margarine, that muck you cook with instead of proper butter.'

'No, that would never do,' I chided, giving a mock shiver. 'The very thought.'

She grinned at me. 'Or Marmite. I can't eat that. Or Bovril. I don't like some seafood, either. Those cockles and whelks you get at the seaside. All vinegary and tough. Yuck! I'm not big on mushrooms, too.'

Did I know that? I didn't remember her ever telling me she didn't like mushrooms. Then again, she always said I wasn't the best listener. Well, according to every woman I'd ever known, they all said that about men, didn't they? *You never listen! You always leave the toilet seat up!* And so on and so on.

She pushed my coffee over to me. 'There's some bread left. I could make you a sandwich.'

'Thanks. But listen, you don't have to. I don't expect to get fed every time I come.' That should get me brownie points.

'It's no bother. I can't sell it tomorrow, anyway, as it won't be fresh. Ellie was going to take it home. She must have forgotten.'

'Why don't you sit down and I'll make my own sandwich?' I said.

She stood there hesitantly, and I walked over to her, put my hands on her shoulders and pushed her down gently until her knees bent and she sat on a stool. Her tiny shoulders felt barely there, through her thin cardigan.

'Feels weird, though. Me doing nothing and you getting food.' She cradled her cup of tea in both hands.

'Just tell me where everything is.'

'What are you having on it?'

'What is there?'

'Um, cheese—'

'That'll be fine. In the fridge?'

She nodded. It wasn't too hard to find everything and knock up a quick sandwich. I cut it in two and handed half to her.

'I should pay for this. Or you should take it out of my fee.'

She ate her half without complaint. I remembered she loved cheese. She once said, 'I have to have it every day or I'll die.'

I'd replied the same, but replaced 'cheese' with 'you'.

'So, we'll finish it tonight, all being well,' she said.

'Mmm. Looks that way.'

'What will you do after? For money, I mean?'

I shrugged. 'Dunno. I've been looking round, but nothing's come up.'

'Perhaps it will, when people see this. I could spread the word. I'm sure shops around here would love bespoke pieces for their interiors. Even if you do cheat on the hand-painted bit! I could put a little label on the bottom corner with your name and number. It could say 'Carl Frost: open for commissions'.'

She underlined the imaginary words in the air.

'Sounds like a good idea. Thanks.'

I lingered over my coffee, wanting to stretch the time with her. Could I make a move on her tonight and kiss her? Would she be horrified and throw me out? Maybe not, judging by the way she was dressed. I could be wrong, but it looked like she'd gone to a bit more trouble than normal.

We went back into the café, and I automatically glanced at the windows. There were no gaps at the edges of the blinds. The old, fun-loving Sarah wouldn't have baulked at getting down and dirty in the shop. It would have fuelled her sense of adventure, but now I wasn't sure. I couldn't read her like I used to. She'd changed. There again, why wouldn't she have, after everything she went through? I had.

My eyes dropped to her stomach. It was hard to imagine the seed I'd planted growing in there. It was hardly there before it was gone. I couldn't imagine what that must have been like for her. She didn't have time to get used to it before she'd lost it. The Sarah I knew would have been devastated.

She dragged the board onto the tables and I grabbed one end to help her, hauling it into place. She couldn't stop looking at my arms; was it the tattoos or the muscles she was drawn to? She'd loved my physique. Couldn't get enough of it. But now, I was half the size I used to be, in terms of muscle. And it had to stay that way.

She took the lead on the design. In the end, I mainly passed her things and watched her, and just enjoyed being with her, as always. I'd missed this so much when I was hiding out in Brazil. It felt right, the way it should be. But it was far from right. She thought I was someone else. I watched her happily doing the detail work; bits of glitter here, a shadow or highlight there with a fine paintbrush. She was always like that when she was decorating one of her cakes.

'I'm addicted to videos on YouTube and stuff on Pinterest. I wouldn't have had a clue about this sort of thing before,' she said.

The finished result did look good, I had to admit, as she stood back to appraise it.

'What do you reckon?' she said.

I folded my arms and squinted, as if I knew what I was on about. 'I love it.'

The last bit of work is what she really needed me for; to fix it to the wall. She stepped back as I did the heavy lifting, but I was aware of her eyes on me the whole time, especially when my T-shirt rode up. It made me feel weak, and I struggled to hold the thing in place long enough to fix it. But finally, it was done.

I stood next to her as we both admired it. Leanne, as ever, was napping on the banquette seating off to one side.

Sarah squealed, and her hands flew to her mouth. Her sensual mouth, capable of giving so much pleasure. At that moment, I ached so bad for her I thought my legs might collapse. But still I stood there. Being someone else. Carl bastard Frost.

'It's turned out better than I ever imagined. Thank you so much.'

'The pleasure has been all mine. But it does look good, doesn't it? I'm pleased with it.'

'I'll get your money,' she said, picking up her handbag and taking some notes from it. She counted it out meticulously, but I didn't care about one pound of it. I needed her. If I couldn't have her, I'd die.

'Thanks,' I said, shoving it into my front pocket.

Did she want me to leave now? Didn't look like it. Instead, she sat on a chair and gestured for me to do the same.

'It'll be weird you not coming here to do this,' she said, leaning forward with her arms on the table. Again with the tits! I tried not to look, but I couldn't help it.

'It will.' I needed to be bolder, so she couldn't fail to get the message. 'I'll be in for coffee, though. And your cakes.'

'That's good. There'll be some freebies coming your way.'

'In that case…'

She laughed, and I held her eye. She didn't look away. I could be wrong, but it looked like a slight shiver just went through her. She slipped off her cardigan. Her body was resplendent in her tight top, and I could see the tiny hairs on her arms standing up.

'Is it just me or is it hot in here?' she asked.

So she hadn't got goosebumps from being cold then.

'It's just you,' I said, leaning back and making myself comfortable.

'I've enjoyed our chats,' she said. 'Sorry if I've seemed a bit like the Spanish Inquisition at times. I'm just interested. Or nosy, as other people call it.'

'Ask me anything you like.' My eyes roamed freely over her body now. I just couldn't help it. And hers were doing the same with mine.

'Are you seeing anyone?' she asked, blushing bright red. 'I've been dying to ask.'

I shook my head. 'Are you?'

'No.'

Leanne let out a soft snore, making us both laugh.

'Fancy another drink? Something a bit stronger?' she asked.

'Definitely.'

She got up to go into the kitchen and brushed past me. There was more than enough space, so it must have been intentional. Then she was gone. Should I follow her? Was she expecting me to?

Paralysed, I sat there, stuck to the seat. Before long, she was back, carrying an open bottle of red wine and two glasses.

'Is this okay?' she asked.

I nodded. I'd drink anything with her. I'd go anywhere with her and do anything for her.

'Yeah,' I said, my voice hoarse and ragged.

She poured, and I couldn't tear my eyes away from her. The feeling, the attraction, wasn't even this strong the first time round, was it?

'Cheers,' she said, her glass clinking with mine.

She was sitting close to me now, her thigh touching mine, just like that night at the Christmas party, the night of the vintage silver dress. Our first kiss. Before it all went so wrong. She didn't move her leg, and I didn't move mine. My mind went into overdrive. She must be feeling it. She had to be. All the signals were there.

'Are you ever going to kiss me or do I have to wait forever?' she said.

I put my glass down. She stood up slowly, and I pulled her onto my knee. Then my lips were on hers, my hands tangled in her hair, and she was making those little noises, like she used to make. I was careful not to do anything I did before, but how did you kiss someone differently? I had no clue. Instead, I just went with it, but not as forceful as the old me. I was more cautious, more tender. But the passion was still there. She must be able to feel it. Her body pressed tightly into mine and it was all her doing. She really wanted this.

She broke away and grinned. 'Thank God for that. I was beginning to think you weren't interested, and I was imagining it. Or maybe that you were gay, and I'd got you wrong.'

I cleared my throat. 'Oh, I'm interested alright. And I'm not gay, thank you very much. I think you're actually pretty amazing.' My Derry accent just got stronger. I'd be saying *begorrah,* and *top of the morning* next.

'Really?' She smiled, relaxed now. She was still on my knee and I kissed her again, for longer this time. I couldn't believe I was actually holding her after all this time. It'd been forever.

'I really, really think you're amazing,' I whispered into her ear. 'Almost as amazing as this wine.'

She gasped and slapped me on the arm. 'The wine is better than me?'

I pulled her back to me. I couldn't stop kissing her. But I daren't go any further tonight. I needed to let her set the pace.

It didn't matter. She was back in my life. Her taking the lead like this had completely taken me by surprise. She had changed.

'I want to see your flat,' she said. 'I've been intrigued to see where you live.'

'Have you? It's most definitely nothing special. But yeah, you're welcome to come round anytime.' *And I'll gladly help you out of those clothes and into my bed.*

'I'd love to get out of here. If I'm not in the cafe, I'm upstairs. I'm beginning to get cabin fever,' she said. 'But my friend is coming up from London in a couple of weeks. I can't wait to see her. And my parents are coming here for Christmas. So, I'll have to pencil you in.'

'Yes, do that. Pencil me in.' I reached past her, picked up the permanent marker pen, and handed it to her. 'Or better still, write me in with that. What's your friend's name, the one coming to see you?'

'Lee. Well, Leanne. She's been my best friend forever.'

At the sound of her name, Leanne looked up sharply, no longer snoring. I didn't react. Dogs did this sort of thing all the time.

'That'll be nice for you. Have you missed her?'

'Yes, I have. But not as much as I thought I would. I've just been so busy since I got here.'

'I had noticed. You never seem to sit down.'

'It's just the way things are at the moment. Listen, though, the cafe is closed on Mondays, now. We've been working seven days to get it up and running, and it can't go on. Poor Ellie barely sees her daughter. I could come round to yours on Sunday after we close, if you want. Then I wouldn't have to be getting up at five on Monday morning.'

Was she suggesting she would sleep over or just that she could stay up late? I searched her face, but I couldn't tell. Whatever. I didn't mind.

'Brilliant.' I grabbed a napkin and a pen and jotted the address down. 'It's not far from here. I could come and get you, if you like. Walk back with you.'

'No, don't be daft. I'll find it. It's not hard these days, is it?'

'No, what with technology and everything.'

275

'I'm curious,' she said. 'How come you're single? I'd have thought a guy like you would have someone in his life?'

'With this?' I pointed at the scar on my face. 'Let's face it, it doesn't make me ideal meet-your-mother material, does it? Anyway, I could say the same about you. Why are you single? You're absolutely stunning, if I may say.'

Her face closed up, and she looked at the floor. 'Well, there was someone, not so long ago. Someone I loved very much. But he hurt me very badly. Almost put me off men for life. There's been no one since. Then I met you.'

'He must have been insane. I would never hurt you. Ever.'

'That's the funny thing. I don't think he meant to. It's complicated.' She shook her head.

'If you want to talk, I'm a good listener.'

She kissed me, her hands either side of my face. Her thumb traced my scar so lightly I could barely feel her touch. Then she ran her thumbs over every bit of my face; my eyelids and eyebrows, my nose, my lips. And finally, my beard.

'I've just realised, I've never seen you without your cap.'

She pulled it slowly from my head, revealing my close-cropped blonde-dyed hair. It was the one thing I'd deliberately kept on. What if she recognised me somehow?

'I wondered what your hair was like.' She brushed a hand over my scalp. I closed my eyes and leaned into her touch.

'What there is of it, you mean.'

'Why do you shave it off? You don't look like you're going thin? There again, my eyes aren't that great!'

I frowned. 'God, you're so blunt.'

'Sorry.' She giggled, her eyes going from my hair to my beard. If she wondered why one was blonde and the other brown, she didn't say.

'I just like it short. It's easier to keep,' I said.

She got off my knee and adjusted her clothes. 'Well, that was interesting. And fun. I've been wondering what it would be like to kiss you since the day I first saw you.'

'Ditto. And what's the verdict?'

'Nice.' She bent down and kissed me again. My eyes snagged on the freckles scattered over her nose. 'But now I have to kick you out.'

'I know, I know,' I grumbled. 'You have to be up at five.'

I put my cap back on. Then I reached out and grabbed her, holding her close. She laughed and let me kiss her again. It felt so natural. And I could do this anytime I liked. She broke away from me.

'Come on, Leanne,' I said to the dog. 'She's kicking us out.'

Her head jerked up. 'Did you just call the dog Leanne?'

I froze. 'I don't know. Did I?'

'Yes.' She giggled.

'It must be because we were talking about your friend earlier.'

'Must be.'

'What's she like, then, your friend?' I asked, as I put my coat on.

'Oh, let's see. She's tall and slender, with fiery ringlets, like in one of those classic paintings. She's like a warrior; she once socked her ex right in the mush! And she's the best friend ever. But she's a pussycat, really. If you ever meet her, you'll love her.' She pulled up the door blind to fumble with the lock.

'I'm sure I will,' I said, even though it choked me.

And then I was out on the street, shivering in the cold, frosty night, the heat she'd created in my body dropping away fast.

I waved as she locked the door and dropped the door blind back down.

'Yeah, I'm fuckin sure I will.'

277

39

IT HAD TO BE tonight. According to the kit, I was ovulating. My temperature had been rising for a few days and I had a nagging pain low down. With me only having one tube, I was banking on it being the right side this month, although, according to what I'd read, it didn't necessarily work like that. The egg with no tube could find its way to the other side. I didn't understand it, but that's what it said online, and I was glad. I was throwing caution to the wind but what was life for, if not for taking some risks?

It was Sunday, early closing, and I was on tenterhooks all day, watching the clock creep around to mid-morning, then lunchtime, then mid-afternoon, then finally, closing time.

All day, Claire and Ellie had been giving me odd looks, wondering why I was so jittery. I hadn't told them a thing and nor was I going to. At least it seemed Claire had got over her rejection and cheered up. She was back to her old self.

The first time they saw the slogan on the board, they absolutely loved it.

'It's brilliant. You two did a good job. I'm impressed,' Ellie had said.

'So am I. I'm not sure I could have done it any better myself,' Claire had said. Praise indeed! Then she'd added,

'So I guess he won't be coming round here much anymore,' and given me the side-eye.

'Dunno. He's a customer. He can do what he likes,' I said.

I almost threw them out of the door at four o'clock, refusing their offer of opening a bottle of wine in the kitchen and relaxing.

'I've got a bit of a headache, actually. I think I'm going to lock up and have a lie down.'

I must be getting better at lying, as they didn't say anything. It didn't make me feel good, though.

When they'd gone, I rushed upstairs, had a quick shower, applied make-up, and put on something sexy. He had to sleep with me. I didn't think he'd object.

I knew roughly where his flat was, with Google maps telling me the way. I left early, wanting to enjoy the walk there to clear my head. The route took me past the Minster and down The Shambles, and I looked in all the shop windows as I passed. It was already dark and only the pubs and restaurants were open, music and laughter spilling out through the doors.

It took me thirty minutes to get to his flat outside the city walls and I stood a few doors down, readying myself. Was I crazy? Probably yes. Should I be doing this? No. Most definitely not. But I wanted my own child filling my arms. I wanted this child.

I took a deep breath and walked up to his door. It opened immediately when I knocked on it. He must have been waiting, as eager as me.

'Come in,' he said, stepping back to let me through.

My phone rang, and I looked at the screen. It was Mum. I'd have to ring her back. If she knew what I was about to do, she would kill me. But she couldn't ever know. No one could.

He leaned forward, pulled me into him and held me like he'd never let go.

'I can't tell you how much I've been looking forward to this,' he said.

Lulu barked furiously, wanting some attention. I broke away and fussed her, giving her a huge cuddle. He stood with his hands shoved in his pockets, shuffling from foot to foot. He looked nervous.

'Let me take your coat,' he said.

I unzipped it and took it off. He breathed in sharply at the sight of my dress, the one that clung in all the right places.

'Wow, you look fantastic! I love your dress.'

'Well, one has to make the effort,' I said. 'You look nice yourself.'

And he did. He was wearing dark blue jeans and a casual short-sleeved shirt in the palest lemon, the top two buttons undone. It showed off his dark skin and his tattoos. Tonight, I'd get to stroke those tattoos, like I'd been dreaming of. Who would have thought tattoos could be so sexy? I'd never particularly liked them before now.

'I can't tell you how happy I am you're here. But I'm really happy you're here,' he said, looking at me like he'd won the lottery.

I stared back at him, deep into his green eyes. The urge to make love to him was so strong I could hardly stand it. But I wasn't going to rush it. I wanted to take my time. But it didn't mean we couldn't have a little fun in the meantime.

He held out his hand for my coat, which I passed him. He went to hang it up on a coat hook near the door, hesitated, then slung it over the back of a chair.

'I hope it doesn't get dog hairs on it,' he said. 'She sheds a little bit, occasionally.'

I shrugged. 'They'll come off.' I didn't care about dog hair.

'Have a seat,' he said, pointing at a slightly grubby cream sofa. 'It's not my furniture, by the way. It's a furnished flat.'

I sat, fiddling with the bottom of my dress.

He hovered in front of me. 'Do you want a drink or anything? I haven't done any food. I thought we could go out.'

'I don't want a drink and I'd love to go out. Or we could just order in. What do you fancy?'

He sat down next to me. 'I fancy you.'

He kissed me so gently I thought I might melt. *Come on, Sarah. Keep your head.*

For the next hour, we cuddled up together on his sofa, hands intertwined, just talking about rubbish, and kissing and touching. I was no longer nervous or scared. Instead of going out to eat, we ordered in some Italian from down the road. It was good, and a relief not to have to bother making it myself.

Neither of us asked the other questions about past loves, childhoods or our backgrounds. It was like some unspoken agreement between us. The clock ticked round slowly, and I savoured every moment, especially the bit where he would take me to bed. Then, finally, after we'd washed up the dishes from our meal and drunk half a bottle of wine each, it was time. We just knew.

He stood, extending his hand, and led me upstairs to a small, unassuming bedroom. I didn't care. I wasn't here for the decor. He let me undress him without trying to take off my clothes and he stood before me, just wearing his boxers. At last, I stroked his skin, tracing his curves and contours while he stood still, like a statue. Then he did the same to me until we were both naked. At that point, I turned out the light, and we worked on touch alone.

'I want to see you,' he said.

'No. Not yet.'

He didn't argue, just kissed me and covered my body with his.

'I won't find a condom in the dark,' he said, pulling away and groping for the lamp.

'You won't need one. I'm on the pill,' I said. 'Just come here.'

He did as I asked, and then he was moving inside me. It was just as I knew it would be. It had to be dark, so he couldn't see the tears in my eyes. If one night was all we'd got, I'd use him until he was wrung out and squeezed dry.

The connection between us, along with the act itself, was fantastic, as I knew it would be. But I knew it wouldn't be happening again. I wanted a baby, nothing else. I didn't want him. Well, I did, but I couldn't have him. I didn't have an issue with having his baby, though. I believed in nurture, not nature. Why would a child take after a parent it had no contact with? I couldn't believe that a baby was born bad; it just didn't add up to me. I didn't believe Chris, or his sister, were born bad. So, if it worked, I could have the good bits of him all to myself. My thoughts went to his horrible sister, Shay. From my one and only meeting with her, I was mighty glad I'd never have to see her again.

After one of the best, most moving nights of my life, I lay still, listening to him breathe. Was there a conception taking place in me right now? Was all the activity going on inside belied by the stillness of the two of us lying here in the dark? Had we made our child? He was deeply asleep when, as I heard a clock somewhere outside strike six, I crept out of his bed, down his stairs and out of his life. The dog, asleep somewhere in the house, didn't bark.

I closed the door quietly behind me and hurried away through the dark streets, straight back to my flat, where I hurtled up the stairs to my small kitchen. I didn't have long.

In a sealed plastic bag in a cupboard was the cutlery, plate and cup he used the first time he came to the cafe. It had been here, unwashed, ever since I cleared the table while he was sitting outside. I'd known instantly it was him. If there had been any doubt at all, making love to him in the dark with only the feel of it to go on had confirmed it. It was him. Only he had ever made me feel this way.

I stuffed it all into a carrier bag and rang for a taxi, waiting at the top of the road for it to come.

'Fulford Road. The police station, please,' I said to the driver.

'Okay,' he said, pulling away.

It was still dark, and I looked out of the windows, seeing nothing. One more night with him had broken my heart. I hated him so much for what he did, but I loved him more. If I was pregnant, I'd be happy. And if not, then... So be it.

Outside the police station, I paid the taxi driver.

'No need to wait,' I said. 'I don't know how long I'll be.'

I walked through the bare canopy of trees all around, through sodden leaves that covered the ground, and into the red brick building. It was empty inside; no drunks or druggies or people bleeding, having been attacked. I'm not sure what I expected.

'Yes, how can I help you, love?' asked a woman behind a desk.

I swallowed hard. It had to be done. 'I need to report the whereabouts of a man wanted for murder. He absconded from London earlier this year. I have his DNA in this bag. His name—yes, um, it's Chris Gillespie. He's wanted for killing three people, one of them a child years ago.' My words were falling over themselves in my haste to get them out.

She looked at me over the top of her glasses. 'It sounds like you'd better take a seat,' she said.

I passed the bag over to her, shaking uncontrollably now, and with tears bursting from me that showed no signs of stopping any time soon.

'Are you alright?' she asked, looking alarmed.

'No,' I said. 'But I will be. I will be.'

40

'DRIVING LICENCE AND VISITING Order, please.'

I hand the documents over to the unsmiling prison officer, who studies them, holds my driving licence up and compares me to the photo. All the while, I struggle to control the tremors affecting every part of my body, now made worse by removing my coat, which, along with my bag and phone, I'm having to leave in a locker. All while standing in the cold.

I can barely believe I'm here: me, outside a prison, lining up with the other cons' families. Cons! Listen at me with the lingo. My right leg is shaking so much it's a wonder it's holding me up at all.

Behind me, a hum of everyday chatter, and even occasional laughter, can be heard. Who the hell can laugh in a place like this? It's as if I've stepped out of the real world straight into hell. When my taxi first pulled up at Wakefield prison, I thought I was going to be sick at the thought of going inside. My legs moved without any intervention from my brain.

I've been queuing for ages, due to the strictness of the security measures for a Category A prison. The instructions I received before visiting included a long list of things I wasn't allowed to bring in, including food and drink.

284

Somewhere behind me, a child starts to wail. Imagine bringing a child here. It's the last place I'd bring mine.

'This way,' says a prison officer, indicating that I should follow. I close the locker door and follow him inside.

Just the very fact of me being in here is making me feel I've done something wrong, committed some crime or misdemeanour, or am about to get found out for something. It's horrible and does nothing to settle my nerves, which are stretched tight and being plucked at every turn.

I shouldn't have come. I should NOT have come. Yet I had to. I'm the one who instigated it. It would have felt cowardly not to.

In front of me is a body scanner, like those at airports. A green light above it indicates it's ready. I walk through it and, thankfully, it doesn't beep. Then, I'm patted down as well, arms outstretched, and shown into a waiting area, where everyone who has been in the queue before me is also waiting. At least it's a bit warmer in here.

Behind me, next through the scanner, is a young woman who can't be more than eighteen and is heavily pregnant. I watch as she steps through it. Her eyeliner is thick and black, and her hair is pulled back so tightly the corners of her eyes slant backwards, giving her a feline appearance.

I wonder if she's visiting the father of her baby or her own father. Neither is ideal. One thing is for sure; I'm not going to ask her. She has a wild, unpredictable look about her that makes me think she's no stranger to kicking off.

The scanner beeps loudly and she swears as two people in uniform close in.

'I haven't fucking got anything!' she screams before they lead her through a door to God knows where. 'You're not putting your fucking fingers inside me!' she screeches before the door closes and the noise fades away.

I catch the eye of a weary-looking woman behind me. She attempts a smile but gives up quickly. I can feel my eyes stretched wide.

'What was all that about?' I ask her.

She sighs and hunches her shoulders up around her ears, like she's seen it all a thousand times before.

'Drugs, more than likely,' she says. 'She's probably just got caught trying to smuggle them in.'

'Really?' I say, shocked.

'Your first time, is it, then?'

I nod. Is it that obvious? Who smuggles drugs into a prison?

'How was she trying to get them in? They take everything off you.'

The woman smiles again, probably at my naivety. Her eyes drop meaningfully down to my crotch area and then back up. I gawp and she nods.

'It's always there, front or back, depending on... well, I'm sure you can work it out.'

'This way,' a male voice shouts, making me jump.

I turn back as a prison officer waves us forward into a large area. Everyone in front of me is shuffling through. There are maybe fifty of us, if I had to guess.

The room we're in now is full of tables and chairs. I realise they are bolted to the floor. Nothing is movable. Most of the tables already have men sitting at them; one chair at one side and two or three opposite.

'Move further in, please,' commands another prison officer. Screws, I think they call them, but to be honest, my whole concept of prison life is based on films and TV—Porridge, which my dad used to watch, and The Shawshank Redemption. I have no idea what to expect, but I know I don't belong here. I feel like a minnow in with the sharks. Some of the other visitors are acting like this is just a day out from the rest of their lives. Maybe it is. None of them look as frightened as I feel. But Wakefield prison is notorious for high-risk prisoners (lots of serial killers) and sex offenders, the ones you read about in the high-profile trials. I couldn't believe they'd sent him here.

I scan the room for Chris but can't see him. He's been here a few months now. It took me weeks to arrange this visit and get it accepted, as I had to be fully checked out. He knows I'm coming. He had to agree to see me.

Where is he? All around, visitors are embracing the prisoners. Mothers, sons, fathers; all hugging. My feet feel glued to the floor as I look around. The thing I'm dreading most of all is facing him and looking into his eyes. Will they be green or his own brown? They'll have to be brown, surely? Why would he keep the green contact lenses in here? That was another thing I'd known when I'd first seen his eyes. The green colour hadn't fooled me at all. Coloured contacts are easy enough to find. They use them in films all the time, don't they? Some people use them for Instagram, along with all the filters, though why they bother, I don't know.

Right next to me, an older couple are hugging what is probably their son. The younger man is weeping and so is his mum, if that's who she is. God, seeing your child in here is even worse than visiting your parent, isn't it? How much of a failure must you feel if your child ends up inside? At least if it's your dad in here, it can't be a direct correlation to anything you did, I suppose. But if it's your own child, is it how you brought them up? I've been obsessed by the nature or nurture question lately, but I haven't changed my mind. It's nurture for me, all the way.

No one knows I've come here today. I just said I had to take the day off and left it at that. Wisely, everyone kept their mouths shut, not wanting to upset me. At least it meant I didn't have to lie.

Then I spot him at a nearby table. He's sitting forward, resting his elbows on his thighs. His head is down, looking at the floor. I make myself move. With my ears ringing and legs shaking, I walk over to him and stand there. I remember all the other visitors, flinging their arms around their loved ones. Down by my sides, my nails dig into my palms. A prison officer nods at me, indicating I should sit. I sit.

He doesn't look up at first.

'Hello Chris,' I say.

He looks up slowly. Gone are the shorn blonde hair, the beard, the green eyes. Although, of course, the scar is still there. And the tattoos will be there, of course, under the sleeves of his baggy sweatshirt. It looks like it's dropping to bits, with its stains and fraying cuffs. He hasn't been in here long enough for it to look like that from new. I wonder how many people have worn it before him. The jogging bottoms are in the same state. He'll hate wearing second-hand clothes. Every minute spent in them will make his skin crawl. With his OCD, that alone will be punishment in itself. The bib he is wearing, denoting his prisoner status, reminds me of the one I wore for netball at school, in P.E.

He doesn't speak, but his eyes flit all about him. What's he looking for? He looks terrified. My throat closes up, and I can't breathe. This is way worse than the films I've seen. This is real life. His real life. And I put him here.

No. No. He put himself here, I remind myself.

He sits up in the chair, pushing himself back. If he's attempting to look in control, once his default position, it's not working. He swings between looking defiant and looking terrified. It's the most unsettling thing yet. He looks like a different person.

His eyes eventually settle on mine, although he still doesn't speak. I know he blames me for this. Along with everything else, I told the police about the letter from his mother, the one that said she'd seen her son driving the car that killed the girl all those years ago. He hadn't actually admitted that when I'd confronted him that day, as I'd realised at that precise moment that he'd killed Adam, and the conversation had taken a different turn. The letter from his mother wasn't enough evidence in itself, as it could have been no more than the rantings of a delusional mind.

It was taken into account, though, and there was more than enough evidence he'd killed Luisa, and mortally wounded Adam, to put him away. He'd pleaded guilty and not gone to trial. In sentencing, the judge had declared him an extremely dangerous man and a menace to society, with the recommendation he serve an indefinite period without parole. The insinuation was that he should never get out. The judge had gone at him hard and hit him with everything he could.

Chris's fingers run through his hair, now thick and dark, and swept back from his face, but there's no disguising the haunted look in his eyes. Behind that is something else. Hatred, maybe? Distrust? Reserved only for me? Then it's gone.

'So,' he says finally. 'Why did you ask to see me? To rub it in and twist the knife some more?'

I look away, straight into the eyes of a man seated at the next table. He's dressed the same as Chris and stares back at me with dead eyes. He's much older than Chris. How long has he been in here? There's no life about him. He looks like he's lost the will to live. Will this be Chris in twenty years?

Chris's question hangs in the air. I don't know how to answer him.

'I had to come,' I say, tears welling up and spilling over. 'We have unfinished business.'

His left leg is jiggling like mad under the table. I can hear the sole of his trainer rubbing on the floor. Fast, like a pneumatic drill. Up and down. Up and down.

'What unfinished business?' His nostrils flare as he glares at me. 'What else is there? I'm finished, if you hadn't noticed.'

He lifts up a hand and hooks one finger in the neck of his sweatshirt, tugging it away from his skin as if it's choking him. There's a flaking patch of skin on his face just under his scar, and he looks pasty. Unhealthy.

'It's going to be a long, slow slide towards the grave for me in here,' he spits out. 'Thanks to you. Life's too short to not eat the fuckin brownie? That's not true in here. It's interminable. It's going to go on forever.'

'Chris,' I say, unwilling to get drawn in to his self-pity. 'You're in here because you killed people. Including that little girl. You know it, and I know it.'

'I should have stayed away,' he's muttering now. Then his eyes shoot back to mine with laser accuracy. 'Tell me. How did you know it was me?'

I bite my bottom lip. I can't believe he'd thought for one second I wouldn't know him anywhere in an instant.

'I looked totally different,' he says, his words tumbling out. 'Sounded different. Walked, moved different. Even changed the way I smiled, for God's sake! So how? Come on; what gave it away?' His eyes sweep the room again, like he's checking for danger, then look back at me.

I glance down at my own hands, at the bitten fingernails and ragged cuticles. Then I look at his own.

'Your hands,' I say. 'The first time you picked up your coke at the cafe, when I came outside. See the cuticle on your left thumb. It's crooked. As individual as a fingerprint.'

He frowns and looks at his thumbs, as if seeing them for the first time.

'Your hands gave you away. Not just that one cuticle. I know your hands, Chris. Also, your mouth—your lips, your teeth. No beard could hide that enough. I know every bit of you. All the tattoos and scars in the world won't change that, or the way you smell, no matter what aftershave you douse yourself in. But first, it was your hands.'

He opens his hands and gazes at the backs of them, stretching his fingers out. 'Well, fuck me!' he mutters. When he looks at me, the hatred has been replaced by tenderness. It's frightening how quickly he can change.

'I came back for you, Sarah,' he says, softly. 'I couldn't stay away. I loved you too much. I still do. Always will.'

I believe him. It's the same for me, although I won't tell him that. What good would it do? And my love is tempered with hate and loathing, too. They make strange bedfellows, but I've got used to it. I've had to.

His eyes flash back to mine as realisation dawns. 'Hang on. You're saying you knew from the first instant?'

I say nothing. Here it comes.

'So why didn't you shop me straight away? Why flirt with me and play with me? Was it to torture me? Make me feel you'd fallen for it?'

'No.' A tear falls from my eye and drips onto the table. 'No.'

'You even gave me one of the cards I made for you. Did you think that was funny? Did it make you laugh?'

'No.' I lift my chin. 'But it showed what a good actor you can be. You didn't show anything when you saw it.'

He leans forward. 'Why then? Why did you sleep with me?'

I need a tissue. I reach for my bag, but, of course, it's not there. Instead, I wipe my eyes on my sleeve. From the side of the room, one of the prison officers watches me. His face shows no emotion at all. His eyes are flint in a granite face. How long does it take him to get ready for work every day, to show this face to the world? Or does it come naturally now? He gives me a tiny nod, raising his eyebrows, asking if everything is alright. A little spark of humanity escapes. He's on my side. I nod quickly, then look at Chris again.

'I had to be sure. I was ninety-nine percent sure from your hands. To do that with you was the only way to be absolutely certain.'

He's crying now, too. 'You could have left it. Kept up the pretence. We could have had a good life together. You know I'd never hurt you. But you had to do it, didn't you? Maybe that slogan should have been *Life's too short not to do the right thing*. That's you to a tee right there.'

'Chris, we're not talking about stealing here. We're talking about killing. Innocent people.'

He shrugs. 'Accidentally, yeah. I never meant to kill anyone. It wasn't murder.'

'You pleaded guilty, Chris.'

'I was advised to. They said it would go better for me. But it was manslaughter. They said if I…' He shook his head. 'It doesn't matter.'

He's going to be in denial for as long as he lives. *It wasn't my fault. I didn't mean it. They pushed me to it.* I can't live with that for the rest of my life and I would have had to if I'd lied for him. It was one lie too far.

Funny, but the fear I'd had of him finding me disappeared the moment he did. I relaxed, safe in the knowledge that I knew exactly where he was. No more wondering and worrying. He was hiding under my nose. I also knew then he wouldn't kill me. Every second I'd spent with him, I felt safe, like before. I can't explain it. He protected me from everything, but mainly from the bad side of himself. I don't think he was ever capable of killing me. He'd kill himself first, and that's what's so hard to reconcile.

When I walk away this time, I'll never see him again. Unless he does get out. I'm never coming back here. If I did, each time it would take more from me, and I'd end up like the other women here, with their thousand-yard stares, misplaced loyalties, and haggard faces. This place steals souls, and I don't want to be that person.

'I know you did what you had to, Sarah, in the end. Deep down, I knew that if you recognised me, you would do what you did. I knew that before I came back. And I came anyway.'

He looks at me, more like the Chris I fell in love with, and suddenly I wonder whether I did the right thing. I could have tried to live a lie and been loved by him. But, ultimately, I know I couldn't have. Nothing can change what he did.

'You took too much from me,' I say.

He shakes his head and looks at the floor. 'I know I did. I violated you. I took your trust, your love, and betrayed it.' He raises his head and looks me in the eye. 'But you took something from me, too, didn't you?'

My whole body goes rigid. Does he know? He can't do.

'What did I take from you?'

'My freedom. My liberty. My trust.'

He doesn't know. 'I didn't take them, Chris. You threw them away when you didn't value life.'

He's silent. Then he says, 'I don't know if I'll survive in here. I'm in with nonces and nutters, the worst ones you seen in the news. I don't belong in here. It's not safe.' He drops his head and lowers his voice. 'If anything happens to me...'

He's shaking, and my heart gives a massive lurch. It couldn't, could it? He's exaggerating. He has to be. It's a British prison, not a Hollywood film where they sharpen plastic toothbrushes into shanks on concrete floors and plunge them into each other.

'If I ever get out, if I survive this, keep my nose clean and do my time... show them I'm rehabilitated—what then? Could there be a chance for us? Say yes, Sarah. It's all I've got to keep me going. Please say yes.'

I know it must be a ludicrous idea, him getting out. But the idea of us being together and him having paid for his crimes, well, that's something else entirely.

'Never say never,' I say. Even now, I have the urge to reach over and grip his fingers in mine. I jam my hands under my thighs. We're silent for what seems like ages.

'So, what's it like in here, really?' I ask him.

He shakes his head. 'Terrifying. You don't want to know.' He looks away across the room. His eyes are haunted.

He's probably right. I don't want to know. All I'll do is go away and think about it. Maybe ignorance is better, and he's granting it to me. I don't ask again.

'Oh, did you get the picture I sent?' I ask.

'Yeah. Thank you.'

'Time,' shouts a prison officer.

I feel like I've only been here five minutes. But this is it. No chairs shuffle as the visitors stand up. The hugging and embracing starts up again. Will he do the same?

He doesn't move, so I stand up to go.

'Well… bye, then,' I say. The room swims as my eyes fill. I blink hard, struggling to keep it together.

He nods and looks away. *Don't look back. Just leave him here.* At the door, however, I do look back. He's sitting hunched over once more, in the same position as before, but instead of gazing at the floor, he's watching me, his face inscrutable.

I join the line of people once more, the urge to cry choking up my throat. This is my queue. The queue to leave hell and re-join life. Back to my new beginning. My heart is breaking at the sight of him, but it's done. And I have so much to get back to.

41

I WAIT FOR MY taxi outside the prison, my coat buttoned up tight under my chin. Still the chill penetrates deep. There's no sign of the pregnant girl from earlier. I don't know what will happen to her or her baby if she is found smuggling drugs in.

I shiver, now thinking of Chris. What will his life be like in jail, and how will he learn to survive it? I suppose the answer is he'll just have to. I can't see him settling in there, though. He's too free-spirited. He'll most likely try and fight the system and everyone in it until he either learns or his spirit is broken. The dead eyes of the man at the next table come back to me. How long might it take the light in Chris's eyes to dim and disappear?

It's a horrible thought and now I'm crying again. The taxi driver pulls up in front of me without commenting on the tears running down my face. He's probably used to it if the prison is a regular run for him, and why wouldn't it be? It's good business, after all.

'Where to, love?'

'York, please. The train station.'

He looks pleased, as he should. It's a lucrative job for him, all the way from Wakefield to York, but there was no way I was going on public transport and risking crying my eyes out in front of strangers, and I haven't got a car yet, even though Dad keeps badgering me to get one.

'You'll need one up here. It's not London, you know,' he's said, more than once.

The funny thing is he would have let me use his today, but that would have entailed telling people where I was going. So I'll just have to fork out for the taxi.

The walk home from the train station will give me time to clear my head and hopefully, any lasting redness around my eyes will have gone, too. I just hope that, when I see my mum, I won't burst into tears and start it all over again. Some days, I long to tell her the truth, but it would crush her, and I can't do it.

I'm quiet on the drive back. Thankfully, the driver isn't one of those who wants to chat. Or maybe he is, but not with people coming back from prison visiting. What must he think of me? Another loser with a lowlife for a boyfriend? Maybe I am, or I was.

'Is here okay?' he asks, pulling up outside the station and parking in a taxi bay.

'Great. Thank you.'

I hand him his money and walk back onto the road. There's another bridge over the river to take me back to the city centre, and I stop on top of it, looking down. It's a beautiful day. The only thing about it that's black is my mood. I feel like this is it now. The visit, while I was planning and preparing for it, took up my time and energy, and now there's nothing. It's how people feel after funerals, I think. A big, long empty stretch of nothingness, with the person they loved gone forever.

Except I don't have nothing. I have a lot to be thankful for. My family. My work. My friends. Zac.

I hurry along now, suddenly desperate to get back to those who love me. The streets of York are familiar to me, so I make good time back to the cafe. I walk to M&S and pick up a luxury bunch of flowers for my mum and some whisky for Dad. Without my parents, I wouldn't have anything. The lure of the Humpty Dumpty baby shop tries to pull me in, but I walk straight past it, the illicit thrill no longer there.

I walk through the door of the cafe feeling much brighter than when I left the prison. Claire doles out plates to a table, and Ellie is serving behind the counter. They both smile when they see me, even though the curiosity as to my whereabouts is evident in their faces.

'Alright?' asks Ellie.

'Yeah. I'll just nip upstairs to see 'His Lordship'. Be back down in a bit.'

'No need to rush,' she says. 'There aren't any emergencies here.'

The part-timers, lovely Olwyn (from the WI, who now works here, and Martin, a young lad fresh out of catering college whose dream is to be a pastry chef), must be in the kitchen. Martin rarely comes out of it, saying it's his natural habitat. He's certainly got a good teacher in Ellie. She's making it her mission to teach him everything she knows and has nothing but praise for him. Olwyn does two days a week and Martin four. I think Olwyn would do it for free. She now calls us her family and loves her time in the cafe. She still has a keen head for business and has helped steer my decision making a few times.

I smile at Claire and point upstairs. She gives me a thumbs up and continues serving. At the bottom of the stairs, my heart quickens and I skip up them, bursting through the door and into the sitting room. Mum is on the sofa with Zac, who's looking well fed and sleepy. Well, that won't last. His eyes swivel and find mine, then his mouth twists and he burps softly. At three months, I know he isn't smiling properly yet, but it seems like he is. His eyes lock onto mine.

'Oh, these are for you,' I say, putting the flowers down next to her then taking Zac. 'And I got Dad some of that whisky he likes. To say thank you for everything.'

I sit down next to her as she picks them up.

'Oh, Sarah. Thank you. But you didn't have to.' Her hand reaches out to touch the paper they're wrapped in.

I can feel her eyes on me. *Please don't ask me where I've been, Mum. Just leave it.*

'How has he been?' I ask.

'He's been just fine. He's just had his dinner, haven't you, my beautiful boy.'

I sit him up to burp him and rub his back, unable to stop myself pressing my cheek onto his downy head. A tiny grumble and a snuffle comes from him, and I close my eyes, inhaling deeply. His smell is intoxicating. It's the best smell in the world. The smell of my baby is so delicious I want to bottle it.

'Where's Dad?' I ask as more air escapes from Zac's tiny body. It's amazing how much can be in there.

'Where do you think?'

I glance around the room and realise what's missing. 'In the park with Lulu.'

'Correct. That dog gets more walks a day than I have cups of tea.'

'No, Mum. That's not possible.'

I told the police I would give Lulu a home. They didn't argue. It was one less thing for them to sort out, I suppose. Claire and Ellie know who Lulu is, of course, but they don't know where Chris (or Carl, as they know him) has disappeared to. I just told them he was leaving York, couldn't take the dog, and that I'd offered her a home. Lulu will spend the rest of her life with me now, being loved and cared for. She's such a young dog, she and Zac will have years together. But when Dad saw her for the first time, he fell totally in love with her, and she did the same with him. Now, they're inseparable. But it's my bed she sleeps on at night, curled up tight against me, like I suspect she did with Chris. I wonder what stories she could tell about how she came to be with him. If only she could talk.

Zac is gearing up to wail, I can just tell. He's a terrible sleeper, never settles, and wants my attention all the time.

He looks so much like Chris that my heart aches sometimes when I look at him. His personality is very much Chris's too, with his constant demands for attention. He loves me to sing to him and rock him. It's the only thing that settles him down, although he seems fascinated by my dad, who works miracles with him.

Regarding Zac's paternity, I told everyone I'd used a sperm donor, and, unbelievably, they accepted it. After a positive pregnancy test, I'd sat my parents down and told them that having a child to replace the one I lost was all I could think about, and that I hadn't wanted to find a partner. They were surprised and shocked, but it was done. But I may have to tell Leanne the truth. Out of all of them, she knew Chris. Zac grows more like his dad every day and she'll probably guess the next time she sees him. She's my best friend and I know she'll keep my secret. But I'm not looking forward to it.

I wasn't sure, even when I got to the prison, if I would tell Chris he had a son. I meant to, but something told me not to. Okay, he may have a right to know, and when he said I'd taken something from him, I thought he meant Zac. Which I suppose I did. I took from him the means to give me a baby, sure, but his responsibility ended there. If he knew, my life would be endless rounds of prison visits, with a baby in tow, then a toddler and young kid, only ever seeing his dad in that place, like the kids I saw earlier. No way. It was hard enough for me to see. What chance would a kid have? He'd be scarred for life.

The door bursts open and Lulu scampers in, followed by my dad.

Lulu runs around the room, checking out who's at home, then jumps onto the sofa beside me and Zac, her tail wagging so hard it shakes her whole body. Maybe she misses Chris. Who knows?

'Hey, sweetheart,' I say to her, leaning down to fuss her. Zac grimaces, reddens, and fills his nappy, by the sound and smell of it.

'Great! Did you wait for me to get home to do that?'

His head lolls back and to one side, his eyes searching for Lulu, who he adores. She, in turn, loves nothing more than curling up next to him, and I trust her with him completely. She doesn't have a nasty bone in her body, and she brings me such joy every day. Between her and Zac, I have the best bits of Chris every day. The worst bits are rotting in prison and I have to leave them there.

'Hello, love. You're back then? How's my little boy?' he says, lifting Zac off my knee. He sniffs him, then quickly hands him back. 'Yours, I think,' he says.

I stand up to take Zac into my bedroom to change him, Lulu hot on my heels. I can feel the glances between my parents, Dad silently asking Mum if I've told her where I've been. A slight widening of her eyes tells him *no*.

I close my bedroom door and lay Zac on his changing mat. Lulu jumps on the bed and sits, her tail wagging slowly.

'Your daddy got the picture of you I sent him,' I tell her. 'I bet he looks at it every day. It might be on his wall.' I know she doesn't understand a word I say, but I talk to her all the time.

Zac squeals and kicks his legs out hard while I try to strip his dirty nappy off. He thinks it's all a big game. When I got pregnant, I knew it was meant to be, although I stupidly hadn't given a moment's thought to the practicalities of how I would manage to run a cafe and look after a newborn. Truth is, if Mum and Dad hadn't stepped into the breach, I probably couldn't have. They sold their home in London and are living with me in the flat, at least for now. The spare bedroom now has a double bed in it for them, and they look after Zac in the day while I work downstairs. It's more than I would ever have expected of them, and I can never repay them. Yet I haven't seen Mum this happy in years. It's like she's come alive. And Dad… well, he's just Dad, happy to go along with things if that's what Mum wants.

What happens if or when I meet a new partner? Well, we'll have to see. But for now, I couldn't ask for more. Well, other than for things with Chris to have turned out differently, I suppose, but for that to have happened, he'd have had to be a different person, and miracles just don't come that big.

But for now, I have everything I want. I'll probably meet someone else to love one day. Someone kind and good and decent. Someone not Chris. But I still have Zac.

42

THE HEAVY DOOR IN front of me swings open on massive well-oiled hinges, and a slice of sunshine, cutting between two buildings, hits my face the moment I step outside. It's weak, but I imagine I can feel it warming my ageing bones. I sniff deeply and close my eyes. It's not what I *can* smell that's heaven, it's what I *can't*. No more unwashed bodies and feet, no more boiled cabbage, shit, and piss. No more pounding of feet on the metal staircase. No more wails in the night, for God knows what reason. No more screaming. The sound of a man screaming leaves a mark on your soul like no other.

I open my eyes again, still blinking in the sun. The last time I was out of here was last year, to go to my daughter Shay's funeral. I can't even remember when the last time I'd seen her was. I'd stood there in the drizzle, with a few of Shay's no-good, druggie cronies, and felt absolutely nothing. She'd never been to see me in prison. None of them had.

There's no one waiting for me here. I wasn't expecting anyone, anyway. But it doesn't matter that no one is here now. What matters is that my conviction has been overturned. I'm exonerated. A free man. I take another step away from the prison exit as the screw says, 'Have you got your travel pass?'

I hold it up for him to see. It means I can get the train somewhere.

'Don't let me see you back in here again, Joe. Now piss off,' he says. As screws go, he was one of the better ones, but I'm happy to never see him again.

I laugh. 'No fear.'

Then the door slams shut behind me and I'm alone. I turn a slow three-sixty degrees, running my eyes over the horizon where the gaps in the buildings will allow. After years of being locked up, all the open space is daunting, and my insides clench tight. I'd forgotten how vast freedom really is. I clutch my holdall tighter before I start to walk away, up the long road to—where? Just where am I going?

Realisation hits me like a tsunami. I can go wherever the hell I want. And do whatever the hell I want. I can go and see my darling son in prison, my only living relative.

We have unfinished business, after what he did to me. And I don't like unfinished business. I have a score to settle.

With him.

Watch out Colin, I'll be seeing you very soon.

Read on for an excerpt from Look Now, The Webcam Watcher Book 3…

Sarah

'ARE YOU REALLY sure you don't mind us going out?' I asked Mum, swaying slightly as I entered the living room. I stopped abruptly, and Leanne bumped into me from behind.

Mum smirked as she picked up the remote and muted the TV. 'Looks like you two have already started on the booze. And of course I don't mind. How many times do I have to tell you?'

Lulu jumped off the sofa and danced around our feet, excited barks escaping her. She picked up her ball and dropped it at my feet. As I bent to throw it, I had to grab the table to stop myself overbalancing. The two large gin and tonics I'd slugged back on an empty stomach had gone straight to my head, and Leanne, the lightweight, was no better. I took a step forward and bumped into the sofa, making Zac, who'd nodded off in Mum's arms, jump awake.

Mum slung him over her shoulder and patted his bottom until he twisted his head to one side and dropped off again. She grinned. 'Hmm, this ghost walk you're going on? Are you sure you two won't be the scariest things on it?'

'Very funny! Will you be alright on your own?'

She tutted loudly and rolled her eyes. 'I think I'll manage. Your dad will be back soon, anyway.'

I hadn't noticed he'd gone. 'Where is he?'

'He's just nipped out to get us some wine. 'We're watching that new drama on telly later.. She dropped a kiss on Zac's head. 'When this one is in bed.'

'I don't think we'll be out that long. The ghost walk is only an hour, then we'll be back after a bite to eat,' I said.

'Where does this walk thingy start from, again?' Lee asked, her fingers fumbling with the zipper of her coat.

'Outside The Jacobean pub,' I said. 'It's just a few minutes' walk.' A loud hiccup erupted from me.

Mum tutted. 'It's like you two are back at school, stealing nips of my vodka and then acting all innocent.'

'We never did that. I don't know what you mean,' I said, winking at her.

'Just go and enjoy yourselves. This little man will be in bed soon, anyway,' Mum said.

I opened my mouth to speak, but she cut me off. 'Yes, I know the baby milk is in the fridge.'

'How did you know I was going to say that?'

Mum just looked at me.

Leanne successfully zipped her coat up, picked up her bag, and slipped it over her shoulder, where it promptly fell straight back off.

'Do you know what?' she slurred. 'I'm just going to put my purse and my phone in my pocket and not bother with the bag.'

Zac let out a loud wail in his sleep and suddenly, I didn't want to leave him. What sort of mother got tipsy and swanned off out, leaving her baby with her mum, who wasn't in the best of health herself? But Mum glared at me as I took a step towards them.

'Don't you dare, Sarah!' she said, patting the sofa cushion beside her. Lulu was on it after a flying leap, spilling Mum's tea in the process. She pushed her arm forward, and I pretended not to notice the drips falling onto my new carpet. 'I'll clean it up. Now go, or you'll be late. What time does it start, again?'

The clock on the wall read seven twenty-five. She knew damn well it was due to start in five minutes.

'Okay, we're going,' I muttered, pulling my coat on and winding my woolly scarf around my neck. I threw my bag diagonally across my body, and we left, Leanne breathing down my neck as we rushed through the cafe and out of the main door.

We linked arms as we made our way down Lendal, towards Stonegate. With the Christmas period long gone, York was quiet, the Christmas shoppers now replaced with tourists and drinkers. Our boots clicked on the pavement as we hurried to the pub where the ghost walk was due to start.

Now free and looking forward to an evening out with my best friend, I swallowed down a bubble of laughter that arose in my throat. Outside a pub halfway down, a small crowd had gathered.

'That'll be them,' I said, pointing. 'Now, act sober and look interested. We don't want to get chucked out, do we?'

Leanne sniggered. 'Do you think they get many pissed patrons on the ghost walk?'

'I don't know. If we don't speak and just nod, no one will know, will they?'

She barked out a loud laugh, and a man walking by us turned his head.

'Sssh,' I said, the urge to laugh now becoming so strong I couldn't help giggling again.

We drew nearer to the group, and it was then I spotted her. She must be the guide taking us on the walk. She was dressed in what appeared to be black leather, or pleather maybe, with a corset top and long skirt. I think they called it Steampunk. A long, dark-red coat the colour of claret swept the floor. It was open at the front, revealing a giant, crepey chest that threatened to spill out of the corset. She was leaning heavily on a red-tipped cane, and I wondered how old she was under her thick make-up. A black, wide-brimmed hat with feathers all around the crown topped off her look.

'Oh my God!' Leanne muttered next to me.

A snort escaped me, and I quickly turned it into a cough. Mrs Steampunk saw us, and her smile widened even more. 'Are you for the tour?' she asked, blinking. She wasn't half bad at the old cat-flick, I thought, noticing the winged liner tapering from the corners of her eyes. Much better at it than me.

'Yes,' I said, pulling a ticket out of my pocket and waving it in the air. I made a concerted effort to not sway as I stood in front of a shop window that contained rows of handbags. Lee caught my eye, and I looked away quickly, fixing instead on the others in the group. There were twelve of us altogether; not bad for a damp March night.

'Right, I think that's everyone who booked,' Steampunk said, consulting a piece of paper. 'We'll be off, then. It takes about an hour, a bit longer on a better night. But we'll have fun, anyway. Is everyone ready?'

A few people chorused 'Yes', and she set off at a much faster pace than I was expecting, holding her cane aloft and shouting 'This way' in a booming, theatrical voice.

'I'm never going to keep this pace up in these boots,' I said to Leanne, who was hanging onto my arm as if for dear life.

'Me neither,' she panted.

Steampunk had now disappeared around a corner and was striding towards the Minster, her heeled boots echoing loudly on the pavement.

'Are we going to the pub after this?' asked Leanne.

I turned to her. 'Are you turning into an alkie or something?'

'No, course not. But it's been ages since we had a girls' night out.'

'Alright. You've twisted my arm. I haven't been out in ages, since I went with Claire to have a curry before Christmas.'

'Perils of being a mum, I suppose,' Lee said.

She was right. But I actually preferred being in with my little family: Zac, and my mum and dad, who kept saying they were going to look for somewhere of their own, and I kept begging them not to. I loved having them around. The thought of it being just Zac and me in the flat scared me, for some reason. But, deep down, I knew it wasn't practical for us all to live together in the long term. There were only two bedrooms, and Zac would soon need the one my parents were sleeping in. It wasn't ideal having him in with me, even though he slept through most nights. If I met some bloke one day, he wouldn't want to share our bedroom with a kid, would—?

I bumped into a man in front of me and was jerked back to the present. The group had stopped in front of a small church not far from the Minster, and the guide looked like she was winding up to go on stage or something. She was strutting up and down, seemingly soaking in the attention of the group. I noticed some of the male members were quite taken with her cleavage as it weaved from side to side. On closer inspection, she looked younger than I first thought.

She was talking about Guy Fawkes being born in York.

Lee's head snapped round. 'I didn't know Guy Fawkes was from here, did you?'

I shook my head and shrugged. 'No. Unless she means a different one.'

Leanne scoffed. 'Yeah, that'll be it. There's probably loads of them!'

Steampunk smiled indulgently at us, and I realised she'd stopped talking.

'Sorry,' I said.

'Thank you. As I was saying…' she carried on. To be honest, what she was saying was interesting, but I just couldn't stop my mind from wandering off. I glanced up and down the dark streets. A man hurried by with a small dog and nodded at Steampunk, who nodded back but didn't miss a beat. He must live around here, then. Probably sees her every night.

'S'cuse me,' Lee said, putting her hand up.

Steampunk didn't look too impressed with being interrupted. Well, you know what these thespian-types are like, hogging the limelight.

'Yes?' she asked, somewhat snappily. Lee wouldn't like that.

'Where did you get your dress from? It's very nice.'

I rolled my eyes. Trust Lee to be thinking about clothes. She'd probably been eying the woman's costume up since we got here, wondering if she should run up something similar to sell in the vintage clothes shop she worked in back in London.

'It's specially made,' Steampunk said, softening a bit at the compliment. 'Now, follow me to a very special place for the next part of the tour.'

And she was off again, her hips sashaying as she strode away from the Minster and down a tiny alley I'd never even noticed before.

'How old do you reckon she is?' I whispered to Lee.

'Fifty-ish, do you think?'

'Dunno. Maybe, yeah. She's certainly keeping the blokes' attention, isn't she?'

Lee sighed and looked down at her chest. Even in the padded anorak, there wasn't much there. 'I'd love boobs like that,' she said.

'Don't be daft. I don't hear Sam complaining.'

She looked away. I knew it! Something wasn't right. She'd been here almost a week now, and whenever I brought him up, she changed the subject.

FROM THE AUTHOR

I am a thriller writer living in Yorkshire in the UK. After years working as a dog groomer and musician (not usually at the same time), I discovered a love of writing that now won't go away. I recently decorated my office in a lovely shabby chic pink wallpaper, as I wanted to have a beautifully inspiring place in which to sit and plot how to inflict unspeakable suffering on my poor unsuspecting characters. Only they don't know that yet…

I love connecting with readers. As a writer, it's one of the best things about the job. It makes all the time spent thinking up stories to share worthwhile. I'd like to say a massive thank you for taking the time to read this lil' ol' book of mine. I hope you enjoyed reading it as much as I did writing it. If you feel moved to write a review, I would greatly appreciate. It really does make a difference to authors.

I strive for perfection. If you find a typo, I'd love you to tell me at info@stephanierogersauthor.com I hope you'll stay with me on this journey. We're gonna have a blast!

Printed in Great Britain
by Amazon

22122928R00179